THE POET KING

MARK NELSON

HADLEY
RILLE
BOOKS

THE POET KING
Copyright © 2017 by Mark Nelson

Cover art © Tom Vandenberg
Edited by Terri-Lynne DeFino
Map of Perspa © Ginger Prewitt

ISBN 978-0-9971188-6-5

Ebook edition alao available

Published in the United States of America and the United Kingdom by

Hadley Rille Books
Eric T. Reynolds, Publisher
Olathe, Kansas 66062 USA
www.hrbpress.com
contact@hadleyrillebooks.com

Dedication

In addition to my best friend and wife, Carol, who gives meaning to all my words, this one is also forJoseph Barat, fellow poet, Stygian, kind soul, quiet hero, and well-spring for all things Devyn.

Acknowledgements

The early drafts of this novel came as a surprise burst of energy after finishing the second. It lay there,waiting attention, an uncertain mass of words that lacked clarity and purpose. The changes that occurred in book two of the series, *King's Gambit* brought much of that badly needed focus to this volume. The story holds true to itself now, and certain characters realized more of their potential alongthe way. None of that would have happened without the sharp eyes of my editor, Terri-Lynne DeFino, who prodded and poked me to find the real story within the story. Indirectly, I hold her responsible for helping me discover the word-mass that became the fourth and final volume in the series, *Pevanese Mosaic*.

That *The Poet King* will now see the light of day is also due in part to the amazing power and strength of Eric T. Reynolds, the owner and publisher of Hadley Rille books, and his wonderful, supportive family. Much of HRB's fantasies deal with heroism, but none of it compares to the real-time challenges Eric and his family had to overcome and continue to surmount. This novel is, in part, for them and the other members of the extended HRB family. May we all continue to find words and value in this small press relationship!

I would also like to thank some early readers, including Jessica Carter and my lovely wife, Carol, for patiently reading three different versions of this story while it evolved. Let it be known: Readers Rock!

The Goddess Renia of the Tears gave forth an elemental sigh, well-pleased with the choices made by the mortals fretting out their days in the realms below. Blood saddened her. From her spectral lids flowed a gentle stream, seeking with her offering to provide surcease from the trauma for the souls afflicted.

Minuet of the Arrows, her familiar, joined her.

"They have done well, mistress," said she.

"Poor souls beset by greed's threat. Too much blood, my Minuet, and too hungrily accepted by the ever thirsty ground. Borimon and Tolimon tax me, my dear."

"But there is a king, mistress, chosen not claimed, made not born. Surely that must count for something?"

And the goddess heard wisdom there, and hope, and drew strength from both. She took a breath, another, a third of content and ease.

A low chuckle disturbed her peace. Tolimon, god of mischance and mischief crouched in the corner of her terrace.

"They will always disappoint you," he said, his voice sinuous and sly. "Man is poor clay. Too easily made, too easily broken. Like their promises."

"Like as not, for you," she responded, gliding away from the terrace edge to her couches. "You take too much pleasure in their pain, Tolimon. They have flaws enough, why make them worse?"

"Their nature, lady, I but play with their nature. Man is an inconstant thing. Short lived and graceless, in the end."

"Because of you."

Tolimon bowed. "Lady, spare me your gifts or reproach alike. I am of the shadows. Secrets, lies, deceit, the silence of the dark—these are my domain. Take you the light if you wish. Man carries his darkness within him even in the light of his day. Weep for eternity, you will never wash Man's darker side away."

"I do not seek to wash anything away. Man's gifts are his own to explore, both the light and the dark, trickster. Move you the shadow whispers if you wish, I will bathe Man in gentle tears so that he can at least make his choices in wisdom rather than fear."

Tolimon frowned up at her, and Renia sensed his unease and jealousy of her adamantine calm. Always he sought to fret her designs, no doubt thinking them simple and naïve, but now she fixed him with her thought and let him know she worked otherwise to his interpretation.

"So?" he sneered, slinking away. "You give them choice only? Frail hope, lady. No wonder they turn from you."

And Renia of the Tears smiled, a deep, cosmic swelling of power and peace, and Tolimon shrank before her to an insignificant but nagging whisper.

"True, little fear monger," she said. "Choice is ever Man's final gift. And though at times they turn from me and listen to your lies, it is also true that, through choice, they turn back as well."

She turned away then, reclining on her couch, dismissing him from her thoughts the way the sun burns away the cloud on a mid-summer's day.

Deeply she breathed, gathered her tears anew, and let them leach from her immortal self in a flow to once again nurture Man to pity and peace.

Chapter 1: An Uneasy Crown

Demona Anargi reined back her mount and paused before the slope that led down to the ford over the Nala river; the channel narrowed here a half day's ride west of Pevana. She thought back to the last time she had seen it, a muddy, churned up froth splashing about the spokes of the wagon provided for her comfort. Now, at the return, the paltry line of horsemen led by Gaspire Amdoran, Lord of Collum, barely caused a disturbance in the current.

So much for ambition.

What began as an adventure with so much promise ended in a desperate race towards uncertain sanctuary. Demona looked across the river where Gaspire waited at the crest of the first terrace watching the column's progress. Even at a distance, Demona could see his tired, saddle sore anger. For three weeks he pushed his ragtag collection northwards back toward Pevana at a pace that killed horses and men in order to stay ahead of Gaspire's cousin.

King Donari Avedun.

Laughable, given the man's drunken past. Poet. Fop. He never missed a revel, and yet now events had turned him into a threat. Any reference to his cousin spiked Gaspire's ire, his jealousy and fear palpable, which he took out on anyone near. Demona learned quickly to absent herself at such times. His rage daunted her at first, but he reminded her of Sevire, her late husband, and she knew how to deal with such men.

Demona wiped her dusty brow and let her horse advance to the water's edge to drink. The closer they got to Pevana's settled lands, the more her thoughts turned to what she might do. The crushing defeat at Lyranden Bridge was a dull ache now. She had to plan, a rare occurrence in her life to that point.

She urged her mount through the stream to the far bank. If the Prelate's banner still flew above Pevana's walls, then that would be a sure sign the seaward attacks had also failed. If Donari's ascension were true, and Gaspire's attitude seemed to suggest it, then that meant policies over-turned, an arrangement with Sylvanus and the south, and Donari's return home with a new crown.

Demona speculated on the implications for such men as Gaspire and Casan. They could be dangerous, but they could also be useful. More than once on their northward road, Demona caught Gaspire staring at her, as if measuring her value and fitness for a task he had in mind. He looked like a man who had learned a hard lesson from the failure at Lyranden Bridge: if once you have an advantage, never let go of it—especially for honor. Demona took his scrutiny, but kept her own thoughts to herself. To her, Gaspire was the kind of warrior who believed the tact found at the end of a sword or a spear point sufficient to his needs.

She glanced down at the water swirling by her horse's legs; she was in way over her head. Hints of understanding tantalized her, but each new thought exposed her limitations. She faced dissembling on a grand scale now out of necessity. Donari's threat to her baby motivated her reasoning. She needed allies to dissemble for her, and realized Gaspire fell short of Donari in that regard. *But if Casan was in Pevana.* If she and her baby were to survive, she would need both a warrior and a dissembler. Gaspire and Casan would do, perhaps.

They will need money, she thought as she climbed the bank and trotted past Gaspire. Her horse stumbled on a loose stone as it crested the bank. Demona adjusted, her horsemanship another thing that had improved out of necessity, and placed a hand to her mid-section as though to reassure the unborn child nestled there. She kept pace with her thoughts, imagined House Anargi looted and abandoned after Sevire's death and her absence.

Ransacked, likely, but I know all of Servire's hidey holes. And I kept a few of my own besides. I'll get Gaspire his money. I don't care how he might use it as long as it serves my needs.

She straightened in the saddle, her developing purpose serving as spinal support and motivation to never be taken for granted again. Her old life was gone. She had survived wrack and ruin. She had choices.

I'm still free.

Gaspire and Demona rode in through the Land Gate of Pevana side by side to bemused, confused looks from the guards. There were no officials there to greet them despite the fact their approach must have been watched for several leagues. Gaspire pointed out the mixed liveries of the troops at the gate, Pevanese and Northern, neither looking too steady.

"Look at them, cowed and wondering," he sneered. "I suspect they must have been part of the Lord Prelate's force that made it back. They have the look and smell of defeat and distrust. Useless."

Demona kept her silence as she followed him through the gate square and on up the cobblestone street to the hill. Gaspire curbed his mount next to hers.

"I need a place to keep my men from talking over-much. The camp near the Maze is no good. Too many eyes and ears."

"House Anargi," she said, considering. "I hardly think the servants would have kept the place up, but it is large enough to house us mostly out of sight. I would like to take a last look at my home."

Gaspire flashed a fake smile. "Perfect! And it is close to the college temples. One last night in your marriage bed, mistress?"

"I had my own rooms, lord, and will use them once again. Sevire's sheets, if any survive, I will leave to you."

Gaspire's derisive chortle mocked her. "And I thought we had grown so close over these last weeks! Don't push me, woman. The only thing that keeps me civil with you is the baby you claim you carry."

"*Civil* is not how I would describe our time together since Lyranden bridge."

"You will have to take what you can get, lady."

"Roderran's child will get what it needs and deserves, my lord, and I know what my role in that will be."

The momentary flicker of doubt on Gaspire's face pleased Demona.

"And what role do you see for yourself?" Gaspire scowled. "You may carry Roderran's child, but you are still just Sevire's cast-off strumpet, a dead king's dalliance."

"I could give birth to a king."

"Who will be a bastard and friendless."

"So be his friend and legitimize him. You need my child, Lord Amdoran. I've seen your looks. This child means power. We need each other, don't you see?"

Gaspire's scowl weakened.

"Take me home," Demona continued, a little shocked at the steadiness in her voice. "If I am right, the servants will have not found all of Sevire's secret places. I ask much, but I may have much to offer in return."

Gaspire's look softened. "To House Anargi, then!" He smiled. "And after, perhaps we both should have a word with the Lord Prelate."

She nodded acceptance and clicked her mount to a quicker pace, heading up the sloping street to the area just below the citadel.

Home. No, not home.

She searched for the right word. Gallina came to mind.

Prospecting. But unlike those hapless miners, I know just where to look.

They had to break the lock on the gates to the Anargi estate. Weeds choked the crushed rock driveway, and the shrubbery and flowerbeds had that overgrown fullness that spoke of neglect. Demona had been gone barely three months, but the changes to the place seemed deeper to her. It was as if Sevire's corpulent, powerful personality had kept the inner rot in the place from showing outwardly, but at his death the corruption proceeded apace, perhaps even faster than normal, as though catching up with time or making recompense for past miss-use.

The house itself loomed like a ruin, dark and dusty; the halls and rooms strewn with debris, broken vases, torn tapestries and toppled decorative statues, most of them busts of Sevire at various stages in his life. Now all lay about forgotten and despoiled. Someone found a store of paint during the looting and left a derisive farewell to both Sevire and herself.

Her inclusion in the invective surprised Demona somewhat, but then she let it go. Although a prisoner in an unhappy marriage, her lot had been much better than those forced to serve in the house.

Yes, Sevire had much to answer for. This is their justice. And fear and distraction kept me from seeing or doing anything. Fear.

She stepped over a twisted end-table that sheltered the cracked remains of yet another Sevire bust chiseled smooth by a skilled hand, a testament to vanity and wealth. Someone had rubbed excrement on the features.

Fear and money ruled here. I've no more time for fear, but I do have time for money.

She left Gaspire to settle his men and slipped away, up the stairs and down the hall to Sevire's rooms. The mouse-nibbled remains of his final feast still lay on the table, dried crusts and sunken remains of hot-house fruit festooned the space around his normal seat. During her time in the palace, word reached her about how he really died. A hunk of cheese caught her attention. Demona made out the imprint of fingers pressed into its cracking sides.

His, most likely; a last grab for more.

The insight disgusted her because she knew herself guilty of similar lusts, but the events of the spring and the baby in her womb changed everything. She refused remorse when she left Sevire, and she would refuse sentimentality now. She looked around the disheveled room. Things were tossed about here, too, paintings ripped and torn, some holes in the walls but no sign of anything secret revealed.

She smiled and tipped over Sevire's great chair, built heavy and stout to take his bulk. Beneath the seat she traced a finger along the inner edge, feeling and then finding a small, raised slat of wood. She grabbed a knife from the table and worked the tip beneath the lip and pulled back. A slight click released the edge of a drawer; she pulled it free and placed on the table. In their last months together, Sevire kept her close but kept his other jewels closer. Three finely worked silk bags filled the drawer. One held diamonds, one held pearls, and one held a collection of precious, colored stones cut and ready for setting. It was a fortune by itself, worth more than anything Sevire had ever possessed put together, and he sat on it every day of his fat life, eating his way to solitude on a cushion of compressed carbon, chortling over the joke.

But he never took into account his wife. Demona stuffed the bags into her pockets, shoved a few strays she found in the drawer down her cleavage and turned to go.

And nearly collided with Gaspire, his large frame filling up the doorway.

"Taking a last look around?" he asked. He had put off his armor and riding gear. "I've set men to heating water. The kitchens are a mess, but we will do well enough." He advanced into the room. Closer, until he had Demona backed up against the table. "I've sent word to the Lord Prelate. We have a few hours, how should we use them, lady?"

Demona snatched the knife up, held it between them. Gaspire took another step and though her hands trembled, she pressed the tip to his sternum. He froze and stepped back a half-pace, frowning.

She fought to keep her voice steady. "My lord, I'd like a bath, thank you, but you flatter yourself if you think I'd take you after Roderran."

There had been lust, also, in all those speculative looks on the trail. He backed away further, glowering yet under control.

"I should have bent you over my saddle when I had the chance."

"But you didn't, and now you know you can't. But you still doubt me."

"I've always doubted you, bitch."

His futile anger, held in check by his own station and the knife she raised to point at his throat amused her. This was a form of power she understood. He repulsed her, despite his physical presence, but she needed him. She fished out one of the bags and offered it to him.

"Patience, lord, I'll not grow fat for awhile yet. I told you I have other things to offer besides my body. You will need men. You will need to pay them. Take this in earnest, Lord Gaspire, and let me have my bath alone."

Gaspire took the bag, hefted it and spilled some of its contents onto his palm, and his eyes grew round at the size, shape and number of the gems. He returned them to the bag.

"There is more of this?"

"Give me my bath and an hour and a few strong men and I should be able to find enough gold to perhaps make a difference in our hopes."

"You ask me to trust you when I could just pull this place apart and find more of *this*," and he hefted the bag for emphasis, "without waiting for you to show me?"

Demona smiled and waved the knife, a pointy rejection.

"You haven't the time, lord. Remember who comes behind us. And I do not think you would be foolish enough to try and beat it out of me. We both know you cannot risk harming my child."

Gaspire growled, foiled. "Again with the child. You best not bleed, girl, or you will bleed in earnest for toying with me."

"We have been in earnest since Lyranden Bridge, Gaspire. I admit I need you. Admit you need me. Truce?"

Gaspire's face progressed through a series of expressions as he sifted her words. Then he smiled, a genuine, feature softening gesture. He bowed and backed away to the door.

"Truce," he said turning to go. "I will see to it you are not disturbed. Collect your things. I will be your strong arms. Then we will see the Prelate." He shook the bag. "This changes everything."

Washed, refreshed and with what remained of her more useful clothes safely stowed in some travel bags, Demona accompanied Gaspire down to the Prelate's rooms in the college. Work had gone on in their absence, a large bell tower loomed above the main temple to the King's Theology. Casan met with them in his office, sitting at his ease with a glass of wine at his elbow. His flinty eyes glinted from underneath bushy, pale eyebrows as he scrutinized them.

"Why is she here?" he rasped.

Before Gaspire could answer, Demona seized her chance.

"I carry Roderran's child, Lord Prelate." She leaned forward, ignoring Gaspire's warning hiss, forcing herself to a boldness that was more front than real. "I've been off my time since just after we left with the army. But there is more." She leaned back in her chair and looked pointedly at Gaspire, who briefly narrowed his eyes in a sneer before reaching into his vest for the bag of jewels.

"Here is the *more*, my lord," he said, placing a single diamond on the table. "There are thirty others like it and the promise of more to come."

"Roderran's child and Sevire's wealth," added Demona. "My *gift* to *our* cause."

Demona expected a cold rebuff, but the Prelate surprised her with a smile. "Of course," he murmured, rubbing his boney chin. "I should have guessed it sooner. The boy kept about his business before he died. And if it is a son..." He left the thought unfinished.

Gaspire broke the silence. "We have a chance, even now, my lord."

15

Casan's beady eyes fixed on him. Demona tamped down her unease. She had grown quickly used to Roderran's bluntness, the direct use of his power and personality, but these two men were of different quality altogether; Gaspire, a shadow of Roderran's raw physicality, and Casan, a wizened knife-blade of intrigue honed razor thin for the purpose. They could help her, and Roderran's child. They could also destroy any hope she might harbor.

Always there is 'free' and then there is 'not quite free'. And I am caught in the middle of the web.

Casan ran his index finger idly around the rim of his wine glass. "I agree. We appear to have a *cause* after all. Let us be brief," he rasped. "I suspect failure, Roderran dead or taken? Correct?"

Gaspire nodded. "Correct. Sylvanus trapped us. I lead a remnant away. He had to have been killed. They proclaimed Donari King. I heard it distinctly."

Casan brought his hands together, and Demona saw the tension as he pressed them together against his pursed lips. Roderran had been Byrnard's king and protégé. The two of them had plotted and campaigned together for years before this most recent, tragic adventure. For all of Roderran's faults and weaknesses, Demona suspected Casan had loved him like a wayward son. His loss hurt. Demona let a hand stray to her belly, for though her loss was more recent, it was no less painful. If anything, Casan's pallor took on a more sickly hue at the news, but the firmness never left Casan's eyes. If anything, they grew even more steely grey.

"So, it was defeat," the Prelate continued. "It was for us as well. The Desopolisan's caught us with some fireships. That weakened us. We did not have the men left after to overwhelm them. It was a near thing, but once we broke...I was lucky to retrieve a handful of ships from the harbor. We made it back several weeks ago. We had contrary winds. The city is restless without a strong hand. I have set watch on the place, suspended the city council, and placed my men on the walls and in the harbor." He smiled wryly. "I thought it best to eschew the palace. I serve as Prelate and Teacher to any who ask. Thus, these humble rooms," he finished with a sardonic wave of his hand.

"We are set to it, then," Gaspire said. "Donari may be a week or less behind me. He wears a crown on his head. I don't doubt many in the army have sworn to him. I left a column of loyal men marching behind me; I doubt many will make it back. This place will prove no sanctuary for them. I have a small mounted group with tired worn out mounts. And her." He gestured at Demona.

16

"Yes," Casan agreed. "We have a chance. The northern fiefs will never acknowledge Donari. He's too soft, too foppish," he paused, "too southern. In that, my report of him has done some good."

"So you are determined to work against him?" Gaspire asked.

"He is not my King. And nor is he yours—or you wouldn't be here smelling of her bath salts." Casan pointed his finger at Demona as he spoke, and she felt the gesture like a knife thrust. "No, you and I, and this lovely, rich, lady here must shrift to work something. And soon, before he can settle into whatever rule he intends. We will need to make a cause for resistance."

Gaspire smiled then. And Casan smiled in return, a long, slow, devious grin that brought color back into his cheeks, smoothed away age-lines. He turned to Demona.

"Are you certain?"

She nodded, once, decisively. "I was late before the battle. And I've missed my time once again since."

Casan nodded, thinking. "You must understand, my dear, how serious this is. If you are mistaken, then I suggest you get yourself truly pregnant without delay and make sure of it away from here. Any child you carry can be our cause." He turned to Gaspire. "The slut may have found a way to be useful after all."

"My lord!" she protested. Casan waved her words away dismissively.

"You will play your part in this drama. Get round and motherly, and pray, even to the Old Ways Goddess if you have to," he added with a chuckle, "that you shove out a boy at the right time to ease any questions folk will have. And there will be questions."

"Questions?" Gaspire asked. Casan sat back in his chair, his expression satisfied.

"To which we will raise support in the north to answer," he responded. "Or rather, *you* will raise support to answer. You need to get her and your men out of Pevana as soon as possible. Go north. Keep this woman and her womb safe."

Gaspire nodded. "If we are quick, and smart, we could parley this into something unpleasant for Donari."

"Perhaps," Casan sneered, "if you had been a little quicker and smarter at Lyranden Bridge, we would not be having this conversation.

Gaspire fussed in his chair, sputtering as if summoning words to protest.

"I did what I could," he hissed finally. "I saved what I could. Roderran was a fool, and, and, yes, I admit it, my lord, I was fooled as well. My men paid for it. It was a lesson I will never forget."

Casan arched his brows. "Fooled? Such heartfelt honesty is weak and out of place for a man in your position, Amdoran. You must embrace ambition now or fail utterly. We both have had a hard slog back from unpleasant days. You want power, and that is an emotion with which I am quite familiar." He took up his glass and drained it. "You have been doing some thinking, and that is both dangerous and useful as long as you do not think and act yourself and others who follow you into further disaster. I enjoyed fifteen years campaigning and politicking for Roderran. Since we are being honest here, I admit I am tired. I'm old, Gaspire, and I miss my king. This last misadventure took something from me, I think. I enjoyed burning Tierne and Heriopolis, but the rest was unfortunate. I, too, have learned a few lessons."

He paused to refill his glass, and Demona noticed he had never offered them refreshment.

What are you, old man, besides weak and lonely?

"But I do have enough left for one more throw," Casan continued. "I think you will have some time to prepare something in the north. I might be able to forestall Donari somewhat from my presence and capacity. He will need the services of my people if he is to set up an administration." He cackled a little. "And won't he find that prospect galling? Ha! He will be so concerned with spies and mistakes he won't know where to turn. That, too, may buy us time. Everything is up in the air, my lord, and when it all hits the ground let the unwary and ignorant take warning. In less than a year, you could be leading an army back over the hills."

"But what if the child is a girl?"

"A minor inconvenience, but if it comes to that, find yourself a redheaded male infant! If we control the image and flow of information, we will turn Roderran into an icon and his child," he graced Demona with a nod, "or the child we produce into a cause worthy of romantic poetry and heroic sacrifice. Poor Donari will not know what to do or where to turn. Too bad for him."

"What of the queen?" Gaspire asked. Casan shrugged.

"Like our lovely widow here, the queen was an after-thought for Roderran. As soon as you get back to Perspa, find the barren bitch and get rid of her. See to it her father has a heart-attack or something. You will need to make use of knives in the coming months. Make no mistake; there will be blood, but that aspect never seemed to concern you in the past. See that it doesn't now."

Gaspire smiled grimly. "Old man, I have never concerned myself with blood. Remember that as we work together on this. We know much of each other—enough to slit each other's throats in the clinch. Give me time and a Regency, and I will give you power as a plaything for your dotage."

The Prelate recoiled at little at the change in Gaspire's tone. "My lord is ambitious and insulting," he said acerbically, "but is not without merit. We will keep faith with each other, then. Send word only by loyal followers. Use whatever resources you can contrive to form a base for action."

"Get me time."

"You shall have it." He picked up the jewel. "You apparently already have funds. Now, go find the men you will need." He turned his cold eyes to Demona. "And you, mistress, take care of what Roderran stuffed you with. Truth or lie, you are part of this now. I have no illusions, Demona, but I have made more from lesser stock than you."

Demona leaned forward, took up Casan's glass, and twirled the stem in her fingers, creating a candle-lit, dancing swirl. Casan's glare turned toxic, but he made no move to snatch the glass back. Courage flared along with the motion. She dained the measure and set the glass down with a decisive click.

"You are wrong, my lord, about me, about the king. He was happy with me and pleased at the idea of a child. There was real warmth, love, even. But you would not know about that, would you, old man?"

Casan stared at her, took up the glass, and turned it over on the desk. "We are finished here. Get me my cause."

Demona preceded Gaspire out the door, feeling for all the world like a target had been affixed her back.

Chapter 2: A Homecoming

The bodies, decapitated and despoiled, proved to Donari that he had no hope of overtaking Gaspire's column. It brought home to him the danger he faced if he could not secure his rule. Gaspire would seek power, would likely cull enough men for a try at the crown from the north fiefs. Those lands would fall to lesser sons, perhaps, after the losses at Lyranden Bridge. Gaspire would exploit that weakness. Donari ordered the bodies buried, seeing in their interment the possibility of his own and the price of failure for all who rode with and supported him.

He had doubts despite the crown fixed to his helm. The man who helped put it there, Sylvanus Tamorgen, Tyrant of Desopolis, could yet prove unfaithful. There were advantages to him if Gaspire plunged the north into civil war; even more if the conflict ended the Avedun line altogether. Donari fingered the notch in the circlet, a reminder of Sylvanus's last stroke, and quelled such negative thoughts. They both had taken risks for peace.

And there is the sad joke; two men fit to rule but who would rather not. And the older man stole a move on the younger and so decided the thing.

The column moved on and two days later came to the river. Donari thought Gaspire might try and hold it against him, but they crossed without trouble. More news awaited them at the crossroads where the road branched north to follow the King's Way out of Pevana's valley and over the ridges to the northern fiefs. The fork showed signs of the recent passage of a large force, both mounted and on foot.

The torn turf eased his mind. He did not want to have to fight his way into his own city.

Devyn Ambrose, the dour young man who had so recently reinserted himself in Donari's life, curbed his mount alongside. In the days after Lyranden Bridge, Donari came to appreciate anew the man's wit. Senden had been right about him, but Senden had been right about almost everything and still paid with his life. Devyn had been there, at least to avenge if too late to save. Donari fought against bitterness towards the young man at first, but those ill thoughts faded with the northward miles. He was not Senden, not even Senden's replacement; just a question full of potential. As Donari grew more used to his presence around the nightly fire, he found himself remembering those chaotic days of the Summer Festival. He took increasing solace in the way the three of them, he, Eleni and Devyn, connected to partially ease Senden's loss.

I need time.

He turned to Devyn in greeting, the younger man's face breaking into a smile framed by tired eyes and several days growth of facial hair.

"My lord," he asked deferentially. "What news?"

Donari gestured to the tracks and disturbed turf. "Gaspire has come and gone for good or ill."

"And what of Casan?"

"The Lord Prelate could be anywhere if he survived the fight at Desopolis. Your Talyior seemed to think he did, which means he might have arrived in Pevana already. He's cheeky enough for that. North would be safer for him, and us, I suppose."

"And the people?"

"They will not have heard any clear word. Gaspire has been there before us. If Casan was there to meet him, then folks have heard what they want them to hear. Lies could be a problem."

"And what will you do, lord?"

Donari looked over at Devyn, took in the frank expression, and decided on complete honesty.

"I will do what I have to do, for all of us." He touched the battle crown. "This circlet of gold is quite heavy, Devyn, but to lose it now would be disaster. I see no alternatives. I have to think of the innocent. Everywhere I look I am reminded of the sums registered to my account. Folk offer me service," he finished with a rueful smile, "and it is up to me to provide them something worthwhile to serve."

"Your people love you, sire," Devyn offered. "Your homecoming will give them hope."

"Hope?" Donari countered. "I need to give them more than that, Devyn. They may have loved me as Prince, but will they still love me as King? They have been ill-used by those in power. I need to be more than another Roderran to them."

"You have my service, sire, at need, though I, too, wonder what that might be."

"Let us get home," Donari said forcefully, "and see what paths present themselves."

Devyn bowed in the saddle and let Donari move on ahead.

Service.

Donari's thoughts lurched to Senden's body, soaked in preservative wine and packed into a rough hewn coffin that trundled along at the back of their lone wagon; a constant goad to Donari's conscience. More than anything else, *that* image pressed him. To finish the one service he could still do for his friend drove him and made his grief a constant thread that wove itself in and out among the moments of each day on the trail.

He found hope in Eleni, in her acceptance of him as he was, flawed and needy. Their pace kept them apart, and yet Donari felt their connection growing daily. They shared meals and words. At times he would catch her watching him as he coursed the column, urging his tired men and their mounts for more speed. And those looks held such understanding. He took them and the courage they communicated gratefully, and tried whenever he could to return the favor. A touch, a passing smile, an hour's talk around the nightly campfire and shared warmth beneath shared blankets determined the extent of their physical intimacy, providing just enough to combat grief and exhaustion and fear.

The column spread out along the road leading over the flats to Pevana's tilled fields. Donari spied Eleni and sidled his mount over close. She rode with the reins in one hand, her right, with her left hanging down to her thigh. Donari reached over and took her hand, raising it slightly and giving it a gentle squeeze.

"Almost home," he murmured. "I have a rather large tub that should serve for both of us." He laughed at the shocked look she gave him, which quickly fell to a warm smile.

"Will you scandalize your people so obviously? What will Cryso say?"

He laughed and let her hand drop. "The people will know you for one of their own, and Cryso will ask if we need extra water and soap!"

She gave a little chuckle. "Well and good, my lord, a bath, then. And then I could use a real bed although I would not trade all the mosquitoes and tree roots of these last days for anything."

"Nor I," he said. "And as for a bed, I have a rather large one of those as well."

They reached the land gate by late afternoon, the spring sun just beginning to pass over the mountains westward. Two banners flew over the parapets, the Avedun dolphin and the red flag of the King's Theology.

And there is one question answered, at least.

The sight of that red banner, flying saucily on a level with his own, sent Donari's ire rising with the dust from his horse's passage. The gates swung open to reveal his people clustered about the gate square. He pulled back on the reins before passing under the arch. A confrontation awaited him at the other end; the beginning of a different sort of race. He marshaled his thoughts, checked the circlet on his helm, and tried to feel like a king as his horses's hooves hit the cobblestones.

Silence greeted him. A sea of stony faces hemmed in the gate square. Donari pitied their uncertainty. The last time a king rode into their city presaged conflict and defeat. Perhaps they thought they knew him, even loved him as Devyn suggested, but that was when he was prince. The crown on his helm changed everything.

He walked his horse along the edge of the crowd. He stared at faces he recognized, tried to smile in his old way, tried to show them that he was still their lord and prince. He stopped before a woman who reached out a timorous hand to touch his stirrup.

"My lord," she asked. Donari had to lean down to hear her. "My lord, where is my man? We've heard no word."

Her question brought forth others. An old crone joined the woman.

"Yes, lord!" she rasped. "Where is my son? Roderran took him south. Have you brought him back again?"

Other voices joined with hers.

"Where is my father?"

"And mine?"

"Is my brother alive?"

"All will be made clear!" he said with as much force as he could. "Many fell, but not so many that all need despair. Captain Avarran leads them back. Be patient for the while. If wagons and horses can be found, I will send some of you south to meet them and help them home. Bring your petitions to the palace, and I will see what I can do."

The shouted questions slowly faded away, but the looks of concern and confusion did not.

He spied the Prelate's carriage.

The Prelate's guard crossed spears as if he threatened the beady-eyed old man who glared at him from the back seat. Donari stopped short, stared fixedly at Casan before swinging away to motion Devyn and his standard bearer closer.

"Put yourself in the center of the square, please," he said pleasantly. He turned back to face the Prelate. "All those in northern livery will swear fealty this day, or they will leave this city."

"My guard serves the King's Theology," Casan responded. "And as such are not subject to your will."

Donari smiled. "I'm sorry. Roderran's colors were red. I assumed we were past such foolery. Fealty, my lord, or they leave."

"Roderran--"

"Is dead," Donari snapped. "And I know Gaspire has already informed you, or else you would not have shown your face here in those

24

robes attended by these *guards* as you call them." He turned away to address the crowd. "How long since Gaspire Amdoran was here?"

Silence at first, then several voices at once from different parts of the crowd responded.

"A week since, sire!"

"Slunk in like a rat!"

"Took men and horses!"

Donari raised a hand for quiet. "I do not know what tales he may have spun in his brief *stay* among you, or what report the Lord Prelate Casan has let out, but hear now the truth!" He pointed to his standard. "This is the symbol of the royal house of Avedun! Roderran fell in folly and battle, and many followed him; many of them our brothers. Alliance we have, now, with the south. Sylvanus of Desopolis stands with us. I claim the lordship of Perspa as is my right as sole heir of House Avedun! North and South, united, my friends. Peace." He swung his eyes around the crowd, stopped when he found Eleni, sitting her horse among a cluster of his men to one side of the gate arch. "We will have peace if you will have me. I claim a crown, friends, but I will not rule unless you wish it. So, will you have me? I may not be much to look at, but I am yours to command!"

For a pregnant moment it seemed the crowd held its breath. Then certainty washed over Donari as folk, like a human wave, took the knee. Variations of *yes* filled the square. Donari leaned over to make his voice heard to Devyn.

"Cut me down that red banner, if you please," he said. "And be quick about it."

He rode back to the center of the square next to the standard and watched as Devyn ran up the stairs to the battlement, drew his blade and with a single blow parted the lines, sending the Prelate's colors fluttering down to the square in a message that went beyond words.

Again, Donari raised a hand for silence. "I am king in Pevana!" he roared. "There will be only one standard above my walls!" He pointed an imperious finger at the Prelate and his guards. "There will be no more armed priests! Fealty or leave."

He swung his horse around, waved his men behind him and made to pass out of the square. He passed close by the Prelate, who had stood in rage when his banner had been cut down. Donari slowed as he went by.

"None of your false piety, Casan. Be a priest if you like, but you will bend a knee to me. Tomorrow, lord, we meet. Maybe I'll trammel up a cushion for you."

"You are a fool," the old man snarled.

"Perhaps," Donari responded genially. "But I am king, and you will kneel."

He clattered off, leaving the Prelate sputtering. Eleni and Devyn followed in his wake.

Eleni caught up to him when they began to mount the hill to the citadel. "That was a fine show," she said. Donari gave her a sidelong look followed by a smile.

"It seemed appropriate, given the situation. We have troubles ahead, my dear, but I intend to make them rather than receive, if I can."

"What will you do with Casan?"

"Accept his false fealty and keep an eye on him. I confess I hoped to find him gone north with Gaspire. He taunts me. Martyrdom might serve his intentions, but I will not be my cousin. That he is still here suggests a plan with Gaspire. Hardly surprising."

"Unpleasant and dangerous."

Donari looked squarely at her then. "Again," he said, "not surprising. We have been dealing with unpleasance and danger for long enough now to know them."

"More fighting?"

"Perhaps. Gaspire will need to raise men. Avarran will return with the rest of the troops. Sylvanus has promised some by ship. We will be able to defend ourselves in time. I have things I will need to try. Letters to send."

"That sounds like a bad play."

Donari laughed as he drew up to the gate.

"Yes, all too predictable, but the scenes will have to play out. I'm too weak to go take power. I will have to ask them to come. If Gaspire is persuasive, most will refuse. Then, Eleni, we will fight."

Chapter 3: A Meeting

In the morning a strand of Eleni's hair fallen across his nose tickled Donari awake when she turned over to snuggle in the hollow of his shoulder. He lay still for a minute, reluctant to move and wake her. With his free hand he smoothed away her hair and contemplated the mural painted on the ceiling. A montage of Pevanese life ran from end to end. Rows of vines descended tilled slopes to the river, horses grazed in fields, laborers unloaded shipping at the harbor piers, farmers hawked produce, and artisans peddled wares at a busy market. He knew those scenes from his youth, but their tone stood out to him now. The figures all bore eager faces as they engaged in positive and prosperous activities. They represented ideas he knew he must safeguard as king just as he had when he ruled as prince.

After images of the dream he had awaken from teased back across his thoughts: Sylvanus laughing in gentle sarcasm, Devyn looking intent and curious, Casan and Gaspire's faces blending into a phantasm of old and new evil. Everything pointed him to action, but he faced limitations until Avarran made it back with the rest of the army.

And then my options expand.

He took a deep breath to steady his thoughts and sought for ways to best use the coming days. Eleni slumbered on his shoulder, her breath warm and moist. Of her, he had no doubts. She would be his queen in defiance of northern probity. She felt right nestled against his chest. She pushed his mind as much as she touched his heart.

Despite his tenuous situation, Donari accounted himself a lucky man.

He gently rolled Eleni over and eased himself out of bed, crossed the room, and stuck his head out the door. As he expected, Cryso was there, sitting on a bench across the hall, dutifully waiting for orders. At the sound of the door opening, he rose fluidly to bow.

"Good morning, my lord," he said in his most deferential voice. "Will you and Lady Eleni require breakfast?"

"Cryso! My apologies, man. I lost track of the time. Have Cook send something up. I also need a message sent to the college. It is time I had a chat with our Lord Prelate. Pick a fair spoken fellow to deliver it. Usual salutation, all that, but make sure the man stresses that this is a royal summons. I want Casan here in two hours."

"Good, my lord. You will find your best ceremonials in your dressing room. Plus, I took the liberty of cleaning out Roderran's things from the chambers he used. He left behind a robe that may prove useful."

Donari smiled his thanks. "Indeed? My thanks again, Cryso. Very good. See to my message and then come back and help me. I want to look the part for the Prelate."

"Directly, sire," Cryso responded, bowing himself back and away down the hall.

Ten minutes later Donari, fully dressed, gently teased Eleni awake with kisses to her forehead, eyes and lips. She smiled sleepily, tracing his jaw-line with an outstretched finger when he drew back.

"Good morning," she said softly, her caress morphing into a vertebrae spreading stretch. "You are dressed already. Why didn't you wake me?"

"You were exhausted, and I had some thinking to do. There is breakfast on the table by the window seat. Have one of the maids bring you something from your rooms. I have a job for you, my dear. I have a meeting this morning with the Prelate. I want you there to record it. I want to show him where I think his place is now. Having things on record might put him off enough for me to work him a little."

Before he could finish speaking, Eleni tossed off the bed clothes and reached for her robe. He watched admiringly as she wrapped her shapely curves, struck anew by her beauty, even with her hair disarranged by sleep. She caught him staring and smiled.

"What, my lord?" she asked, eyebrow arched in a manner with which he was quickly becoming familiar. She had learned to read his moods in their time together.

"Eleni," he began, choosing his words carefully. "I want you to know I have two reasons for asking you to attend. I want your eyes and ears, but I also think you have the right to face this man. He was Corvale's handler. He set in motion much of the sadness we have experienced since the winter. "

She leaned across the bed and kissed him then, once, deeply. "Thank you," she said. "I am doubly armed and doubly warned. I want to be there. Make him squirm. I will take all the more pleasure, then, recording it." She moved away gracefully. "Is that eggs I smell? Real coffee? Bread? Do you have time to eat?"

She left him amazed and besotted, staring at her retreating figure. He moved to the door, raising his voice as he turned the knob and opened it.

28

"I have taken what I need!" he said loudly. "Help yourself, but have Cryso take you to my study along with your pens and pad. You've an hour, more or less." Her muffled reply followed him out the door.

Donari made a fast circuit of the palace, checking things he knew Senden would. Guards were well-placed. Those of his party billeted in the palace had been well looked after. Devyn and several officers were finishing a quick meal in the kitchens when he swung in through the door. He waved them back into their chairs when they made haste to rise.

"Stay," he said. "I will need a meeting to settle protocols this afternoon. I want those of our men who are able to assume patrol duties, relieve any who may have been placed by the Prelate or by Roderran's orders. Secure the harbor, both landward gates and the palace. Take a muster. If we have the men available, place groups in the major city squares for the day. This is our city, but some in it may not be our people. I want to make sure of things; especially if the meeting with the Prelate goes like I think it might."

The men, young but hardened survivors of the campaign, settled themselves.

"Finish your cups, gentleman," he urged, "and then set about seeing to things. We are home, but I cannot trust we are home safe until Avarran comes up. We may face trouble from the north over all of this. I need the city made as secure as possible in the interim." He hooked a finger at Devyn. "A word, Devyn? Walk with me?"

They fell in step with each other as they walked down the hallway towards Donari's study.

"How was your rest?" Donari asked. "I know I was completely done in yesterday."

"As well as could be expected," Devyn responded, "given that I slept in a dead man's bed. I found it restful, in the end, and instructive."

Donari gave him a sidelong look. "Instructive?"

"I learned a few things, sire."

"As in?"

"As in I feel myself pointed at something. I think I am meant to be here, my lord."

"Strange," Donari mused, stopping by one of the great windows that looked south over the city. "I have been thinking the same thing since we turned for home." He turned to look squarely at Devyn. "We will have many things pointed at us once the northern lords understand how things have changed. This city will fill up with eyes, probably has already if I read our Lord Prelate correctly, and I will need to keep ahead of them. Senden knew this city and my mind better than anyone else. I don't expect you to be him, but between you and Eleni--" He left the thought unfinished for he saw comprehension come over the young man's face.

"My lord," Devyn said. "I doubt there is anyone besides Senden who knows this place as I do."

"I heard part of the tale. I think you are uniquely placed, Devyn Ambrose, to help me save my crown. I need you out and about today and over the days to come. I need you to smell out information I might be able to use. In some ways, this crown Sylvanus granted me handicaps me. I have to play the statesman. You don't."

"I am no assassin, lord."

"Of course you aren't. You are a poet of Pevana! And you swore fealty to me on the slopes above Lyranden Bridge, and I will require hard service of you, maybe, but I will never take your honor. That was my cousin's way. I intend a new way if I am spared. So, will you be my eyes and ears?"

Devyn paused a moment before answering, moving to the window to stare out at the city scape spread below. Donari joined him, leaning on his hands against the sill. Above, the midmorning sun burned away the coastal haze. Roof tops shed steam as they dried. Smoke from ovens and fires snaked upward to drift seaward in the sun-born land breeze. Donari waited, patient, aware of the personal choice the young man next to him faced. In the distance, he could see the great open space created by the renovation of that portion of the Maze that had burned. Devyn seemed to have noted the same, for he smiled and turned with his answer.

"This is my first day home in ten months," he said. "I have places I need to visit. Of course, I am your man, sire. I'll be off directly. When shall I report to you?"

"Tonight. Earlier, if you uncover anything vital. My thanks, Ambrose."

Devyn bowed and made to turn back toward his rooms. "I am commanded," he murmured. "That it is also my own wish is a double grace."

He walked away, leaving Donari alone with his city view and a growing sense of responsibility. Donari tried to envision where next to place his feet in the political maze. He forced himself away from the sill with an exasperated sigh. The meeting with the Prelate waited for him. Despite the unpleasant anticipation, he might gain at least the beginning of some answers. He continued down the hallway to the back stairs that led down to his study. A page, breathless in haste, caught up with him as he set foot on the first step.

"My lord," the boy said, stuttering and reaching for breath. "Cryso sent me to tell you the Lord Prelate has arrived. He waits for you in the main hall. He demanded Cryso open the door to your study and let him in, but Cryso begged off. The Prelate seemed somewhat put out. Shall I return and see to it, lord?"

Donari smiled at the image of a ruffled Casan. "No, let the Prelate wait." Donari searched for the name to go with the boy's eager, familiar face. The feckles clinched it; a rarity in olive-skinned Pevana. "It's Drue, isn't it? And your House?" The boy rewarded his guess with a blush that intensified the effect.

"My king," Drue gushed, lingering over *king* as if testing the savor of a new word. "My father is the Merchant Ander Manelli."

"Ah, House Manelli, is it? Well, Drue-lad. No more running. If you are to serve me, you must know that at times it is important to at least give the appearance of control. Come with me now and catch your breath. See me settled at my desk, and then you can show the Prelate in with proper style. Afterwards, ask Cryso to bring in something red with some cheese. The Lady Eleni Caralon will also be coming to act as my secretary. See to it that she has enough ink and pens for the purpose."

The awed young man escorted him to the back door to his study before releasing him to his other tasks.

Donari settled himself at his desk. He chose the study rather than the reception hall. What they had to say to one another did not need a full audience. Drue re-entered, his eyes round with tension and excitement.

"Sire," he said. "The Lord Prelate Casan is here." Donari gave the lad a wink, took Roderran's notched battle circlet and placed it on his head, took a deep breath and motioned the boy to open the door.

Casan swept in sporting full ceremonial garb complete with ermine robe and his theologian's cap. But all the finery could not hide the man's lack of color and the new wrinkles pinching the flesh near his eyes.

"My Lord asked for an audience? Why here? Could it be you fear that piece of bent wire on your brow might slip off?"

Donari did not respond at first, choosing rather to stare coldly at the bent figure bristling in front of him while he weighed how best to respond.

"Drue, a chair for the Lord Prelate, if you please. And show Lady Eleni in when she arrives. Thank you." He dropped his voice into a more authoritative tone to address the Prelate.

"Interesting choice of words, priest, but at least they sounded honest. Please note, I did not *request* an audience. Rather, I *required* a meeting, and you are here. What we have to say to one another is best kept to only a few ears. Sit. Talk. That is what we must do now. Sadly, I could not find that cushion, but no matter."

Casan eased himself into a chair and leaned back, affecting calm and control.

"Your humor is in poor taste, young man," he sneered. "Such arrogance is foolish."

Donari fought back the urge to chuckle.

"I left mirth at Lyranden Bridge, Casan, and I do not require your opinions on taste."

Casan's eyes flared daggers.

That's right, you old bag. I am not what you expected. Robes and a hat cannot hide the truth of you!

The Prelate sagged back into his chair as if conceding a throw.

"Forgive my tone, my lord. I am an old man, and the man who bore that crown before you was dear to me. I have heard what happened. What was done with his body?"

"Buried, along with nearly four thousand of his men, most of the northern nobles and joined by nearly fifteen hundred Desopolisans."

"Could you not have brought him home?"

"Could Gaspire have? No, don't protest. I did not bring my cousin's body. I chose not to."

"You chose?" The words came like the crack of a whip, a moment's lapse, revealing both Casan's grief and anger at Donari's assumption of power. It was a small slip, but it allowed Donari to keep his expression impassive.

"Yes."

"By whose volition?"

"My own, as king."

"By whose hand? Sylvanus? Is he making Perspan kings now?"

Donari fought down a sudden urge to lean over the desk and slap sense into him. Roderran would have, which is why he chose otherwise. Instead, he leaned back in his chair, calmed his heart beat and cooled his rage.

"Roderran's folly cost him his life and the lives of many who followed him," he said. "Sylvanus took him in a fair fight, offered me the crown and peace with the south. He did not need to, but he saw an honorable way out of the chaos of *your* policies. As I am Roderran's heir, I took the crown. As I am king, I accepted the offer of peace."

"Even though my force was even then attacking Desopolis."

"And being beaten, as it turned out, by a bunch of garrison troops and the ingenuity of a wandering Pevanese poet."

"How can you exult in such loss?"

"Forgive me, Lord Prelate, but I have felt *such loss* as you put it for the better part of the last year while you and Roderran set in motion the disaster that befell us. I miss the men; they were innocent dupes to failed rule. I even miss my cousin. If I could have limited his excess and saved him, I would have. I would have even forgiven him the attempt he made on my life, or was it you, my Lord? Corvale was your creature after all, wasn't he? Please, don't insult my intelligence by denying it. You came here wrapped in your priestly vestments as if they granted you immunity." He forestalled a response by turning his attention to the door, which opened to admit Eleni. "Ah, Eleni, please come in. Drue, a chair near that side table if you please. My secretary, Lord Prelate, to keep us both honest, as it were. Mistress Caralon, the Lord Prelate Byrnard Casan; Lord, Eleni. You may have seen her. She was the first female scholar at the university."

Casan shifted uncomfortably in his chair. His jaw worked, creating an impression of an aged bird of prey chewing on something unpleasant. The wrinkled pallor in his cheeks flared tinges of red.

"What is the meaning of this, *sire*?" Casan asked. "What are you up to?"

Donari gave him a thin smile that turned genuine when he looked away to Eleni.

"Up to? Remember to whom you speak, priest. She is here to record our words. I intend to bring truth, Casan, to all my people. She is here also to keep me from killing you outright."

"Blasphemy! I am the Lord's representative!"

"Blasphemy? To expose a lie? Retribution, rather. Corvale killed her husband. Would you like to answer her? No? Are there really any accidents in all of this? You have much to answer for, Casan, and so I will let you live. You see? I am not my cousin after all."

Casan did not respond at first, and in the pause Eleni's pen flew along its page, filling the silence, hinting at suppressed emotions. The Prelate seethed at such baiting; his eyes darted about as though searching for an escape, but instead words came.

"Hard words, my lord," he growled, "but they also reveal your weakness."

Donari frowned in exasperation. "I never claimed strength," he said, quietly at first but with growing conviction. "I did not ask for the crown. I did not ask for you or your hired incendiaries. I did not ask for war. But I am more than willing to fight, priest, for a real peace. For that, I will be king."

"A king of what? A middling city? A collection of southern ruins? The north will repudiate you! You are a king in name only. The Perspan throne sits in Lomillar, not Pevana."

"And you are a priest in name only. Shall we repudiate your status and remove your robes and hat, sir? Shall we decree an end to the experiment in theology and return to orthodoxy? Gaspire might be able to find enough spears in the north to make a try at us. I expect him to, eventually. I'm sure the two of you discussed the idea. But remember, Casan, most of the senior northern nobles now molder in southern dirt. You burnt several cities. Shall I burn your churches? Without them you are nothing, and without Roderran, what is that faith in the end? Emptiness led by empty vessels; men who lost their honor and their way in the quest for power. And," he finished, "the king's seat is wherever I place my bum, regardless of location."

Casan slumped

"The faith is real," he said, but his voice had lost most of its bluster. "The people believe. I am their spiritual leader, now."

"Where does it read in your holy tracts: *Thou shalt rape and pillage and engage in dynastic murder*? Answer me that, holy man."

"My lord goes too far," he grated between clenched teeth. "I will not accept--"

"You will accept everything," Donari interrupted, "because your king has said so. Calm yourself, sir. We are not finished."

"What else have you to say, *sire* that you have not yet said?"

"This: I will let my people choose. You may keep your *faith* even though we both know how false it is. But let it be a true faith then. From this moment onward, all security measures under your control are ended. There will be an end to priests guarded by bully boys. You may chew on your plots, Prelate, but you will find them less than nourishing."

Casan's eyes ceased their darting, as though arrested by curiosity mixed with caution.

"My king shows wisdom and kindness?"

"Expediency."

"Lord?"

"I have a task for you. In three days time, I will hold a state funeral for Senden Arolli. Representatives from all faiths will speak. You will give the main eulogy."

Casan sputtered. "What, are you mad? The man was a commoner! A sneak! I cannot, will not countenance such a thought."

"Ah, he may have been a *commoner*, but he was no common man. He was my friend and a hero to the crown, and on your life you will speak for him and speak well."

"But, but doing so…"

Donari smiled, a fine mixture of hate and real genuine pleasure. "Yes," he said. "You see it now, don't you? I spare your boney knees. Speaking for Senden will send a clear message to all that you support my crown and beneficence. I wonder how that will play out among your northern contacts? I could kill you. If you had a conscience, you know I would have just cause. But this is much better. Better even than some false vow of fealty."

"Three days." Just two words, flat, dull.

A small victory.

"Correct. You will send a copy of your speech to Lady Eleni here at the palace for safekeeping and posterity. I think our little meeting is over. You may leave."

The Prelate struggled slowly to his feet, looking even older than when he first entered the study, and bowed just barely enough to avoid insult. He ignored Eleni as he shuffled out of the room.

Donari stared at the door a long moment after it closed. He rubbed his right temple, eyes unfocused, lost in thought; the only sound in the room the scritch of Eleni's pen on the paper as she struggled to complete the record. Donari waited for her to finish. She raised a worried frown to him when she put down her pen.

"I am sorry," he said. "I hadn't meant to bring up Tomais or Corvale. That was a slip. I know it hurt you. Forgive me."

"I was startled, that's all," she said in reply.

"I wanted him to really see you. I needed him off his center. I think it worked."

"Yes," she said with a wry smirk. "I think it did.

"He is still a venerable old snake. We but scotched his tail a little. He has venom enough left for the purpose. I suspect he learned as much from me as I did from him."

"And what did you learn, my lord?"

"I learned he intends to work against me. But he hopes to do so while staying in Pevana, now, that I did find a little surprising."

"And what did he learn from you?"

"That I am stronger than he expected, more determined and more dangerous than he ever suspected. But that won't keep him from making a try at me. Of that I am quite certain."

"Is that all, you think?"

Donari rose, walked around his desk to where she sat and took first her pad, then her pen, and then raised her up to take her in his arms.

"If there was more," he whispered before he kissed her, "I am sure we will discover it soon enough."

Chapter 4: A Day for Devyn

Devyn left on his errand partially rested but disquieted by his night in the palace. The staff put him in Senden's old, spare rooms. To Devyn, it seemed as if Senden left very little of himself behind when he accompanied Donari on his final adventure. There were a few books, a sword, some spare clothes in a closet, mostly black, a good pair of light boots, which he set aside, and a small notebook in a drawer. He almost sent for Cryso to ask for another room, but then he glanced through the notebook. What he saw there kept him up despite his road-weariness, for the notebook held Senden's thoughts and commentaries about the service he rendered Donari and Pevana's people.

There had been nothing salacious in the writing. Senden recorded things in terse descriptions and bald expressions. As Devyn read, he felt like he recovered something he had once lost. He and Senden met only a few times, and yet he remembered Senden's lack of surprise when Devyn found him dying after Jaryd Corvale's treacherous ambush. The images stayed with Devyn the entire journey back to Pevana. One of the entries toward the back of the notebook gave him his shocking answer and sent him into a dream-troubled sleep. It dated from last summer: *Another temple fire last night. Renia's, down on the east side above the Landgate Way. Pulled a fool out of the smoke. Maybe the burns on his arm will teach him a lesson, if he lives. If he does, then I may have just saved my replacement. Although as to that, he has the air of an ascetic about him. He will need to learn how to balance caution with daring.*

To read about himself through the pragmatic eyes of another disconcerted Devyn at first, but later in the account he found another short note referring to the finals and their leave-taking: *Cheeky pup thumbed his nose at Casan. Two against the world! Youth! Word has it they rode out on stolen horses. Ambrose: he's the one.* Devyn's dreams that night replayed scenes from the last year; a series of vignettes viewed through a prism of changed perspective, Senden's perspective. He realized then it was not just Kembril's shade that urged him to come back. Senden, too, in his sardonic way, had sent out a similar summons fate saw fit to answer.

He was home. He had tasks.

Devyn chose to walk when he left the palace. It seemed like a better option for his needs. It had been ten months since he and Talyior rode south. He noticed some of the immediate changes when he rode in with Donari the day before. The hazy mass of the Maze that used to loom like a shadow in the southern parts of the city was gone, replaced by barracks and a cleared space visible from the palace gate. He paused there for a moment, breathing in memory, reorienting himself on the rhythms he used to accept as a matter of course. The scene presented him felt like words running out in a stream, familiar, known, like the touch of a favorite garment, yet altered subtly to account for sinews just that much larger, vision that much broader, the same yet different. Poetry, though altered, still rose with the mist leaching off the damp rooftops of the city.

He sauntered down the hill, taking his time while he had it to spare. Pevana may have smelled like home, but most of the Pevana he knew as such had gone up in flames last summer. A gravesite called to him. Eleni told him the tale during their return journey, and he intended to spend a few minutes with Kembril. He wanted to save that for later. He had some wandering to do first. At the base of the hill, he took a side street off the intersection and headed off toward Malom Banly's stable. Eleni still kept all his collected words. Her praise pleased him, but he did not feel the need to repossess them. They were from a former time. He was a different person now with a different purpose. He felt certain there would be different words, at need.

He chose to come at Banly's from the alley that ran along the outer corral, close to where he had his nook in the back stable. He did not need to see Malom. He wanted to see what sort of horseflesh was still to be had in the city, and he wanted to see if chance had preserved any of his things, and one thing in particular.

The back corral stood empty, a sure indication the herds of Pevanese stock drafted for Roderran's campaign had not been replaced. As he climbed over the fence, Devyn recalled how Talyior came upon him that day last summer, lost in mid-practice in the space near the little stone altar rescued from Renia's burning temple. Now it lay tipped over on its side, weedy vines partially covering one lip. Devyn knelt to pull away the growth and relived that night when he first met Senden Arolli. Thoughts of Senden and Talyior roiled. Past and present mixed in flux. Part of him wanted to hear Malom's garrulous voice ordering him to train the newly broken colts, to return to what he knew best and closest, to step aside from the path of words and ambition, but the greater part of him recognized the futility of such notions.

It was impossible for some to come all the way home.

His sleeping space had been cleaned out. Not even the old field desk remained. In fact, it appeared no one had replaced him. The place felt lifeless. He found an old burlap sack, placed the bowl in the bag, slung it over his shoulder and retraced his steps back to the alley. He knew where his bowl belonged.

He walked down the alley and turned left to take the main street back towards the city center and the cleared area that once formed part of the Maze. And as he turned he nearly ran into Sanya, the baker's daughter and his former lover. She bore a large basket of hard rolls, one of which toppled out as she swerved to avoid him.

"Devyn!" Her hand flew, not to the falling roll, but to her very-pregnant belly. "I'm, I'm surprised to see you!" She made to bend down to pick up the fallen roll, but Devyn forestalled her.

"No more surprised than I," Devyn replied, picking up and brushing off the roll before replacing it in the basket. "Hello, Sanya."

She stared at him in silence for a moment; her expression shifting from alarm to awareness, to anger and appraisal, not unexpected after an absence of nearly ten months, and all spiced by a glimmer of the flash that used to grace her eyes. But the effect faded quickly, replaced by a pinched dullness that spoke of weariness.

"You're back," she said, shifting the basket to her hip, almost defiantly exposing her gravid condition. "They say Donari has returned as king. There was a battle. Was it victory or defeat?"

Devyn smiled away the accusation in her tone. "I came back with him, Sanya. And yes, there was a battle, very terrible. And I suspect there was a little of both victory and defeat in the outcome. Time will tell."

As he spoke, he watched her face fall as she took in the possibilities of what he said. No doubt the father of the child she was soon to have had marched with the army. He made a brief gesture toward her belly.

"So," he said lightly, "it appears there have been changes. Whose? Avarran's?"

She raised her chin in false pride. "Not yours, to be sure! And he! Na, far too noble, that one, despite all my efforts. But you, leaving without so much as a word! Gone all these months. Harsh, Devyn."

"Unavoidable, Sanya, I really had no choice. I had enemies."

"But you never came back."

"Sanya," Devyn began, but Sanya interrupted him.

"Never mind," she snapped. "It doesn't matter anyway."

Theirs had been a physical relationship that never got beyond the beginnings of real care. Sanya had wanted more, but Devyn never encouraged her. He felt a little guilty all the same. Sanya had brought him to manhood; at the least she deserved his kindness.

"Sanya," he said, his voice dropping to create a soft tone. "It will always matter. Tell me, who is the father?"

His words seemed to break through her bravado, and real concern washed over her face.

"He was one of the Lord Amdoran's cavalry officers. He rode south. Amdoran was here a week ago. My man wasn't with him."

Devyn catalogued that piece of information along with the insights from the stables, for the latter explained the former. His mind flashed back to the field at Lyranden Bridge and the carnage of Amdoran's charge. More than likely the father of Sanya's child was one of those casualties.

"I am sorry, Sanya. I have no news for you."

"As I said," she replied. "Was it victory or defeat? Donari a king. My man dead. My child goes fatherless."

Devyn shook his head ruefully. "Sanya, I don't know what to say. All will sort itself out eventually, I am sure." He paused, weighing his words. "Was it that way for you and your man? Love?"

Sanya smiled, a wan, familiar look. "A little," she responded. "And I sensed that he's dead or won't come back. So, I will have my baby anyway, man or no man. What sort of world the child will come to…" She left the thought unfinished, letting her voice trail off as she looked away.

Devyn reached up then and gently brushed away the single tear she let escape her lashes. The gesture brought her eyes back to his, fixing him with an intensity and need he found daunting.

"Devyn," she whispered. "What am I to do?"

Devyn smiled. Sanya had always been a rough sort, earthy, a little coarse, but genuine. She would survive and thrive as a mother if her world held enough peace to give her and her child a chance.

"Have your baby," he said gently, "in peace. Donari is home now. He is king and will bring change if he is spared. I intend to see to it that he is."

"Are you grown so powerful then, horse-boy?"

Devyn bowed slightly.

"I serve him directly," he said. "Powerless as ever, but with a purpose."

Her smiled deepened. "Words," she scoffed good-naturedly. "Always the poet. You are different, Devyn, changed, but in that you are the same. Words."

Devyn shifted his burden. "They are my trade, my dear, have been since I left, actually. Renia bless your baby, Sanya. Peace to you."

"Are you back to stay?"

"Sanya," he began, but again she forestalled him, reaching a hand to his forearm.

"Ah, now, I don't mean that," she said. "We are past that, I think. Besides, you don't have the look of a father yet. I," She placed her free hand on her swollen belly, "*we* will manage well enough. I only ask because this is your home, such as it is."

Her words of release made him feel strangely sad. She had no idea what Donari brought back with him from the South. Her world stood as good a chance of faltering into civil war as it did prospering in peace. To Devyn, she was the face of the service he would give to Donari. She was Pevana; her baby the hybrid soul of north and south.

"I am home," he said, turning to go. "For as long as my king needs or allows. Luck to you, Sanya, and to your child. Renia grant he, or she, comes to a world at peace."

"And you, Devyn Ambrose, and you. Luck and life, friend."

He watched her waddle away and wondered which burden weighed the heavier: the one burning his shoulders or the one burdening his heart.

Devyn stood looking down at Kembril's grave, the altar bowl in its sack by his feet and his hands grasping the tines of the wrought iron fence enclosing the site. Ever since Eleni told him about the aftermath of the fire, Devyn had tried to prepare himself for this moment. And still tears came. He stood there for a long time, taking in the precisely engraved headstone, the border of stones, some of which still bore burn marks from the flames that took most of the Maze, and the carefully clipped and tended grass that grew in the space. Fresh cut flowers lay gracefully on the mound.

Devyn noted the contradiction: a beautiful, endearing resting place for his mentor and friend that bore little resemblance to Kembril as he had been in life.

"Ah, Kem," he muttered around his tears. "They honor you, but there isn't enough dust or shade."

He took the bag with the altar bowl and lowered it over the fence and followed. Taking extreme care, he took the bowl and his knife and scooped out a hollow depression in the turf before the headstone. Using the burlap sack, he cleaned off the bowl as best he could before placing it in the space he created. He put the fresh flowers into the bowl and sat back on his haunches. The fence would have to go, eventually. Kembril never dealt with walls or barriers in life; he should not have to in death.

Still, pleasant enough for rest.

He looked around the wide space around the gravesite where once there had been a clearing created by the huge, ancient oak tree. Turf and bare earth commanded the space where the Maze hovels used to ring the area. Barracks and horse lines loomed to the south. To the west and south, the remnant of the Maze still marched its labyrinth of poverty and piety down toward the southern walls. Whoever saw to Kembril's internment chose well, but it lacked one essential element.

He moved behind the gravestone and scooped another hole in the ground. Then he reached into his shirt and drew out a small leather bag. In it was a single oak nut. He found it near where Senden fell to Jaryd Corvale; putting it in his pocket had been an afterthought of sorrow, but now he felt as though he were completing a pattern as he placed it in the hole. In time, with luck, Kembril would have his shade again. When he finished planting his hope, he sat with his back against Kembril's stone. Words came:

> I breathe centuries of memories
> When I review all that I had from you.
> And in the stories and lays
> I used to mark my days--
> A constantly changing view.
> And over hills unknown
> Through thoughts full blown
> I spoke of things fine and true
> To the high and the low
> The quick and the slow
> They all point back to you...

He closed his eyes, put a hand to the stone and kept vigil.

Sunlight, beginning its westward slant teased him back to the now. As he sat there blinking away the vestiges of reverie, he grew aware that a small group of children squatted in a semi-circle facing him on the outside of the fence. For a moment the scene transported him back in time and the faces, showing various stages of cleanliness and innocence, stared back at him with his own eyes. Almost, almost, he felt as though he were perched upon a regal tree root summoning the words with which to enchant an audience. But his better sense knew such a vision partly just a product of the place, a memory of other stories, other words, other days. He took a breath and let it go as a sigh. His action brought a response from his audience. Some of them scooted closer. All of them fixed him with eager eyes.

"Please, sir," one who looked to be the eldest among them said. "Why do you sit with the dead?"

Devyn did not reply at first, for the question, so genuine and soft in its utterance, nonetheless caught him off guard. He checked the sun's position. He had been sitting against Kembril's tombstone for over two hours lost in resting thought, but he forgave the time because exhaustion sometimes took forms other than physical.

He smiled at the children. He sent thanks to the shade of his former mentor. He had been about other purposes for too much of his recent past, a servant to his king, but he had his own needs to meet as well.

"I was paying honor to a friend," he said finally. "I have been away too long. I heard of the care given to this place and came to make my own offering."

A little girl child, probably no more than six or seven years old, piped up from the edge of the group. "My maman says we hav't keep the Old One's place clean," she said. In her tones he heard the tenor of the Maze reborn, beauty hidden beneath dirt and poverty. "He tol' us stories. I can't climb the fence yet, so I find flowers."

"They put a fence up to protect it from the horses," said the oldest boy who had spoken first. "My sister brings me the flowers, and I climb in and see to things. We miss the old man. He told us great stories," his voice caught, "before the fire."

"I remember," Devyn said. "I was there. A very great fire. A very great price to pay."

"I remember you," the boy said. "You are Ambrose the poet. You were his friend. We saw you, before."

"Yes," Devyn replied. "I was his friend, and he mine, more than a friend. I miss him, but I thank you for the honor you do him, children. He is well repaid, I'm sure."

"We miss him, too," the little girl said. "And his stories! Would you tell us one?"

"Tasia!" snapped her brother. "Don't be rude! He hasn't time for us."

"You hush, Bastin!" Tasia squeaked. "We haven't had a story in forever. I was jus' asking." Other children in the group took up her cause, adding their voices in defense of her request.

Devyn's quiet laughter silenced their argument. "Peace!" he chided them gently. "Peace brothers and sisters."

He checked the sun again and climbed over the fence and sat, back against the wrought iron tines, facing their expectant faces.

"I have time to spare for a little tale, my friends. I will tell you the first tale Kembril ever taught me. This is the story of how Renia's minion, the daring Minuet, got her bow and barbs and set about piercing the fates of Men. Settle closer now, and off we go."

He took a deep breath, inhaling the taints of all the real and imagined impressions from those days when Kembril's words kept him alive.

"Once upon a time, back in the days before men made of this place a city, back before there were kings and princes, ships and trade, before just about everything, a fair spirit came into being as a thought from the mind of the goddess Renia. So surprised was Renia to discover what her thought had wrought that tears sprang unbidden to her eyes and fell in a gentle spill down to the slumbering shape before her. A teardrop each landed on the shape's brow and eyes, causing it to wake. Another splashed against closed lips, causing the mouth to open, a breath to be taken and words to come forth.

'My Lady,' the shape whispered, gazing up in awe and love. 'You called me. What is your wish?'

And Renia sat fair amazed at the slip of life before her. 'You come upon a wish,' said she. 'You are a note, a melody, and I find you fair and dear. I shall call you Minuet, for you are small yet precious.'

"And so it was that Minuet came into the world and set about helping Renia order her domain. And many were the tasks the Goddess set her, and long were the journeys she took, bringing light to lands which before had loomed as shadows within shadows. Her footsteps were color, her breath light and air. Her goddess's tears she collected into channels, creating the rivers and streams that flowed from the purple hills to the sea. And Renia set her to planting seeds of all kinds, and so were sown the trees and grasses, the vines and all manner of growing things. And Renia bethought herself and lo, wild kine and surefooted beasts passed among the tree woven slopes and along the fallow plains, and Minuet escorted them and watched over their progress and thought it good to help bring order from chaos."

"My Maman says I am chaos," one little boy chirped, breaking the spell momentarily.

"You shut it, Tam!" his fellows cried. "Don't ruin the story!"

"Nah, nah," Devyn eased. "Our Tam is more part of this tale than you realize, for Man is something of Chaos, you know. Even disorder is part of the pattern. Listen now." He settled his back to a more comfortable position and continued.

"And so it came to pass that Renia grew aware of the influence of another force in her design. Casting her thought far and wide she knew then the power of Tolimon, the God of conflict and strife, in whose image the shapes of Man now walked across the lands Renia ordered. And where Man walked death stalked, for Tolimon gave Man restless power but no conscience. The fair Minuet also surmised this and sped to her lady, 'Mistress,' said she. 'Such horrors have I seen. Your works are marred; the land itself bleeds.' And Renia set her tears flowing anew to serve as solace for her servant tried and true, but the effect was not what she intended, for Man, as Tolimon created him, would be stubborn and easily distracted from wisdom and reason. She put her mind to work on what she might do to counter Tolimon's mischief."

"Long and long Renia thought while the shadow and effect of Man spread throughout the land. And Renia could see that such powers she possessed would not be enough to fully remove the stain of this new life sprung from Tolimon. And in her teary extremity, Renia's thought alighted upon a partial remedy. From the wellspring of her mind she produced a bow of strident white and a quiver of arrows tipped with light.

'Take you this bow,' said she to Minuet. 'And with it these barbs of lofty intent. Though we cannot remove Tolimon's Man, we can at least prick him to a partial notion of order and good, for we must make it understood that chaos is but a shadow life, as much the tree as the wood. We will call these arrows Conscience and the blows they impart, however gentle or harsh, Fate. With these, you shall snick Tolimon's threads and thereby seek to wend Man to our design. Off with you, now, fair Minuet. We will have our Man and our Order yet.'

"And so it was that Minuet became the huntress of Design, and through her bolts she weaves the fates of men into Renia's plans. And such it is that chaos never lasts and always falls to conscience's better thoughts, thanks to Renia of the Tears, and the Arrows of Minuet."

Devyn's youthful audience sat in rapt silence as the timber of his voice faded to silence. Then as one they all smiled and erupted in a cacophony of thanks and requests for more. But he had run out of time. He still needed to get to the Golden Cup in time to listen in on the afternoon talk. Telling his tale made him thirsty, which added impetus to his decision to rise and leave.

"My friends, that will have to be all for now, but I promise to return from time to time for more stories. Keep watch on our Kembril here as you have done. Flowers in the stone bowl, perhaps a little water on the turf about his feet. Na, na" he continued, waving down their shrill protests.

He leaned down conspiratorially, drawing them in with a smile and a gesture. "We have Donari as our king, now, as I am sure you have already heard."

They nodded breathless agreement.

"And I am sure you would like to help him if you could." More nods. "So, I want you to keep your eyes and ears open for things that don't feel or sound right. Like what you might ask? Nothing evil. Nothing dangerous. Just, if you notice strange types, because I know you keep track of comings and going, yes? Then take note. Get word to me.

We may face threats, you know, to Donari, to all of us. If we can find out those threats beforehand, then maybe we can stay safe and have more time for stories. Help me watch over our home." The nods grew more solemn with each word. He had no real fears for their safety; the Maze-born knew what it took to survive. In the future, if anything in the southern parts of the city moved, he was sure to hear of it.

When he finished speaking, they departed like a breath, less a satisfied audience than a motley collection of new-hatched amateur spies. But under the present conditions, Devyn had to get his information as he could; too much depended on the knowing. He watched them scurry off toward their homes, skirting the barracks buildings and disappearing into the shadows of what remain of the old Maze beyond. All but one. The little girl, Tasia, nearly tripped him when he turned to leave.

"Thank you," she said in her birdlike voice, reaching out her tiny hand to touch his knee. "That was good. Jus' like the Old Man. Minuet is my favorite."

"It was my pleasure, Tasia. Now, catch up with your brother. I would not wish you to get in trouble with your mother." She flitted off, and he turned his feet west towards the *Golden Cup* and his final stop.

With the first sip of the mug of beer at *The Cup*, Devyn knew himself well and truly home. Of all that he saw and sensed that day, only the taste of Saymon's ale had remained constant. He actually let loose a small sigh as he swallowed. He settled back into the corner booth so he could survey the room, ordered a plate of that day's fare and set himself to review what he gleaned from his day's wanderings.

Devyn scouted all four of the major stable establishments in addition to Banly's. No more than a score of sound mounts remained in the city. Gaspire had looted liberally, and Donari would find it hard to equip and mount more than a company at this point. And judging from the paucity of available horse flesh, Devyn felt certain Gaspire led more men out of Pevana than he brought in with him. The few men in northern livery were attached to Casan: an irritating but nominal presence. Even if he had the material available to follow Gaspire, Donari stood an even chance of being outnumbered should he catch up with his cousin. As Devyn parsed it, lacking horses and men, the king had no options until the rest of the army arrived, and that might not be for another month.

The northern army had done more than just occupy Pevana. Sanya. Devyn was sure there were other newborns or babes on the way from northern fathers. Pevana had always been something of a hybrid place with its mixture of northern politics and southern attitudes. The coming generation would blend blood into the mix. Devyn found the prospect intriguing. New times meant a new song for Pevana to sing if Donari could survive as king.

Sanya, folk he observed, and especially the looks on the faces of the children he encountered at Kembril's grave spoke of Pevanese pride of place, affection and support for their prince turned king, and a willingness to survive. Even the faces and chatter of the patrons who began to fill the Cup for their evening glasses, dock workers and tradesmen, even the four prostitutes over in the far corner, all seemed normal enough. Talk around the room held topical matters mostly, but it was early yet. He would nurse his food and brew and wait for a quiet word with Saymon before he left. Perhaps the scene was too normal.

A plate and two mugs later, Saymon Brimaldi himself brought over an uncorked bottle of wine and a pair of glasses and slid into the booth opposite Devyn. The large, bearded proprietor fixed intense, deeply recessed eyes on him as he casually poured a measure into both glasses. He pushed one over, taking a sip from his own as he did so.

"Welcome back," he rumbled through his beard. "The Prince's money run out?"

Devyn laughed as he accepted the glass. "Months ago," he said. "It is good to see you, Saymon. And I am sure you are aware of the change in Donari's title?"

Brimaldi smiled in turn. "Oh, yes, that spread like wildfire yesterday. We've had little news otherwise. I assume things went ill in the south?"

"That depends on how you look at it."

"How do you?"

"Roderran underestimated Sylvanus, made mistakes, and they cost him his life...along with a large chunk of the army, both northern and Pevanese. It was a debacle."

"And out of it Donari becomes king?"

"That is a longer tale; perhaps for another time."

Saymon stared at Devyn for a moment as though weighing the efficacy of pressing him for more, then he shrugged it off.

"Fair enough" he said, sipping again. "When that time comes, we will crack another bottle of this and set to. You obviously have stories about you worth listening to. You've come back a master of yourself, young man, changed, if I may be so bold."

A compliment from Saymon was a rare thing, and this one startled Devyn, made him feel a bit transparent.

"My thanks, I think," he replied. "Life has become both simpler and more complicated."

47

"I daresay. Where is your friend, Talyior? I last saw him here, collecting on a bet against you, as a matter of fact."

"He found a girl, rather well-connected you might say, in Desopolis. I expect him here in a few months, perhaps. There is to be a peace conference. Sylvanus of Desopolis swore fealty to Donari on the battlefield."

Saymon quirked an eyebrow.

"Yes, that is correct," Devyn continued. "It was one of the strangest moments in a series of strange days and well worth the bottle you have offered for another time."

"Man who brings bread to the palace also bakes for me," Saymon said. "He reported other news, sad news." He paused pointedly. "Senden Arolli?"

"I saw him fall."

Saymon hung his head for a moment at the confirmation. "He was a friend, of sorts. Sad. What will the king do? They were close, I hear."

"Donari has taken steps to find a replacement."

"You?"

"In part."

A slow smile grew on Saymon's face. "Well, from poet to spy in the blink of an eye!" He chuckled.

Devyn breathed a laugh as well. "I serve Donari now. Whether I can replace Senden, I have no expectation, but my king needs me, us, to help him."

A lifetime of serving and observing people stared back through Saymon's eyes. The man's beard hid more than secrets and food crumbs.

"Us, you say," he rumbled.

"These are dangerous times, Saymon," Devyn replied, leaning forward to add emphasis to his words. "There is peace, but with whom is debatable. Pevana is now the king's seat. There will be factions. He will need news where and when he can get it. I hope to get it for him."

"Senden's replacement in truth, then?"

"If you like, at least in effort if not effect. Can you help me? Can you help your lord and king?"

Saymon took a longer pull from his glass, motioned for Devyn to finish his, and then poured both of them a half measure.

"You are far from the drunken rhymer I saw last year. Donari chose well."

Or Senden did.

"So, then," Devyn said, keeping his voice low. "Will you get word to me if you hear of anything untoward?"

"An appeal for king and country?"

"For a friend?"

Saymon clinked his glass against Devyn's, holding it slightly raised in toast. "For a friend," he said. "For the memory of a friend." He drained his glass and slid to the end of the booth. "And for king and country. The rest is yours if you wish. If I hear anything, rest assured you will hear of it. Welcome home, lad."

Chapter 5: Farewell

Eleni Caralon sat in her rooms in the palace transcribing notes into her journals. She wrote to slow her racing mind. So much change in so short a time, and then Donari's contest of wills with Casan quite upset her balance.

She stayed near Donari's side throughout that first day back, assigning written directions to clarify Donari's verbal orders, observing the formal oaths of fealty in the main hall, and recording the reports from various sources military and merchant. While Donari seemed to take in the mountain of information easily, Eleni struggled to keep up and soon limited herself to just writing it all down. But she did not worry overmuch because she knew insights and trends would come as she collected her notes and thoughts on paper later. If Donari needed her input, she felt reasonably secure she could process things intelligently, eventually, if not immediately.

They spent the late afternoon hours preparing the details for Senden's funeral. Such instructions as necessary had to be written out fair and given to the copy-boys for reproduction and posting about the city the next day. But the activity served to remind Eleni of another funeral.

Tomais.

Doubt spread like an ink stain on paper. Tears threatened but did not come. Then memory of the message in that last, reviving dream before she agreed to follow Donari resurfaced and kept her from losing control completely. Tomais would never begrudge her happiness, and that idea helped to save her from the pit.

Love creates answers even for a soul perplexed.

She rose, stretched, and walked to the big window that looked south down the hill. All of the best rooms in the palace shared the same view, it seemed. These rooms had belonged to Donari's mother. Now they were hers. She traced a finger on the windowsill and tried to feel at home. Vain thought. And yet she knew she wanted to stay. The position she held with Donari suited her skills perfectly. The emotional ties between them complicated things in ways she was just beginning to understand. He was king, and should he survive to rule, he would need a queen. She, a seamstress-poet turned historian, was supposed to write about dynastic politics not experience them. The falling darkness turned her window into a mirror, and as she stared at her subtle reflection Eleni wondered if she were looking at a mistress or something other and indeterminate.

As she stared at her reflection, she saw the door behind her open. The maid, Anlise, glanced at her before moving to turn down the bed. Eleni half-followed the girl's movements. Anlise was the same little slip of a thing who served her more intimate needs during her recovery from Tomais's death. And that felt odd, too. The notion of servants went against her normal, self-sufficient habits.

"Thank you, Anlise," she managed with good grace. "I was just thinking of bed, actually."

"Then I am glad I anticipated you," the girl responded over her shoulder as she folded back the covers and fluffed the pillows. "Cryso would never let me hear the end of it if I grew lax in your absence." She turned with a satisfied look, holding her nose up proudly. "Welcome back, mistress Caralon."

"It is good to be back. And it's good to be *clean*. I've seen enough dirt and dust, I'll tell you."

"And blood, if the hall rumors are true."

The changed tone brought Eleni up short.

"Yes, and blood." She remained seated, strangely unsure. "But Donari hopes to put an end to all that. We have all seen too many dark days. I still recall my own, from before. I don't know if I ever thanked you properly."

"Service freely given, lady. We here in the palace are set to serve, and both the Prince and Cryso--"

"King, Anlise. Donari has accepted the crown."

The girl flushed at the correction.

"An old habit, lady, forgive me. We all have to adjust to the changes you've brought back."

"There is nothing to forgive, Anlise, and your king would be the first to say so. But, yes, there have been changes and more in the offing, I suspect."

"But are all changes good?"

"What?" Eleni rose at the comment, wanting at that moment to push a little, drawn by the girl's intensity. "Is there something I can do for you, you seem--"

But she did not finish her statement, for Anlise had stepped back toward the door, demure once again, her face transformed into a decorous, porceline mask.

"No, mistress," she said from the doorway. "There is nothing you can do for me, good night."

The door snicked closed. Eleni stood there, nonplussed at the slight emphasis on the word *nothing*.

The next morning, Eleni took her ease in the palace gardens, an expanse of gently falling ground that ran west from the palace to the citadel wall. Flower beds breathed perfume to her as she wandered the crushed rock pathways. Sea air teased at the edges, mixing salt with the sweet. She completed a circuit and started another, thoughts untwisting with every breath. Her life with Tomais had been filled with love entwined with industry. They experienced joy and intensity, but with each driven by their own talents, those moments of *slow*, the solace of shared silence, had been largely missing.

We could have used a few turns in this garden, Tomais and I. We loved too fast, or maybe we were meant to. Renia knows, perhaps.

She sat down on a bench placed in front of a small fountain, a marble oval with four dolphins caught in mid-leap spouting gentle streams from their mouths. Everywhere she looked now she saw Donari, House Avedun. A profusion of blue and white dominated everywhere yet laced with just enough other color to create a mesmerizing, natural tartan.

Is this my life now? She asked herself, taking a deep, filling breath. Once, again, and then again, exhaling to at least calm if not peace.

Yes, her deepest self responded, Renia-sent, *Yes it is.*

She sat back, closed her eyes and let the sun seep through her lids, willing her pulse to slow, for time to pause so that she could sift through all the threads, find their ends and tie them off into one, manageable pattern.

She almost succeeded when a footstep on the path and a slight cough broke her concentration. She opened her eyes to find Anlise standing before her.

"Mistress Caralon?" the girl asked. "Cryso sent me to find you. The king requests your presence in his study."

Once again, disquiet flitted by on butterfly wings at the subtle emphasis on the word, *king,* and it came through not as effort but reproach.

Her eyes. That voice. She is too young for jealousy. What could make her seem so angry?

Such thoughts accompanied her as she left the garden, re-entered the palace, and walked down the short hallway to Donari's study. A guard stationed at the door opened it for her and bowed her in. Donari looked up and smiled as she drew close to the empty chair at the left side of his desk. Devyn occupied a chair on the right.

"Ah! Eleni," Donari said, waving her to a seat. "Good timing, my dear. We've had some news." Eleni noticed a short stack of papers and her spare pen and ink bottle had been placed there for her. She took her seat.

"News, my lord?" she asked, taking up her pen.

Donari waved a paper.

"Letters from the south," he responded. "Sylvanus Tamorgen sends us greetings and updates."

"As in?"

"Our tyrant turned vassal assures us that work has begun in earnest repairing the damage caused by Casan's assaults."

"The man should be tried and hung."

"Quite correct, I'm sure," Donari said, chuckling. "And yet I think there is more to be lost in making Casan a martyr. But, if Renia grants us the grace, we may yet exact payment." He waved the letter again. "But there is more. Less lives lost in Heriopolis and Teirne first reported, and so the work there proceeds quickly. Sylvanus met with the surviving leadership of both cities as well as representatives from Eadna. He expressed surprise at how readily all of them had taken to the idea of unity with the northern crown. Pretty amazing, when you think about it." Then he focused on the paper and read the final lines aloud.

"*Representatives from every city will send a delegation to the conference, but I fear that may not be as soon as either of us would wish. There is fever in Teirne. Shipping is also in short supply. I will send a first portion of those captured at Desopolis and Lryanden Bridge. Beware. Bad cases may remain. You've some hard choices to make, King. Luck to you. Lyvia and her young man, Talyior, send their regards to Ambrose. That is an intrepid soul, but I'm sure you have already noted his talents.*

Sylvanus."

Donari handed the letter to Eleni. "A copy for the records, I think."

"Of course, as soon as you need."

She placed the letter in her pile of papers, looking from face to face. Donari leaned back in his chair with a pleased expression. Devyn blushed and fidgeted. Eleni grinned at his discomfort.

"Sylvanus is right, you know," she assured him. "*Intrepid and talented* comes pretty close to the mark."

"He flatters me," Devyn responded.

Donari laughed outright. "Don't blush, young man. Sylvanus Tamorgen is a dissembler of the highest degree."

"A powerful ally," added Eleni.

"And a terrible enemy. Let's not disappoint his hopes. And I do see hope in his words, friends. Time may work against us as regards Gaspire and the north, but I think the south will be with us at the pinch. I could use some of those men he says he will send. Renia grant that he finds the shipping soon."

"But until then?' Eleni asked.

"Until then we need to make the most of what we have. We stand on our convictions, use his pragmatism as a model for our own, and survive."

"But time, sire," Devyn began.

"Yes, time," Donari mused. "I suspect we have the summer to prepare. Gaspire cannot allow me a full winter here without some action. What concerns me in that letter is the hint of delay. Gaspire and Casan will keep in contact. I want the roads and the harbor watched for unusual activity. If Avarran can come up with the van of the army, and if I can convince enough of them to stand by me, then we will see next spring, perhaps."

Eleni took up her pen and began making notes. She scribbled a moment, then caught Donari's eye. "So you expect Gaspire to move?"

Donari nodded. "Oh, yes, he will move. I know my cousin. He will come before the weather turns if he can find the men. And he might. A company of Roderran's left-overs marched out this morning."

"Sire, was that wise?" Devyn asked.

"Perhaps not, but I did give my word down there in the gate square. I meant it: I intend to give my people choices. Now, I want you to review your report for Eleni." He touched her left hand as she set pen to paper with the right. "Listen, my dear, as you write. I will want advice from both of you."

Devyn launched into the tale of his yesterday wanderings, complete with story and speculations. Eleni's pen flew over the page as she struggled to get it all down. Donari probed him ceaselessly, drawing out bits here and there to test their relevancy, forcing Devyn to draw conclusions from his collection of sense impressions.

Eleni's respect for Devyn grew as he related his tale, for he touched on some of the same questions she faced. Pevana had changed for both of them. The idea of *home* for both of them now depended on Donari's influence in their lives. She looked again at Donari, this man, this king she knew she loved, impressed anew by his intellect and curiosity, the sheer power of his personality. To be in love and in awe at the same time unsettled her, but only momentarily. Love was so much more powerful.

She put her pen back in its bottle when Devyn finished and smiled with genuine good feeling at Donari.

"Gaspire does not stand a chance," she said, boldly reaching for his hand.

Donari gave her's a squeeze in thanks. "I hope you are right, my dear. The first real test comes tomorrow." He let go and pushed another piece of paper over to her.

"What is this?"

"The text of Casan's eulogy for Senden. The funeral is tomorrow morning. I want this in the record, too. We will see if Casan can play the role of a real cleric."

Eleni scanned the page while Donari finished with Devyn.

"So, to prepare for what may happen tomorrow, Devyn, I will require bodies in the press for Senden's procession. We need to reset our security here."

Devyn left. Eleni finished reading the Prelate's intended speech and rose to allow Donari to embrace her. She leaned into the kiss he place on her brow.

"Letting that man speak is a risk," she murmured into his chest.

"From now on, everything is a risk," he answered. "But I want Senden to have this one, last revenge before rest. Casan may rage, but he is no fool."

"But you could be made to look the fool if he speaks amiss."

She felt his arms tighten around her, silencing further comment.

The day of Senden Arolli's funeral dawned a subtle, graceful expression of high spring. It was June first. It was also Senden's birthday. Eleni dug up that piercing piece of irony as she prepared the broadsheets for placement about the city's main squares. She found it somehow fitting that a man who spent his life tying loose ends together for others should go to his final rest with his symmetry complete.

She moved through the scenes of the day as an actress trying hard to immerse herself in her part, and desperately hoping no one would see her persumption. As the king's *more-than-secretary-but-officially-as-yet-not'*, she kept to her place in the procession that set out from the palace to follow Senden's casket on its dray, separated from Donari by city elders and other heads of houses. Her heart shadowed his in ways beyond physical. She moved in an indistinct murk, clouds of emotions buffeted by unseen forces ghosted over her: grief for Senden, love for Donari, guilt, regret and sorrow for Tomais: lost in a self-created mist. The only way out was to survive the day.

The procession left the palace proper and turned up the slope, making for the Avedun plots where a space had been provided. People lined the way. Many had known Senden, despite the nature of his position. His association with their prince, now king, had been such a part of their city's history that he achieved a sort of notoriety even as he moved about his stealthy tasks. He was a son of Pevana, and the people honored his path to his final rest. Eleni understood why Donari eschewed a service in the temple. He wanted as many folk as possible to see and hear the Prelate present his coerced eulogy. Donari did not feel in the least bit sacrilegious combining piety with politics in this way. The Prelate had made a second career doing so. She watched him pass, head bowed in reflection, no doubt remembering all the days of their convoluted bond. She wondered if he felt a little guilty, as she did, that the pace of their days precluded more time for grief.

Senden. Tomais.

She looked up to check the area as the procession passed through the cemetery gate. Donari's orders had stripped the walls for enough men to line the way. She did not feel especially vulnerable, but then Donari and Senden felt their preparations more than adequate on that fateful day when Roderran arrived at Pevana. The similarities perplexed Eleni. She caught a glimpse of Devyn Ambrose walking along the top of the cemetery wall. The image reminded her so much of Senden that it hurt.

Ahead the procession arrived at the prepared gravesite with its temporary stand and a pulpit. And this, too, was part of the plan Donari and Eleni developed. Donari would not ascend. That space was reserved for the Prelate. Donari wanted to share the moment with his people, and he wanted the Prelate to be as humiliatingly visible as possible. As the dray carrying Senden's casket rocked to a stop next to the grave, the Prelate himself, looking resplendent in his full ceremonial robes, emerged from a coven of red-clad priests and struggled to mount the platform steps. Eleni thought he looked tired but defiant as he clutched the railing. They locked eyes; the old man's baleful and bitter, the young king's a mask of serenity and regal accord.

"My lord king?" the Prelate asked. Donari deigned to answer but nodded once, raising a hand in the air to still the crowd. Into that gathering silence, the Prelate took breath.

"Good people of Pevana!" he began. "Good citizens of Perspa! Loyal subjects to our King! Harken now as we lay our treasured son, Senden Arolli, in the place of his eternal rest. Let this be a lesson to us all, of whatever faith, creed or persuasion, that those who fall in the service of others deserve our love and respect. Their sacrifice ennobles us all, and it is meet that we reflect and earn the fruits of their labors on our behalf."

"Our departed son, Senden, served as our gracious king's chief protector and aide, and we must here this day gird ourselves to take on the chores he has put aside." Again, he and Donari locked eyes, and Eleni thought she saw a ghost of a smile, the barest hint of a gloating smirk, behind the Prelate's glance. Donari kept his face impassive.

"Ware! Ware I say to all you folk!" the Prelate thundered on. "The burdens of responsibility are not lightly undertaken. They reveal the inner soul. They tax your courage. Let Senden Arolli's example show you the way, for in all things he was committed, courageous and intrepid. And these are qualities we will all need to exhibit in defense of our freedom, in the furtherance of our peace, in the continued support of our most gracious king. Let all here bow their heads and make solemn promise, solemn, sincere vows of fealty and love for king and country, as our fallen Senden did every day of his life."

He paused and signaled with a be-ringed hand and attendants stepped forward to lift the casket off the dray and lower it into the grave. As they lowered, the Prelate continued, pitching his voice so that it carried effortlessly.

"And so we lay our heroic son into the earth and commit his spirit to the hereafter. May he rest in peace, and in homage to his memory, may we all live in peace. Let a stone be placed for him, let earth be scattered for him, let the maidens bring flowers to adorn his resting place. Farewell, Senden Arolli: king's friend, noble servant, worthy, worthy soul."

The Prelate fell silent, and again locked eyes with Donari. For a long moment, each stared at the other, and Eleni could not resist raising an eyebrow; she thought he heard a note of sincerity there at the end. Then Donari nodded, satisfied, the deed done. And at that moment tears came to his eyes, and to her's as suspended grief washed over the assembly. People near saw them, and shed tears as well while the attendants set to with spades to lay the earth over Senden.

Eleni suspected Casan had sent messages speeding north; probably after he finished composing the artistic pack of lies he just presented. The greater gain came in how the local folk perceived the Prelate's words and how they might translate them in their market place gossip and tavern conversations. But even more helpful would be how the northern provinces received the news. No matter how many missives Casan sent speeding north, he could never explain away what he said, how he said it, and how the people heard it. Donari could pull Casan's military teeth by disarming his acolyte guards, but it was sweeter meat to have the old man pull his political teeth out by himself by virtue of his own words. Eleni thought Senden would appreciate the subtle maneuver.

Eleni walked along in the mob just behind Donari, careful and decorous. Though she might wish it otherwise, the unspoken rules of life for a royal maintained their grip for now. Even though she ached to hold his hand, she contented herself with sharing an unspoken thought and made that suffice for the touch. Donari smiled at her over his shoulder, just a brief grin that she returned: a shared lover's secret. They paced back toward the palace and the rest of the day's duties, holding each other handless but connected.

After persevering through his humiliation at Senden's service, the Prelate spent the rest of the day in seclusion attempting to recover his equanimity. It had been insulting enough to have to commit the words of Senden's eulogy to paper, but actually saying them aloud and in matchless style, taxed him beyond all patience. He had to catch himself toward the end; he was so good in the act he almost believed what he said. Thankfully, he managed to leave once he finished and so avoided the insufferable graveside small talk. The quick return to the college in his carriage, a bumpy, lurching misery, further reminded him of the day's cost: Power. Face. His age exposed to the gossipy mob. Donari's ambivalent countenance baiting him, one hand placed pointedly on the detestable casket and its iniquitous contents, watching, listening to every word, judging, testing, nodding acceptance and dismissal in the same gesture.

And all those people, gloating over my discomfort, crying their insipid tears, honoring that dead miscreant. I'm glad I avoided breakfast this morning. Otherwise, I would have vomited for sure.

The weight of his failure forced him to toss off his heavy ceremonial robes just to climb into the carriage. He called for paper and ink as soon as he returned to the college and spent the rest of the day writing out his hate, exhausting his wrath so he could at least sleep that night.

That evening a small trading vessel slipped out of Pevana's harbor. Once clear of the headland it tacked north and headed up the coast. Among the wine casks in the hold, a cleared space held a palate provided for the young King's Theology priest who sat clutching his stomach with one hand and the small bag of seditious letters in the other. His would be a queasy, miserable voyage, but his discomfort paled in the face of the misery the letters he carried might bring.

Chapter 6: Rebellion Raised

Compared to their breakneck pace to reach Pevana, the journey north proceeded much more to Demona's liking. Gaspire Amdoran added half again as many men to the column. Most were indifferently mounted, which slowed their pace, but Gaspire did not seem to mind. Once his group cleared the settled areas around Pevana, he relaxed and gave commands with less snarl. He kept them at it beyond normal hours every day, but Demona found it easy to keep her seat.

It helped that the King's Road was a true road and not a primitive track through the hills. By the time they crested the ridges and descended through the pine forests on the northern slopes, she had the measure of the man with whom she traveled.

He still lusted after her, but the bag of jewels stashed in a pocket next his skin altered his methods. Gaspire actually talked to her as they plodded along. He flashed smiles and attempted small witticisms, gave her space around his fire, and made sure her tent was set up first. She thought of her own stash.

Maybe Sevire was right: money changes everything.

Still, despite the easy miles, Demona's anxiety grew. She needed to establish her own credibility before she grew too fat with Roderran's baby. Her sharp give and take with Gaspire when they hunted up Sevire's jewels gave her some measure of confidence. Up until that moment, her life had been a series of submissive scenes largely directed by men; the dalliance with Talyior the lone exception. Roderran's child would take away her physical tools. She needed something else. *Silence kept me from Sevire's beatings, but words worked with the king.* She spied Gaspire up at the front of the column. He rode at his ease relaxed and assured, homeward bound after avoiding deeper defeat. Roderran was dead, but he, Gaspire Amdoran, was very much alive and in possession of important means to important ends. To Demona he had the look of a man who might be talked to. She resisted an urge to run a hand through her hair as she heeled her mount to more speed.

Words it is, then.

She drew up alongside him.

"Mistress," he said with one of his newly minted smiles. "Dust too much for you?" He laughed, perhaps the first genuine sound Demona had heard from him. "As a boy I read tales where the king always rode at the front, the place of honor and greatest risk. But I think those tales were mostly wrong. The leaders rode in front because the air was better. Dust and horse dung never seemed to make it into those tales. Small wonder."

"Small wonder?" Demona asked, intrigued by Gaspire's sudden voluble manner.

"Dust and dung just aren't very noble, despite being real parts of any journey or battle. There is always dust." He looked at her. "Everything begins in blood and ends in dust, don't you see?"

"I did not take you for an introspective."

He laughed again, reached into his pocket and fished out one of the jewels he had taken from Sevire's house. "I'm a realist, lady. I left two thirds of my men at Lyranden Bridge to add the weight of their dust to the earth. I know blood and dust as well as any who have hung a sword at the hip."

"So it is all about fresher air?"

He put the jewel away. "Not all. There are some things the poets get right, but mostly, yes. Go ahead, take a breath and see for yourself."

She urged her horse ahead of his on the road. They had just topped a rise, and below her the lands fell in long, gentle slopes pierced by the road. To the west, dark pine woods cast a green shadow before thinning out to grass covered downs. To the east, the hills rolled like a geologic wave toward the sea, a blanket of grasslands set about the lower heights. Another range of hills, purple with distance, branched northward, falling in turn at the end of sight to a great gap.

Demona possessed a sketchy knowledge of geography. Her life with Sevire never commanded she look at a map, but she knew she looked out over a goodly portion of the northern fiefs of Perspa. Collum, Gaspire's lands, ran back beyond the pine woods to the mountains westward. Sorreel's rolling plains spread north and east, and that line of hills branching off the main ridge formed the border between Sor-reel and the coastal fief of Emdar.

A kingdom, if I have a son. Perhaps a place to disappear in if I don't.

She took a breath, another, and let the expanse tease her into daydream. *Security. Power. Life.* Gaspire came up alongside, breaking the image.

"You are right, my lord," she said. "The air is much better, as is the view, from the front." She gave him a challenging look, convinced of her earlier summation of Gaspire's worth. "From the front, lord. Don't think to use me beyond *my* wishes. You laugh now, but until you have Donari's head on your spearpoint, this is still defeat. Casan is a rude old man without his power. We, lord, you and I, will make this king."

Gaspire frowned. "Again, you presume much. What is to keep me from taking your wealth and following Casan's advice about presenting a timely child on my own?" He tried to assume a superior tone, but Demona saw through it.

"Call it a mother's intuition," she said. "Or call it woman's way. You want *this* baby, and I am part of the package. From the front, lord, together. No secrets. No lies. I have lived through abuse and seen defeat. I want victory."

"You've changed. I almost miss the strumpet in you."

She laughed. *Why did I ever think men were difficult?* "She is still there, Lord Amdoran. Mind your manners and maybe I'll show you."

Her thrust struck home. Lust and grudging respect played over Gaspire's features like clouds dappling sunlight. "When?" he husked.

"When I am satisfied and comfortable. When I know *all* of your mind, lord."

"Ask."

"You and Casan were vague back in Pevana. What are your intentions?"

Gaspire scanned the view without responding, then gave her a sidelong, calculating look.

"Vague? You presume a role, lady, when all Casan and I require of you is a service: birth that child and make it a boy. That is all. You heard him back in Pevana."

"That is not enough, lord."

He faced her directly. "I might offer you more since you've been so generous," he soothed, patting the place where he kept her gifted jewels. "But you will just have to wait. Perhaps we could make the interim as pleasant as possible for both of us...and your child?"

Gaspire wanted power, but he also wanted her.

"Are you sure you can take him?"

Gaspire let a steamy hiss escape in response as he swung his horse around. "Him. And you."

He looked back down the road to where the column had begun to catch up with them. "As for your other questions, we are two days from one of my lodges above the river, within sight of Lomillar. We will stop there. I hope you managed to scrunge some unguents and perfumes from your estate, Demona, because you will need them."

"A bath and a day will be, as you say, lord, pleasant." Demona let her voice deepen, just so, couching in sound a promise she knew he wanted.

Gaspire relaxed. "I will send someone ahead to forewarn my people. Enjoy your time in front. My scouts tell me we have not been pursued. We are safe for the moment. Lead on, mistress." He sketched a mock bow in the saddle and rode off.

Demona took his advice and urged her mount to a faster walk, intent on breathing and thinking as much as possible in the interim. She felt she could handle Gaspire's naked ambitions and obvious lust, his mercurial anger and lack of patience, but a gallant Gaspire, a Gaspire open and direct, pushed her off her center.

Demona rode with eyes fixed ahead but thoughts leaching behind.

Gaspire's lodge, surrounded by outbuildings set among scattered trees, loomed at the summit of a small rise with pasturage spread out below. As Demona followed Gaspire into the courtyard, she looked north and spied the great bridge spanning the Eloe River and the city of Lomillar spreading up the contours and slopes from the river bank.

It was larger, noticably larger than Pevana. Qualms followed her as grooms advanced to help her dismount and see to her horse.

Gaspire waited for her at the top of the portico steps. Behind him two servants held open the great double doors to the main hall. The architecture fit Gaspire well: rough yet well appointed, a warrior's haunt. He had bragged to her on the road about the size of his fief, given to him when Casan ascended to his role as Prelate. Demona suspected Gaspire might be a harsh lord but not cruel.

The smell of roasting meat drifted to her through the doors, and Gaspire's estimation in her eyes rose considerably. An older man, white haired and slight, stood next to Gaspire as Demona approached.

"My steward, Osir," Gaspire grunted by way of introduction. "From the smell, I'd say my man reached you in good time."

Osir bowed slightly. "He did indeed, lord. And we had two of the lads come home with several deer yesterday. It seems they hung for the purpose. We've culled a few cattle as well. By the time your men take care of their needs, all should be ready. Welcome home, lord."

Gaspire checked the sun's position and gave Demona a considering look. "Well?" he asked. "Bath or food?"

The day's ride had been the easiest of the journey, and Demona did not feel weary. The smells decided her mind for her.

"A basin of warm water and a cloth, for now, and food after, thank you."

"See to it, please, Osir. Then sit with us while we eat. We have much to discuss."

"We, lord?" Osir asked, looking sidelong at Demona.

"Yes," Gaspire grated. "*We*, as in we three. There have been changes, Osir, changes and opportunities."

"Changes, very good, my lord." Osir responded, bowing them in through the doors. "We have had some word of events in the south. A small craft made it up river two weeks ago. Most thought the tale too outrageous to believe."

"Believe it," Gaspire asserted. "The king is dead. Donari has claimed the crown. I intend to make his reign brief. Look sharp, Osir, your retirement will have to wait. Expect demands on our resources. For now, food! I am famished."

Osir bowed them in. Servants showed Demona to a room with a small basin ready with warm water and clean towels. There was a bed, a chest for clothes against the wall, a window that looked north to Lomillar. The room possessed a ruddy comfort drastically at odds with how she had spent the last month of her life. It would do nicely.

She washed her hands and face, removing as much of the trail grime as she could. The first touch of the wet cloth on her face felt like one of Renia's caresses. Her estimation of the manor's potential rose considerably when two servants brought in a large metal tub as she was leaving. They assured her water had been placed on the boil and should be ready for her later.

Dinner was more intimate than she expected. Places had been set for Gaspire, Osir and herself around a small table near the main hearth. Candles and a low fire lent a red tinged glow to the scene.

Demona found a hunger she had missed on the trail. A clean face and hands and the promise of real cleanliness afterwards served to whet her appetite when servants offered her venison slices swimming in garlic butter. Small potatoes, roasted with their skins intact and sprinkled with spices graced the dish along with a selection of steamed vegetables. Fresh bread, her first since before Lyranden Bridge, galvanized her attention so much that she commandeered the butter dish and spent several minutes slathering the chunks she tore off the rustic loaves.

She looked up to find Gaspire smiling at her over the rim of his wine glass.

"What?" she asked. "I'm hungry. I see your plate is as full."

"I've never been outpaced at the table by a woman," he responded. "And yet you manage a compromise between dainty and ravenous. But more importantly, watching you just now confirmed some things for me. Only a pregnant woman would eat as you do, and the grease on your nose is quite fetching."

Demona nearly bit her tongue. First gallantry, then flirtation? Without taking her eyes off him, Demona took up her napkin and deliberately wiped away the offending grease.

"Perhaps if we had eaten better on the trail, I would not be so obvious. Your man here outshines you lord." Her thrust hit home. Gaspire glared at her over the rim of his cup then turned to Osir.

"You have had news, you said. How did the city take it?"

"As I said before, lord, most refused to believe it. Your arrival will have an effect, I'm sure."

"But will they rise in Roderran's memory?"

"With a good reason, perhaps."

"Would the king's son provide the reason?"

Osir turned to Demona. "Much could be done, I suspect."

Demona did not much care for his calculating stare.

Why are all men so alike?

And yet she knew her own answer even as she asked the question.

Not all men, just the ones you encounter when you run with jackals.

"I bear Roderran's child," she said. "That should be enough."

Osir nodded, accepting the reproof. "Yes, mistress," he soothed. "I'm sure once the people see you in company with my lord, all will be well."

Gaspire tossed one of the jewels Demona gave him. "This might also help matters. Take it. We will spend a few days resting and refitting. I want to make a suitable entrance. Use the jewel to set tongues wagging in the city, but keep enough back to gain entry to the palace stables. Mistress Demona cannot enter Lomillar mounted on a nag. Do what you must, but get me one of Roderran's carriages."

Osir took the jewel, drained his glass and rose to leave. "As you wish, my lord. Please, finish the wine. I will check on the progress for the lady's water."

"My thanks, Osir," Gaspire murmured over the rim of his glass. "You've done well. Get some of your more useful young men to horse to spread word. All men who would see the north unsullied by southern perversions must come to Lomillar."

Demona finished her meal in silence as she processed the gist of the dinner-time talk. Gaspire poured her some more wine.

"You asked for truth," he said. "There will be a council of the remaining lords; a collection of old men, many of them now grieving sons left dead at Lyranden Bridge. We will need to be persuasive. The carriage should help."

"What of the Queen? Roderran said he put her away before he marched south."

"He did, and she and her troublesome father will need to be dealt with. I've given thought to that already. The queen has brothers, but more of your jewels will work there."

"You trust Osir?"

Gaspire nodded. "Absolutely. One of the few, actually."

"He wonders, I think."

"Wonders what?"

"Why? Why make all this trouble?"

"Because," he answered. "I am a northern lord. I went with Roderran to take the south. And we were undone by treachery. Sylvanus gave Donari his crown, Roderran's crown, Perspa's crown. Better heads than my foppish cousin have borne that circlet. How can he rule? I am a better man, and I will prove it by making the child growing in your belly a cause and eventually--"

"Eventually?"

Again, Demona's question gave Gaspire reason to pause, but only for a moment.

"I know I am no king," he said, his voice unusually contemplative. "I'm a fighter not a diplomat. Donari will call this treason. We need to sell the honor of it." He paused to drink. "I do not like my cousin; it is that simple. More than blood was spilt in that southern adventure. We lost our pride. I hate feeling weak. And yet I suspect things are mostly even now. Casan's assault damaged the southern cities. Sylvanus may have opportunity, but he lacks the men. Roderran bled the Pevanese white before Lyranden. Donari doesn't have the men to force the north to take the knee, either, at least not yet. There is a space of time here a daring, resolute man, or woman, could use."

"I want only what every true northern lord would want," he finished in a soft but determined voice. "I will not serve a southern king, and that is what Donari is, will be, soft, womanly, a purveyor of poetic platitudes and gentleness. Such a one will not hold us. We've folk enough, men enough, to decide our own fate. I do not need to rule to resist. I can be well satisfied to help in the recovery of our honor."

"So," Demona interjected. "You become a maker of kings like the tyrant Sylvanus. A worthy occupation."

Gaspire frowned. "Be careful, mistress, your condition does not protect you. I need your baby, but I don't necessarily need your tongue. We've a difficult task awaiting us in Lomillar. Show your grit but keep it civil! Yes, as you say, I will be kingmaker if I can. Power is power, Demona, and I will have my portion."

"But will you share?"

Gaspire finished his glass and rose to leave. "That depends," he said, "on how long we continue to dance around each other."

Demona returned to her room to find the promised bath ready and steaming. She slipped into the tub with a deep sigh. For most of her adult life she had grown accustomed to a daily soak and maidenly ministrations. Since Lyranden Bridge, there had been just the one, inadequate experience that one night back in Pevana. She had to wash her hair by herself. Life in the company of hard men and the hard times they produced made her miss the caress of hot water.

She examined the slight bulge in her belly, sent new hopes that it would be a boy, and let her thoughts linger on the memory of the father. *Roderran.* What did she owe him? Abuse and neglect sent her to his bed willingly. Affection surprised both of them. She took solace in that remembered fire, her proud words to Casan in Pevana. And in those words she now understood she acted now out of both self-preservation and loyalty. Her baby was the idea Gaspire needed to use for power, but she saw the child as a means to keep Roderran alive. Their short time together constituted the longest string of satisfactory days in her life. She ran her fingers lightly over her womb.

So many compromises, so many variables, little one. How will we face them?

She considered Gaspire's dancing comment, took up a cloth and soap, and began washing the road dust and the effects of a sexless month away; the suds forming a sensuous sheen on her arms and breasts. *Gaspire.* It might not be unpleasant. She ran her hands once more over her belly and leaned back to let the water envelope her up to her chin.

It's time.

The water rinsed away the last of her illusions. Gaspire had only waited until he could be sure of the pregnancy.

And so have I, in a way. Forgive me, Roderran.

She noticed how the soap made the bathwater murky and saw there a metaphor for her future. Nothing would be clear unless she made it so, but that meant she had choices to make.

Twenty minutes later she sat combing the tangles out of her hair with a cotton robe tied loosely about her. She listened without surprise to the heavy tread coming down the hall. At the sound of the knock and the handle turning, she calmly put down the brush and rose to face the door. As Gaspire entered unbidden, she gently pulled on the tie and let the robe slip to the floor.

Chapter 7: Confrontation

Demona's purloined carriage clattered over the bridge and in through the outer gates of Lomillar. The sheer size of the place intimidated her. It sprawled up the terraces above the river, easily many times as large as Pevana. That stood to reason. Lomillar was the chief city of the realm, dominating the confluence of three rivers and five provinces. Roads led to it. Power spread outward from it. Demona shrank back against the seat cushions, questioning her ability to somehow make her future there.

And yet she found solace in Gaspire riding alongside, resolute and firm at the head of a score of his best mounted and armed retainers. He surprised her the night before by holding his own against her charms. He could have been crude, even brutal, but had treated her with tenderness.

Demona made sure to say all the right things afterwards. Some skills never left the artist. Some alliances required unique payment. Gaspire would be enough for her purpose, on many levels, but he was no Roderran. She kept that thought foremost in her mind as the carriage trundled along; a silent reassurance to her unborn child.

Your father was a king, and you shall be a king!

But Gaspire would be regent if the child were to emerge a redheaded male. Demona knew there were men scouring the countryside for other pregnant women as insurance against a stillbirth, or worse, a girl.

Their arrival in Lomillar exceeded her expectations. Worried townsfolk lined the way into the city, pressing up close and reaching up to touch stirrups or stare at Demona through the carriage window as the column forced their way through the press. She did not see many armed men in sizeable numbers but recognized the livery of Trenar and Sor-reel, which meant the presence of the two old lords who had lost their sons and heirs in the south. Trenar also meant the presence of Monica Trenar, Roderran's estranged widow, which might present a challenge.

Demona quailed at the thought of killing a woman, but she could not allow the Queen to become the focal point for resistance to Donari's rule.

She has proven herself barren, anyway, as I have proven myself otherwise.

Her carriage ascended the gentle slope to the palace perched on a terrace above the river and rolled to a stop. Demona stared upwards at the imposing columns, bass relief carvings above the portico, the massive wooden doors reinforced with wrought iron. It reminded her sharply of Roderran, thoroughly male, cut, bold and decisive.

He ruled from here.

Gaspire handed her down. "Remember, say as little as possible," he said out of the side of his mouth.

"Worried?"

"Not about you. The lord of Sor-reel is here, Tareegan, an old friend. You met his eldest son in Pevana." He pointed. "That's him next to the door. The one next to him is your worst enemy in this: Monagir, Lord of Trenar. Watch him! I do not see the lords of Hallar or Emdar. Both men lost sons at Lyranden Bridge. They are coastal and likely heard the news first. I will need them, eventually."

They reached the double doors to the main hall. Gaspire introduced Demona to the older man, who bowed over her hand graciously while, behind him, the Lord of Trenar leaned on his cane and glowered.

"Welcome, my dear," Tareegan said. "If what Gaspire tells me is true, you bear our hopes. Perhaps my son will not have died in vain."

Tareegan led them into the assembly hall where Perspa's kings met with lords of major and minor houses to conduct the realm's business.

Roderran's throne, empty, dominated one end of the room from a raised dais. Several rows of tiered seats made of deeply auburn hardwood ran along the wall. For Demona, the place projected a dark physical atmosphere of hard manners, hard words, and for the enemies identified there, hard times. Demona imagined Roderran leading one of those meetings: a brash, shouting, gesticulating chaos of proud, warlike men and their arrogant expression. And all under his sway.

Gaspire led her to a chair placed close to the throne but on the floor. A clear message to all assembled. Demona took her seat and tried to assume a bold expression, willing herself to meet the collected stares.

Gaspire returned to the center of the half-empty room. The faces turned to him ranged from the wrathful to the timorous, but all of them had questions that they began shouting all at once.

The noise rose. Gaspire let it, keeping his face impassive, his eyes ranging the room to take the measure of the men he faced. The corner of his mouth twitched, but so slightly Demona could not be sure it truly did. He raised a hand. Slowly. The din faltered, grew quiet. A space around him cleared.

"Sit," he told them, his voice clipped, precise. "Sit down and calm yourselves so that all can hear."

Grumbling, those in attendance settled themselves again in their chairs. Gaspire walked out to the center of the space, pointed at Tareegan of Sor-reel.

"What have you heard?"

The older man rose to respond.

"One of the small transports I sent south to join the fleet put in to one of my seaward villages almost a month ago. After the failure at Desopolis, they sailed with the remnant back towards Pevana. They got separated and blown off course and chose to come home rather than put into port. They talked of many ships and men lost. I sent word to all I could, calling for a meeting here, and then letters reached us a week ago from the Lord Prelate telling us that Roderran had fallen in battle and that you were on your way with survivors. So, is all this true, my lord?"

Gaspire grimaced. "It is as both your sources have told you: disaster and defeat and treachery. I saved a remnant. Donari is crowned but by Sylvanus's hand. My lords, I suspect treason. Though he is my cousin, I have doubts about Donari's allegiance."

"But he is the king's near cousin!" one of the lesser nobles shouted. "He is the heir!"

"By policy, yes," Gaspire responded, his voice scathing and derisive. "And Roderran trusted him. Small trust, I say, and ill-earned by Donari. My wing cut to pieces by Sylvanus's dishonorable wiles. Our brothers and sons, my lords, buried in the pits that took them and their mounts in mid-career. And Donari kept aloof from the tragedy, held back when Roderran met Sylvanus man to man in the field, held back when Roderran fell. He waited for Sylvanus to rip Roderran's crown from his cloven helm before he advanced to accept it, *submissively*, from the hand of the victor. I have no patience for cowardice, and I will have no truck with blood-treachery. Though Donari be my cousin, I will never accept him as my king. He is no blood of mine."

He paused and turned back to Demona. His changed timber impressed her.

A point for you, lord.

She settled back in her chair to enjoy the rest of the show.

"What happened to the rest of the army?" someone blurted out. Gaspire turned to the voice and paused before replying as though making an effort to control his emotions.

"I must admit, my lords, I fled after Roderran's fall," he continued finally. "I'm not proud of the fact." He swung around to include all in his response. "It was a slaughter once the pits halted our cavalry. Roderran led the foot forward to try and break through; brave but vain. I shudder to recall it. It is a notched circlet Donari bears, my lords, marred by more than Sylvanus's sword blow. It is tainted by betrayal. Treachery! Treachery I say!"

There were loud grumblings as he finished, but Demona knew he had only just begun. That this bunch of callow fools and younger sons should respond at all encouraged her.

Gaspire walked over to her as the noise rose. Demona graced him with a smile. In a land where treason functioned as a normal stock in trade, half the men in the room earned their station as a result of civil strife, dynastic murder or contrived accident. Gaspire stood next to her chair, right hand placed casually on the back. Together, they let the rumble grow.

Gaspire's words had teased the timid, pushed the active to the tipping point, that moment where the wave hung at the crest before plunging into the surf. Gaspire removed his hand from her chair back. She grabbed his forearm.

Not yet. Not quite. A moment longer. Squeeze it, lord, the way I squeezed you just before. I see it now, that connection between sex and power. How simple! How easy!

Surprisingly, Gaspire let her hold him back. When she judged the time right, she loosed him and rose as he moved back to the center of the floor. Gaspire stood there, dark, bold, hand raised for attention, waiting for the noise in the room to subside, capturing each group with a grim look, jaw thrust out. Within seconds he regained their complete attention. Demona remained standing.

"Well, friends," he said into the silence. "I see my news has touched a nerve or two. Good. Northern lords are we, my friends, and we know the fruits of loyalty and the perils of betrayal. Roderran was our king, and our loyalties to him were well placed. If not for treachery, he would still reign. Instead, we have Donari, soft, distant, infirm, the creature of Sylvanus of Desopolis!"

"Mark me, friends," he continued. "He will send for us to make our obeisance, and the letters will come on scented paper in southern characters. My question is: how will you receive the summons? I've told you my own mind in this. I would know yours."

More grumblings followed when Gaspire finished. These, though not universal, quickly rose into heated comments. In the midst of the uneven din, old Monagir, Lord of Trenar, father of the queen treated so shabbily by Roderran, struggled to his feet and called for attention. Demona felt doubt rise with him, willed him to silence but in vain. The lords ignored him at first, but then some noted his effort and took up his call, and soon the room returned to silence as all waited to hear what the old man had to say.

"I came here at the request of my daughter, the queen," he began, his voice tremulous at first but gathering force as he warmed to his subject. "Roderran was king but no husband to my daughter. For that I spurn remorse over his death. He suffered a fool's fate, and I say it now clearly, despite how some of you might take it." He cast a baleful eye on Gaspire. "I rue, rather, the thousands lost that he took with him. Where are they? Does Donari claim their allegiance? Are we suborned, as our Lord of Collum suggests? How is it he alone returns to excite us to reject Roderran's heir? And yet I, too, have my doubts about this newest Avedun to take the scepter and the manner in which he took it or had it given him. Understand, lords, I am sick of the entire clan." Again, he paused to glare around the room. "But I am also a northern lord, one of you, and my daughter is queen of this land. Are we to forget her in favor of a policy that grants power to Donari of Pevana? Trenar will neither submit to Donari or to any other Gaspire might rise to the diadem. I will cleave to my daughter, the rightful Queen of Perspa."

He finished with a cold glance at Demona and let the weight of his words sink in, and in that silence Gaspire stepped forward.

"My brother lord of Trenar is free to have his opinions," he said. "But I ask all of you here to remember this: The Queen is barren. Can we support an empty vessel in our extremity? What hope there? No child from her will follow. Better Donari than that, I say." He raised a placating hand to still Monagir's ire. "Harsh words, my lord, and I am sorry to have to say them. I hold you ever in esteem, sir, despite being part of the 'clan' you have come to so despise. But the facts are unavoidable, as I am sure all here are aware. The queen is not our leader. She cannot raise and train men. Roderran put her aside out of necessity, so that she might be free of the politics of breeding."

All eyes turned to Demona as he spoke. She raised her chin imperiously, straightened to her full height and placed her hand dramatically, with an actor's timing, on her midsection in a message unmistakeable.

"Revolt is no easy prospect," Gaspire continued. "Order, rule, stability—these are things not lightly put aside. Men need a cause to risk their security, wealth and futures. We have suffered a tragic blow in the failures I witnessed in the south. I lost friends, boon companions all, men of my own household. Everyone here, eventually, will have to face the effects of those losses. We are not supplicants!" he shouted, raising his hands. "We are a proud and warlike people. Are we then to submit to southern treason? Roderran wished to spread our sway to the whole peninsula! I will not allow the reverse to happen to Perspa: southern ideas, southern manners, southern politics spread throughout our valleys."

He motioned Trenar to sit. The old man hesitated at first, drew breath as if to contest, but then sank slowly back into his chair. Demona stared victoriously. No one else sought to rise and dispute Gaspire's opinions. Demona moved to his side as he continued with growing confidence.

"I am not the stuff of kings. I am a soldier. The Lordship of Collum is more than I deserve. I wish serve my people in any way I can. I will resist Donari when he calls me to kneel and make the oath. I choose, rather, to support and raise another to the rightful place vacated by Roderran in his death. I will fight for Roderran's heir."

"But Donari is the heir!" someone shouted.

"But the queen is barren!" someone else added from off to the side. Gaspire did not deign to turn to face the speaker, choosing rather to include all there in his response.

"True, and more apologies to Trenar, but I speak of an heir nonetheless." He turned to Demona, took hold of her arm above the elbow. "I speak of an heir, lords. It grows in the womb of the Lady Demona Anargi. She accompanied him on the trail. She bears Roderran's child."

"But it is a bastard!" screeched Monagir of Trenar, jowls quivering with rage. "You would foist a whore's bastard on us? You are insane!" His outburst stunned the room.

"Trenar will not stay for this!" the old man continued loudly into an uncomfortable silence. No one rose to support him. He brandished his cane at Gaspire. "The queen, my daughter, will not stay for this. My folk filled Roderran's ranks, despite his behavior towards her, out of loyalty and hope for glory. And for what? To die at the ambitious whim of an Avedun king? I and mine have had enough of that strain. They are a pestilence upon our country, I say. You claim treachery, but where does the betrayal begin and end? Trenar will not stay for this, I tell you. You will have naught of me. I quit this assembly!" Then he spat at Gaspire's feet and shuffled off out of the room.

Demona wondered how Gaspire fought down the urge to take his knife and slit the man's throat right then and there. She could feel the tension in his grip as around them the room erupted anew into noise and chaos. And yet, despite Trenar's outburst and departure, she knew they still had them. Gaspire showed them they did not have any other choice. Gaspire let go of her arm and stepped forward.

"Every man is free to choose!" he shouted after Trenar disappeared through the doors. "What alternative do we have? I tell you Donari is a southern puppet. He cannot be our king! Not even royal blood can expunge his fraudulent rise, my lords. I offer you a cause: an innocent babe that bears the blood of our King. His mother is a peerless beauty. I brought her out of the wrack of Roderran's ruin. She has come to us looking for sanctuary, a place to bring her child into the world, to give him to his father's people to love and support, and in time raise him to the station apportioned him by virtue of his blood. I say Donari is more bastard by his behavior over these last months than the unborn child sleeping in Lady Demona's womb. Again, apologies to my Lord of Trenar, but I would rather Roderran's blood from a tavern wench than place myself and all I have at the bidding of such a one as Donari of Pevana."

Silence reigned as all there digested the import of his words. Finally, Sor-reel broke the silence.

"What you propose is outrageous, but perhaps these are outrageous times. My lords!" he cried. "We must all take counsel of our thoughts. Perhaps Gaspire gives us a way out from calamity. Understand, all of you who lost sons, brothers, fathers; we face dark days if we do not submit. I sense our weakness in all our voices. And yet I am of a mind to follow Gaspire's lead. I would support a Regency in memory of Roderran, but I am old. I may help start this thing, but it is you who will finish it...you and your supporters...if they can be found. I foresee war, friends, but I would rather that than the dishonor of swearing fealty to a king wrapped in southern charms. Let you think on this and choose."

He turned to Gaspire and Demona in closing.

"Let rooms be prepared for the lady. Let word be sent to Hallar and Emdar. We must see about this my lords."

Words swam around Demona like irritated schools of fish as the assembly broke up. Groups of men left talking among themselves, others stayed, offered her curious, cautious greetings before leaving. Gaspire loomed, a protective presence, as the place slowly cleared. In the end only Tareegan, Gaspire and Demona remained.

The lord of Sor-reel sighed. "This is madness," he said. "Are you sure you know what you are doing?"

"I am doing the only thing I can, the only thing that pride and honor will allow me to do," Gaspire responded.

The old man stared at him for a moment, his face a study in grief and curiosity. He bowed to Demona.

"Then so be it. But Trenar has cause for his anger, Gaspire," he said. "Roderran used that family ill. He could be a bitter impediment."

"I will take thought on that. He is too weak to do much more than whine, anyway. I expected his response."

Tareegan shook his head sadly. "Alas for my old friend and comrade," he whispered. "Dark days, my lord."

"But with fortune, better days may follow."

"So you say."

"So I hope, lord. Otherwise, Reegan's death will have been in vain."

"Did you see him fall?"

"Yes, next to Roderran. He used his shield to cover the king. It was a noble death."

Tareegan frowned. "I've grown tired of that word," he scowled. "It came too often to Reegan's lips, as I recall." He turned to Demona.

"Hardly a gracious introduction to Perspan politics, my lady, but you did well."

"You are kind, lord," Demona responded.

"Kind?" the old man scoffed. "No, not kind. Pragmatic, perhaps. I will reserve kindness for the birth. See to your health, madam."

He stalked off, calling for his carriage and retainers. Demona stared at his retreating back, parsing both the compliment and the threat. She and Gaspire left the hall and moved outside. At the base of the steps, men assisted the lord Monagir into his carriage. Demona caught a glimpse of a woman, swathed in black lace, reach out a pale hand to help the old man to his seat.

"The queen," Gaspire said to her questioning look. "Mourning black, how very touching."

"She must hate me."

"Hate you? Of course, but that can only be expected. To tell you the truth, she is putting on as much a show as we are. I think she hates Roderran, both the man alive and his memory dead, more than anything else."

He moved to the steps as the royal carriage rolled up.

"Take heart," he said. "We have made a good beginning. And once I start spending your money things will move quickly; especially once we get you settled in the palace."

"Palace?"

"Of course. You heard Old Trenar. The whole lot are out. Once folk hear that Roderran's heir is brought home for his birthing, they will insist. You'll have your comforts yet."

Demona let him lead her down the steps, her gaze still fixed on the departing Trenaran carriage. She recalled Casan's last words back in Pevana, felt a chill despite the sun's warmth.

"A good beginning, you say," she said, gripping his hand to step up into the carriage. "I must trust your judgement. And yet I wonder."

"Wonder?"

"What will happen next?" she asked, pointing to where the queen's carriage trundled out of view.

Gaspire followed her eyes, then helped her settle onto the cushioned seat.

"An accident," he answered.

Chapter 8: Questions of Legitimacy

The Prelate Byrnard Casan pulled several candles in closer to read the letters from Gaspire Amdoran. Casan had fretted for over a month since Amdoran took his men and the woman, Demona Anargi, north to foment a response to Donari Avedun's crowning. The loss of face at Senden Arolli's funeral forced him to keep his silence while Donari re-established his administrative control. Trusted adherents trundled out of positions of authority and replaced with men of the king's choosing, several building projects, a church and missionary center for the King's Theology de-funded, and the renovation of some Old Ways temples reminded Casan, daily, of the grinding loss of power and influence. Folk now avoided King's Theology services, donations dried up, and the priests he sent out more often met scorn and ridicule than acceptance. He felt cut off from news and information, his trade in power since taking the cloth, as it were. Forced into a fuming, relative passivity by his lack of resources, he still searched for ways to annoy Donari. But after a month of nothing, doubt nagged at him and whispered its lies in his dreams at night.

He left the warmth of his bed to receive the letters in his office. He would not be able to sleep anyway once he read the contents; better to sit and think in his favorite chair than toss among the pillows and sheets. The contents of Gaspire's terse report did not disappoint him.

Lomillar, June 30th.

My Lord Prelate:

We made good time coming from Pevana, the Lady Demona kept up well, and we arrived before Lomillar's walls with time to gather ourselves.

I made my case. Trenar challenged me, but his age betrayed him in the end. He and his hapless daughter met with an accident. There are ravines on the road to Trenar.

Trenar has gone up in flames. It seems the old man's relatives were just waiting for him to go. The youngest surviving son stands no chance. Cousins were at each other within a week. A useful distraction, I think.

Sor-reel stands with us. He grieves for his son but has promised me men and supplies. I am well-pleased in the old hero. He at least has lost none of his drive, even if he has trouble mounting his horse these days.

Demona's pregnancy shows, and, smart bitch that she is, she has been careful to wear clothing that shows off her condition. I wonder if she has any idea how short-lived that power will be once the brat takes its first breath?

If I can get the men and get them in place, we might challenge Donari before she comes to her time. It is a risk. Or is there some other thing we might do before she whelps?

All here have received Donari's letters requesting fealty. I used mine to wipe my arse.

I have taken precautions against disaster. I have five women with child who confess to be as far along as she. Several report red hair in their family's history. Perhaps Roderran was busier than we imagined?

GA.

Casan reread the letter three times; each time with a brief thrill as he reached the end. Old Trenar and his daughter out of the way presented Gaspire's plot with a number of advantages. They could have disputed the truth of the Anargi woman's baby. They could have split support and siphoned off men and supplies. No Trenar meant no major break. The baby might as well be legitimate.

Legitimacy.

The thought bloomed for him with such intensity that he burst out laughing. He let himself cackle on for a few minutes, considering the audacious beauty of it. Here he was, hand-bound by Donari's manipulations, and an *accident* that removed a barren problem presented him with a chance pregnant with possibilities.

His pen fairly flew across the page as the ideas sprang, coalesced and flowed in a constant motion-thought, an unprecedented fraud, a glorious temporal joke on Donari and his romantic notions of rule. What chance did romance have against political experience? Casan laid it all out succinctly: the articles of dissolution, evidence of a war trail marriage, survival of the state.

When he finished, Casan stared at the document reverently, convinced of its perfect absurdity, but he went to his bed afterwards equally convinced it would work.

For the first time in a month he slept soundly.

In the days Senden's funeral, Donari quickly set about establishing his royal authority. He sent letters north explaining his desire to establish Pevana as the new capital of a united peninsular realm. He and Eleni labored over the wording of those first missives. Donari knew he would face resistance from elements in certain fiefs beyond the hills, and so he took pains to refrain from peremptory language and strove to reinforce his position with logic. He tried to paint a picture of peace for all his people, for in his mind the north and the south needed each other. Northern raw materials, southern foodstuffs; trade would be the final arbiter of the peace he hoped to forge. Donari had Eleni pour over his drafts, nudging and pruning them as needed. The effort showed him yet another side of her. She found the small things in his straightforward prose that he missed and helped him inject his humanity into the words. She made him better, and he loved her all the more for it.

He took her advice and let her retreat from openly proclaiming their connection. She dressed as a woman in royal service, keeping up the appearance of being Donari's private secretary. Donari chuckled at her timidity because he fully intended to marry her once he gained enough breathing space and security to flaunt tradition. He understood the need to keep himself unattached as a matrimonial bargaining chip. He only entertained the notion at a surface level, however, for he found it utterly distasteful. He knew what he wanted, and if he had to play the distant king to the watchers and speculators in the city then so be it.

He knew all the secret passages in his palace anyway. Decorum could only delay, not eliminate, their time together. In the nights, when time allowed and prying eyes removed themselves from the scene, they managed to find one another. And so their bond grew; a love spiced by work's excitement and the growing reality of Donari's rule. But his desires depended on northern sufferance, and responses to his letters came slowly or not at all.

And then the army marched home, and it was as if the earth itself breathed a sigh of relief.

Donari rode out with an escort and wagons filled with provisions to meet them. He wanted to measure the minds of the Perspan survivors and see how they reacted to his crown. He needed men badly but needed loyalty more. Avarran's messages mentioned hardships on the road home. He could not allow rebellion to march freely through his gates. He would feed them, talk to them, and give them an honorable choice. He knew he could count on his Pevanese footmen, but many others in the train were leaderless northern levies. If he could show them the sort of ruler he intended to be, perhaps some of them would swear to him or at least see how different he intended to be from Roderran.

The risk is honor. Roderran never bothered with it. He would slap an appropriate number in chains and cow the rest.

Donari could not bring himself to act that way. Peace could not attend a rule so begun, and peace stood foremost in Donari's hopes.

He did not even put on armor when he rode to meet them. Weaponless, his only defense their deference; his only shield his integrity. He knew he flaunted fate in acting thus, but in his mind the region had seen enough of blood and martial destruction. Roderran had begun and ended his rule with military campaigns. Donari wanted to begin his with the opposite.

As Pevana's prince, he had liked to think of himself as a poet, always keeping hold of those early memories with Kembril and the vibrant life of the city. He had words, then, but could he rule as the poet king?

He wanted to. Perhaps it was a fool's hope, but poets are dreamers.

He met the army settling into camp at the crossroads connecting the track to Pevana with the King's Road. He stood atop one of the food wagons as the ragged, haggard band collected before him. He stared out at a sea of faces, some hollow-eyed some pinched with curiosity.

He stood there for a long moment, letting them get a good look at him and the crown gracing his brow, willing his hands to leave off trembling, waiting, with his poet's sensibility, for the right moment to speak. Timing and tone meant everything to the story-teller attempting to win over an audience. Donari swung his gaze once over the crowd, and then again. He drew destiny's breath and tested his fate.

Before Donari could speak, a single spear lofted up from the mob to stick pointedly in the space before his perch. Men shouted in outrage and alarm. Avarran barked a command and a file of Pevanese rushed forward, locked shields, and lowered points at the now roiling mass of angry, confused men.

Donari fought down a wave of dismay. He stood as tall as he could, spreading both arms wide, both symbol and target, and trusted words.

"Soldiers of Perspa!" he exclaimed. "Welcome home. Home, I say, after long days and misadventure! You have proven yourselves loyal to the lord who led." He paused for breath and to let the import of the past tense set. "I speak here no ill of Roderran, my cousin. I am not he, my friends. That there was dispute between us I am sure there are those among you who would so assert. I will not deny it. I did not agree with him, but he was my liege-lord. I obeyed his commands. I regret his death, but I do not regret this crown. I would have you understand my mind, all of you, before you finish this march."

This first effort met with some vague grumbling and shaking heads, but not from the majority. Donari let the effect of his words work their way to the back ranks before continuing. If nothing else, he knew he had their attention. The whole mass shuffled forward as if to better hear.

"No doubt you have had ample time to talk amongst yourselves during the long march home about how things have transpired. Sylvanus defended his people and yet in the moment of his ascendancy, he took a harder road. True, he gave this crown to me, but I remind you now I am, by all the laws of our land, Roderran's heir. I am Donari Avedun, King of Perspa, and I intend to rule. You all heard the words of Sylvanus at Lyranden Bridge field. Hearsay and history, slippery words and falsehoods branded him '*Tyrant*'. He stood in the way of Roderran's dreams of conquest. And yet in victory Sylvanus saw wisdom. Where Roderran sought to conquer and impose, Sylvanus saw the need for peace. Trade, not blows, is what we need to exchange in this land, men. Think back to the graves at Lyranden Bridge, think back to the graves of those who expired along the way back, think back on the reasons why you left your homes at Roderran's behest and consider how it might have been, and might yet be, different."

He allowed his words to linger. He had to get them thinking of fields and families rather than blades and revenge. He could not win all of them over. On the surface, he must appear too passive, too aligned with Sylvanus for the hardliners to accept. He had to brazen it out; a hard choice for a hard time.

"I do not demand fealty's oath from you." The raspy tremble in his voice nearly betrayed him. "I ask it. That is why I have come to meet you here, in the open, so that all may hear and choose. I have brought provisions for you. I want you to take your ease this night, talk amongst yourselves again as you have heretofore. But tonight you talk knowing all the truth. I am my own man, but I agree with Sylvanus of Desopolis in that we need peace. All sides bled at Lyranden Bridge, cities burned all along the coast. All are made weak enough, I think, to consider the value of peace. Will you also consider it? You men who call yourselves '*northern*', whose lords and captains may have fallen at Lyranden Bridge, I ask that you sort your minds carefully. I ask you to see the larger view in this."

Again, he paused for breath and to let his words sink in.

"I understand loyalty to kith and kin. This is no longer about Trenar, Sor-reel, Hallar, or any other plot of land attached to a name and a sigil. I say we have been too long separated by leagues, hill ranges, and attitudes. I would heal those wounds, shorten the distance between the minds of my people northern and southern, for make no mistake: Sylvanus of Desopolis gave me his fealty when he could have done otherwise, and I will hold him to his word. He will come, and all the southern lords with him, to Pevana to forge peace, reaffirm vows, and look to the days to come."

He put a foot on the wagon bed rim and leaned over his knee like a performer drawing those closest to him into his confidence.

"Let us spend this night in talk, friends. Let us eat and think and choose. If I have not won your service now, here, then I lay no claim on you. You will be free to take provision, select leaders and continue your journey, unmolested, back to your homes. If there will be strife, I will not start it here. I seek the goodwill of all men in my rule. Understand that above everything else. Do what your heart bids you with my blessing. No! Hold!" he cried, raising a hand to stop them, for like a wave men, singly and in groups had begun shifting space and taking a knee.

"No, men," he urged, pleased at the effect his words had drawn. "Not yet. I will not shame those who still doubt by this sunset show. Let us all consider carefully what we will do without passion or violence. I claim sanctuary of this camp for all, and in the morning, let the captains come to me with report of their men's minds. And for those who claim no leadership, let them come as well, and then all who would may make their oath, and I will gladly accept them into my service. Until then," and he swung his arm to include the commissary men who had accompanied him, "let food be prepared, let my tents be set, and let us eat together as brother warriors at least."

He scanned the crowd one last time before he descended from the wagon and saw a mottled sea of hopeful faces interspersed with dark brows and ambivalent, unscrupulous looks. And yet the assemblage broke up quietly, and men set about organizing that evening's meal. If nothing else, Donari's efforts bought at least one more night of peace.

In the biggest gamble of his life, the dice still danced.

He spent the evening eating and moving about among the men but attended by Avarran and two guards. The survivors in the Pevanese contingent greeted him warmly and pushed food and drink at him repeatedly. Their response gratified him. Despite the obvious wear and tear of their experience, many held themselves proudly as he passed. With such men, Donari felt like he stood an even chance in any conflict. But most of the others Donari encountered looked tired, confused, and leaderless; a tragic state for common soldiers. Still others gave him silence and mistrust bordering on defiance. To these he took care to smile, take his ease and move on. Some he sensed softened their looks at him as he moved about, but when he passed on to another group his back itched nonetheless.

One young man in particular stood out; Donari judged him barely in his twenties, but his men responded to his command with complete trust and respect, for they rose smartly and stood to with a sharpness missing in other groups. The young leader saluted Donari and stood spear-shaft straight to await his inspection.

"Your name, sir?" Donari asked, drawn to pause by the precision of the moment, aware of the tension in the men's bearing, especially in the eyes of their young leader.

"I am Hallan, youngest son of Hallaran, Lord of Hallar, sire," he said, his face twitching as he finished, as though he had to strain to add the nominative. "These are all that remain of my father's levies."

"Yes, I remember you now. I saw you with your brothers in Roderran's camp once."

"Hillar, the eldest, and Hilmar...sire." Again the pause, and to Donari it held a mix of grief and rage.

"And they fell at Lyranden Bridge?"

"Hillar was impaled on a stake in one of Sylvanus's dishonorable pits. Hilmar took an arrow in the eye protecting Roderran before the earthworks. They died following their lord, sire." And with the third use of the term came the pent up anger and disgust. Donari felt its sting and knew nothing he could say could ease the man's pain or win him easily to his cause. He studied Hallan in silence for a second or two, weighing his next words carefully.

"They acted with honor," he said finally, nodding his head as if to affirm his conviction and soften his intent. "And I will not insult your feelings by saying they were misled. They sought glory in arms. I am sorry they paid such a price."

"There is no honor in being slain by an arrow or a sharpened stick."

"War and death are no respecters of station, young man," Donari responded firmly, his tone rising to match that of Hallan's. "Many fell on both sides that day. If a man meets his destiny face to front, what matter the means of his death? Roderran's fall was the stuff of fables, Hallan, understand that. More often than not, death in battle comes as a surprise to the one who falls and is rarely worth a song."

"Your crown is marred, sire, as is the way you came by it."

Donari smiled at that, for he knew Hallan's words cut to the core of his difficulty. Treason's taint, however unearned, lasted. Reason as he might, he knew there was no way he could persuade Hallan or his men. Donari's spirits sank at the notion.

"I, too, followed my Lord's orders, sir," he said sadly, "even though I found them foolish and wasteful. I grieve for my cousin, your brothers, and all those lost in that campaign. It need not have been that way, and I would rule differently if I am spared."

"Halmir cursed you just before the arrow took him."

"And I likely would have cursed him if our roles were reversed. I don't ask forgiveness, Hallan. There is blame enough to go around, yes, and shame, too, I'll not deny it."

"My father, Roderran, others, they all said you were soft, a fool."

"Of course they did. How could they say otherwise? I spent no time at court. I met your father but once: a hard man from a hard land. Reputation is a malleable thing in politics. Do you know me Hallan? Is it softness that brings me among you, unarmed, scarcely escorted? All I ask is that you make your choices *knowing* me and not just my supposed reputation." He stepped back a pace and raised his voice to include all of Hallan's party. "That is all I ask of you this night. Eat, rest, think. On the morrow freely give me fealty or take provision and my earnest wishes for a safe journey home. Your lord will have need of you."

He looked directly at Hallan. "For your lord father has lost enough of his sons, and I would not be the cause for further loss. I commend you, Hallan, for the care you have shown your men. Take counsel with yourself, for I would have one such as you in my service."

Donari thought he sensed the slightest softening in Hallan's eyes, as though the barriers of suppressed anger and inexperience gave way in the face of freely offered truth. But the effect was transitory and quickly blinked away.

"I have my duty to my father and these men to get home," he said, raising his chin proudly.

"If you go, I do not know what mischief you will find once you clear the hills. Gaspire of Collum precedes you. Go home. Serve your father. Give him report of me and my hopes. Should we meet in peace then we will be well met, but if you return as part of open rebellion, then you shall learn how soft I am. Renia's grace on your path, sir."

Hallan's eyes searched Donari's for a moment.

"I, I will consider all you have said, sire," he said quietly.

The young soldier's last *sire* came with less pause, less venom than the first. Donari nodded as he walked away.

A small beginning.

Donari scrutinized Jason Avarran over the rim of the glass from which he sipped. The wine helped rinse some of the day's bitterness away, and his war leader's steady presence acted like a boon to his troubled thoughts. Regardless of how the morning went, having Avarran back gave Donari hope.

"I don't know anyone else who would have done as well with that motley crew," he said, taking a seat in a camp chair. "You've done miracles, my friend."

Avarran, armorless, sprawled in his own chair on the other side of the fire. The irregular light cast the man's face in shadowed relief but could not hide the intense weariness. New grey showed in the man's beard and temples, and yet he was only a few years older than Donari himself. The eyes that rose to meet his own, though still clear and precise, looked as though they held bitter memories.

Avarran took a drink, seemed to savor the flavor for a second, and then drained the rest in a gulp. He reached for the bottle in the grass next his chair and refilled before responding.

"Renia's Grace, but that is good, sire. We were reduced to water alone all too soon on the way back. A good wine is the only cure for such dust. My thanks."

Donari glanced over his shoulder to where Drue waited to serve.

"Let's have that plate of cold beef and another bottle, please!" he said. The boy complied, placing a tray on an over-turned crate midway between the two men, took the new bottle and refilled Donari's glass, and retreated back into the shadows.

Avarran took a slice and munched thoughtfully before swallowing with yet another pull from his glass.

"The miracle is how good all this tastes," he said. "If there is more of this for the others, you might win some of them over."

"There's plenty and to spare. Small recompense for such a hard road. And don't give me the lie. Your face reveals how bad it was."

Avarran nodded agreement. "It was a challenge, my lord. Much mistrust, a lot of fear, and dark words up and down the column. I think some perished just from the shock of defeat."

"That spear."

Avarran grimaced, the twist in his features accentuated by the firelight.

"My apologies. I should have expected something of the sort."

"None needed. Disarming them would have sent the wrong message before I had a chance to talk."

"True, but that spear was a message itself."

"But it was only the one. I will take hope in that." Donari took a piece from the tray and chewed on more than just the beef. "How do you think I did, after?" he asked, swallowing.

"Give the local troops a bath and a week's rest, and they would march on Lomillar for you," Avarran replied. "But as for the others, I am not sure. Too many of them lost friends on that field. We buried scores on the way home. If we had faced enemies, we would not have made it. Too many nobles and captains fell. They followed me because I made them, and our troops were still united. They had no choice in the matter. I'm sure that rankled on the road."

"Do you think some of them will stay?"

"Some, not all. The Collum bunch have no love for you and never will."

"Gaspire will prove a problem, I agree."

"So clap the fools in chains. Why send them home to swell his ranks?"

Donari smiled wanly. "Weren't you listening?" he said. "I have to let them leave even if it leads to civil war. I cannot force them. Peace needs to be a voluntary action."

Avarran shook his head ruefully. "They will see it as weakness, my lord."

"Perhaps, but maybe enough will see it for truth. What of that Hallan?"

"He is a good man, though young. Despite his parentage, he did a hero's work keeping his men together. If he lives, he might make a strong war-leader."

"Will he stay?"

"No, my lord. I highly doubt it. Too young to go against his fathers wishes"

Donari frowned into his glass. "Damn," he muttered. "I know you are right, and I know we will have to watch those that do stay after tomorrow. I invite treachery inside my walls, but I have to give them a choice. I have to live my words."

"It is a risk."

"Yes, but I can do no less, I think. I cannot begin my rule with more betrayal."

Avarran finished his glass and rose. "Then sleep well, my lord. I think you bought a night's grace at least. The men are talking. Regardless, I say get us home, get us fed, and let me get a force ready to guard the hill passes as soon as possible." He bowed at the tent flap and turned to leave, but Donari stopped him.

"I owe you more than I can express, Jason, for leadership and counsel, both of which I value highly. Again, you have worked miracles since the spring. Get to your rest. Here," he said, offering him the other bottle. "Take this with you. Small recompense but earned thrice over."

Avarran took the bottle gladly, some of the care and concern Donari had seen in his expression fading beneath the smile he gave in thanks.

That image alone helped Donari sleep that night.

Donari arose a little after dawn. With Drue's aide, he dressed carefully for the part he must play. This time he would appear armored and crowned: the image of red, Avedun splendor and Pevanese blue. He almost laughed at the half-quizzical, half-critical eye the stripling gave him before nodding decisively and sweeping aside the tent flap. He exited to find the Pevanese troops drawn up in rows to either side of his tent.

The morning sun glinted off burnished helms, a reflected glory that made him pause in surprise. And the faces beneath those helms stared back at him with clear, determined eyes, as perfect in the moment as the gear they bore so proudly.

Avarran stepped forward, drew his sword, and knelt. And at his motion the rest followed, spears forward, sword points down.

"This is another miracle," Donari said with wonder in his voice. "They must have been at it all night to achieve this."

"I found a few more bottles last night for motivation," Avarran responded. Then he deftly reversed his blade, presenting the hilts to Donari, before continuing in a louder, more formal tone. "Our oaths were given long since, sire, but let you know now that all here renew that pledge to their lawful king. Our swords, our lives if needed, are yours to command."

Donari took the hilts. "Most impressive!" he said, pitching his voice to carry. "And I accept your oaths gladly. Care in peace or strife, as I live so shall you. Now, shift yourselves. The time has come to know the minds of our northern brothers."

At his command they spread their masses apart, creating a bay into which advanced the various companies and groups to give Donari their decisions. And they were small groups at first; mostly younger men in search of a purpose. Almost half of the survivors from Emdar made their oaths. The old veteran they elected to speak for them explained the split apologetically in a gravely voice.

"My lord," he said, avoiding eye contact. "I am Tamson Greeve, an' the lads asked me to speak for them. Many have families, lord, or lands awaiting them. They cannot choose other than to go home, lord. Some of the younger ones will stay and enter your service if you will have them. You said think and choose, lord, and we have. Those that leave asked me to lead them. I've a woman back home, I do, lord, but I will take fair report of you to Emdar. More than that I cannot promise."

With that he left, and those that went with him filed in behind. Those who chose otherwise advanced and did their obeisance and so set the tenor of the morning as bit by bit the men of Perspa's army came forth to make their choice. The men from Collum and Sor-reel did not bother to even send a representative. In view of all there they dressed their ragged ranks and marched off, and the direction they took gave Donari his answer.

Of the men from Trenar, a goodly few made the oath, which surprised Donari given how poorly Roderran had treated the queen, daughter of their lord. There were quite a few individual men who claimed no former lord, and Donari took them, too, despite the warning tingles they sent down his spine. Group by group it went until finally only the men of Hallar remained. Into the space between the Pevanese wings advanced Hallan, son of Hallaran.

He stopped several paces away and stood there, grim-faced and yet his eyes betrayed his emotions and the hand that gripped his sword handle was white with tension.

"Hallan of fief Hallar," Donari said gravely. "The morning is come. What say you and yours?"

"The morning has come, my lord," he answered. "And I am here to take my leave of you, with honor, if you will, unlike others that now march ahead. I would have you know why, sir."

"Keep your honor, lad, and tell me."

"Last night you spoke fair, lord, and we spent much of the night debating amongst ourselves. For my own part, I see your honesty, and perhaps I could serve such a one as you, but I am not free to choose in this case. My men need me to get them home, and until my lord father tells us otherwise, you are not our king."

Donari kept his expression impassive even as anger and pity contested for control. Anger for the rejection; pity for what he could see it cost the young man to speak so.

"You and yours have chosen. So be it. Safe journey to you. Give our Royal regard to your father, and say to him that I grieve for his lost sons. Say also that I rejoice in the return of his youngest son, who in his bearing does his father honor. But remember my words at our parting last night: should we meet again in conflict, I will not be so patient."

A smile teased the corners of Hallan's mouth. "My lord is gracious, and if we should meet again, in peace or strife, I hope to return honor with honor regardless of the outcome." Then he bowed gracefully, turned on his heel and walked away. His men shouldered their spears, and the whole, grim procession marched away.

Donari stood in growing despair. Nearly two-thirds of the northern troopers marched to uncertain news when they got home. Before the fall, he suspected, they might come marching back to take his head and crown.

Hallan's departure struck the deepest; he sensed something of himself in the young man. The outcome may have been a foregone conclusion, but that did not temper the disappointment.

He had no doubts about Gaspire's intentions in Lomillar, if that is where he came to roost, and no doubts as to what sort of rebellious mischief he could instigate if enough of those now gone gathered to his standard. It would take time to gather a force sufficient to protect Pevana, but what if he was forced to march north and contest the issue? Reconstruction siphoned off Southern help, and even if Sylvanus could spare the men, would they be enough to counteract this leave-taking? If the northern lords ignored his summons, he would need to frame a response. He walked on tenuous ground. If he were not king of the whole region, then he might end king of none of it. And who would lament his fall? Who would succor his city burned, his people homeless and helpless? The image assaulted his spirit like an easterly gale, cold, dark, bone-chilling.

Avarran moved to his side with a sigh and sardonic chuckle. "Well then," he said. "That's done. I hope they all fall into a ravine."

Donari smiled wanly. "You don't mean that. You are just disappointed they did not thank you for getting them this far in one piece. Rather cheeky of them."

"Humor, after such insult?"

"Did you mark young Hallan? I wager there are others like him in that column. Who knows what time will bring? I will keep my small hope, thank you."

"Well, as for that," responded Avarran. "If you had any doubts about your legitimacy, you can put them aside."

"What do you mean?"

"Every king must have his rebellion to deal with. They respect you enough to see you as a threat. I doubt a mere prince would get such a rise out of them! May I give the order to strike camp and march for home, sire?"

"See to it."

Within an hour, the depleted host took to the road to cover the last few leagues to Pevana. Donari rode among them taking note of their bearing. They were good men. And yet he could not keep himself from reigning in at the top of a small rise to look back. In the distance, he could see the dust just beginning to haze the road as the northern companies paced along, a sinuous variable in a game of royal politics.

Chapter 9: Demona in Lomillar

Demona Anargi contemplated the cut of the new gown in the full length mirror and frowned. Her thickening waist ruined the lines, and yet that bulge was the only reason she received the gown in the first place. She swung side to side, trying to avoid looking too intently at her profile. The dress lacked some of the finesse she used to find in Pevanese fashion. In fact, she found much of Lomillar somewhat dispiriting. The clothes were thick woven and plain, generally, and the people went about their daily tasks without cheer at least as much as she could tell.

Once Gaspire installed her in rooms in a wing of the palace, he placed maids at her service and guards at her door. They accompanied her wherever she went, herding and warding her at all times. They rarely let her leave the palace grounds. She exacted her revenge by requesting creature comforts like the gown whose cut she did not quite like.

Demona motioned absently and her maids assisted her out of the garment. She waved off the next one offered.

"No more, Telis, none of these will do," she said, wrapping her robe around her naked frame. She hugged the cloth about her breasts, turning more tender now, and starting to swell a little. "I need something lighter, something more suitable for the weather."

Telis, a thickish, matronly creature with a husky voice, scowled as she gathered up the offending gowns.

"But these were from one of the best dress shops in Lomillar!" she protested.

"Then we will try one of the other ones!"

"My lady makes odd requests."

Demona turned and gave her an icy stare.

"Lord Amdoran set you to see to my needs. I want comfort for my unborn child, your future king. If the council wants to keep me caged here," she gestured with disdain to the room at large, "in this stifling palace in a city that never seems to gather a fresh breeze, then they will put up with a few requests." She took a light robe proffered by one of the other maids and moved to the window.

"Of course, my lady," Telis grumbled. "I'll send a few of the girls out again and see if they might find something more to your southern tastes."

"Oh, and Telis," Demona said lightly, still facing the window. "We must do something about the way you address me. This muttering

90

just won't do." She looked over her shoulder in dismissal. "It won't do at all. Look to it."

Real anger flushed over Telis's face. Demona raised an imperious brow. The woman nodded grudgingly and thumped out the door, drawing the other maids with her in a chastened gaggle, leaving Demona alone.

And what sort of victory is that, I wonder? Reduced to harassing servants. Hardly the stuff of successful intrigue. Roderran would have just laughed at me. Sevire would have criticized me for being too gentle. And Gaspire won't care as long as I continue to bloat and grow rounder.

She stared out the window. Below her the city bounced from terrace to terrace under the noon sun to the river bank and the great bridge that spanned its width. Even to her untutored eye, Demona could see Lomillar had its advantages, despite its lack of style. Three smaller streams, cutting from the highlands of Trenar and Collum, combined at their confluence to form the river Eloe. Gaspire told her the city served as a conduit for river trade and had been located originally to exert maximum influence on four of Perspa's six northern fiefs. There was power here, latent due to recent events, but real and accessible for her benefit if Gaspire and Casan's plot ripened.

She checked the sun's position again and thought about taking a walk, but the need to alert her handlers gave her pause. No matter the leagues and changes in her life, it seemed as though all she ever exchanged was one set walls for another.

Walls, changes.

Her mind wandered down old paths, around familiar landmarks of memory to a summer of words and the poet who gave them to her over the garden wall of her husband's house.

Talyior. I have him to blame, or thank, for all that has happened. I wonder what sort of poem he might come up with now if he were to walk through the door?

She teased a tress of her hair, tracing the past in its tight curl.

Talyior.

The name always seemed to lurk on the edge of all the events in her life since that crazy summer's affair. A grin lifted the corners of her lips.

And here I sit in a northern palace, and he is Renia knows where.

A knock on the door broke her reverie, and Lord Tareegan of Sorreel entered. His appearance startled her. Heretofore their interactions had been social, casual words in the company of others. What she knew of him she had gleaned from Gaspire's perceptions. His entrance, alone, now gave her pause, but he advanced, smiling genially, motioning her to take a seat at the table next the window. He took the other.

"And how goes your dress shopping, mistress?" he asked. As he spoke, however, he began tapping his fingers on the table, his old, cracked nails creating a clicking anti-rhythm at odds with his question's tone. Demona clutched her robe a little tighter.

"Well enough, thank you," she answered carefully. "I'm surprised; such interests seem beneath a lord's notice."

Tareegan grunted and leaned back in his chair. "You would be surprised what is worth a lord's notice, mistress," he said. "I've been known to check the linens in my house for wrinkles. I've also mucked out my own stables a time or two, just to make sure things there are what I want them to be."

"And are things always what you want them to be?"

"Yes, and if they aren't I change them."

Demona heard the threat in the man's tone, but she had come too far to let an old man daunt her.

"Your attention to detail is admirable. Now, as I am sure you've noticed, I am hardly dressed for visitors. It must be a northern custom to intrude on a woman's privacy. Is there something I can do for you?"

Tareegan's old eyes danced as he chuckled over her indignation. "Well then. Gaspire was right about you. You are quite the spitfire." He nodded approvingly. "My apologies."

"For what?"

"For doubting you. To be honest, when you first arrived here last month I questioned the whole affair. I thought the idea of a child from Roderran preposterous under the conditions, but you've grown on me along with that belly of yours."

Demona clutched the robe tighter, insulted by his familiarity.

"I suppose I should be pleased to have convinced you."

"Yes, you should," Tareegan interjected. "But enough of that. I am convinced you bear Roderran's child. I suppose I always did, but these times require proof beyond the word of others."

"So you don't trust Lord Amdoran?"

Tareegan glanced out the window. "Of course not," he said, speaking to the view. "You have moved among us now since Roderran took you on the war trail. None of us here in the north trust our brother lords. We've been conditioned from when Roderran's father sat in the chair. That is how rulers rule, mistress. Suspicion is a great tool for leverage."

Demona relaxed a little. This was ground she had begun to understand. She reached across the table and touched Tareegan's elbow.

"I think I see, lord. I am part of this *leverage*, and you don't trust Gaspire. And yet you know what he seeks to accomplish."

Tareegan frowned. He leaned forward, suddenly intent, all pretense abolished from his wrinkled face. "Yes, and I can see, now, what Roderran saw in you, and why Gaspire comes to your chambers after hours. You are lovely, and you've learned how to dissemble." He shook his head. "I almost pity you, lady, to find yourself between two such men as the Lord Prelate and Gaspire."

"But you aren't like them, of course." Demona made the sarcasm in her voice obvious.

Tareegan nodded diffidently. "Good!" he said. "Your spirit is not just for show. See that you nurse that spirit for what will come before the year is out. There will be civil war, death north and south. That is the world your baby will engender with *his* first breath. I think I understand you a little."

"My lord, you barely know me."

"I have means to the information needed for understanding."

"Of course, my maids."

"Servants in my house."

"My guards?"

"Gaspire's. Call it part of our compromise. I am the elder lord, but I will allow him precedent. He might think he is taking it, being masterful, but I did not survive Roderran's reign for nothing. I have my own agenda, and it includes avenging my two sons. Gaspire may have the gullet for what he intends, but he is too easy to read. You are a bit less so, but only just. Remember that, lady. You asked for help for your unborn child when you came among us a month ago. Can you rely purely on Gaspire? Take thought about who your friends are in this matter."

"What are you suggesting?" Her question hung in the air between them. Tareegan's words and increasingly cold tone dissipated Demona's sense of command like mist burned away by the sun.

The silence stretched, uncomfortably tight as that last gown she had tried on. Tareegan's flinty eyes, shale grey and surrounded by wild, bushy brows, furrowed intently.

"I think we understand one another, Lady Anargi," he answered finally, his voice softer but no less chilling. "Not everyone wants to see yet another Avedun on the throne. Donari is a bad bargain in a sad, sad business. And yet your child would not be solely Avedun would it? It could serve many purposes. Gaspire's. Casan's. Or mine."

"Or my own," Demona asserted, surprised by her own candor and courage. Tareegan was not a dress to be altered, or a man she could seduce. Dominated? No. Assimilated, perhaps. Or removed altogether if necessary.

"Or your own, yes. One must always take into account the wiles of a mother protecting her young, or in this case, prospective young. Yes, I rather like the description. You can keep your illusions about that if you want to, for now."

He leaned back with a satisfied smirk, and threads of meaning to a complex pattern slipped from Demona's fingers even as she sought to tie them off.

Tareegan continued. "I have news. Lord Gaspire has sent word from Trenar. He has been up there bashing heads. The remaining sons of old Trenar have been at each other." He waved his hand dismissively as he rose to leave. "Dogs snarling over a fleshless bone, in my opinion. But the truth of it is there will be no more flames from the highlands. Gaspire has them quelled, and they have agreed to send troops for his cause."

"Why are you telling me this?"

Tareegan looked knowingly at the discarded gowns. "So you can find the right dress to greet him in when he arrives to tell you, of course! Don't be silly, woman. Gaspire will return from this little triumph randy and chortling." He winked an insult. "You might enjoy both attitudes when he next knocks on your side door. He will think his designs march along swimmingly. He might grow impetuous. And *that* will not do for *my* hopes."

Demona rose to follow him to the door. "And what can I do about that?"

Tareegan turned with one hand on the door latch. He ran the index finger of his free hand once, gently down the inside of her robe, his fingertip making a whisper's touch along her left breast. The gesture, sensuous yet at odds with his aged appearance, made her recoil.

"Fuck him out of this martial exuberance in the ways you know best, my dear," he said. "A move too soon will fail here; a move too late, likewise. We must gather our friends, each of us, and let the proper time announce itself. He returns in two days. Until then, my lady."

He left. And as Demona closed the door behind him she felt a chill form in the small of her back; a small pain as the half-formed fetus in her womb stretched out its little arms and legs in search of more room and scraped against a tightness that persisted. She took a breath, another, her mind reeling as she tried to parse how to deal with Sor-reel's revelations.

Two days. I will need a dress, and must make arrangements for a suitable banquet to celebrate the news.

94

She looked around the room and saw her body framed in the mirror. The pain settled, receded a little, but did not go away.

"Oh yes, little man," she whispered, dropping her hands to her belly. "Things are beginning to happen--to both of us."

Chapter 10: Symmetry

After Donari returned with that portion of the army that swore allegiance to him, Pevana progressed into a summer slowness that hinted peace. Word and presence arrived from Emdar in July in the form of Bindon Celion, the eldest surviving son of the old Lord Tondry. He sailed into port in a small craft flying Emdar's pennant, bearing messages full of kind words but little substance.

"Your noble father sends greetings and gentle words, Bindon," he said, forcing a gracious smile. "But he stops far short of acknowledgement and aid. Did he share the contents of this with you?"

Ties economic and filial bound Pevana and Emdar. Both had prospered, but Emdar was still the smallest fief in the realm; its lands limited to the sweep of hills and dunes framing its harbor-city. Necessity made it a timid player in the present political game.

Bindon nodded his head once; his face a study in ambivalence "I have, my lord," he said, his voice fair and at odds with his piratical look. "And I beg you to receive it in the spirit of the connection between our houses."

"What?" Donari scoffed, gently. "No *sire* from either your lord father or yourself?" He noted a quick tightness in Bindon's jaw and joshed away his asperity. "Nah, nah, we will put aside such questions for now, I think. It is enough, perhaps, given the time and nature of my crowning, that he sends any word at all. That he sends you with it, well, we will take that as a boon true. Forgive me if I seem harsh."

"And my father bid me add this, then, in addition to the words in the letter," Bindon said, his look softening. "That my lord is newly crowned with a doubtful circlet, however real the blood that bound you to Roderran, he admits is compelling but should be considered at a council of lords. The north is new in its grief. Our king and so many of the high and low lost…to aspire to heed your royal summons is just not possible. My lord, my father sits in his rooms and tears his beard at our losses. The remnant of our foot only made it back a week before I sailed. He is sensitive to your call, but surely you must see the difficulty with Sor-reel at our back. Gaspire of Collum has sent out his own word, disputing your rights. You ask for fealty, but to do so could bring down the wrath of the rest upon us."

"I would come to your aide."

Bindon blanched, his face glaring white against red hair. "With what, my lord?" All are weak, but we are the weakest, even with our folk unhurt. The shambles of a beaten force guards your walls. Promises of southern peace cannot do us good in the short term. My father begs for time, my lord, to sort this situation out. He rejoices at your return to Pevana, he wishes to renew our ties of old, but he cannot take the knee, not now."

"You mean he won't unless I prove I can survive first?"

"My lord, please."

Donari waved his unease away. "Enough. Between the two of us, man, I cannot blame him, but this crown I now bear requires firmness. In time you and your father will take my oaths or feel my displeasure. I am Perspa's rightful king."

"Perspa's kings rule from the King's Seat at Lomillar."

"I do not intend to rule from Lomillar," Donari growled. "I bring the south and peace with my rule. I cannot be just a northern king. Take my thoughts back to your father. Let him sift his grief and come to see his duty. I need Emdar. My peace needs trade in your ships. He risked his sons to follow Roderran's folly; let him risk the rest to follow me. For if I fail, civil war will cumber this land, and this spring's disaster will turn to next spring's treble calamity. Think on it, Lindon. Stay as our royal guest until I can find words to write your father in response to this." And he crumpled up the letter and tossed it aside. "Be well-advised: my next missive will be more forceful. I will take the north if I need. I do not fear Gaspire and his feeble ambitions. "Rooms have been readied for you." He motioned Drue forward. "Young Drue here will see you settled and refreshed. Though you refrain from calling me your king, still a king's greeting and benison I give you. And that, too, is something you should think on. Good day, sir."

He reviewed the interview after Bindon left and felt both a thrill and a chill receiving this first reply. He had sent his requests by ship to the northern ports, addressed to each of the major lords of the land, calling all to account for their absence from his new court. He knew better than to expect alacrity. He played a rigged game here. Emdar's guarded response served to deepen the silence from the other regions.

No surprise, Tondry is a realist. He patronizes me because he has to.

He let out an exasperated breath, bent to retrieve the crumpled letter, and stalked down the hall.

"I'm too much of an idealist," he muttered to himself. "Roderran would just lope off enough heads to make his point. I must wait, ignorant. What I need are eyes in place to get me real news. Speculation does not serve."

97

Drue returned from seeing Bindon settled in his rooms and stood respectfully waiting new orders. Donari waved him closer and handed him the letter.

"Take this to the Lady Eleni and ask her to join me in my study. Then go find Devyn and do the same."

"Yes, sire, at once. Will that be all?"

"I wish it were, lad, but for now it is enough."

Drue bowed and practically ran from the hall. Donari followed more slowly, chewing on his thoughts. Cryso hovered expectantly by the doors. Donari raised a hand.

"Whatever it is it can wait," he said. "Send word to Avarran down at the cantonment. I will need a meeting tonight. Send some sturdy lads with a glass out to the headland. I want to be informed of any sails from whatever direction the moment they are sighted. I need some space to think."

"As you wish, sire," Cryso deferred with just the slightest hesitation. "Messages have come from several of the merchant houses. I have placed them on your desk in your study. Those that brought them seemed intent on a response, but I will put them off with a glass and a visit to the kitchens."

"I especially don't have time for that lot. My thanks, Cryso. But don't give them the good stuff! Take a glass of that for yourself."

Cryso bowed acknowledgement and left. Donari continued on to the foot of the stairs alone once again with his thoughts.

And in the end that is how it must be I suppose. If the rule is mine, so are the choices. And the results.

He mounted the carpeted steps slowly.

Eleni put down the draft of the state letter she had been working on, flexed her fingers, frowned down at the words and then rose and walked to the window. Behind her, Anlise busied herself changing out the bedding. Eleni had grown accustomed to the maid's presence since her return. The girl went about her tasks with quiet efficiency that rarely intruded on Eleni's concentration.

The mid-day summer sun beat down on the tile roofs of Pevana, and Eleni wondered what the autumn might bring if they were granted that much time. In the month since Avarran returned with the army, life in Pevana regained some of its slower, sensual pace. Though badly worn down by their travails, the returning men helped stabilize Pevanese society. Shops reopened. Eleni noted flowers in abundance. The fields outside the city showed signs of tending, as did the acres of vines on the slopes above the river. As with the northern folk, there were tragic gaps in the ranks, but folk quickly succored the grieving and life went on with a semblance of its former grace.

She let her eyes wander over the shoulder of the hill, walls, and rooftops beyond and below. Just outside the citadel, opposite Donari's private rooms, the new bell tower for the King's Theology Temple rose like an offending digit bewebbed by scaffolding. To Eleni, it all seemed like a petulant protest; a weak attempt at one-upmanship. Donari laughed it off as unimportant, but Eleni remained unconvinced.

Bricks and mortar could be turned into symbols. That scaffolding is just too obvious.

Although Senden's funeral pulled most of the Prelate's teeth, Eleni felt certain he still gummed the ends of old plots in search of new irritants. With Donari too busy to bother with him since that time, Eleni and Devyn took it upon themselves to organize a watch on Casan's activities. A week ago Eleni returned to the College to tidy up the loose ends of her academic responsibilities and sneak a look at the activity of the place.

She managed to avoid confronting the Prelate directly when she went to conduct her business, but she did see him engaged in earnest conversation with a bevy of red clad acolytes in the Library's main floor seating area. In accordance with Donari's edict, no one showed any arms, but neither Donari nor Eleni harbored any illusions that weapons still lay in stockpile. Few of the men Eleni encountered in the library exhibited any priestly qualities. Their bowl cut locks did nothing to soften their features; many of them looked as though they would hold their own in a tavern brawl. She could not imagine them engaged in any ecclesiastical discussion that did not also involve their fists. She remembered filing the insight away in her mind for another time, but in the bustle of her days forgot to mention it to either Devyn or Donari. She looked again at the scaffolding and made another mental note to do so that day.

Donari might call it a small omission, but small stones falling loose from great height have been known to bring the avalanche.

She heard Anlise finish with the bedding and the slight rustle of her dress as she moved to join her at the window.

"My lady enjoys the view?" Anlise asked deferentially.

Eleni blinked at the question. Anlise normally kept her thoughts to herself. The bulk of their conversations trended to the phrasal; limited interactions that focused on tasks done or expected.

"I do indeed, Anlise, today especially. My former home had a balcony that faced east. I used to love getting up early to greet the sunrise."

"Do you miss your old home?"

The question sent Eleni back to the day she and Gania packed away all her memories of that former life: tears and grief, hope and fear encompassed by change. She placed flowers on Tomais's grave after her return, but never went back to the home they had shared.

"That was an old life, a different me," she said quietly.

"This faces south and west."

"Yes," Eleni responded, brightening. "And it holds the light wonderfully."

"For your records." Anlise gestured to the piles of pages and Eleni's ink and pens. "Such detail."

Eleni shrugged. "It is what I do. The king expects a detailed record of these days."

"Why?"

Eleni turned at the abrupt expression. Anlise's face remained impassive, however; her eyes appeared nothing more than curious.

"Details are my stock in trade, Anlise, but I take such care with the king's accounts so that men in later days will have a clear understanding of the events that happen during his reign."

"Why should the king care what men think?"

"What do you mean?"

A smile teased over Anlise's lips. "He is king. He rules. Why should he worry about questions?"

The odd tone reminded Eleni of when she and Anlise had talked back in the palace garden during her recovery from Tomais's death. There had been something about Tomais's burial rites, a tic about faith, and a hint of judgement. She smiled to cover her silence.

She turned again to the window, gesturing to the unfinished bell tower.

"Donari is not Roderran, Anlise. You have served in this palace long enough to know him when he was Prince of Pevana. For him, the crown just intensifies the care. We all get to make choices now. And that is one of them. Our Lord Prelate is a persistent spider. I wonder where he found the money for the work?"

"I heard a priest in one of the public squares say once that destiny, at times, must be provided for."

"High sounding words for coerced tithing."

100

"You do not approve, my lady? I should think a poet would appreciate beauty, and what it costs."

"As I said before, we all get to make choices," Eleni responded, nettled. "I'm sure it will be impressive."

"It will be beautiful once it is done," Anlise said, voice growing rapt. "A soaring testament to the power of faith."

Again. That tic. The slightest inflection on the last word. *Share no secrets with this one.* Eleni turned her gaze away from the pretentious spire, took a breath rather than respond, and tried to let the sun and warmth dissipate her flicker of unease.

A soft knock on her door broke her away from her reverie. Anlise moved, frowning, to see to it. Drue, practically out of breath and his hair in need of a combing, entered.

"Lady Eleni," he said, pushing by Anlise. "There has been a ship from Emdar. The king requests you meet him in his office, and please bring your writing things with you."

The boy's manner brought a pointed tisk from Anlise.

"Drue, that is no way to come in to a lady's room!"

"But the king said!"

"Still, I don't see—"

"That's enough, Anlise," Eleni soothed. "It is nothing, really." She glanced at the maid, who had followed Drue, and wondered if her frown deepened due to the boy's presence or the mention of the northern fief. A question framed itself in her mind, but Drue's rasping enthusiasm broke the string. She checked her hair and face in the mirror, took up her pad and basket of ink bottles, and hurried out the door.

Eleni re-read the letter from the Lord of Emdar three times before returning it to Donari with an attempt at a smile. Devyn sat nearby, watching, from one of the deep chairs near the fireplace. The three of them had repaired to Donari's study after a disappointing morning spent reassuring the city elders that open war did not yet threaten their valley. No fire burned in the grating, the room lit by a combination of candles and late-afternoon sun.

Eleni sat at Donari's desk amid a clutter of notes and transcriptions. The door opened, and Captain Avarran slipped in. Donari waved him to a chair.

"Well," he said finally. "That was a rough bit of work. Eleni, I thought your pen was going to ignite from the friction. You really did not have to record everything from those pattering old fools."

"I wanted to make sure I got it all down," she said. "You never know when you might need a well remembered quote. Some of them might need to be reminded what loyalty means."

Donari snorted. "Yes, I suppose you are right. But I think that lot will stay loyal. Without Sevire's misguiding hand here to lead them astray. Old Cumber, the wheezing, bald fellow, is worth a little tactful restraint. His son serves with Avarran here, actually. If I have need, they will find me men, money and munitions."

"His son is a good kid, sire," Avarran explained. "He doesn't have the old man's caution."

"Good, but let's not underestimate the value of caution."

"So you think Emdar's letter means problems?" Devyn asked.

"Oh, yes," Donari responded. "If Emdar is reticent, despite the actions of their fighting men earlier, then the likes of Collum and Sor-reel will be openly against me. If they send any message at all, I now doubt they will come in person, then I expect them to be variations of the same thing: rejection pointed and final. We may be defending the passes by fall or at best by next spring."

Donari paused, and Eleni redipped her pen and looked up, sensing something in the offing.

"Sire?" Avarran inquired.

"Caution in others might be wise, in us, perhaps otherwise, perhaps even foolish," Donari continued. "We are tired. Folk need to get back to their fields and trades. Marching north is out of the question." Eleni's pen flew across the page.

"I agree, sire," Avarran said. "But just manning the city walls gives Gaspire freedom to make the first move."

"Until we can claim southern help, we have to let Gaspire have his space. A pity, but there it is."

"What would you have me do?"

"I need eyes in the hills. I want the King's Road watched. Can you find the men?"

"Of course, my king, none would refuse a royal command."

"I want volunteers. Younger sons, single men. I will not take husbands and fathers away for this."

"As you wish, sire."

"We've had a month to refit our herds. Find mounts for them. Hilltops. The roadway. There may be skulkers out there doing the same thing for Gaspire."

"I am told he took a fair number of the two year olds from the herd when he went through, but I can find enough for the purpose."

"See to it, please. I want them in place by the time young Bindon leaves for home."

Eleni scratched away, recording the commands as Avarran rose, bowed and left.

Devyn coughed, stretched his legs out. "So much for Avarran's tasks," he said. "What do you need from me?"

"How have your city wanderings gone?"

"Fruitful."

"And?"

"And I feel like I have the pulse of the place now. I have taken a handful of the lads about the palace and set them to keeping watch on the various sections of the city." Eleni started when he touched her elbow to get her attention, so deep had been her concentration. "I even have a man in the university for your needs if you ever have need when there." He sobered. "Senden's notes have been helpful, and surprising. I must admit I rather enjoy being a spy. I guess the Maze taught me more than just how to survive."

"I can well understand," Donari responded. "Perhaps in this case surviving and spying run to about the same thing. I need information. Have your man in the college sniff around the Prelate. Not knowing northern counsels galls me. I am sure he has been in contact with Gaspire. Perhaps you might turn up something there for us."

"I will see to it directly, sire."

"Please do, and then rinse the day from your face and come back. Dinner. The three of us. Let's enjoy the evening."

"An excellent idea," Eleni added without looking up from her writing. She barely noticed the creak from Devyn's chair as he rose and left quietly.

Eleni finished her last sentence, put down her pen, stood, and walked over to sit on the arm of Donari's chair. She ran her hand familiarly through his hair.

"I have already added spy to my other titles," she said. "Casan has a few too many over-large thugs reshelving books these days."

Donari frowned. "Other titles?"

"Mistress, secretary, cheeky widow; *spy* seemed appropriate."

"And you did not tell me?"

Eleni bent and kissed his forehead. "You've been taxed. We took it upon ourselves, Devyn and I. No harm done."

Donari closed his eyes to the movements of her fingers. "You will be guarded," he murmured.

"I will not risk you. No more visits to the library, please."

"I always have Drue and one other with me."

"Not enough. And you are not my mistress, dearest, never think it."

"But others must, not that I care." She sighed. "It seems I'm cut off, then. I will have to let Devyn sneak about the library stacks and shelves for me."

"I will keep you busy enough."

"And risk your virtue?" She let herself slip from the chair arm into Donari's lap.

"Worth it."

She kissed him, the pressure of their lips creating a different kind of tension that had no time for plans, plots or peril. And yet when they parted, she could see Donari still had questions.

"Have I missed anything?" Donari asked. Eleni leaned away but found an answer right away.

"Yes, yes you have," she asserted. "You mentioned *normal* with Avarran before he left. I agree. I don't know why I didn't see it earlier. But I saw hints of normal from my window today: fields and vines getting attention. Movement in the markets. But it is just that, hints. It is as though the city can't allow itself to slip back into remembered patterns."

"But Eleni," Donari interrupted. "Can you blame them? Today's news should make that clear. There has been too much change and too much uncertainty. They see war clouds."

"What they see is their prince turned into a king. *Normally*, right about now their prince would be making proclamations about the Summer Festival and the sites for the Poet's Competition. July is passing, Donari."

Donari frowned. "You can't be serious. How could I distract them so obviously?"

"How could it be a distraction to give them what they need the most?"

"But there is no way I could put aside all these other matters."

Eleni leaned in and kissed him again, playfully, on the tip of his nose. "You don't have to. I propose another title for myself: Mistress of Revels. I will see to it. You'd probably have me write the directives out anyway. All you'd need to do is sign them."

Donari shook his head. "Eleni," he began.

"You know I am right," she asserted. "I've heard you talk about nothing but men, arms and weapons since you returned. That is only part of the equation, love, and what better way to remind them they are in your thoughts than by insisting they continue happy traditions?"

Donari frowned, but then the value of the idea blossomed for him. "Renia's Grace, but you are right! Still, there is risk, but I think we can manage it."

"Of course I can," asserted Eleni.

"Yes, of course, *you* can," Donari agreed. "Well, then, we've even more plans to make tonight and all the more reason to dine together. Cryso!" he shouted. Instantly, the study door opened, revealing Cryso's unflappable visage.

"You called, sire?"

"Have Cook send dinner up to my terrace for three, no, make that four. You will be joining us. Eleni will need your help."

"I am to join you, sire?"

Eleni found the sudden transformation on the older man's face strangely humanizing.

Donari took Eleni's hand and led her passed the sputtering servant.

"Cryso," he said, chuckling. "You surprise me. After all these years and you get flustered over an invitation? These are changed times, indeed. Yes, send word and join us. Call it a royal summons if you must, but I think you've more than earned a glass."

"As you wish, sire, I am honored."

Donari winked at Eleni. "Oh, you'll pay for it, old friend. I'm about to dump more tasks into your lap. Join us!"

Bindon Celion stayed for a week of tours, fetes and meetings with Donari and his Council. Donari made certain guards attended his northern guest at all times. They showed Bindon the keels of the four new galleys laid in the shipyard, the bounty assembled in Pevana's markets, and the natural bustle of Pevanese life. Eleni's notices about the Summer Festival helped the effort. Donari wanted Tondry's son to return home with a tale that contradicted the one his enemies spread.

Since February of that year, Donari's life had been filled with metal, munitions and war. He longed for days when the most important thing on his schedule would be to decide which concert by school children to attend. The silence from north of the ridges grew more and more settled and serious with each passing day. He did what he could.

Avarran's small mobile force from the survivors of the southern battles went to the hills to ride patrols and keep watch from the heights. The fishing fleet, decimated by the manpower demands of Casan's naval campaign, slowly got back to pursuing the schools of whitefish and pilchard that swam in the currents outside Pevana's harbor. Among those craft were other boats charged with keeping watch on the horizon northward. Behind this flimsiest of screens Donari and his people sheltered and tried to resurrect the disturbed threads of their lives.

At the end of July, a week after Bindon sailed for Emdar, Donari received letters bearing the seals of Collum, Sor-reel, Avedar, and Trenar delivered by a haughty messenger escorted by several of Avarran's men. The northern letters all held variations of deliberate insult and political repudiation. Amdoran's response held the most import, however, for he included a copy of the Prelate's Proclamation exposing and legitimizing Demona's pregnancy.

He shared the stunning news with Eleni.

"Much comes clear, with this," he said, waving Amdoran's terse missive. "It seems I have a bastard cousin on the way."

Eleni took the paper, her face paling as she read its contents.

"No wonder Casan was so defiant when we returned."

"True. He and Gaspire must have known all along. They will paint this as redemption rather than rebellion."

"But will the people accept it?"

"We have to assume the worst, I fear." Donari rubbed weary eyes. "This news changes every perspective. I thought I won a throw by forcing Casan to speak at Senden's funeral. More fool me, now, I suppose."

"Is it as bad as all that?" Eleni asked, rising.

Donari took her into his arms. "Gaspire beards me, love. Casan's influence in the north is proven. Men will rise to my cousin's call in support of Demona's child." He sighed into her hair. "Roderran's follies continue even after he is dead. Renia's Tears, Eleni, the child is innocent no matter its parentage."

"What will you do?" Eleni murmured into his chest.

Donari tightened his embrace. "Wait and see, hold fast to the things we know, and pray for success."

The next day, ships flying Pevanese and Desopolisan colors cleared the headland and tied up at the wharf. They held Sylvanus and an embassy of southern leaders along with nearly five hundred well-fed, rehabilitated Perspan troops. Donari held those letters crushed in his left hand while with his right he accepted their fealty. Despite the near certainty of civil war, Donari felt at peace.

Chapter 11: Choices of Life

Donari met Sylvanus and the other southerners across several long tables pushed together in the Palace Hall along with Avarran and several of the senior heads of Pevanese merchant households. Eleni sat poised to record the proceedings at a table set nearby. Everything depended on clarifying and cementing the odd relationship begun so surprisingly on the field at Lyranden Bridge. The careful, calculating looks from the southerners reminded Donari just how much he and Sylvanus risked.

"Let me make myself clear, gentleman," he began, touching the notched battle circlet that still served him as a crown. "I wear this symbol. House Avedun rules Perspa, but this will be an altered region if I am spared and my hopes realized. I know how I come by this bauble, and I accept the responsibility. Lord Tamorgen spoke at Lyranden Bridge of a king for all, north and south. Bold words and bravely spoken." He smiled warmly at Sylvanus. "Let us hope he is a man farsighted. I hope to prove his faith in me during the days to come."

"Young man," Sylvanus chuckled, taking up his goblet raising it in good natured toast. "You've made a good beginning with this wine! Were it not for the larger issues that face us, I would make the voyage for this alone."

Donari raised his glass in return. "Then let us make a binding accord so that the vines that produce it stay unburnt for future pressings. My deepest thanks to you, Lord of Desopolis, and to all of you for your trust in coming."

"We follow Sylvanus's counsel in this, sire," wheezed the old lord of Teirne. "Your folk have helped us repair and salvage much from the conflict. And yet we hear that the firebrand himself, this Lord Prelate Casan, resides yet in this city?"

The old man's flinty words struck Donari like a blow to the face.

"Yes, sir, the Prelate leads his church, and, for now, oversees certain parts of the university."

"Why, sire?"

"He was an arm of Roderran's folly, lord. He is powerless now."

"His fleet burned my library. They slew many of my folk. He has much to answer for."

"And he will answer, in time, sir. But he is the head of a growing faith, and I have sworn to allow my folk to choose in such matters."

"Is that wise?"

"Was it wise for Sylvanus to hand me this crown? Who can say, yet, what is wisdom and what is folly? I will not rule as my predecessor. Casan galls me, but I have isolated him. His failure in the south discredits him. He is a toothless cleric, sir, and yet I fear the northern response if I make him a martyr. He stayed in Pevana seeking to annoy me. I watch him. I limit his power."

Before the lord of Teirne could respond, Sylvanus coughed and waved him down. "King Donari has his cousin, Lord Gaspire Amdoran of Collum to deal with first, my friends," he said. "I can attest to the danger he poses. And now we hear of this child. Further danger. We will face conflict. Better to face it here, in support of a king who will rule for us, than piecemeal behind our battered southern walls. I urge patience in the matter of Casan."

Donari gave Sylvanus a grateful look. Sylvanus smiled and winked, a gesture Donari found oddly comforting.

After the tense beginning the rest of the meeting progressed equably. Both sides agreed to exchange future trade. Indeed, the tables fairly buzzed as the talks broke down into individual discussions between folk hammering out particulars. Over at her table next the wall, Eleni's pen flew across her pages as she struggled to keep up with the flow of information. Donari thought her look of rapt concentration particularly fetching. He scanned back across the table, caught Sylvanus's eye and rose, gesturing toward a sideboard that held more wine and sweetcakes. Donari poured for both of them.

"My thanks, lord," he said. "That was awkward."

"Perhaps it is I who should apologize," Sylvanus answered. "I left that part out of my letter to you. Old Hazan there was the least willing to accept things. Understandable, you'd have to agree. Teirne suffered first and worst from Casan's attentions."

"Understanding doesn't make it any less uncomfortable. Casan vexes me, but I meant what I said. I have to leave him be for now."

"I had to let him ask his question. Eventually, you will have to provide him an answer. I think he would find 'peace and prosperity' particularly mollifying."

Donari laughed at little over the edge of his cup. "And you? What would mollify you, lord?"

"The same, of course. Your Talyior and my Lyvia have been busy. Along with the restoration, they are planning a wedding. I'd enjoy enough peace and space to fully experience the novelty."

"A wedding!" Donari exclaimed. He looked back to where Eleni sat scribbling away. *A wedding, of course.* "Shall I grant him a title?"

Sylvanus grinned. "I suppose I can no longer be 'the tyrant of Desopolis,' can I? I hadn't considered it, to be honest."

"Call it a compromise to northern sensibilities. Perhaps one day, all such things as titles will pass away, but for now I fear I must make you a Duke."

"And my headstrong daughter will become 'Lady Lyvia'. Ha! She'll hate it. I love it."

"So, tell," Donari said, tossing off what was left in his glass. "Do you still think you made a good bargain back at Lyranden Bridge?"

Sylvanus sobered appreciably. "Doubts come with authority. I think you already know that. But I can assure you I have never had any grave doubts since that day. Your Talyior, the good will of the men you left behind, even the grudging honor of some of the ones captured at Desopolis all speak against doubt. I think I chose well at Lyranden Bridge. Besides, from the way you handled Hazan, I think perhaps my doubts would no longer matter."

Again, the man's perspicacity impressed Donari. *He would make a bad enemy.* "No," he agreed. "I have it now, and daily I grow more assured I must rule, and I will with your help.

They had both made a bargain at Lyranden Bridge, and with honor came loyalty. Sylvanus took up the flagon and poured again for both of them.

"Sire," he murmured, raising his glass.

"Does the word come hard for you?"

Sylvanus took a long, deliberate swallow. "I'll get used to it," he said. "I hope I have opportunity to use it again."

"As do I. But you mean something different."

Sylvanus swirled the liquid in his cup, then fixed Donari with a frank, worried look.

"You are in trouble," the older man said. "You hid it well across the table, but your real confidence is thin, yes? This child the Anargi woman claims she bears?"

Donari turned away so to hide his expression from the others in the room.

"Yes," he responded, pitching his voice low. "I'd hoped for more men from the lot that returned with Avarran. The north is closed to me as yet. The woman went south with Roderran. There truly could be a child, and Casan has made it a cause. I don't know exactly what Gaspire is doing, but I assume he will rally sizable numbers using the baby. If it comes to battle, I think we will be sorely pressed."

"Find me the ships, and I will send what I can, when I can."

"Would you accept a command from the king you have made?"

Sylvanus coughed a laugh. "Of course, 'sire', command."

"Come yourself. Soon. Put a saddle on every nag you can trammel up and start them north."

"Again, shipping."

"Then gather what you can and come overland. Anything added to my few squads of cavalry would make a difference."

"No small command, sire. See? A third time and already it trips off my tongue like love words."

"Sylvanus, I know you and the others have suffered grievous hurt, but all our fates will be determined here in the north. If we are allied, then get me men to face what comes."

Sylvanus finished his wine, nodded agreement. "I will do what I can."

"Pray that it will be enough. I want to build, my lord Tamorgan. This land has seen too many flames this past year. And if I face one more throw in the game, then I want all my dice on the table."

Donari drained his glass. A motion at the door drew his attention. Devyn Ambrose entered and moved to his side.

"Sire, Cook says all is ready."

"Excellent! Perhaps we can smooth away some of those frowns. I'll collect Eleni, then." He looked from Devyn to Sylvanus and back again. "Ah, I suspect you two have some catching up to do as well. I'll leave you to it."

Devyn Ambrose and Sylvanus loitered by the window while Donari led Eleni and the others to the feast. As the room cleared, they followed. Sylvanus paused at the door and shook Devyn's hand warmly, a deep smile fracturing his salt and pepper beard.

"Well met, young Devyn. I see you have found your service. I am glad my gambit worked out so well. I knew I placed my trust in an enterprising man."

"And I, lord," Devyn responded. "And I also rejoice at the news Talyior prospers. He needed a place. Tell him he owes me a tale."

"I will, my boy, though I would not be surprised if he and Lyvia came back with me when I return with men. She was not pleased at being left behind or Talyior, either. I am in some unease about my reception when I return home!"

"My lord will handle things, I am sure."

"Perhaps," Sylvanus agreed. "But we are in changed times, lad. I may have one adventure left in me: this king-making business and the north. My daughter and her love life will best me, I think."

"As I recall, you were looking forward to becoming a grandfather."

"And that, in time, will be a grand adventure, and more in keeping with my meager talents. Serve our king, young man. I am sure we will meet again."

Chapter 12: The Mistress of Revels

Eleni took one last look in the mirror and adjusted the wide brimmed sun hat slightly before allowing Anlise to fix it securely with a long pin. The southern lords had sailed the day before. By the time their ship cleared the headland, Donari rode out Pevana's land gate with Avarran and an escort of his precious cavalry. Before he left, he gave Eleni her own marching orders.

"Since you claim the title, *Mistress of Revels*," he said, kissing her goodbye, "then you get to set about organizing something. But remember, my dear, for some there are painful memories attached to the festival. There are missing faces and missing places. And that bears careful consideration. Take the measure of the city while I'm gone. I agree we need to do something. Perhaps a little laughter will serve us well."

Eleni took extra time preparing herself for the day. She had to project confidence and compassion, and a miss-placed hair or the wrong shade of color on her lips could send the wrong message. She hoped to persuade folk back to joy. She managed a convincing wink at the mirror. Behind her, the door opened revealing Anlise, punctual as ever, and just as spiritless. Eleni decided she would not let the girl's asperity blunt her enthusiasm.

"Right," Eleni whispered to her reflection. "Laughter it is." She swung around, gave Anlise a bright smile and swept up her basket of writing materials. "Come, my dear," she said. "We've a party to plan."

Donari's favorite page, the effervescent Drue, met them in the hallway, and the three of them proceeded out to the courtyard to a waiting carriage and driver. Two guardsmen curbed their horses nearby. Once Eleni and the others settled themselves, Eleni waved the driver on and the carriage trundled off.

"We have a number of stops to make today," Eleni told the others. "I'd like to surprise Donari with some firm plans when he returns."

"Where first, my lady?" Drue asked.

"A few social calls to some of the houses major on the hill, a quick pass about the city's alehouses and then back, unless something else catches my attention."

"Do you really think you get people to listen?" Anlise asked. "The great houses don't even know you."

"No one knew me when I took over my father's business, either, Anlise, but that didn't stop me from making a reputation. I know my way around Pevana."

She gave the girl a brief, pointed grin, but Anlise didn't get the message. She sniffed, decorously, just barely skirting insult.

"My mother loved your work, my lady, but as I recall, you still entered through the servant's door. It is a different story when you come through the main entrance. You are asking for their money and time, not making a delivery."

Eleni forced her smile even wider in response. "Ah, true, to a point, my dear. But the fact remains that I have always known what do once I get inside, regardless of the door I used. Anlise, are you sure you want to go along on my little expedition? Shall I have the driver stop and let you out." She looked over her shoulder. "Oh, yes, it would still just be a short walk back to the palace. I'm sure Mistress Denna could find some task for you. Drue," she said, giving the boy a surreptitious wink, "Isn't today washing day?"

"It is indeed, my lady," Drue responded enthusiastically, "And I believe Mistress Denna intended to do all the rooms in the west wing."

Eleni arched her brows. "Ambitious! Think of all those sheets! So, Anlise, what shall it be: a nice ride about the city helping me and Drue keep track of things or soap and stirring paddles?"

Anlise's eyes flared. "That won't be necessary, Lady Eleni," she said. "I meant no offense. It's just that, with all the troubles from before, the pall has never left the city. Folk have suffered. Trade is practically nill. That is hardly cause for a summer festival."

"I disagree with you, and the king agrees with me. Now is the perfect time, actually, to show our people that life goes on as before in spite of flames and war and uncertainty. What better way to show our northern cousins, should they hear of it, that Pevana will keep to her ways."

She let her expression soften. She really did not want to argue. "And I am not just a seemstress turned secretary, Anlise. Folk know of my connection with the king, and I know the lower city. If I can make people listen, then I think I can get us our festival." She ended warmly to remove any lingering sting. "If all goes well, I might sew you a new dress!"

"That would be," Anlise smiled stiffly, "delightful!"

Eleni had to fight back growing disappointment by the time they finished visiting the last of a half dozen of the richer houses on the hill. Though they received her decorously, none of the heads of household she talked to expressed whole-hearted enthusiasm for her plans to hold a Summer Festival. All of them had suffered in the aftermath of Roderran's foolishness. Some had lost sons in the conflict. All had lost treasure. Roderran had looted efficiently. Eleni listened to the various, apologetic expressions and wondered how Pevana would survive if Donari failed to cement his rule.

She directed the driver to head down into the city, hoping for a better response. In the few months since Donari's return, the common folk made shift to recover their lives. But Eleni's sensibilities told her uncertainty still ate at the city like a canker, and even the prospect of joy in the form of the festival seemed a risk few were willing to make.

She and her little group made a circuit of the alehouses and inns where festival activities normally took place. Some of them had fallen on hard times just like the families on the hill. Some grieved for sons and workers lost in the south. Others suffered from less skilled replacements and less trade. More than a few looked in need of a paint job and refurbishment. She ignored Anlise's constant, sniffing disapproval over the general lack of flash and cleanliness. Eleni knew about dirt and the common man; such things were part of the life, and she was not after appearances. The genuine smile is all the brighter for a little mud, after all.

About the only place that seemed unchanged was Saymon Brimaldi's *Golden Cup*. Its understated sign and entry beckoned to her like a memory. Images of that fateful night returned; that mix of temerity and love that initiated her present adventure. She decided she could do without Anlise's sneering and ordered her, Drue and the guards to remain outside. She swept in alone and took the fact that half the common room's tables were full of mid-day patrons as a reason to hope.

Saymon greeted her with a smile and left off tending the bar to join her at one of the booths.

"Mistress Caralon," he rumbled through his beard. "I see quite a lot of young Devyn. It is good to see you under my roof again."

Eleni suppressed a desire to laugh. The timbre in Saymon's voice reminded her of happier times when she and Tomais would frequent the place. Saymon's burly, unpretentious prosperity served that part of the city well. Eleni ran her fingers over the wood of the table, gouged and well worn but clean and sturdy, just like the proprietor. Together, Saymon and his house functioned like a lodestone of the real for Pevana. Although the Tree had vanished in its flames, The Cup remained: a haven of good food and spirits. Solid. Stable. Eleni was glad she chose to leave it for her last stop.

"Oh, my friend," she sighed, relaxing back against the cushioned seat. "It is *good* to see you again."

Saymon gave a low chuckle and motioned to the bar. A very pregnant serving girl waddled over with a bottle of wine and two glasses.

"Thank you, Sanya," Saymon said, popping out the cork. "There's a stool there by the door to the kitchen. Pull it over and mind the bar for me, please?" The girl nodded in thanks and left.

Eleni looked a question.

"A recent addition," Saymon answered. "Changes, as you mentioned. Now, that sigh sounded like it needed a glass," he went on, pouring for the both of them. "As I said, I've seen quite a bit of Devyn but none of you."

"Many changes, Saymon," Eleni replied, sipping delicately. "I hardly know where to begin."

"No need, mistress. Devyn has told me some of it. I'm sorry about Tomais, and yet you return as something different." He raised his glass. "Here's to happy changes."

Eleni blushed at the compliment. "I'm not sure what to say about that. I can't imagine what people might be thinking. Those who know me, at least."

"Are you here to find out?"

"No," she answered, surprised by the question. "Something else entirely, although now I wonder if there isn't some connection." She had not seriously considered how folk might take her affair with Donari, what they knew of it, anyway. Obviously, word had spread about her altered status. Though they had been discreet, the palace was full of eyes and, like Anlise, judgemental conclusions. In her quiet moments, thoughts of those whispers rankled, but she did not let them stop her. Just as his choices forced Donari to act, so too did her choice to love him.

"I guess I've been looking for something all day and haven't found it until now, here," she continued.

That brought a rise and fall of Saymon's bushy brows.

"Looking? What for?"

Eleni sipped from the glass and fixed her eyes on his. "How strange," she said. "I've been looking for support for the summer festival, thinking some joy might do the city the most good."

"But?"

Eleni placed her glass carefully back on the table. "I think I've also been looking for a reason to be happy, myself."

"Is it such a big step from the *Cup* to the palace?"

"As I said, my friend, changes. I confess to feeling unsettled. Right now this table top feels more solid to me."

"No luck elsewhere?"

"Grudging support at best."

"Hardly surprising. There hasn't been much cause for mirth since last summer."

"Exactly. That is what I told Donari when I broached the idea. This place needs to find itself again."

Saymon kept his eyes on her's while pausing to take a measure from his glass. "Good idea, but--"

"But what?"

Saymon sat back, a slow smile creasing his beard. "Don't forget how Pevana works."

"Meaning?"

"Word gets around faster than a royal coach. I've had three people in here today describing you and your entourage's progress."

"Donari insisted. Not a good idea?"

Again, Saymon paused to drink before replying.

"Not exactly," he responded finally, surprising her yet again. "It is a good idea for safety, perhaps, given your new status. There are unsavory bits and pieces still in the city. And yet not such a good idea if you really want to know the mind of the place. The Maze is largely gone, but its ways still persist."

Eleni stared at him. *Risky,* her better sensed whispered. *Necessary,* responded her innate independence. Donari would be furious, but the idea of a full on summer festival flared brighter. She would never reach the people jouncing about with armor and the image of authority. The festival was all about casual rebellion in jest.

The idea of flight swelled for her into an objective. She took up her glass, swallowed the dregs and rose to leave. "Your back door still out through the kitchen?" she asked.

"Of course, mind telling me where you are going?"

"To see another friend," she answered, squeezing his shoulder as she passed.

Eleni relaxed once she gained the shadows and narrow places of the alley. This was familiar ground to her. She knew every foot of the region abut the harbor walls all the way to the edge of where the old Maze used to be. When she was a young seamstress struggling to live up to her father's reputation, speedy deliveries helped. She knew every shortcut through and around the area. The house she and Tomais built lay just two streets up and one over. She heard Saymon's admonition to take care but felt more secure in her innate knowledge. Besides, she needed to test the pulse of the city, and how better to do so than to question Gania Landare, who knew everyone and everything from the harbor to the land gate square.

The idea, so quickly crystallized in Brimaldi's tavern, settled into a calm conviction as she paced down the alley. Her progress had been noted and followed, most likely by more than just the gossip traders that reported to Saymon. If she really did have a footpad on her trail, they would have to know the ins and outs of the lower city better than she did. Outside of the surviving Maze children, there was only one other person she could think of who might. She thought she stood an even chance of passing undetected to Gania's and an equally even chance of regaining the citadel's security before the watch found her. Once Drue and Anlise realized she had given them the slip, they were certain to raise the alarm.

She smelled the midden pile behind Gania's house before she saw it and turned left between two houses and then again right, regaining the main street from the harbor. The sun was nearly set behind her when she reached the walk way leading to Gania's front door, and there, as if in realization of Eleni's earlier image of her, stood the woman herself, sweeping the stoop with dearly remembered, aggressive strokes.

"Renia grant me freedom from dust," Gania grated through clenched teeth. "If it isn't one thing it's another. Tenant can't pay, and the wind brings foul air. The rain over flows the gutter, and everyone's boots track in the mud. Lyssa gets a cough, and I have to spend my sunset moments sweeping. Bah!"

Eleni stopped at the end of the walk before the first, intensely swept step.

"Hello, Mistress Landare."

At the sound Gania froze, mid-sweep, and looked up from her work. Her eyes grew round but just for a moment, then they relaxed, crinkling back behind folds of wrinkled skin as the ponderous woman broke into a broad, open-mouthed grin.

"Well, then," she said peremptorily. "There you are. Two months back or more and just now coming for a visit?" She looked up and down the street. "And alone. You are still full of surprises, seemingly."

"Gania, I'm sorry, but things have been so unsettled--."

"And you've been too busy to see to old friends!" Gania huffed, but her dancing eyes belied her tone. "No matter, dearie. You are here now, and that's enough. Will you come inside for a cup? I've water on the boil for tea."

"Yes, gladly!"

Gania swept Eleni into the kitchens, sat her at the table and in a trice set out two steaming cups and a plate of small cakes. Then she plumped herself down opposite and fixed Eleni with a look that defied deception.

"So, word has it you have moved up in the world," she said, breaking off a piece of one of the cakes and popping it into her gap-toothed mouth.

"That's strange," Eleni replied. "Saymon Brimaldi said much the same thing."

"Ha! I daresay. He gets most of his information from me, so, not so strange, maybe." She leaned a little forward and swept her greasy hair back behind her ears. "So how is it the king's consort shows up at my front stoop unescorted? And him rode out just this morning? Not safe, young lady."

"It seems nothing is much secret in Pevana these days."

"Don't be foolish, girl," Gania wheezed. "You know better than that. Secrets don't keep in Pevana, never have, never will. We've always been so."

"How are things here?"

Gania leaned back. "Well enough, I suppose. Some of that lot I told you about before still owed me coin when they marched. I'm told most of them fell at that battle, where was it?"

"Lyranden Bridge, I was there. Terrible."

"Were you then? Yes, Lyranden Bridge, that's right. Just deserts, I say. Cheap bastards."

"I'm sorry…"

Gania waved it off. "Not your fault, obviously, and there's others who suffered worse than poor me." She tilted her head and gave Eleni a knowing look. "But if you've been out and about this day, I suspect you have a sense of it, yes?"

"Yes, sadly."

Gania nodded agreement. "Sad indeed. It's like the well water has gone sour. Too many afraid, old folk around, hankering after the lost, wondering what sort of king Donari will be, how he came to the crown at all, and what it might mean for the future, or if we even have a future."

"Gania, I was hoping to organize the summer festival to help, somehow."

But Gania ignored her. "And you showing up here like an apparition, better dressed than when you left with a look on your face like you was some miscreant come home late for supper! Not wise, mistress! These streets are not safe anymore for such as you."

"Such as me?"

"You left the prince's secretary. You return as the king's consort. Not safe."

118

"But this is my home," Eleni began. Gania held up a meathook hand and stopped her.

"Not anymore."

The raw truth hurt; such an abrupt cutting off. Eleni pushed aside the urge to dispute the facts, but her better sense suspected Gania had the rights of it.

But still. Am I truly homeless?

She let the sweet tea rinse away the bitter thought. "I wanted to talk to you," she continued. "I need you to talk to others. I didn't think showing up with mounted guards and a carriage would help either notion."

Gania's habitual glare softened. "And I'm glad you're here, Eleni. I've missed you. Pevana is not the same. You are a sign of the changes, actually, mistress. You want the festival to bring something back. Good luck. If you could bring back the lost, you might have a chance. Too many shadows around here these days. Empty houses, half empty beds, kids missing fathers, girls missing their men. I've only two tenants myself. Times are hard, too hard, maybe, for a party."

"Saymon Brimaldi said he would help."

"And he will, and I'll have my say around the well to as many ears as I can, but I wouldn't get your hopes up."

"I have to try."

Gania stared at her for a long, uncomfortable moment. "Of course you do," she whispered finally. "You're the type."

They talked through two cups of tea and four cakes. True dark swelled in the east by the time Eleni pushed away from the table and made to leave. Gania offered to send for a boy to see her on her way, but Eleni refused. She had escaped one form of supervision; she did not feel the need to willingly accept another. She pulled the hood of her light cloak down to hide her face and slipped down the street.

She walked quickly, intent on reaching the palace as quickly as possible. She reached the intersection and turned right to head to the main avenue that led to the hill.

And then her feet stopped of their own accord in front of her old house.

Not my home. Not anymore. Not safe.

She stood before the door, the moonlight bright enough to reveal its carved, decorative surface. Her hand cast a shadow when she reached out to touch it, and in that moment she grew aware of her exposure; certain that eyes other than the moon's watched her. She knelt and pulled up a loose cobblestone from in front of the door. From the hollow beneath it she took a key, unlocked the door, and went in. As she passed underneath the lintel she understood: her last visit there had been to pack away the past, a hurried, teary exhalation, but the effect proved temporary. Tomais might be moldering in his grave, and she might have moved on to a different life, but unfinished memories still lingered here. She left the door unbolted behind her and went upstairs to her former bedroom. She went out on to the balcony, sat in the leather chair Tomais made for her and let memories take her.

And those memories took her deeply, deeply into herself. She sat there for nearly an hour crying softly on occasion but mostly just breathing, letting images wash over her and remembering.

The moon rose above the headland, unnaturally bright. Its light sent her back inside to wander through the rooms. According to tradition, most Pevanese houses placed the main bedroom on the left regardless of floor, but Eleni and Tomais chose otherwise in order to take advantage of the better view. Gania thought it an oddity when she came to visit. She even commented about it that day back in the spring when she helped Eleni sort through her things after Tomais' funeral.

She ran her fingers gently over the dusty furniture, and marveled at how the place remained unmolested. In a corner, she found some of Tomais' bits of leather. In the closet, half-covered by a pile of abandoned clothing, she and Gania had worked quickly back then in their grief, she found a half finished bit of embroidery. She closed her eyes and leaned against the closet door jamb and lost herself in the darkness of an apology to the past.

The sound of footsteps on the stairs snapped her out of her reverie. A creak on the last step before the top sent her shrinking back into the darker shadows of the closet. She was trapped. She reached instinctively for the dagger Donari gave her, but she had left it back at the palace. Another creak, which meant whoever followed her into the house reached the top of the stairs and took a step onto the landing. The landing opened up the top story of the house; left to the second bedroom, forward to the workroom and right to the master bedroom and balcony. Eleni strained to hear which direction the strangers would choose. If left, there would be silence. If center, there would be a minute pop from a loose floorboard. If to the right, there would be several creaks before they reached the door.

Eleni fought to control her fear. If she heard a creak, she would have mere seconds to beat them to the landing and down the stairs. Silently, she gathered her skirt and hitched it under her belt and slid like a breath of air to just beside the half open bedroom door.

She held her breath, listening for life, waiting for her chance, or if she would even have a chance, to run. She heard a faint murmur and a response, which confirmed her fears there were two of them. Sweat broke out on her brow and trickled down her cheek, and she felt the clammy, adrenaline rush down her spine.

Then she heard a creak, followed almost immediately by a slight pop. She counted to three and trusted to fate and broke for the landing. She practically threw herself down the stairs and landed in a clutter in the shadows at the foot. She spared one glance at the two shadow figures on the landing. She thought she saw naked blades in their hands. One of them made a throwing motion, but the darkness must have spoiled his aim for the blade stuck in the railing post next to her head. Then Eleni was up and out the door. She lunged at the handle in an effort to close it behind her and buy some time, but she missed, overbalanced, and stumbled to her knees. She scrambled up, turned to the right to start running for all she was worth but managed only a few desperate steps before her assailants caught up with her. She felt the pull as a hand closed on her cloak. She drew breath to scream but stifled the sound, lurching aside to avoid the sword point that rushed passed her right shoulder. The next instant she heard a strangling gurgle and grunt, and she stumbled forward, the pull on her cloak ending abruptly. She turned to see a figure rip its blade out of the throat of the man who had grabbed her. Blood spread in a shadow arc as the figure spun deftly to take on the other pursuer as he rushed out of the house. That man tried to pull up short but still took a thrust to a shoulder as he scrambled back and sideways. With a grunt and a curse, he hustled out of reach down the street and around a corner.

Eleni stood there, too stunned to continue her flight, completely surprised by her rescue. Her rescuer lowered his blade and turned back toward her.

"Devyn Ambrose." She let loose his name in an exhaled breath. "How did you—"

Devyn cut her off with a gesture and bent to examine his victim. He wiped his sword blade clean on the man's shirt.

"Later," he said, taking her arm and leading her back up the street. "I suspect those two acted alone, but I think it would be unwise to loiter here. Come." He quickened their pace. Eleni let him lead her, but not without several backward glances over her shoulder.

"Who were they?" she asked.

"The one who grabbed you looked like one of Casan's disarmed bully boys. I saw him in the crowd behind the Prelate at Senden's funeral. The other fellow, not sure, but he was no priest. I should have taken him in the heart. Too agile. Perhaps one of Donari's recent oath takers might have had second thoughts, or no thoughts, about his fealty or honor."

"How could I have been so silly?"

Devyn flashed teeth unnaturally white in the moonlight. Despite his exertions, he looked remarkably calm. "I am not going to ask what you were doing out here in the middle of the night," he said. "But Donari probably will. I think I know why you snuck off without a word. Every time my tasks take me out beyond the citadel walls, I find myself making an excuse to swing by Kembril's grave."

Eleni blushed with shame, thankful for the dark. "But how did you know? Did you follow me?" she asked.

Devyn breathed a laugh. "Your escort returned to the citadel lathered and anxious, calling out the guard and all the extra maids to go out and try to find you. I ran into Drue, who managed to calm down enough to let me know where they lost you. I made a guess, ran into some of the 'little birds' I've set to watch things for me. They said you'd snuck into a house near the harbor square."

"I needed to talk to Gania Landare, an old friend. Alone." Eleni touched Devyn's arm, stopping him. "Little birds?"

"Some of the Maze children. They get me news at need. The best of them is a seven year old bundle of sauce named Tasia. She watched you go into what I assume is your old house."

"Yes, I sensed something of the sort, and when I didn't leave, she went to find you."

"Correct. We were at the corner here when we saw two shadows go in after you. I sent her to find the watch and came after you. A close thing."

"I was stupid."

"Donari warned you, but do not be so hard on yourself. We are home, but it is not the same for us. Donari has changed all of that. I was a child of the dust and stables. Now I find myself becoming adept at sneaking into all sorts of places, giving orders to others and making choices. I swear by Renia's Tears, if Senden's clothes were a bit smaller I could wear them."

Devyn's tone allowed Eleni to relax. Good feeling rushed over her. "Well, I am still something of a seamstress."

"You know what I mean," Devyn replied. "We are moving in different circles. No matter how comfortable we get with the new lines to our lives, there are still old rhythms that pull on us. As hard as it might seem, Eleni, we need to choose what world we want to live in."

Eleni felt embarrassed and foolish. She had lost control of herself for a moment. Her feelings for Donari welled up inside of her as she paced along. Had she met with an accident tonight, she could only imagine what it might have done to him. She made herself a target, one of the untoward risks when one loved a king.

"I'm sorry, Devyn," she said, shivering and giving his arm a squeeze. "I want Pevana to get back part of its soul. I ran off to get a sense of it. The house drew me, as if I had something left unfinished." She looked back down the street a last time. "And now it is, I suppose."

They turned the corner and moved up the main way toward the hill. They paused when they saw the royal carriage coming toward them, horse hooves and wheels a-clatter.

The carriage arrived. Drue, gawking, practically leaped out the door to assist her.

"Mistress Eleni!" he gushed. "You gave us quite a fright."

"I'm sorry, Drue, but I had to follow an idea. I didn't mean to put you and Anlise out so."

Drue's mouth worked as though chewing on something unpleasant. "No need to apologize to me, mistress, but Anlise might be another matter. She was mad enough to sour butter."

"Did she blame you?"

"Of course," the boy replied, helping her into the carriage. "But that's normal for her. I'm used to it."

"Yes, so I have begun to notice. We will have to see her mollified or changed. In any event, thank you. You are too good to me, Drue." Eleni patted his knee as the boy settled onto the seat beside her.

"I wish I could do more, mistress. The king asked me to look after you, after all."

"Did he?" Eleni looked up at Devyn, who had come close to secure the carriage step and door. "It seems all of Pevana has been set to watch over me."

"Donari needs us, Eleni," Devyn said. "And we need him. That truth means we have to choose."

"Yes," she responded. "I understand now. I chose to live after Tomais' death. I cannot take it back. Every choice now has to be a choice for life."

Devyn leaned in close and pitched his voice low.

"Donari does not need to know of this," he said. "I'll make up something about those two bodies; it need not get back to him."

Eleni reached up and brushed her fingers along Devyn's cheek in thanks, smiling and shaking her head.

"Choices, my friend. Truth is also a choice. I love him too much to lie to him."

"He might get upset."

"With reason."

"He will saddle you with more guards."

"And I will take them."

Devyn bowed. "Luck to you, lady."

"Thank you, Devyn."

The driver turned the carriage around and set off for the palace. As the hill, now bathed in moonlight, loomed before her, Eleni felt something give way. It felt like a final stitch in a healed wound snipped and pulled away from the skin, painless but for the memory of pain.

When word got back to the Lord Prelate Byrnard Casan the near miss with Eleni Caralon, he took out his frustrations by berating his immediate servants until he grew hoarse and exhausted. Casan dismissed his fools and collapsed into his chair, a bit mortified over his loss of control. In former days, he used to command his legendary temper to better effect, but now he sat there and struggled, alone, to calm his rapid pulse and catch his breath, wondering why it was taking so long to do both. It had been only the first stratagem, and a small setback at that, but he felt deflated all the same, as if suddenly grown aware that time was a variable he had neglected to consider. *What if I do not live to see Donari finally humbled?*

Ironically, the prospect of failure actually calmed him. He wiped the adrenaline sweat from his brow with a silken handkerchief, dragged a sheet of paper from a tidy stack next his elbow, dipped a pen into the inkpot and began writing down his thoughts to further arrest their spasmodic career. In his own, spiteful, conniving way, Casan wrote himself into inspiration like the true poets of Pevana; a mirror image of them in that moment. Theirs was the poetry of honesty, his, the poetry of deceit.

But just like them, when he finished he sat back satisfied and surveyed his results. News of Eleni Caralon's escape attended the announcement that the Festival of High Summer would take place on its traditional dates. Casan determined his next try would occur during its resultant excess and chaos. He did not need to burn down half the city this time. All he needed to do was find a willing archer. He settled in his chair mentally back in control although, physically, he still felt enervated. He decided he was hungry. He lacked energy to shout for service and made do with several feeble rings from a bell he kept hidden in a drawer. Even that effort left him a little shaky.

The soup still tasted good, however.

He met with certain others through the meal, trusted men, heretofore not utilized directly. They were some of Corvale's group of incendiaries, placed by him to oversee his former henchman's activities. Since his return, he kept them assigned to tasks in the bowels of the university to keep them from sight and question. Two of them were among his most trusted operatives, both of them having served him in the field during his previous career. They knew his mind better than most and quickly took up the vein of his next ploy as he unraveled its particulars.

The festival would bring Donari and Eleni out again. There would have to be a procession, outdoor revels, and a scabeous competition of poets. Surely, Donari could not allow himself to be seen cowering in his palace for fear. He would have to show himself to his people to reassure them of the normalcy of life under his kingly rule. He would feel the need to assert his courage and send a message to the north that life in Pevana had returned to its prosperous, happy nature. Despite his fears, Donari would come out, and he would bring his woman with him.

Eleni fretted over her notes too nervous to concentrate. It had been a week since her misadventure at her old house. Eleni felt certain Donari already knew about it. Anlise came to announce the king's return, and the look on her face all but confirmed Eleni's fears. She gave up trying to write, put away her pens and took to pacing nervously back and forth from desk to window.

She heard footsteps in the hall, and then Donari burst through, face ash-white from road dust, fear and anger. She held up a hand in supplication.

"Donari, I—"

But he would have none of it. He brushed her hand aside and crushed her in his arms.

"What were you thinking?" he said, his voice harsh with emotion. "I left clear instructions. You can't do such things, Eleni." His words and embrace gentled. "None of this is worth it if you go and get yourself taken or killed. You are a target, too, my dear."

"I know it, and I am sorry." She broke away, chin up, searching his eyes, reassured by the love she saw there. "I should have known better, but that day had been so frustrating. I got trapped by a memory, I suppose. Devyn saved me; at least *he* didn't disobey you."

She backed away as she spoke. His expression softened.

"I know what it is like to feel trapped by an old life," he said. "And I realize time has not been fair to you, but I will not lose you now, Eleni. I cannot do anything about your past." He drew close again, reaching into his shirt pocket. "All I can do is look to our future, *our* future, Eleni. I will have no other."

He brandished a ring of gold set with a single, large diamond. He took her hand before she could stop him and deftly slipped it onto her ring finger.

"I think it is time I trapped you in my life," he said, raising her hand to his lips. "If you would have me."

Tears welled and Eleni fought for breath and words to protest, stuttering.

"But...Donari...what will the people say? The dangers--."

"Politics?" he finished for her. "No. Not now. Pevana will love you. The north doesn't matter."

"How can you say that?"

He took her back into his arms.

"Well," he said, lips moving against her forehead. "I am the king. And I want you for my queen. There's just one thing."

"What?"

"You haven't said yes."

She took his face in her hands and kissed him then, long, deep, breathing in his scent, his hope and his strength. She felt his arms reach around her waist to press her against him.

"Yes," she sighed. "But you've made a bad bargain, my lord."

"Let's let time judge the matter."

Eleni laughed and all tension fled, replaced by a joyous certainty.

"Well, one thing is clear anyway."

"What thing?" he whispered.

"Whatever the crown has cost you, you haven't lost your poetry."

He swept her up, moved toward the bed.

"Pevana should have a poet-king," he murmured, "to go along with her poet-queen."

Chapter 13: Decisions

Late July brought languid days to the restive north. Demona wrapped herself in lace and light cottons and contemplated the growing bulge in her belly. Now early into her sixth month, she began to notice the more she showed off her proturberant belly the more obsequious the behaviors of those she encountered. Servants cooed and asked after her health and folk reassured her that she bore the dearest treasure in the north and everyone looked to protect and preserve the child in her womb. But Demona needed more than words.

And then letters from the Lord Prelate arrived certifying the legitimacy of her baby. Gifts poured into her chambers in the royal palace. Letters from lords she knew only as names arrived with gratifying frequency, and even Gaspire began treating her with more than usual gentility. He began asking before entering her rooms. He touched her with hints of tenderness and opted for discretion when they took their pleasure of each other. She surprised herself by liking the changes. She reviewed her experiences with Roderran and Sevire and realized they lacked real tenderness, and even her dalliance with Talyior ran more to the manic than sensitive. She took stock now and made connections on how best to orchestrate the rest of her pregnancy and the days beyond. Slowly, with small steps of logic and awareness, she warmed to the idea she might be the mother of a king.

For a woman whose life heretofore consisted of barren sensual pursuits, collecting baubles and surfeiting a rapacious but now dead king, such thoughts were heady departures. As her baby grew within her, Demona's expectations expanded. She listened closely when Gaspire prattled about plans. She actually started looking at maps. Now those names and regions meant resources and men, future tools she needed to learn how to use. Lost in the world for most of her life, Demona now found herself well and truly in it, and curious.

She sat at her dressing table as the evening began to overtake the day, preparing for a visit from Gaspire. He spent most of his time on the road or in the camps situated astride the King's Road south of the river. But when he managed time in Lomillar, he made sure to spend choice moments with her. She read his intentions clearly. Bed the vessel, reap the power. He made that clear to her on more than one occasion. And yet the lovemaking waxed mutual. Her hormones raced now, and when she clasped him to her she did so with genuine lust. Gaspire was no Roderran, but in her condition he worked well enough, prickly back hair notwithstanding.

Tonight would be different; there would be questions after pleasure. Demona dipped into the bottle of scent that had so ravaged Roderran's reserve with the full intent of making Gaspire hers. The mystery of woman often left the hardened warrior defenseless. History stemmed from secrets whispered across the trysting pillows. Scandal, for the powerful, possessed a certain posterity.

Forewarned by practice and forearmed by knowledge, Demona knew Gaspire could not withstand her. She touched scent to her cleavage, just so, like a skilled hunter placing the final tension in the snare. She passed the early hours of the evening brushing her hair and enjoying a light meal of her favorite things. When the knock came just before midnight, she actually smiled.

She took him, matched him, controlled him. In the end she kept him, agonizing, on the edge of climax, riding him, her belly a third presence in the act. And at the moment of highest pitch she paused, squeezing him inside her in a way that drove every man she had ever bedded to beg for one last furious thrust. Demona loomed above him, her forehead damp with her exertions, her hair falling in an eldritch, magical cascade about his straining features.

"Are you mine?" she asked, her voice bereft of any sensuality, matter of fact, composed. "Are you mine, lord? Mine and my child's?"

Gaspire's eyes refocused on her at the sound of her voice, his dark face further shadowed by the curtain of her hair, his jaw tense as he struggled for control.

"Yes," he gasped.

"Will he be your king?" She relaxed her hold as she spoke, and tightened again when he hesitated. "Will he be your king?" she repeated.

"Yes, yes!" he moaned. "Demona, please."

She smiled. "And will you defend me and this king?" She relaxed, moved slightly, a promise. He groaned, thrashed his head side to side, rabid. He tried to thrust into her, to finish, but she put a hand on his chest and rose just off him, a warning.

"Yes," he frothed. "Woman, anything. I swear it."

"Yes, you will swear it, my lord, now and again before the other lords. I want Tareegan to hear. I want oaths. Sureties." She eased back down on him, slowly, grinding with each syllable.

He grabbed her hair and pulled her down on him.

"Do not push me, bitch," he snarled.

But Demona knew about pain. She knew how to seal it off at need; a gift from Sevire. She let a gasp escape her lips, took the pain, compared it to memory and found it wanting.

Even your cruelties fall short, my lord.

In the same motion she relaxed. Nothing. He might as well have been trying to impale a bucket of lukewarm water. He must have noticed the change. His hand fell away.

"What?"

Demona teased her fingers in his chest hair, grasped some.

"Do not push *me*, lord," she whispered, yanking out the hair. And as she ripped Gaspire's offending follicles, she tightened once again, spasmodically, plunging herself down the length of his member.

She held him as his useless seed exploded into her. He hung below her, breathless, face pulled back in a rictus mimicking pain. She waited for his spasms to pass. He returned with a gushing breath and collapsed back on the pillows.

"Borimon's balls, woman, you have never done that before."

Demona kept him in her, held up the tufts of hair, let them fall back onto his chest.

"And if you ever want to feel that way again. Swear."

Gaspire sighed in defeated satiation, and Demona knew.

"I swear," he said, his voice now direct, rasped with his normal growl. "I swear to protect you and that child pushing down on my bladder. I swear I will make him such a king as the north has never seen. I will be your champion. I will see him crowned and to his majority."

"And?"

He paused for a breath, another, and a third. "Woman, I would do so even without all *this*." He cupped both her breasts, caressing, strangely gentle. "There is power here, between us, that serves us both."

"What of the other lords?"

"I will require them to swear along with me."

"And if they refuse?"

"Then I will pound them until they do. Satisfied?"

She noticed he was still hard inside her. She raised an eyebrow. *That* was different. She began to move again, slowly, seeking her own pleasure now.

"Yes," she breathed. "I am satisfied."

Demona entered the council chambers alongside Gaspire later that afternoon. Her booted feet clicked a precise rhythm. She advanced to her seat below the throne and swung around theatrically, letting her light cloak billow away from her body exposing her expanding contours. She swept the room, let them scrutinize her, noted the altered looks this time, appraising, speculative, almost respectful. And there were fewer of them, as well, just the major lords and a handful of the more important merchants. Tareegan openly smirked. The lord of Avedar, Loren Bastalli, ran thick fingers through a shaggy salt and pepper beard. Demona held his eyes despite her unease. They had yet to formally meet, but the man sent a note to her once word reached him of Casan's bull of legitimacy. Of all the letters she received then, his had been the briefest and least artistic. Demona decided he looked like an aged badger.

I already have Tareegan and Gaspire, my lord, and I will have you before this meeting ends.

Gaspire cleared his throat as if to speak, but Demona put a delicate hand imperiously on his forearm to forestall him.

"Welcome, my lords," she said. Gaspire tensed next to her, but she squeezed his arm to remind him of his promise. He seemed to understand and relaxed.

"Welcome," she continued. "To my council."

"Your council?" barked Bastali. "Amdoran, what is this?"

Tareegan laughed openly. "It appears our lady has taken the Lord Prelate's sanction to heart, my lord! This could get interesting."

The Lord of Avedar was not mollified, however. "I've come from knocking Trenarese heads on my borderlands to talk about Gaspire's intentions not to bandy words with a pregnant tart."

Demona did not answer. She looked intently at Gaspire and waited. He cleared his throat again, shook off her hand, and took a pace forward.

"The lady Demona Anargi bears the king's son. We all have received that word. I pledged to uphold her child's claims, to ensure her safety, to serve as Regent to the child, should it prove a male."

"You, Regent?" the lord of Avedar growled. "Since when did you become a politician? Spurs and spears, as I recall, were all you boasted of in your younger days."

Tareegan stepped forward. "Now, now, my lords, let's not wrangle. Our lord Amdoran has returned to us a changed man." He glanced at Demona as he spoke and winked. "And has learned some hard lessons."

"Lessons," Bastali scoffed. "I daresay. But he failed the test at Lyranden, didn't he? What lessons there, eh?"

"We've gone over that, Avedar."

"Yes, I know, Sor-reel, but I still question his fitness. He's obviously…gone over everything this woman has to offer. I'll wager the

130

only position he can command is the one where she's on top! He can bed her if he chooses, but that hardly qualifies him for a position of power." He laughed at his own crude humor and swept his gaze around the room to include the others in his mirth.

Demona stepped forward and backhanded him, the ring on her finger cutting his cheek and gouging a trough through his beard. He stepped back, stunned, and put a hand to his face, staring in shock and surprise at the blood on his fingers. He snarled and raised his fist for a blow and advanced. Demona retreated.

Gaspire's meathook fist took him full in the face, and the angry, grizzled lord crumpled to the floor, blood already splurting from his broken nose.

"That will be enough," Gaspire rasped. "No one is to raise hand against Lady Anargi. I have given my oath! As will you. Now. Here. Even this foolish lout." He nudged the bleeding and unconscious Bastali with his boot. "Someone send for water and towels. He will need to make his kneel."

Tareegan knelt by the fallen man's side, assessing the ruin that was his face.

"If you've left him enough teeth for the purpose," he said in reproach. "Was that really necessary?"

Gaspire looked at Demona and grinned. "Yes," he said, ignoring the growing murmur behind him. "Yes it was." He reached down his right hand, the same hand that just broke his brother lord's face, and took her's, gently, bent over it, and kissed it like a courtier. Demona marveled at the action. She could see the blood and the torn flesh on his knuckles.

"My lady," he murmured.

"My Regent," she answered.

She settled back in her chair, beaming at the collection of faces now turned to her in curiosity and concern.

Yes, gentlemen, I am not what you expected. And that is the fun of it.

"My lords," she said, coolly official. "Let's take Lord Tareegan's words to heart and not wrangle. Much has changed, as you can see, and my Lord Gaspire needs to clarify things for you."

Gaspire stepped forward as those assembled retook their seats. Servants helped Loren, who had recovered enough of his senses to keep a cloth pressed to his bloody face, out of the hall. Gaspire waited for the doors to close before continuing.

"Right. I'm sure I'll have to answer for that," he said. "But I will not brook insults to the Lady Demona. You have your evidence. Casan's writ of legitimacy holds. Curb your tongues, gentleman, or I will serve you in the same fashion."

Silence greeted his words. Demona felt a moment's disquiet before she realized the silence meant acceptance rather than revolt. She relaxed, but as she did so a different kind of tension twisted itself into notice in the small of her back. As before, with her uncomfortable chat with Tareegan, the pain sparked then quickly dulled but did not go away completely. She took a deep breath to calm herself. Gaspire looked a question at her. She waved him to go on.

"I've taken reports all morning since I returned from Trenar," he announced. "And things are returning to normal. Markets have reopened. Caravans of food and materials arrive daily. This activity is positive, lords, and feels like a new, fresh wind. Let us use that wind to our advantage."

Murmurs attended his words. The few heads of merchant houses present nodded sagely. Tareegan whispered to his aide. Commerce would help fuel the north's rejection of Donari's reign. Prosperity in the wake of a king's death could only help those who sought to rule after.

Even the knowledge the whole thing was more than half a sham did not overly concern Demona. She liked the tone of Gaspire's words and the assembly's reaction. Gaspire stretched his available troops dangerously thin to lend support to the decrees sent out ordering the folk to get on with the business of life; effectively quelling any further upset to the established system of rulers and ruled. They had done well. Even the internecine debacle taking place in the Trenaran highlands failed to bank their momentum. The children of the old lord spent their men and treasure trying to kill each other off to claim the princely circlet and Trenar's right of place in the kingdom. They did not know how insignificant they would become once her son was born.

Son. Yes, a son. I'm certain of it beyond all reason, but then nothing in my life since Sevire has had much to do with reason.

Demona took solace when Gaspire told her of what went on in Trenar in that none of the rhetoric attending that conflict made any mention at all about the former Queen, dead along with her father in that tragic accident. Even her memory could have been an irritation to their plans. Demona granted Gaspire a point for seeing it first. As he suspected, once the queen and the old man were out of sight, they were out of mind as well. Gaspire had gone north not to quell but to contain the unrest and allow the Trenaran brats to squabble among themselves for a season. With any luck they would kill each other off by autumn and remove themselves from causing further concern. Gaspire's grating report continued, bringing her back to the present.

"So much for the restive highlands," he sneered. "I'll get men from the two younger brothers when I need them. Our main concern is, of

132

course, with Donari and the south. Reports have reached us of a peace council with Sylvanus and the other southern leaders. I have used the news to spur efforts to organize and refit a useful force, some of which is in camps to the south of the city."

"And what of Donari?" asked one of the merchant leaders. "Will he come north?"

"That Donari has not immediately set about pacifying the northern regions suggests weakness and timidity, gentlemen. We razed the valley north of Desopolis. The Lord Prelate burned Tierne and Heriopolis and, though the assault at Desopolis failed, he sailed home unmolested. They do not have the men or shipping for a quick thrust. In fact, Donari seems content to leave us alone, for now. I am told he met the army outside of Pevana's walls and gave every man a choice to swear fealty or go home. Our new king has pretensions to nobility and honor, friends. He is nothing short of a fool, if you ask me."

"He is your cousin," someone in the back challenged.

"Sernon, wagon master," Gaspire bridled, the rasp in his voice falling dangerously low. "All here know my connection to the Avedun family. He is my cousin, and a coward, and as such he is not my king. I have sworn, I tell you. I will have his head in time, and Demona's child will use the crown as a plaything until such time comes as he is fit to wear it and rule.

"Donari loves to give folk choices, but he erred in this, I think. Frankly, I do not understand such foolishness. Power is not something you give away freely. I wonder at times if Donari is not just stupid. I wonder if Sylvanus Tamorgen of Desopolis is not the real force we must deal with.

"I share these thoughts with you, gentlemen, not to council fear. I will not spend my time following such threads. In the end, after all the courteous calls for homage run their useless course, and writs of outlawry and threats of confiscation get published and repudiated, it will all come down to swords. So, let us look to our markets but keep the men practicing at the butts."

Gaspire's words impressed Demona, despite his gruff manner.

And he had been tender last night, after, caressing my shoulder, murmuring his plans, half asleep, into my hair.

Such thoughts circled around in her mind as she accepted the oaths from the lords and merchants. One by one they filed by her chair, bending over her hand, doubtless taking her measure even as she took their loyalty. She met the eyes of every one of them.

The scene reminded her of some of the dances she had attended in Pevana; scripted affairs where looks communicated promise and the pressure of her partner's hand on the small of her back revealed the intensity of their lust. Despite their lofty status, these northern lords and merchants were still just men. She smiled deeply as the last of them lingered, lips brushing her finger tips as though testing a scent.

Just men, and therefore, pliable.

The room cleared until only herself, Tareegan, Gaspire and Kenton Reece, the eldest nephew of Lord Halloran of Hallar, remained. Reece had arrived late the night prior accompanied by a sizeable escort. Gaspire let her read the missive from Reece's uncle, offering compromise and support. Hallar suffered most in the failure at Lyranden Bridge; a bare fraction of their foot made it back home, led by the youngest son, Hallan. Hallar had a coastline to guard; the letter reminded his brother lords of his exposed position. In it he urged them to caution but agreed Casan's proclamation substantiated their moves. Kenton would stay to see to House Halloran's role in whatever plans were set in motion.

Tareegan poured two goblets of wine from the small cask on a side table, gave one to Demona, and sipped from the other. A wry smile crinkled his seamed face.

"My, my," he murmured. "This wine tastes almost as good as that last episode went."

Gaspire moved to the table in turn to pour for himself.

"I saw nothing humorous. Avedar could have been a problem." He wiped blood from his knuckles. "Problem solved."

Tareegan snorted at the comment, motioned for Kenton Reece to serve himself. Demona sipped carefully from her glass, unsettled by Tareegan's look and the continued, low throbbing in her lower back. She thought it might be the baby pushing against its boundaries, but now she was not so sure. She shifted in an effort to make herself more comfortable. The other three men pulled chairs close to hers, and took their ease. Gaspire finished his glass in one long swallow as though tossing off a bitter thought.

"You keep guzzling at that pace," Tareegan chuckled, "and we will run through the last of our Pevanese stocks before winter. That stuff is getting scarce."

Gaspire finished his glass, poured another and sipped more discreetly before answering.

"That will not be an issue, since we might have to take action before then. I'll fill up your cellars by November if I can find the men."

"Why move so soon? I thought we were content to let Donari think himself secure. Is time not on our side?"

"Donari has the south. You've read the reports. In time he will find the men. Right now, we are equal, equally weak that is. The lot that marched north to us needs time to refit. Many of them want to go home. I've paid them, kept them in camp and set them to drilling. But there is another reason."

He looked at Demona.

She looked back, sipping demurely from her goblet. Had she gone too far?

"You're angry." She raised the glass again but winced against the rim as the pain in her back increased. She took a mouthful, swallowed back against the pressure. The throbbing eased slightly. Gaspire quircked a brow.

"Angry? I'm not used to giving women credence. You risked everything just now."

"And yet it seemed to work," interjected Tareegan.

"True enough," Gaspire agreed. "We have their oaths. We will get the men. The quality might not be high, but numbers should tip things in our favor."

"So we are set on our way?" Demona asked.

Gaspire stared at her before responding, and she meet his scrutiny similarly.

Your surrogates won't matter.

"I think I need to move sooner rather than later," he said, looking instead to the wine in his glass.

"Ah!" Tareegan barked. "Now we get to it!"

Gaspire glowered at him. "You are too smug, old man."

"Smugness is the refuge of the old, Gaspire. You've set up the risks. Be glad I and the others agree to share them with you."

"You are an irritating man, Tareegan."

"And you are sleeping with the mother of my future king. Be careful she doesn't cut you off!"

Gaspire stared at him, stunned for a moment by the man's bald exposure. Tareegan waved away the insult.

"Come, come, Gaspire. You have never spent enough time here at court. The walls themselves whisper, let alone the help. What you and Demona do is your own business. Let the people think what they will. The child is legitimate. Nothing she or you do changes that."

Gaspire held on to his anger for a moment longer then let it dissipate into a sardonic smile. And in that moment, Demona thought she saw hints of Gaspire the man rather than the ambitious persona.

"Well, then," he said. "Thank you for your, blessing, not that we need it. But you mistake my mood. I was serious about acting sooner rather than later. Casan's rhetoric validates us. A Donari victory strips all pretense away."

"That has always been true."

"Yes, but what if Demona runs into trouble trying to whelp? I am thinking the promise of a child for the north, and the threat of a child to the south, serve us better than the dangers of childbirth. Can we count on support should she fail to bring the babe to term?"

"That has always been the risk. Donari is still too weak to attempt anything. Are we strong enough to roll the dice?"

Gaspire turned to the waiting Kenton.

"And you, Kenton Reece?" he asked. "Until he shows, you stand for your uncle in these matters. What will he say? What will he do for us besides write letters?"

Kenton frowned at them from behind a reddish beard and a mass of uncombed, gnarly locks that hung down in sweaty ringlets below his ears. He had a rough-edge look of the highlands about him that Demona found distasteful, but she noted his bright, alert eyes. They darted knowingly from Gaspire to Tareegan like a serpent's tongue testing the air for information.

This man is hungry to prove himself.

"You read his thoughts," he growled in a deep, throaty rumble. "He has the northern ports to watch and ward. He doubts Emdar's support."

"Emdar is ringed to the east and south by my lands," interrupted Tareegan. "I have an eye to the border. Emdar will make no moves against either of us if the push comes to war. Halloran must know that."

"But we both lost so many."

"As has everyone!" Gaspire said bitterly. "And we take measures to make up our numbers against further need. We are younger, yes, untried, more so, but we are moving forward. Will he send to us?"

Kenton leaned back in his chair as though stung by the admonitory tone from both of them.

"Hallar has always served the realm. Hallaran stands with us all."

"That is because Roderran and his father taught him the value of honorable service over rebellion," Gaspire scoffed. "I earned my spurs on those fields, and though it may have been twenty years ago, memories of questions remain."

Kenton leaped to his feet.

"Let you not doubt House Hallar!" he snarled. "We bled for Roderran. My uncle still mourns for his sons, and yet he gives his support still. Old arguments have been long forgotten. Let you not revive them. We are a northern people. Make no mistake."

"So you and the letters say," Tareegan said quietly.

"But will he send?" Gaspire added.

Kenton paused, calmed his heaving chest, and finished his glass with a final, decisive swallow.

"At my word," he said, finally, and Demona noted his voice's changed timber: determined, resolved, proud. "My uncle will release five hundred spears and a company of horse to our needs."

Gaspire reacted to the numbers. "That was not in the letter."

Kenton smirked, all anger forgotten. "Hallaran does not commit everything to paper, but he gave it out to me to consider, and decide."

Tareegan chortled. "That is rich, my lord! And so you are close to your uncle's councils, then? Do we have, in you, a man with aspirations? What of Hallaran's youngest, Hallan? We hear he survived the long road home. What of him?"

Kenton smiled grimly. "Hallan is home recovering from his journey. The father's grief will not let him risk the son so soon. I am, somewhat raised, in my uncle's esteem."

"And yet you stayed when your cousins marched south. What of that? Fears for your safety?"

Kenton raised his sword hand to display the calluses and scars. Then he slowly clenched it into a solid fist. While physically impressive, Demona sensed Reece was much the lesser of the three.

He is a tool they shape.

"Lord Hallaran's men will follow me for reasons in addition to their lord's orders," Reece continued. "I've trained them all, my lords. I have been for long now Hallaran's master at arms. Five hundred men, I say. Trained men. On my decision."

"This is not a parade ground affair," Gaspire interjected quietly. Kenton turned a cold look upon him.

"Let you and I repair to the court yard," he snarled. "And let you try my parade ground skills. You will not find me, or any that march to my orders, wanting. You wish to unseat your puking cousin? I and my lord's men will see to it."

Gaspire nodded, seemingly satisfied and encouraged. He raised his glass and drained the dregs. "Then we are decided then. Even without Trenar and Emdar, we move."

"How soon?" asked Kenton.

"We gather and train what we can for an attack through the hills in the autumn."

"That is a risk," Tareegan said quietly. "What if Donari retreats to his walls? A siege in winter?"

"Men in the field can be directed. We can despoil Donari's lands. Keep him fretting behind his walls. We can always march the men back at need. But if we can force a battle before the south can rise for Donari, then we win. Simple."

He rose, motioned Reece to do the same.

"Come with me, Kenton. I want to show you the camps where your brave five hundred will train. Your news pleases me." He took Demona's hand, breathed a kiss and squeezed it just enough for thought. "And the Lady Anargi as well."

Demona finished her glass as Gaspire and Reece left the hall. Tareegan tarried over his, a musing look on his face. Their eyes locked as he rose from his chair.

"That was quite a performance," he said approaching to help her rise. "It worked well enough. You proved your hold on him. Beware Loren. He's wild, and that broken face will not help his disposition. I will set watch on him."

"So you approve?"

He took her hand, bent to kiss it.

"I envy Gaspire his gelding," he whispered over her fingers. "I only wish I were twenty years younger, to share it." He straightened. "You look tired, my dear. A hazard, I assume, that comes from dealing with too many men at the same time."

Demona grimaced at his words, for they cut right through all pretense. Tareegan possessed a disturbing ability to expose her thoughts. The baby kicked again. The pain in her back intensified.

"Yes," she agreed. "I am tired. I think I need to go lay down for awhile. My maids should be just outside."

"Come," Tareegan ordered genially. "I will escort you to them. Take care of that child, my dear. Gaspire was right. The promise works better for us than the product. Rest."

Chapter 14: A Festival of failure

When his duties left him time, Devyn tried to help Eleni with her festival plans. He nosed about the city, listened to the well-talk, and frequented the several taverns where Eleni hoped to hold the poet's competition. He met variations of the same effect everywhere. Folk tested the idea favorably in one breath, and then talked about the missing faces and dearth the next. In the past, the summer festival had served as a celebration of plenty, but though life went on in Pevana, and people professed pride and joy in Donari's ascension, times were still tight and concerns for the future real and tempering. Nonetheless, preparations proceeded with announcements posted to enroll the poets, a number of the merchant families organized banquets, street performers began to collect in the squares to practice and advertise their skills.

And yet to Devyn the whole affair seemed a muted shadow-play. He recalled last year's chaos and ferver nostalgically. There had seemed so much more at stake then to add spice to the words, the sights, sounds and sense of it all. It took Devyn most of a day of meandering about the byways of the city to completely understand it. The biggest difference lay in the people's ignorance. Last year they reveled in spite of the conspiracies hatching about them. Their passion surmounted the flames that consumed their innocence. In the year since, Pevana's people had learned suffering, and that made all the difference.

By the time Devyn reached *The Golden Cup*, he decided he would not enter the competition. Words still kept him company as he explored his changed world, but not with the same sort of magic as before. Donari had given his life a new purpose. Responsibility now whispered in his ear as a counterpoint to the organic rhythms that once braced his youthful turmoil. He wanted those old feelings again. The rush of warrant, the boldness, but time's passage and learning how to kill changed a man. He felt anew Kembril's loss.

He nursed a pint in the same corner booth where, on that magical, glamorous night he rose to tempt fate and find a new friend in Talyior. Saymon bustled about the place directing cleaning tasks and talking through plans for the coming reading. Devyn's sense of detachment deepened even as he watched the activity. Same place. Same tables and chairs. But different.

Hardly the stuff of inspiration.

And yet he saw several lines in the swirl patterns in his glass, but far from motivating him to feel, they just reminded him of the distance he now stood from his own past:

With so much of the game left to play
Woe to the poet with nothing to say...

Dissatisfied, he shook the glass looking for more but only saw brown-tinted foam and liquid. He swallowed the last, bitter dregs and slipped out.

Despite Devyn's impressions, Pevana trammeled up enough spirit for a try at gaiety. Flowers appeared in window boxes as before, open-air kitchens assembled. Pevana's poets signed the lists for the various reading locations but in fewer numbers than before.

The day before the start of the festival, workers found Renly Obiri, the proprietor of the *Gale*, one of the reading locations, in his storeroom sprawled in a pool of his own blood, throat slashed from ear to ear.

The news spurred Devyn to make another circuit in the faint hope the incident was just a sad accident. And yet the collective whispers from his informants suggested otherwise. Just before sunset, little Tasia found him taking a drink at the community well outside Gania Landare's house. She appeared like a sprite, nonchalantly accepted the ladle he offered her, as if meeting him was an affair of casual insignificance. She fixed him with her ageless eyes.

"My brother and his friends were set to help Mr. Obiri unload a wagon this morning," she whispered breathlessly. "They found him. Did you know?"

"I heard," he responded, settling to the ground and leaning his back against the well casing.

"Did you know him?" She joined him.

"A little."

"My brother says he had a temper, but he was nice to me. Gave me a penny once."

"So much? Generous."

She gave him a sidelong glance. "Not funny. He was old. Brother said there was a lot of blood."

"Bad men exist everywhere, Tasia. He might have surprised a robber. I'm sorry your brother and his friends had to be the ones who found him."

Tasia ignored him, her attention drawn by a butterfly that landed on her dusty knee. Devyn watched it beat its red-tinted, ephemeral wings for a moment before launching away. He received the wind of its passing as a summons, a gentle susseration from a spiritual place, to take notice. The butterfly danced before them for a second then the currents of the world took it away.

"Red," Tasia whispered. "So much red."

Her tone made him look more closely at her. She blinked her rabbit eyes at him with a code mysterious.

"Do you mean poor Obiri or the butterfly?" he asked gently.

"I dunno," she answered, rising. "Mamma has friends who go to the big temple to hear the cross old man preach. He doesn't like our festival, I guess."

"The Lord Prelate cannot keep us from our festival."

Tasia turned to leave. "The butterfly is gone," she said, looking at him for the first time, eye to eye, all seven year old serious. "Too much red. Why is Tolimon in the tower?"

"Tolimon, where?"

"In the bell tower of the big church."

"But what do you mean?"

She flittered away, leaving Devyn to parse her words, facing a troubled, sleepless night. And sleepless it was, for just before dawn flames took part of the warehouse of one of the merchant families that agreed to schedule a banquet. By rank chance, Devyn happened to be returning from a look around the harbor wharves and saw the tell-tale glow. He raised the alarm in time to quell the fire. The arsonist chose to set the blaze in a near empty corner in the back.

Message received.

Rumors spread by morning, and concerned missives piled up on Donari's study table. Devyn followed his orders to the best of his abilities, sending what men he could spare to patrol the streets and reassure the people. Donari and Eleni prepared to make a progress through the city to lend their support. Devyn did not much like the idea. Murders and flames; a familiar pattern of blows in a combat begun long before and freshly renewed; Casan had found his fangs. Devyn taxed himself and his few helpers to look, listen, and feel the pulse of the city and its butterfly fluttering of joy.

The final blow came in the form of one of the competition entrants, a young man from one of the leading merchant houses, found stabbed through the heart, the poem he intended to read the next night pinned to his ravaged chest by the blade.

The desire for a poetic competition guttered out like an old candle.

The sequence of banquets got cancelled in the middle of preparations. The quality stayed home behind their locked estate gates. The common people met in the street for food and dancing and ended up miling about asking questions.

Eleni wept. Donari stormed. Devyn cursed himself for not doing more, and yet he knew there was little he could have done differently. The currents of the world had blown the will for revel clean away.

Tantalizing, tainted, gone.

That night he sat with Eleni and Donari in chairs set around a small table on the balcony outside Donari's rooms. They sipped from ornate glasses. A lantern cast their faces in yellow tints and above them summer stars winked down. Below them the city fitfully finished off the three days. Devyn took in the view and found it hardly festive.

"This won't do," Donari asserted, leaning against the railing. "I see your point, Devyn. This smells like the Prelate's work. Sylvanus warned me Casan still has teeth, and I'm not fool enough to think all loyal who swore fealty. I cannot remove dissent if it receives help from without."

He paused to take a drink, letting a frustrated sigh escape with the swallow. "I have to act, despite my weakness. I can't keep all the men I have in the field, and yet leaving the hills undefended just helps Gaspire. Plus," he looked again at Eleni, much more determined this time. "I want to marry. Let the conservatives wail astounded. Let us risk it all for the right reasons. Change has happened. We created a twisted equation these last few months. I want a simple solution if I can get it."

"Donari," Eleni insisted. "We do not have to do this. I've told you."

"I'll not put you through the scrutiny of small minds," Donari asserted.

"But wouldn't the winter gales close the King's Road?" Devyn asked.

"Gaspire knows that as well as we do. I think he will move sooner rather than later. That woman's pregnancy may fail. That might change things. I need information."

"How long will I have?" he asked. But the question was more a dodge than anything else. The reference to Demona brought Talyior's face to mind. Thankfully, his friend was safely south and snared by Lyvia Tamorgen.

"Month, maybe a month and a half," Donari answered. "I will need to move before full fall. If I know what is moving there..." Donari left the thought unfinished, swirling what remained of his wine before tossing it off in a decisive swallow.

"How will I get word to you?"

"Be quick and come back, but take someone with you. You have the measure of the eyes and ears you have placed about the city, yes? Take one of them."

Devyn frowned in response as he ran through the available faces. All of them were too young or too wrong for his purpose. He needed to slip into the northern towns without causing alarm. He needed a pretense and an image that would give him freedom of movement. He looked up at the stars winking in the night sky. They blinked at him mute, inscrutable observers of man's turmoil, useless save as metaphors for poets and lovers. He let the silence stretch on uncomfortably as he struggled to find words to answer his king's request.

"I cannot decide," he said, admitting failure. "There are good men in that crew, but I do not know them well enough yet to choose. May I have tonight to sleep on it?"

"Take the night to think, take tomorrow to talk, but I need you heading north within the week at the latest."

"Can your men secure Donari's safety in your absence?" Eleni asked. Her voice came as though from a shadow, for she had leaned back in her chair out of the range of the weak light from the trimmed lantern.

"Sweet," Donari murmured. "I will have you, of course, since I will not be letting you out of my sight. Between the two of us, I am sure we can avoid any more unusual moments like your last adventure. Avarran will be here tomorrow. I need Devyn for this."

"But think of the danger," she whispered.

"We have been living with danger long enough, my dear, to know it by its middle name. Knowledge is worth whole companies to our cause."

Donari moved to her chair and leaned in to kiss her, and Devyn took the intimate merging of the two shadows as a signal for his dismissal.

"I'll take myself off to sleep and think, my lord. Good night, and you, lady." He left in the wake of their murmured responses.

That night he slept fitfully. He dreamed again the old nightmare of flames and falling masonry, but this time attended by the appearance of a series of faces, distorted by heat waves and imagined light: Roderran, Gaspire, Sylvanus, Casan, Corvale, and the priest he gutted in Gallina. He saw shadow horses, iron-shod hooves striking sparks from unknown cobblestones. Voices whispered at him, snatches of half-remembered verse accompanied by faint musical strains, sounds that reminded him of a flute and a guitar quietly played in tandem. His mind raced his intent into true rest's black forgetfulness just before dawn.

In the morning, he spent an hour walking the citadel battlements trying to make a choice but nothing came clear. Collectively, his small group possessed many admirable qualities; a few of them even Maze survivors like himself. And yet each name failed muster. He stared south to the hills, optionless, bleak. The failed festival deepened the pal hanging over the city as if it now waited, joy suspended, for the next great moment. He let his eyes run one last time over the battlements and red-tiled roofs of the city, searching for even a hint of that once-treasured mirth and bravado he used to know.

Nothing there but the caution of fear.

He picked at a piece of dried moss from a crack in one of the crenallations and pinched it to a flakey dust he let slip into the breeze. It fell to his right. North.

"Right, then," he whispered to the day. "I'll just have to go it alone."

He turned to go back inside, dreading having to inform Donari of his decision.

"Devyn Ambrose!" Devyn turned to find an out of breath Drue before him.

"Yes, lad, what is it?"

"A ship! Desopolisian. Berthed at the quay just now. I've just come. A hundred well armed men, and, oddly enough, a handful of rolled carpets."

"Is that all?"

The boy smiled. "No, sir. And one private citizen who said he knew you."

Devyn shook his head, his grin as wry as it was relieved. Fate had smiled. He had his man.

The two friends sat smiling at each other over mugs and plates of Brimaldi's finest in a back booth at the *Golden Cup*. Somehow it seemed fitting their reunion should take place where their relationship first began.

Devyn picked at his plate while Talyior ate with relish.

"You have changed," Talyior said between mouthfuls.

"And you."

Talyior looked around the common room. "This place hasn't, seemingly."

Devyn followed his gaze. "I recall a slightly different clientele from a year ago," he said quietly.

Talyior snorted into his cup as he drank. "That was a time. Hard to believe how things have gone."

"I trust you are still with Lyvia?"

"Oh, yes. She is, determined."

"And she let you leave?"

Talyior smiled. "Well, as to that, I've earned something of a place in the city as a result of what happened in the spring. Quite surprising, really. She has been amazing. Sylvanus has been patient with me. People seem to look up to me both because of her and maybe those other things."

Obviously, dark memories still haunted his friend. They served to sober his normal jocular good humor; a development not lost on Devyn. He considered telling Talyior about Demona, but decided against it.

"If you are not careful," he said. "They will start giving you real responsibility, like make a magistrate out of you."

Talyior laughed. "And I'll get fat and grow nose hairs that wheeze when I speak in council, like that portly wine merchant we duped last summer before, before things changed." He finished on a down beat and drained what remained of his drink.

Devyn returned the mirth, a low, almost sonorous sound, and refilled their glasses.

"Yes, things, we, have changed. I, too, have found a different purpose. After we buried Senden, Donari asked me to replace him. I've been keeping an eye on things ever since."

"You are too young to be a good spy."

"And you are too young to be a good magistrate."

"Point taken…but?"

"But I suspect in time we may become good at both."

"Well, as for that," responded Talyior. "I may have other opportunities. Funny thing about being the son of a rug merchant; you sometimes find ties to the old life in the strangest places."

"As in?"

"As in a prime lot of merchandise rolled up and stamped with the family sigil tucked away in a warehouse that escaped most of the flames. We found it in the clean-up after the battle. Apparently, my father traded further a field than I knew."

"I heard that was part of the cargo you brought north. So you will be a rug merchant after all? What will Lyvia say to that?"

"She was rather taken by the independence of the idea, actually," Talyior said, his smile reaching his eyes. "I told her I did not want to be a kept consort to someone else's power. I may have earned some gratitude from the south for my part in the conflict, but I think I would like to justify my place even more with a little industry. My father's old foreman, Espan, sailed with me. I intend to see if anything might be left over of my family's things in the north. He wants to make a go of it. Loyalty can surprise you sometimes."

"Agreed."

145

"And what of you? I heard something in the palace when we met with Donari. You've a task?"

"He needs information about what his enemies may be plotting up north."

"And he does not have enemies enough here?"

Devyn smiled at the jest. "We have had our moments here, yes, but his concerns about the north press him, all of us, really. You know that, Tal. You brought a partial answer with you in those men you tumbled out of your ship."

"More fighting?"

"The north has ignored his calls for fealty and conference. There will be more fighting. I am set to find out when and where Gaspire will strike if I can."

Talyior paused a moment before replying, as if he were weighing his next words and sifting them to gauge their effect.

"Alone?"

"Yes."

"Foolish."

"I could take one or two likely lads with me, but I'd rather they stay and keep watch over Donari and Eleni. They, too, plan a wedding."

"Yes, we heard of that. Interesting. You know, I remember she got up rather quickly when I ran her over last year. It seems she keeps on rising." He chuckled in his cup. "Not bad for a bunch of poets."

"Changes," Devyn said. "She is part of them, too. Quite an amazing woman."

Talyior chewed contemplatively on a carrot. "Yes," he murmured. "I agree. I rather like the idea of her becoming queen. It makes sense given all the madness in the world this last year."

Devyn nodded absently, his mind running back to that fateful discussion in Sylvanus' study. Once Devyn agreed to go in search of Donari, he effectively sundered his and Talyior's connection. Love, glory, and a crown all served to separate them. Part of his mind thought it all somewhat funny. Words, the smallest of things the vast majority took for granted as a daily function, drew them together in friendship and shared adventure. Words also connected them to the big ideas, like causes, hopes and battle; the things that united men under single purpose. And yet all Devyn saw now spoke of dissension. How was a man to act when words seemed bent on dissolving amity?

Perhaps heroes were the loneliest of men.

Senden had worked alone.

He glanced up, caught a familiar look in his friend's eyes and wondered even now if he should do the same, despite his earlier wish.

"So, you leave in less than two days?" Talyior asked.

Devyn paused before replying. Talyior bent his head in that knowing fashion at the hesitation.

"Oh, really, nobility? Now? You left me once before, remember? And look at me. The woman is talking marriage!"

Devyn laughed into his cup. "But you are ready for it."

"Oh, cheeky. Insults? And just when I was going to offer to go with you?"

Devyn sat back a little stunned. Love, respect, and honor had found Talyior and taken him far from the dilettante who once pined after another man's wife. And yet the old Talyior was still there, and that meant he still needed to be protected.

"No," he whispered. "I won't let you. Too dangerous. Lyvia needs you. You have other concerns."

"I sailed a fire-ship into a galley filled with men who wanted to kill me. I put a sword point through the eye of a man who held a knife at Lyvia's throat. Don't talk to me about danger. I am in this thing, too. You took off on your own once before and look what happened to you. You're wearing black clothes and using unpoetic language. Ren's Tears, man! You are acting like a spy! You need me to keep you centered on what's important."

"But I think we are both passed tupping serving maids and duping tavern keepers."

"And so we are, but that doesn't mean anything, not really."

"How so?"

Talyior leaned forward conspiratorially. "We used to finish off each other's thoughts, remember? Times may have taken us down different paths, but we are still friends. I know you need me."

Devyn leaned in, infected by Talyior's spirit.

Silly notion, going alone. False nobility, Devyn.

"I always *fixed* your thoughts, as I remember," he jested.

Talyior snorted and a year fell away. "What, jealous? And you with those fine clothes and a desperate mission? Ha. I've seen that play."

Devyn shook his head, realizing in that moment how much he missed his friend's humor. His life had gotten much too serious since that brawl in Desopolis. War and responsibility had a way of taking laughter, the mirth of friendship, out of the daily equation. The goofy grin on Talyior's face, a mix of spirit and the ale he consumed, convinced Devyn that, if he intended to risk his life, he might as well do it with his best friend. Besides, Talyior's reference to their poetic past gave him an idea as to how they might travel in the north. He wondered if his fingers would still find the stops on a flute if he could find one on short notice.

"Fine," he said. "I need you, but what of Lyvia?"

"We will probably be back before she even wonders about me."

"Or dead."

"Then it won't make any difference, will it?"

"We need to leave with the dawn." He smiled in recalled mischief. "And I know where we can get some horses."

Talyior took up the hint, nodding, eyes bright. "And I know where we can get a ship."

"Done."

"Well done."

They left together, squinting and a little woozy in the late afternoon sunshine. They walked back up the city, strangely silent, the need for words quite run out. Devyn ran over the gear he needed to assemble and the general quality of the mounts available in the palace stables. Sadly, there were no more matched pairs belonging to Sevire Anargi to steal.

"Can I send a letter south?" Talyior asked as they paced up the street.

Devyn considered. "Probably best not to. I'm sorry."

"You doom me, friend. Then can I stop off and see Gania? I had half a mind to surprise her with a wet kiss and a grope. But I guess that's out of the question."

"You don't have to go."

"And *that*, too, is out of the question. From now on, the fewer ears the better. Too bad for Gania. You are making me leave behind a trail of disappointed women."

The sun was just about ready to impale itself on the mountain peak to the west when they arrived at the intersection where the citadel way crossed the main road from the harbor.

"I'll meet you at the quay with horses and supplies. Do you have your guitar?"

"Lyvia gave me a new one. Quite nice, actually. Flute?"

"I'll see what I can scrounge. My life has not been given lately to tinkering with stops."

"I will keep to the ship the rest of this day, then."

"Good. I will see to what we need. In fact, some of it is already being assembled."

Talyior paused before leaving, looking around. "Even though we are leaving again," he said with a poignant lilt in his voice. "It is good to be back."

Chapter 15: A Killer's Apotheosis

Devyn watched Talyior walk away, and then turned to ascend the road to the citadel. As he began his climb a small shadow detached itself from a doorway to intercept him. It moved into the fading sunlight; Devyn recognized Tasia.

"Little one!" he said, kneeling down to greet her at her eye-level. "It is good to see you again so soon. What brings you so far afield after dark?"

"I saw Tolimon in the bell tower, again," she said. Her eyes had a wild caste to them, and Devyn could feel her tremors when she reached out a hand to touch his own.

"I've had bad dreams," she continued. "Red. And Tolimon. For days now. An' you told us to watch and I have and I saw him. It felt…bad."

"Have you told your mother?"

The look she gave him came straight from his own past.

"She's too busy to bother right now. Besides, I can take care of myself."

Devyn saw himself in her tense features; too young for such independence but unwilling to give it up. He remembered the fears he faced down during his own time in the Maze. Perhaps that was why she searched him out. Who else would understand?

Something in her tone set his mind on edge. Tolimon was the god of Chaos. In the old stories his presence always meant mischief. For better part of the last month, Devyn, the king, Pevana herself had been perplexed by one crisis after the next.

And tonight was to have been the climax of the festival: ruined by mischance.

He ran over the series of unfortunate events, paired them with Tasia's cryptic references, and suddenly puzzle pieces snicked into place.

Casan.

"You say you saw Tolimon in the bell tower," he asked. "You mean the new tower? At the college temple?"

Tasia nodded. "Yes. He was practicing."

"Practicing?"

"Yes, practicing. He'd point his bow in every direction and draw it back. Why is Tolimon practicing in Renia's city?"

"I have an idea, Tasia. Thank you for telling me."

"It is bad, isn't it?"

He considered telling her the truth but weighed what it might cost her and chose instead to preserve her childhood as best he could.

"Not at all, child. Nothing worth bad dreams."

Tasia seemed to take reassurance. "Really? Good, then. Maybe it would make a good part to put in your next story to us. Will you come and tell it soon at the old one's grave?"

"It would make a wonderful addition, Tasia, and I will surely add it to my next story."

"Tomorrow?"

"No, not tomorrow, I'm afraid. I have some duties to attend to. I may have to leave for awhile."

"Will you tell us a special story when you get back?"

Devyn ruffled her scruffy hair. "I will tell you two special stories when I get back." He watched her dash off, an image of youthful intensity back down the slope, across the intersection before slipping like an afterthought down an alley way, heading back toward the Maze. When she disappeared, he turned his gaze up and over to the right, where the bell tower, newly completed loomed over the upper levels of the city. Why would a helmeted and armed man be spending time aiming a bow from the tower of a place of worship?

He turned in a half circle, taking in the angles, quickly noting the tower's unique placement. The clues slipped into place, clarity coming like Senden's voice in his dreams.

"Do you see it, boy? Plans within plans; that is Casan's way. He never tries but he has another gambit waiting. This was started last fall…"

Quickly now, Devyn took stock of what he knew and what he sensed about the tower and Tasia's words. The elegant spire, still lacking the bell for its cupola, presented many angles for an accomplished bowman, and the city now quartered many such men.

He looked up to the citadel and with a shock realized the tower's height even allowed for a long bow shot into the palace grounds and the king's private balcony. Squinting, he estimated the distance. His conclusions set him running swiftly up the street. Last night clouds partially masked the full moon, muting its lunar glow, but tonight looked to be a clear, star ridden night. Light enough to cast shadows amongst the shadows; light enough to reveal Donari and Eleni taking a glass and their ease. It had become their pattern.

And someone noticed.

A rough plan took shape in Devyn's mind. The light had failed during his chat with Tasia, and his fear told him he lacked the time to warn the palace. Maze-born instinct took over, and he changed course for the college.

Devyn crouched beneath some shrubbery outside a secondary entrance to the university library. The imposing King's Theology temple loomed before him; its lofty walls supported bricks scavenged from last year's spate of temple burnings. To him, the large, unlovely square served as a symbol of who had been in power during that time.

The bell tower actually served to connect the library to the temple, providing the Lord Prelate with a covered walk way to move between his chambers to his ceremonial areas. Devyn would have to access the tower through the library, which meant he had to avoid the priests, acolytes and students intent on their scholarly business.

Devyn slung his sword across his back, checked his belt for the two throwing knives, leftovers from Senden and useful should he need a silent silencing. Devyn checked over his shoulder to gauge the moon's position. The lunar orb, its fullness reflecting the sun's sunset orange, was now completely free of the land and rising into the night.

Time to move.

Like a breath, Devyn slipped to the ground and crawled along the wall. He made quick work of the door lock, opened it just enough to slip inside, and found himself on the library's main floor screened by tall bookshelves. Off to the left a pale glow from a student's candle rose above the stacks and somewhere ahead voices murmured. He eased his way down the wall, hugging the stacks and pausing to check for people. The last thing he needed was to stumble on a half-asleep scholar or one of the late-night clerks resetting tomes.

He made it without incident to where the library's floor plan intersected the bell tower foundation. In the half-light, Devyn made out the lower end of the stairs that led up the inside wall of the building. Here the tower's builders placed an arch that ran through it to exit into the main chancellery of the temple beyond. Light welled from that direction joined to the sound of voices chanting prayers. Devyn doubted the Prelate would be leading such late proceedings. The picture in his mind deepened his bilious disgust.

He waited, stilled his racing heart, slowed his breathing, and reached out with his senses to check the area for unseen presence. Nothing. He slipped into the archway and flowed like darkness up the stairs. He placed his feet carefully near the wall as he ascended to cut down on the chance a board might squeak.

By the time he reached the third landing he realized he was not alone on the stairs. Above him, a heavy tread attended by the slight clank of metal on metal worked its way upwards.

Devyn cursed his hunch and Donari's love for his palace balcony. He kept going, sacrificing speed for stealth now, and hoped the man above would take his time setting up his shot, praying silently to Renia of the Tears to allow him time to get there and foil what surely came. He stole over to the railing and risked a glance upward. A shadow figure stumped purposely up the stairs. Devyn could hear his wheezy breathing, the shuffling step.

No stripling, and not in good shape.

An image formed in Devyn's mind of a grizzled veteran, softened by easier duties but whose skills at long range death remained undiminished.

There is no bell to service yet. No need for someone to be on these steps unless...

Eleni's notes on the assassination attempt when Roderran first arrived at Pevana included Senden's thoughts there had been more than one shooter, but they only found one of them. Devyn's sense of pattern increased with an attendant dread that produced a trickle of sweat down the small of his back. He quickened his pace.

Above, the darkness lightened as the stairway neared the opening to the bell tower. Devyn stole another glance and noticed the steel helmet. It reminded him of ones the Prelate's former guards and bully boys wore. The man reached the top and stepped up onto the covered space. Four wooden pillars held up the dome which lacked its bell. Devyn went to all fours as he followed. Still two levels below, he could hear the man going about his business; a grunt while stringing a bow, the precise clips of arrows being lined up against the solid framing. Then no more sounds of movement; just moonlight quiet interrupted by the man's rheumy breathing.

Devyn eased a knife blade from his belt. He crawled, bug-like, up the final set of stairs. Easing his eyes above floor level, he made out a tall, solid figure standing upright, secure from notice by the distance from the ground below and the shadows cast by the roof above. The man held a large bow with an arrow notched and stood poised, looking in the direction of the citadel.

If Donari is not there, he won't draw.

Devyn raised himself higher and brought his left leg up underneath him in preparation to stand and throw his knife.

The bowman tensed and drew back the bowstring, sighting down its length at a target. Devyn surged to his feet, but the floorboard creaked. The man flinched at the noise, loosed the arrow, and turned to see who was behind him. Devyn threw his first knife but missed, the blade spinning harmlessly before imbedding itself in one of the roof pillars.

The archer advanced, gripping the bow like a club. Devyn had just enough time to regain his balance, duck and roll right and forward. Up again in an instant, he braced himself, second knife in hand. His opponent saw the blade in the moonlight and grew cautious. He held the bow in front of him with one hand while moving sideways toward where his sword leaned in its sheath against the railing. In a surprisingly quick move he threw the bow at Devyn, who threw his knife at the motion. Once again luck worked against Devyn, for the blade glanced off the bow and ricochet off into the night.

Both drew swords and advanced to the attack. The assassin was indeed older. The light of the full moon revealed a seamed face framed by a pepper and silver beard. Neither of them spoke. Sword blades rang as they met. Vaguely, Devyn wondered what folk about at that time might think of the strange tones coming from the tower, as though sprites clanged on a miscast bell.

The intended assassin, though no artist with the blade, possessed size and strength and swung his weapon like a walking stick. Devyn met his second swing early, taking the blade high in its arch and pushing it wide, exposing the man's midsection. Even so, the impact sent a numbing sting from Devyn's wrist to his shoulder, but he ignored the pain and pivoted inside the man's defenses and crushed his nose with an elbow. The man grunted in a shower of blood and teeth. Devyn rotated back, grabbing his sword handle with both hands and slashed back down the archer's outstretched blade finishing with a deadly slash across his neck. Mistake. Devyn knew Donari would have preferred to have the man questioned. The archer collapsed toward death, his helmet rolling away when he hit the floor, revealing a grey tonsure after the manner of the King's Theology priesthood.

Devyn froze, waiting for the alarm that surely should come, but nothing of the sort happened. The fight had been wordless; the only sound the two swords clanging. Impossible as it seemed at first, Devyn accepted luck may have been with him after all. He looked over the railing at the streets below. Nothing moved save a bat after bugs. He shifted over to look down the stairway of the tower. Again nothing. He looked over to where the bowman had aimed. The balcony was awash with moving shapes lit by torches. The sound of voices raised in alarm drifted to him. And then a shape moved to the railing holding a bright flame aloft. Even at that distance, Devyn could tell it was the king.

Alive. Renia's Grace, if I had failed…

Devyn bent to clean his sword on the assassin's cloak, hands trembling, knees weak; the sense of being *placed* as though for a purpose overwhelming.

Renia's Grace, indeed. Or Minuet. What have I become?

All the faces of the men he had slain passed before his inward eye just like in his dream: the priest-bully in Gallina, Jared Corvale, the hapless fool outside of Eleni's house. Was he so experienced, then, that he could coldly act on a hunch and slice a strange man's throat with no personal cost to himself? Had he come so far from the restless poet in search of words? Was he now a killer? And yet what had all his sword training been for if not for killing? All his practice he likened to his verse, all poetry of form and motion, art.

But what happened in the cupola was all about blood, skotching an appendage of evil. His service to the king justified the act. He could have died himself had he not proved quicker and more fortunate.

So this is what it feels like to be a minion.

He stumbled down the stairs, unsure if he liked the idea, promise to Senden notwithstanding . Donari was a good man, a fellow poet, and Devyn rather liked the idea of a poet-king. That soothed him in the end as he slunk down the final flight of stairs to the arch.

He made his way back through and out of the library the same way he came in. The whole episode took just a few minutes from the time he arrived at the shrubbery. The internal journey, however, had been epic. He survived and now must turn to the next task.

Because that is what minions do.

He kept to the shadows once he left the college grounds, avoiding the clatter of palace guards sent to investigate the disturbance. Devyn knew he had to give his report, but he only wanted to do it once. As he slipped up the final slope to the citadel gates, words came to him in cadence with his steps. He thought it ironic. His service largely kept poetry from him, and the festival went off a shadow of his and Eleni's intention. Like his presence in the bell tower, perhaps these, too, were a gift from Renia.

And in those times
Of maelstrom
Confusion and strife
When all about you
Makes you question
How you lead your life;

And is it by desire
Or Design,
Spirit malignant or
Benign,
That you make your
Choices at the door
Of Fate?
Or is it aspiration?
And who is to blame
For dreams
That fall to flames
And words that run
To labyrinths of context
And contention?

Silence won't give
You answers
Fear just makes things worse.
Are words a gift
From the muses
Or another form of
Curse?

You have to follow
The threads and
Just remember
What you came here
For.
Remember all
The dreams and all
Their meanings
That change with
Age.
Hope and Faith
Are unlike words
On a page;
They shift and they sift
And leach away
The after-effects
Of pain,
Making a memory
Of sadness--

And despair
An evaporating haze.

Relate and remember
All the things you've done
And seen.
Understand there's more power
In a gentle laugh
Than in any nightmare scream.

Chapter 16: The Marriage of War

Eleni sat in a crenellation on the citadel wall watching Donari and his escort fade to toy figures moving in a puff of road dust. The assassination attempt Devyn foiled set in motion a week of whirling recrimination and pronouncement. Donari put the questions to Casan, but the old man managed to avoid claiming the archer for one of his own. Conflicting testimony created just enough doubt to force Donari to back off. Eleni felt otherwise. A crown did not limit her reaction. Love compelled her anger. She wanted an end to the threats, she wanted Donari, and she wanted a baby.

The summer heat made distance hazy and faery-like. Eleni focused intently on that dust cloud. At its head the compass point of her life remained fixed and visible, an image superimposed behind her eyelids when she closed them against the midmorning glare.

Donari left her with the task of overseeing preparations for their wedding. She wrote the proclamations that went out to the people to take care with their homes and businesses. In lew of a successful festival, Donari intended to clean up the city for the nuptials they now planned for that October.

"We cannot allow the people to dwell on the bad feelings about the festival," he had said when he kissed her goodbye at the palace steps. "Something hopeful, something positive will serve. Plus, we can beard the old man by making him officiate at our wedding. I'll send him a note to that effect."

In his view, their marriage would serve as a final slap in the face to hide-bound northern probity and the machinations of those who would supplant him. Their move for love would force Gaspire's hand. She agreed, in part. Action was needed. Donari chose to inspect his preparations; she had something different in mind.

Without even realizing it, she had begun thinking like a queen. But she still retained some of her former audacity, that rash, chafing restlessness that motivated her to thrust her words into the mix of the poetic competition the year before. Devyn's man in the college reported little going on with Casan. He preached in the temple but never left the college grounds. Donari professed guarded satisfaction over the calm, but Eleni still doubted. It was one thing to have the old spider watched; another thing to see for herself.

It was time she payed an official visit to the college. Donari was right. What better victory over the Prelate than to make him officiate at their wedding?

His thugs threw daggers at me. This time I will whisper daggers at him.

She decided to take a real blade along just in case.

Once she determined her course of action she moved swiftly. She left the battlements, gathered up the handful of useful young men Donari left behind to 'protect' her and sent them off to burnish helms and clean up their mail. She swept up Drue and sent him off to find her maids and arrange for carriages to take her entourage to the college. She now enjoyed the run of Donari's mother's closets, and the dresses, though a bit dated, were still sufficiently regal to suit her purpose. Eleni avoided pretention, preferring discretion over ostentation, but now she needed to leave an impression. She wanted Casan to see her dripping with authority's trappings, to literally smell her ascension. He made it a habit to waltz around in his faux temporal finery. She intended to match and surpass him.

She let Anlise take an hour to do her hair; a first in her life. She caught several deep frowns creasing the girl's brow as she wrestled with Eleni's tresses. Eleni let it pass as frustration but decided to leave the girl behind when it came time to leave.

By mid-day, coifed, scented and be-draped, she allowed Drue to help her into the carriage for the trundle ride down to the college. A squad of armed and armored horseman escorted her, a gleaming symbol of Donari's power. They clattered down to the main doors of the library, causing a stir in the robed thugs clustered there. With credible efficiency her young men formed a cordon that allowed her easy entry into the building. Despite her rapid heartbeat, she managed to waltz through the portal like she owned the place as indeed she would once Donari placed a ring on her finger and a crown upon her head.

She paced down the hall in a stately charge of lavender folds and glittering jewels. This was woman's war, different, though no less risky and epic than the crash and blood of man's version.

She penetrated into the main entry hall, her escort flowing about her like a gleaming set of martial lanterns in the interior half-light. With a wave she sent a page scurrying off to announce her presence. Calming her nerves, she took hold of her courage and the words she knew she would have to speak. With Drue at her side and a handful of guards, she followed the hapless messenger and swept through the half-open door of Casan's office before she could be announced and caught the old man partly off his guard. He stood behind his desk, clutching a sheaf of papers, four other priests hovered near with surprised, chagrined looks as they took in the sudden disruption. They looked like macabre school boys caught cheating on an assignment.

"Gentleman," she said calmly, inwardly marveling at how cold her voice sounded. "I regret the intrusion, but the Lord Prelate and I have matters to discuss. Drue, a chair please." She turned to the scowling priests. "Sirs," she said carefully with false tact. "If you will excuse us for a time? Outside, perhaps? Drue here and several of my young men will gladly wait with you until the Prelate and I are done."

The priests hesitated to move, all looked quickly to the Prelate, who continued to stare nonplussed. Eleni took advantage of the delay to give a quick wave of the folded fan she held in her right hand. It was a bejeweled affair from an earlier era, but it served her well as a figurative blade. Her men moved to frame the door. The Prelate, gave a quick nod that freed his priests to go. In a moment, the room emptied. She waved away Drue's questioning glance. The door closed, leaving her alone with the Prelate.

Eleni let him stare, noting how his eyes moved from her to the guards back to her, his right eyebrow rising as he took in her presumptive opulence, the royal tone of the dress and her confident mein. She raised her chin to complete the examination.

"Sit down, Byrnard," she snapped. "I won't require a bow and a hand curtsey, this time."

He sputtered. Angry. Drew breath.

"I said sit, old man. Let's not waste time with pompous expressions, agreed?"

The flames died down, replaced by a calculating, black coldness as Casan slowly lowered himself to his chair. He even managed a decorous smile.

"To what do I owe the pleasure of this visit?" he asked.

"Priest, the pleasure is all mine make no mistake. Donari feels himself bound by diplomacy to allow you your life. I do not."

Casan's jaws worked. "Why are you here?" he grated. "You dare interrupt me in my duties?"

She laughed at that.

"You know full well why I am here, old man. And yes, you are a very old, old man. Have you looked in a mirror lately? Your eyes still look pretty clear, but have a care for those wrinkles, my friend, they are getting deep enough to swallow up what is left of your humanity.

"How dare you," he sputtered. "Commoner! Strumpet!"

"Really?" she smirked. "Are you reduced to such hapless terms? I find that ironic, seeing as how you appear to place great emphasis on strumpets. When is Demona due, eh? How much of the tithes from Pevana have you sent north to provide for mid-wives and spears?"

Casan did not bother with denial.

"Enough to make sure Donari will fall when I choose to have him fall. He is not a fit vessel to bear authority. He is a fool weakened by kindness, a shadow of his forebears, and an embarrassment to his more worthy cousin's memory."

"You hate his wisdom and independence," she said, leaning forward, undaunted. "You hate him because he is not your creation. You hate him because his ambitions do not reflect your own. You hate him because he has bested you in every turn."

"He let me burn nearly all his useless temples," the Prelate replied. "He could not stop Roderran's gambits. He is a fraud."

"Smoke dissipates, priest," she answered. "Even a slight breeze clears the incense away from all of your elaborate rituals in that gaudy chapel you cadged together. Purloined masonry, sir. The stones remember. And the people still believe. You are an affectation after all." She tapped the fan against her heart. "The folk keep their faith here, fool, inviolate in the end. And right alongside the memory of their Tree they keep their love for their lord. Donari allows them to chose, Prelate. That's freedom. In the end they will chose freedom from you and all you represent. Peace has a way of leavening militant religion."

"People are sheep."

"Fortunately, Donari believes otherwise."

"He is no king."

"He is more a king than you are a man of faith. And you know it. It eats at you. It festers like a canker, chewing away at your vitals like the worms that reduced Roderran to the stuff of the earth."

This was rage poetry to her soul. All the sorrow of her former life, and all the danger threatening her present, originated with this one, spiteful, wizened old man. Hate swelled, pushed. She balanced on the edge of feeling just like him, and the image scared her just enough to save her. She took a deep breath, rose smoothly, releasing the clasp that held her light carriage cloak, and walked slowly around the desk. Casan's eyes followed her, wary, furious. She stopped next to his chair, letting her scent wash over him like truth.

"He's more of a man than either you or Roderran ever hoped to be," she said quietly. "You have tried to kill him or discredit him since the day you came to Pevana, and he is still here. I saw Corvale's head on the ground, covered in blood and dirt; his last surprised, confused expression frozen on his face. I described it in detail in my account. I mention that now because the look on your face is eerily similar."

"Woman," Casan rasped. "You go too far. You are worse even than the slut Roderran got with child. Do not try to impress me, bitch, you are a bauble, easily disposed of."

Eleni leaned in. Casan could dissemble, plot, agitate, but he could not fight like a woman. This was battle of a different sort; one he was not man enough to win.

"Remember when power was an aphrodisiac?" she whispered. "Remember when you still had a use for your cock, how hard you got? Did you rise when Corvale killed my husband? Did the flames that took the Maze excite you? Did you feel that urgent need to thrust into something soft and pliant, to dominate?"

"Cunt!" he gasped.

"Oh, yes. You do remember. And you rage because that is all you have left, memories of cunts, frayed ends of fallen plans, images of the power you once used as a pleasure toy. Donari will not kill you, but time will. You are impotent. A failure."

Her words set his teeth gnashing, but her lips moving so close to his ear froze him into immobility.

"Oh," she went on. "If only I could make you understand how exquisite it was that night on the balcony when your archer failed his mark and bled for it? Donari took me there against the railing. He tickled the small of my back with the fletching of that arrow as he thrust into me from behind; like a king, Casan, long, sensuous, firm. We laughed at you. The sweat from his brow dripped down my back and my breasts hung out over the balcony like an offering."

She could feel his quivering fury. She let her lips brush the spiky down on his sagging earlobe.

"When he finished, I held him like a babe all the rest of that night. Like a baby, Byrnard. I would not be surprised if he got me with twins. Twins. Another Avedun generation, but this time free of your taint. My babies will be like the breeze that disperses your noxious incense, old man, and you will be forgotten."

She slipped the dagger out from her sleeve, reached over and placed it on the pile of papers in front of the Prelate. The old man clenched; the tightness in his jaw meant victory. She rose, lightheaded, but kept her voice cold.

"Donari won't scruple to remove you, Casan, but I will. If you want to survive to officiate at our wedding, I suggest you stop trying to meddle in the king's affairs. We will have an outside affair, sir. We are partial to green and blue. See to it."

161

She laughed the whole way back to the Palace. She never felt so powerful, so alive: to dare the dragon's lair and then tweak its tail, delicious fare, lusty. If only Donari had been to hand.

Her claims about conception had been a hope, but her hand strayed to her belly as if drawn by a force. She thought about nothing else during her walk in the garden later. So much for Casan. In her rapture, Eleni didn't feel the spectral snake coil about her ankle, slither up her leg and towards her belly. Her hindbrain briefly considered an image of a rider heading north at a hard gallop, carrying an ire-filled message of death. But joy superseded all else. Eleni Caralon prayed for her portended future. She rather liked the idea of twins.

Chapter 17: Tour

Donari beat dust from his light coat as he dismounted at the small camp nestled in the hills a half day's ride from Pevana. His escort ranged about the space, setting up horse-lines and preparing areas for the light tents they packed with them. This place served the watch post that crouched among the rocks at the slope's summit and looked down the ridge to the plains of Sor-reel to the north.

Donari stalked up the path to the vantage point, his leg muscles protesting the stress of the ride from the city, rueing a summer of relative physical inactivity. He took himself to task as he walked. He asked men to serve him in uncomfortable places like this. He needed to keep himself in better trim. Avarran accompanied him, equally dusty but evincing no such discomfort. Donari added a mental note to express his thanks again for Avarran's good service. The man seemed adept at producing miracles. First the army's return mostly intact, now these forward posts manned by dedicated volunteers.

Donari paused to let Avarran come alongside just below the raised platform of rough hewn beams. Two men in Avedun colors stood to attention at the base of a three-step ladder.

"What do we have here, Jason?" Donari asked.

"An observation post, sire. Six man teams. There should be two others, but I noticed two horses missing." He turned to the nearest soldier, a small, tough-looking trooper with the bow legs that spoke of cavalry service. "I assume they are out on patrol?"

The man nodded. "Yes, sir. They have been gone since mid-morning. We saw some campfire smoke earlier. They went to take a look. They are due back any time now."

"Thoughts?" Donari asked.

The trooper kept his poise at the question; a small point that spoke to Donari of confidence and skill despite being addressed by a king.

"We've seen nothing sizeable to our front, sire. If you climb up, I can show you what I mean."

Donari preceded him up the ladder and saw that it had been fashioned to just clear the level of the rocks around it, providing a panoramic view of the lands about without placing it above the horizon line. Anyone looking up from below would not see the beams.

The northern slopes of the ridge fell in rolling sweeps and forested shoulders to the plains beyond. The region appeared empty. The soil was

163

poor in the hills, rocky with patches of alkali that precluded husbandry. Sor-reel's folk kept to the better ground closer to the river. No tracks connected Sor-reel and Pevana. What trade existed funneled itself through Lomillar and the northern river ports of the Eloe. The ridge line between Pevana's valley and the northern fief was an effective barrier by default. It was the abode of hunters and the occasional woodman.

The trooper pointed off to the left, westward to where a hill nearly as high as the one on which Donari now stood loomed. Its rise created a narrow valley choked by scrub oak. Donari imagined a stream struggled to pass there, filtering around rock and root to find its end in the grasslands to the north. Donari nodded approval. This was a good vantage point. Any sizable force would find passage here difficult.

"The smoke we saw came from that hill, sire. Just the one tendril. We suspect hunters, but it could be our northern counterparts keeping watch on us. We have been here for a month and seen nothing. When that smoke showed up yesterday, we decided to take a look first before sending word. You're coming saved us a trip."

Avarran joined them to take in the view. No more smoke hazed the skyline. Nothing moved to their front, not even a bird on the wing.

"I have a handful of these posts along the ridgeline, sire," Avarran said, sweeping his arm from west to east. "One in the heights north of Pevana to watch the coast and the trails from Emdar. This one commands most of the front facing Sor-reel. I have another westward, closer to the King's Road. Six man teams, with mounts. They are due to be relieved soon."

"You have done well," Donari said. He gripped the trooper's arm to include him in the compliment. "And we have been fortunate, I think, that our northern brothers have not been more ambitious. But your smoke story worries me. Skulkers or scouts, the uncertainty does us no good."

Just then he saw movement among the trees at the valley floor. Two horsemen walked their mounts out from underneath the canopy and began climbing the ridge slope, picking their way crossways through rocks and scattered pines.

"Our missing scouts, I presume?" Donari asked.

"Yes, sire," the man grunted. "And from their pace, I would say they will not have much to report."

Donari and the others descended from the platform and headed back down the path to the camp. The two scouts trotted in just as they arrived. Again, the men's calm demeaner in the face of a visit from their king impressed Donari. Avarran had chosen his teams well.

164

"A single fire," the taller of the two, answered when Donari asked for his report. "Small, just for cooking, we think. There seemed to be two of them from the prints. We noticed marks that suggest they had a third mount with them, probably a pack animal."

"Hunters?" Avarran asked.

The other, younger looking but no less capable seeming than his companion, shook his head in denial.

"We doubt it, sir. We've used the quiet this last month to do some snooping after game ourselves. There just isn't much up here right now. Too hot."

"Northern scouts, then" decided Donari.

The younger looking trooper nodded agreement. "Yes, sire, we think that is the case. But the fire was too small for a signal. Perhaps they've gone in search of a better place for one, or—"

"Or there is no one close enough north for them to signal," Donari finished. "Yes, that would make sense." He turned to the taller scout. "Do you think they saw you?"

"It's a possibility, sire," he answered. "But, again, it's just the one spot. We ranged around the hill a bit and did not find anything else. Those fellows, whoever they are, just arrived yesterday, took a look around and decided they were alone. Their trail leads off westward."

"Towards Collum," Avarran murmured.

"And the King's Road," Donari asserted. "If we read these signs correctly, my cousin is showing an alarming lack of creativity. We need to exploit that if we can."

"I agree, sire. Nothing will come at use through here. As we first suspected, Gaspire will have to use the road."

"But I still wonder about those scouts and the word they take with them."

"And to whom they will report it."

Donari checked the sun's position. "How long a ride to your next post?"

"A day, if we go back down the ridge to use the horse tracks in the valley."

"Are you suggesting a short cut?"

Avarran frowned. "If speed is your need, sire, there is a track along the ridge from here to the next post. Broken ground, a few dicey spots."

"But faster?"

"If we don't run into trouble."

"We are twenty. We will be the trouble." He gripped Avarran's arm to dispel any dispute. "No, friend, save your breath. We have been cautious all summer. It is obvious to me where the push will come, but the sooner we talk to your last team the better."

"As you wish, sire."

"I do wish." He pitched his voice higher to include his escort. "Feed yourselves from your packs, friends. Leave off with the tents. We will not be staying." He paced over to his horse and fumbled with his saddle straps. He brought out a small pad, pen and ink bottle. He gestured for one of his escort to approach. "I will need you to take a message back to Pevana. Give me a moment. You can prepare to ride while I write it."

He sat down on a rock and scratched out a few terse lines. Avarran joined him. When Donari finished, he blew the ink dry, folded the paper and handed it to the waiting rider. The man took the missive, saluted smartly, and fairly leaped into the saddle.

"What do you intend, sire?" Avarran asked, following Donari towards their horses.

"I've asked Eleni to send word south, again, asking for more help. She was also expecting me back, but I want to head west. Gaspire does not fear us, Avarran. He knows we are too weak, or else we would have seen more than the two skulkers reported."

"So you act on a hunch?"

"You have known and served me long enough, Jason, to know how I feel about hunches."

Avarran laughed as he mounted. Donari liked how the act altered the man's expression.

"I do, indeed, sire, or else I would not have suggested that track."

"Are we becoming predictable?"

"No, my king, but we might be getting a little desperate."

"Correct. We need news and action. I need surety to bring the army out to the field. We might find that reason when we come to your most westward post. Onward, sir!"

Avarran gave a single order and within minutes Donari and his escort clattered down the slope to the trail that snaked westward through the hills.

The track wound through a raised valley, a depression really, that separated several higher ridge humps from the gentler slopes to the south. Despite its narrow state and rough terrain, it did keep mostly west whereas the main road and horse track from Pevana kept to the flats near the river that swung south, pushed that way by a spur of the ridge.

Donari and his escort rode quickly but heedfully with riders thrust ahead and kept behind, but the steep ground prevented flankers. He found he kept looking north and up to compensate. His desire for news and action made him read the tale of the scouts ahead of them a little differently from Avarran. No activity for months, then a brief stay by unknowns who do not retreat but pass on north.

They were looking for something.

As he pounded on behind the foreguard, Donari reconsidered his assessment of Gaspire's talents. Something must have happened in Lomillar, and recently, to spark such a ranging move. Perhaps those men had been tasked with searching out possible tracks other than the King's Road. They came, observed the rocky, broken ground and moved on.

Every furlong brought him closer to the passes where the King's Road cut through the ridge. Everything pointed west to where that track exited the hills to follow a tributary stream to the main river channel. There were villages there. They would have to be defended or moved.

A warning shout brought him back to the present. He pulled back on the reins to avoid crashing into the riders in front of him. From behind other riders practically upended him in their haste to provide cover. Donari's horse stumbled. Avarran's face swam into view as Donari struggled to keep his seat.

"Get down, sire! Dismount and keep low!" he shouted. Donari felt a blow to his chest as Avarran pushed him off balance and out of the saddle. He fell in an undignified clump to the dubious safety and cover beneath his mount's thrashing hooves. He got to a knee, grabbed for the reins and fended off Avarran's horse as it swerved and nearly crushed him against the flanks of his own.

"What is happening?" he shouted. "How many? Who? Where?"

"Ware, lord!" screamed Avarran. "Stay low!"

More shouts. Metal clashed off metal as somewhere ahead men traded blows. Donari got to his feet, scanned the slopes, fearing archers, but no tell tale zips came. More blows. Fading.

Not many, then. This was no ambush. Accident?

He controlled his horse's excited surges. His men collected around him. He could hear Avarran's voice ahead giving orders. Calm. No more metal on metal clash. Dust billowed from the trail ahead, hazing the afternoon sun, filtered past Donari's position, leaving him blinking like a newborn awakening from a nap.

Avarran loomed before him. The men warding him during the fray drew back. Donari struggled back into the saddle.

"Did you have to hit me?" he asked.

167

Avarran looked abashed. "My apologies, sire, but I had to get you down."

Donari laughed away the tension. "Effective! What happened up ahead?"

Avarran's relieved smile fell to a frown.

"Something I never expected on this track. A small party, smaller than our own. We seem to have surprised each other."

"Losses?"

"One of our outriders took a sword point in the arm. He should be fine."

"Theirs?"

"Two dead. The rest fled back up the path when more of us came up. I've got a few out after them. I'd say they can't be more than a handful."

"Whose?"

"They wore Collum badges, sire."

The way ahead cleared, and Donari moved up to the scene of the action. Two bodies lay across the path with Gaspire's device on their coat sleeves. One of Donari's troopers held a horse captured in the fight. Donari looked at the hindquater closely.

"Well," he said, straightening up after recognizing the brand. "I would rather have captured one of the riders alive, but I guess we will have to content ourselves with the return of one of the mounts Gaspire purloined."

Inwardly, Donari took himself to task as his men laughed at the jest.

"This bunch was using this track for the same purpose, sire," Avarran explained. "We have been caught watching each other. And yet they come late to the party."

He looked again at the bodies and agreed with Avarran's assessment. This group had been lightly armed. Small shields. No spears. No sign of archers.

"This group was out for information," he agreed. "Gaspire is not ready yet, but neither are we." He looked back at his assembled escort, and saw the youth, the effect of Avarran's training, and the quality gear. "But perhaps," he finished, pitching his voice to carry. "Perhaps we are a bit more ready, if not to attack, at least to defend."

He gestured at the bodies. "Leave a squad to bury these unfortunates. Will we find your men still at their posts?"

Avarran moved up alongside as Donari urged his mount into motion. "To get to our post above the river we will have to leave this track and bear south. These men would have had to come across the northern slopes about the road. Rough country."

"I see this as a sign, my friend. It is time we acted with more intention."

"What are your wishes, sire?"

"Send a man back along this track with word to raise the companies."

"All of them?"

Donari considered. If he missed his guess, then he could lose more than men.

"No, just enough to fortify a camp at the base of the ridge where the King's Road comes down to the river villages. I want men up that road."

"I will see to it, my lord."

"Yes, you will, because I want you in command there."

Avarran rode, silent, for a pace, a second, a third before responding.

"But I won't be able to stop what Gaspire will surely bring south with five hundred men, sire."

Donari turned in the saddle. "You've done miracles since Lyranden, my friend, but I won't require one this time. Just slow them enough so I can bring up the rest. If your men don't catch up with the survivors of this little affair, word will reach Gaspire. Whatever his state of preparation, this will make him think about time."

"Perhaps he will make a mistake."

Donari smiled and urged his mount to more speed. "We can hope, Avarran, we can hope."

Avarran matched his pace. "Better, sire, I will see to it we fight."

And more men die, but fewer, perhaps, than otherwise.

Donari kept the disturbing thought to himself. Watching Avarran's sturdy features relax into concentration, Donari once again marveled at his good fortune in having the services of men such as Jason Avarran and Devyn Ambrose.

I could die with such men, but I would rather rule with them.

An hour later Avarran's scouts led them off the track to follow a shallow water course south. There had been no further sightings of the northern survivors. Another hour saw them to Avarran's westernmost observation post. From its vantage Donari could see the line of the King's Road snaking up and around slopes, disappearing behind a great, rocky shoulder on its way to the pass.

Nothing moved along its length as far as he could see. And yet the day's events had shown him otherwise. There was movement there and more to come.

169

Donari thought of Devyn and Talyior now two weeks into their mission. They had agreed on a month for them to assess what they could and return with news.

Come soon, Devyn. Get me word, soonest. Let Gaspire take counsel of his fears, let the Prelate's snivels infect his plans. Let him come now and have done.

He took a last look at the road, left the observation post and went downslope to build a camp whose foundation held more hope than substance.

Chapter 18: Spies

A week's sailing with a fair wind brought Devyn and Talyior to a sheltered beach at the mouth of the river Eloe. The Eloe drained the north, running across the midsection of the northern fiefs, creating an interior border separating Trenar, Avedar and Hallar from the three lands to the south. They sailed upstream with the tide under cover of darkness and sidled close enough to the southern banks to swim their mounts to shore. To the north, great, terraced bluffs loomed as deeper shadows, but the southern shore held level for many leagues, providing room for a roadway that ran along the banks heading for Sanreal, the river port town of Sor-reel.

Dawn filled the sky behind them as they trotted along. They passed a number of groups marching purposely, answering Gaspire's call for men. Activity on the river mimicked the road as vessels worked upstream in the slack water. On the whole, Devyn found all the alacrity disturbing. What disturbed him even more was hearing references to *the southern woman and her baby* in some of the talk along the road. He checked Talyior's reaction, but his friend seemed unchanged, concentrating on trying to play his guitar when they slowed to walk their horses around congested spots. Perhaps he missed the references, but Devyn decided to spare him the information. Demona was part of their peril but only as a vessel; their real task concerned Gaspire.

When the road neared Sanreal, he spurred ahead and took a path that branched away from the river. The way climbed out of the river valley to run along a rise that overlooked the town. They walked their mounts side by side for awhile to rest them. Below, the day grew bright and warm and filled with movement.

"What we heard in the road talk was true it seems," Devyn said. "I expected something, but not to this extent."

Talyior took a swallow from his water bottle, and handed it to Devyn before replying.

"So you said on our way north. But I gather things a bit differently, perhaps. None of what we have seen has been heading for the coast. I see nothing large on the river. No galleys, friend."

"True, it is obvious that Gaspire will strike over the hills. In that, Donari has read it right."

"Still, I estimate we passed several hundred on the road, and those small craft seemed fully manned and laden."

171

"He's gathering men and material."

"Where?"

Devyn took a swig from the bottle, stared at the river and the traffic threading the road, and nodded as though making up his mind.

"He won't use the sea. He needs a road," he responded, swinging up into the saddle. "All of that is heading to Lomillar."

Talyior took back the bottle, secured it in his saddle bag, and mounted in turn.

"And I suppose that is where we must go, too?"

Devyn smiled at the implied humor.

"I admit, our track record in cities is not very good," he said, urging his horse forward. "But I think Donari will need more than speculation. I'd thought to go slowly, playing and listening, but I don't think we have the time."

"No tavern games?"

"Not this time. We skip whatever charms Sanreal might have."

"A longer road, no music and no beer. Fun."

Devyn laughed, kicking his horse to more speed, gesturing at the scene below.

"Perhaps we will get both music and beer in Lomillar. Let's beat whatever *that* is to the city. First pint on me, deal?"

"Done!"

They rode off, keeping to the low side of the bluff shielding them from the town below. Above them the sun beat down with summer intensity. Dust rose behind them. They pushed a little further south, away from the river line, in search of more unsettled open ground. Within a few leagues the region passed into scrub land that allowed them free reign to ride without fear of challenge.

They kept going well after sundown although a moonless night forced them to pick their way carefully. For the next two days they paralleled the river, keeping the bluffs just in sight on their right. They saw no one; the lands about empty of even the cattle herds that represented Sor-reel's wealth. The western reaches of the fief grew more broken as they climbed towards the highlands of Collum; the border defined by the King's Way, the main north south road from Lomillar to Pevana. Devyn turned back toward the river before they reached that line, following a small, erosional valley that cut up along the shoulder of a hill whose brother heights formed a ridge with scattered groups of trees on the southern slopes that hinted at water. The sun had begun its last westward plunge when they crested the rise to find themselves gazing once again at the river below, winding its course westward between raised banks. Off to the right, still some leagues distant, the massed buildings of Lomillar, chief city of Perspa, spread out along the flats of a wide shelf formed by the confluence of three streams that flowed together to give the Eloe its mighty volume.

An impressive wall, running from east to west and stepping up the terraces to the flatter land above encircled most of the city's mass. But buildings and clustered dwellings seeped down stream along both banks as though life itself had burst through Lomillar's gates to find new boundaries. Devyn thought the place huge, shapeless, and unlovely. It lacked Pevana's red tiles and spires. And yet even his untutored eye could see it was uniquely placed to control commerce and communication for the region. All roads from Trenar, Collum and Avedar converged outside Lomillar's walls. Though sixty miles from the sea, the city still functioned as a port of power and prominence.

"It's big," Talyior grunted. "Somehow, I didn't expect this. It's bigger than Pevana and Desopolis put together."

"It's big," Devyn agreed, "big enough to lose ourselves in, perhaps. To get what we want we might have to."

"I daresay. Look there," Talyior pointed. "The river road swings out away from the banks before the bridge. That's for us, if you still think we need to go in."

Devyn took in the view. The river track bent towards their vantage to avoid a rocky outcropping that thrust up from the southern banks to pinch the channel. Once around that basaltic disturbance it returned to course the river, heading for a causeway several leagues distant. A steady line of wagons moved along that stretch of the road. He followed the line to where it ended at a cross-roads at the feet of a large, many arched bridge connecting the city to the southern shore. From that bridge the King's Road began, a straight, wide way that climbed up from the valley to the rolling lands beyond.

And along those first leagues Devyn saw the cook fires of several camps. And outside of those camps, an army trained.

Despite the heat, the sight gave Devyn a chill.

"That's quite a few more than what Lyvia and I faced at Desopolis," Talyior muttered.

"And almost as many as came to the field at Lyranden Bridge," Devyn whispered. He coughed and spat, the road dust as bitter as the image spread out below. "Such numbers. Avarran and Donari suspected, but they had questions about the quality."

"And to find out we need to down there."

"If you want that pint I owe you, yes."

Talyior coughed and spat in turn. "Might need two."

173

Devyn chuckled sardonically. "Still glad you came along?"

Talyior gave him a look that bordered on disgust.

"That doesn't deserve an answer. I've never been a spy before." He checked the sun's position. "Shall we make for the bridge today?"

Devyn considered the distance. There would likely be guards at the bridge and at the gates into the city.

"In the morning, I think," he responded finally. "More traffic might make it easier to cross and skulk around. Doubtless we might find a use for our instruments as cover."

They retraced their track to where a few trees grew in a dell framed by jumbled, piled stones. By the time they unburdened and staked their mounts it was nearly dark, and they risked a small fire to make a warm meal; their first since leaving Talyior's ship.

They ate and took their ease, discussing how they might handle what they met in Lomillar, reliving old memories of the duels they used to conduct in their former life. They took turns practicing some of the tales they might need; the north favored stories about Borimon and Tolimon rather than Renia. Eventually, their talk faded to companionable silence as the threads of their friendship knit themselves back together.

They let the fire fall to embers as the night sky birthed stars. Talyior took up his guitar and played, idly fingering chords, teasing a wordless rhythm from them with small variations in the sequence. Devyn listened, half aware as he tapped a stick in time. And then words came, and he sang softly:

And on and on it went apace.
Over the hills like immortals they contested,
Trading blow for blow like lovers their kisses.
Blood flowed in a crimson shower
And the death rose flower
Spread its petals to accept the grace.
And the end came at last as a whisper
As the blade slipped through
With a sharp, final truth
To dispel the royal lie,
Leaving the one cousin
Carrion
And the other
King...

Devyn's words trailed away, and Talyior stilled his strings.

"Where did that come from?" he asked.

Devyn broke the stick, tossed it on the coals and lay back.

"I'm not sure," he said. "The sight of Lomillar got me thinking about Roderran and Donari, I suppose."

Talyior gave the strings a final strum.

"They fit," he said, shuffling the instrument back into its leather covering. "Dark, though."

"Maybe later, if we are lucky, we might find some words less dark that also fit," Devyn sighed. "But those are all I have for now."

Talyior grunted as he shifted into his blankets.

"Something to look forward to, but I wouldn't advise using them in Lomillar."

They rose well before dawn and used the darkness to make their way down toward the river track. They fell in behind a group of wagons and followed them the rest of the way. No one questioned them. They rode behind like an escort as the mass trundled over the bridge. The Eloe's water gurgled and swirled against the foundations like a riddle. Devyn watched patterns form and disperse, seeing in the movement something akin to the task he and Talyior faced. They had to parse answers to half-formed questions and then return to the stream of life with the knowledge.

They left the bridge, traversed the short, raised causeway that ended at a wide square before the city gates. Guards waved the wagons onward. They followed. Again, no one questioned their presence. A short way inside the gates they stopped before an inn as the line of wagons turned off the main way to take a street that followed the line of the wall.

They dismounted. Devyn handed his reins to Talyior before going in to inquire about a room.

"That was easy enough," Talyior said, low voiced.

"Perhaps too easy," Devyn agreed. He glanced up and down the street. The place bustled like a hive. "Easy to get in, but getting out again might be another matter. I'll be back in a minute."

Chapter 19: False Interlude of Pleasure and Pain

An aching back, a kicking baby, and the fetid palace air drove Demona from her chambers, down the hall to Gaspire's sitting rooms where she burst through the double doors with a disgusted expression to interrupt what she instantly assumed was a planning meeting. Helms and swords lay piled on a table near the wall, and a group of men flanked Gaspire while Lord Tareegan took his ease in a chair off to one side. Gaspire looked up at the disturbance, a dark look forming behind his beard, but he must have noticed the storm approaching because he wisely held his tongue.

Demona flared to a stop next to Tareegan's chair, ignoring the older man's wheezy chuckle and focused her attention on Gaspire. The men around him shifted as if trying to avoid the fray about to commence. Gaspire leaned forward on his hands.

"Lady Demona," he said with forced control. "To what do we owe this, pleasant, intrusion?" His eyes narrowed pointedly, but Demona had stormed that wall already.

"I want out of this stuffy pile of bricks," she responded baldly. "I'm sick of Tellis and these whispering walls. The gardens here are boring," she gestured to the maps and piles of parchment, "and I'm tired of closed doors. Nothing moves in this city but that carries a sword. All I hear from the battlements are the sounds of hammers on anvils."

Gaspire's brows came together in consternation, and he pointed meaningfully at her rounded belly. "All you complain of is happening on behalf of your child," he growled. "And we are in the final days before marching."

Demona did not back down. She leaned on her hands in turn, bringing her face closer to Gaspire's over the table.

"I don't want to march," she hissed. "I just want to breathe."

For a moment they glared at each other. The other men in the room shifted as the silence grew uncomfortable. Finally, Gaspire broke and settled back into his chair with an exasperated sigh.

"Demona," he said, thinly, warningly, "You have a strange sense of timing."

"My lord, no one else in this room knows just how good my sense of timing really is. I choose my time, sir, and today I want a ride out in the country. I want some wild flowers, a basket from the kitchens and a carriage with decent springs."

176

"You burst in here, interrupt me in council, for a distraction?"

"As you so rightly said," Demona returned tartly, "All of this is done on my behalf. Right now I want an outing. It's hot. This city smells like manure and ashes. I require an afternoon's pleasure. See to it."

Gaspire frowned. "Hallan," he said bleakly, gesturing toward a young, blond-haired officer who stepped forward.

"Since you are but newly come to Lomillar, somewhat tardy, sir, in truth, let you see to Lady Demona's needs today."

Hallan came to stand next Demona, and she appraised him quickly, taking in his fair-faced youth and comely bearing, and yet as he bowed respectfully to her she could not help but notice the pinched look around the edges of his eyes when his briefly met hers. He turned to address Gaspire.

"My Lord," he said in a voice low with suppressed emotion, "I beg leave from such a delightful task. I have my men to look after."

"Your men will be well bestowed with your cousin, Kenton Reece, here." Gaspire gestured to the man on his right, who looked darkly at Demona. She remembered him from the council chamber. Beside her, young Hallan seemed to stiffen as though suppressing anger. He took breath to speak, but Gaspire forestalled him.

"Not a word, sir. I dispose you as I need. See to the Lady's pleasure."

Hallan stepped back and took her hand formally. "An honor, Lady Anargi," he whispered. The calluses on his sword hand rasped slightly against her skin.

"I'll let you gentlemen finish your squabble," she said, turning to leave. She wanted fresh air and entertainment, and young Hallan, with his sweet face and unspoken mystery, looked capable of providing both.

The carriage took them out the northern gate of Lomillar and off on a side track that followed a small stream back into the hills. As Demona hoped, the air was much cleaner, the views much more pleasing, but the lurching progress did nothing to ease the pain in her lower back. She ordered a halt when they crested a rise that revealed the city, the river reach and southern lands spread out below them. Tellis and the other maiden who had accompanied them lay out the sweets and fruit from the basket on blankets they placed beneath a large, sentinel oak tree perched on the summit.

Demona kicked off her shoes and walked about on the grass, reveling in the tingly prickling on the soles of her feet. She paused on the edge of the oak's canopy just inside its shade. Below, Lomillar buzzed with activity. There were camps along the road above the river bluffs. Long lines of wagons snaked toward the gates from several directions. The great bridge was a living thing, choked with folk coming and going. There was a time when she would have made no sense of the scene, but her months with Gaspire tutored her eye, and she now saw purpose in all that movement.

She watched avidly for a few moments, gently caressing her belly. *All for you, child, all for you.*

As if in response to her thought, the baby gave a sharp kick. Demona stifled a gasp and lowered herself to the ground to take the weight off her back. Behind her, Tellis and the other maid continued their tittering preparations for lunch. Demona breathed slowly through persed lips as the pain eased and settled back in it accustomed place in a spot just above her left hip. One breath, another, and the moment passed. She felt the rhythm of heavy footsteps approach. Hallan, helmless and swordless, sat down next to her. The slight breeze teased his hair as he shared her view.

"An impressive view," he said, breaking the silence.

"I'd use a different term."

"I quite understand, given the smells we rode through to get out here."

The humor in his tone captured Demona's attention. She scrutinized his profile, seeing again the pinched crease about his eye, recalled the touch of his hand in hers, and yet she marveled at how that same callused hand now took up a blade of grass and gently smoothed its length.

This one is different.

"I suppose I miss Pevana's sea tang," she said diffidently. "You are from Hallar, you must know what I mean."

Hallan bent his head, intent on his blade of grass or just shy, Demona was not certain, but when he spoke again, there was a hint of Hallar's coastal hills in his voice.

"I do, lady. My father's favorite manor overlooks the bay above Hallar port. I grew up with the sea breeze. There are gulls here, but far inland for my tastes. This place smells more like pigs than anything else."

Demona snorted. "Oh, I quite agree! My rooms in the palace are nice enough, but when the wind gets up, things turn ripe."

"The stock yards are full, lady, preparations."

"I never new *preparations* could stink so bad."

178

Hallan looked at her then, his smile slight, his eyes still a little guarded, distant.

"You have seen war, lady—"

"And mud and blood, coming and going. I much prefer preparations that include perfume and combs, thank you."

Hallan's smile turned genuine, and Demona decided she liked his face. Despite his caution, there was something earnest about him that reminded her of Talyior. Demona could not remember ever having a friend. She wondered if the young man smiling at her might be the first.

"I'm sorry," she said. "You must forgive a pregnant woman her moods. I know I am poor company." She pointed down at the city. "All of that involves me, in fact I'm paying for some of it, but the pattern still eludes me."

The smile deepened on Hallan's face as he explained the scene below.

"Those lines of rolling stock, there, and there," he said, pointing right and left. "Bring foodstuffs. The one on the right brings grain from the storehouses in Avedar. My company passed them yesterday on our way here from Hallar. The one on the left comes from the highlands of Trenar with what could be gleaned from the mess up there." He grunted appreciation. "Those camps across the river are nearly full. Gaspire has been busy."

Demona detected the change in his tone.

"You don't sound pleased. Is it because you are forced to guard a silly woman such as myself and those two gossips back there rather than be part of it?"

He looked at her. His smile faded to caution.

"In truth, mistress, I am not sure how I feel or if I should feel at all."

"What do you mean?"

Hallan held up the blade of grass and released it to the breeze. It fluttered to the ground several feet away.

"I am my father's last remaining son," he answered quietly. "My brother died at Lyranden Bridge, defending the king, whose child now kicks in your womb."

"And you were among those who marched back."

"That was a bitter road, lady."

"Then you've no cause to love Donari."

Hallan frowned, stared hard at the city below.

"You are partly right, lady," he said. "Gaspire gives my command to my cousin, and ties me to your carriage for the day. Forgive me," he

179

smiled ruefully, "for I am unused to such pleasant duty. I mean no offense. You bear the son of my king. That should be paramount for me."

"But it isn't." Demona found his honesty strangely endearing. She looked at him with new appreciation.

Yes, he's too honest, sadly, like Talyior.

And again memories bubbled of passionate words, a young fool and his hopes, innocence in a world bounded by deceit and betrayal. Understanding about the world she inhabited came clear to Demona with a pain equal to the taxing throb created by her troubled pregnancy. It was full of individual visions, personal loyalties that only partially attuned themselves to wider policies and definitions of honor.

This is a good man.

And that good man now turned to her, his expression frank and open for the first time.

"I have a duty to my father, a duty to your child, another to my men and others among my people who will march with Gaspire to more battle and death. Gaspire does not trust me. He trusts my brutish cousin more. That much is obvious. You heard him. And yet I was left behind to save what I could from the wreck of Lyranden Bridge. What Gaspire says and what I saw, what I experienced, are not necessarily the same thing."

"And you think that is too much to risk for an unborn child?"

"I confess I do not know, lady, but I would defend your child's right to live. Gaspire hopes to make him a king, but what sort of king? I've seen Roderran. I met Donari in the fields before Pevana."

Demona put a hand, gently, on his forearm. "I loved Roderran, Hallan, however brief our time together. He wanted this child. I have done what I had to do to preserve this life. I have," she paused, "different memories of Donari Avedun."

"These are confused times, mistress, agreed, and I think the difference is between what one hears and what one sees."

"And what have you seen?"

He stared at her, his face awash in emotion.

"I've seen too many men laid to rest in the pits designed for their destruction to trust blindly any more," he said, his eyes intent, focused on hers. "In what do you trust, lady?"

Demona broke contact and looked again at the scene below.

"In the end, just myself."

The wind shifted, and Demona took in the taints from the stock yards. The sun went behind a cloud. The baby kicked and shifted, and a throbbing pain began in the small of her back that intensified when she tried to rise. She managed to get back to the carriage, but spurned the lunch Tellis offered.

"Hallan," she gasped, settling back into the carriage. "Take me back, now, something is wrong."

But it took time to harness the horses, and by the time they started back, the pain pulsed from Demona's back to her extremities. The ride back was a lurching, jarring horror that reduced Demona to a mewling lump. Tellis had to hold her down to keep her from thrashing about on the seat.

"Hallan!" Tellis cried. "Lady Demona needs something for this pain. There is an apothecary shop just inside the gate. We must stop!"

But all of that came to Demona as through a closed door, muted, distant. Pain formed the limit of her world. Her vision narrowed. The baby kicked. Hard. Again. Demona's vision narrowed. Narrowed. A pinpoint. Nothing.

Chapter 20: Power's Price

Eleni rode easily alongside Donari as they followed the last of wagons bearing the early season grape culls. Along the river, the heats of summer still lingered, but in rows higher up on the slopes, the night chill set enough of the sugar to take some to the presses. As a distraction from daily cares, Eleni and Donari had ridden out to help with the harvest. They worked alongside despite the fact that, for want of men, women comprised most of the work crews. Donari put Pevana's men in the field, but the requirements of life still held sway. And yet, as the wains carried the harvest to the vats for pressing, more than a few folk wondered aloud whether they would still be alive to test the tenor of the wine in a year.

Donari and Eleni's presence among the workers helped to reassure all of them. His order for five hundred to attend Avarran's needs caused murmers and stern faces. The order for two hundred more to haunt the hills about the observation posts produced noticeable strain, and yet the men marched with good will; a test of the soundness of his small army. He saw more of the same in the sounds and faces of those he worked beside, cheerfully irreverent in the face of royalty. Dirt and sweat served as great levelers. He and Eleni returned in far greater spirits than they left in the morning.

"Renia grant us freedom from the Gaspires and Byrnards of the world," Donari sighed, slipping up to his neck in the tub Cryso had thoughtfully procured for them. "I could be happy. Our people deserve peace."

Eleni joined him and ran a leg over his, sending a different kind of contentment surging through him.

"You will. *We* will. I can feel it."

Donari kissed her forehead through her damp hair. The mix of scented water and soap worked even more magic on him than her touch.

"I've sent men from their families on a hunch. Hardly fair when I get to soak here with you."

"Your people will not begrudge you, Donari, you know that. They all know what we face."

Donari sighed again, settled deeper into the water, drew her into him closer and lay his head back against the tub's rim.

"They still deserve better, certainty at least. We harvest and train, but nothing seems clear."

"But you are sure Gaspire will come."

Donari stroked her arm in agreement. "Oh, yes," he murmured. "All signs point to something soon. I've staked my crown on it. Avarran is in camp across the road. And your little adventure with Casan will likely prompt even more alacrity."

He felt her chuckle against his shoulder.

"About that," he continued. "Couldn't you at least wait until you are actually queen before trying to act like one, please?"

Eleni sniggered and splashed him, the spray putting out several of the candles that burned on a stand next the tub.

"But it was so much fun."

"I'm sure, but until we settle with Gaspire, I want you to steer clear of Casan."

Eleni took up a sponge and sat up. She squeezed the sponge over her chest, sluicing away soap bubbles, tempting him.

"I'm sorry, but I wanted him to see that he's put his faith in the wrong strumpet."

Donari gently caressed her left breast. "I'm sure you made your point, my dear." Then he took the sponge from her, dunked it in the water and squeezed it abruptly over her head. "But no more taunting cranky, old men! Practice those wiles on me from now on."

She blew away the water and swung her leg over to straddle him, displacing more water from the tub.

"With pleasure, sire," she said, kissing first his forehead then his lips now wet with the run-off from her hair.

Donari let their friction leach away his consternation. Though beset by enemies before and behind, a victim of his own tolerance, he was still king. He had to trust his choices and deal with it.

He let Eleni tease him to interest. Afterwards, he, too, dreamed of twins. In the back of his mind, however, a thought ran in a constant loop: if they were to see a spring of life and love, they would have to survive the wars of autumn.

Casan ached in many places. Grown increasingly, maddeningly feeble since his return from the southern failure, he fretted over his physical decay like never before. For years he resisted degeneration by adopting a mask of vitality while working on his and Roderran's schemes. His thinning hair and wizened features served a purpose then. They kept folk from taking him too seriously as he worked them for his purposes.

But then the failures of last summer happened, followed by the debacles of spring, and he had been forced to accept the notion that Donari and others could see through his wiles.

The knowledge galled him then, and continued to gall and enervate after the great changes since Lyranden Bridge. Donari checked him at every pass, and now even the bitch who shared Donari's bed dared taunt him with her security and flaunt her profligate sex in his face.

As he shuffled down the hall through the arch of the bell tower to attend rites in the church, he raged against his growing infirmity. He waited while attendants placed cushions in place for his knees before allowing others to help lower him down to the supplicant's position for the day's expected moments of prayer.

And even here he found himself strangely bicameral, for he knew to a fine degree just how fake were the rights he followed so assiduously. He and Roderran thought them up between the two of them over a summer's worth of whoring, drinking and plotting in the year of the old king's death. At the time, Casan liked the intriguing possibility of foisting a faith on a plaint populace as a means to power. And yet here, now, nearing the final analysis as it were, he found himself surprised at his own success.

People actually believed.

He settled himself in the uncomfortable position for prayers and experienced a kind of apotheosis: to come to the end of a tumultuous life and realize that, ultimately, one was a product of one's own machinations.

Faith is malleable, even for me.

He spent a reasonable amount of time in holy contemplation. Doubtless some in the church assumed he meditated and prayed through a set regimen, but the truth was he finished his musings early and only waited for the pain in his knees and back to motivate him to try and rise.

That was one mistake we made, Roderran, all those years ago. We should have allowed for prayers to be said lying down.

He distracted himself from the pain by reviewing the information he received that morning from Gaspire. Its coded contents implied an early move, risking everything on an early battle, and given the Caralon bitch's recent insult, Casan welcomed the news. He took stock of the options left him. He might have but one more chance to cause chaos.

He took a deep breath, inhaling the taint of the incense and took stock of his options. Donari, all but unassailable despite all of Casan's best efforts, remained alive, crowned and loved. Even the woman eluded him, and yet he knew she still presented the best opportunity. As Donari's announced betrothed, she still retained her original status as his secretary, spending long hours working on her records and accounts according to the young serving maid, Anlise.

He looked over his left shoulder, spied her kneeling in her usual place and motioned for his aide to help him to his feet. He had to pause to let the blood return to his extremities before shuffling back down the aisle, stopping beside her pew. He motioned for her to slide in further and sat down next to her.

"How nice to see you again, child, pray continue your prayers."

The girl gave him a quick, wide-eyed look before doing so. She finished her devotions in a rapid whisper, and then settled back expectantly.

"How goes your service in the palace?" he inquired serenely.

"Well enough, my lord," she whispered, "but none of the others are believers. I hear their whispers at my back."

"How unfortunate," Casan soothed. "But we must forgive them for their ignorance. Perhaps in time they will see wisdom."

"I pray for it," she said, carefully. "I just wish others would see the way."

"Well, child, we will have to show them with our conviction. That is how we will lead them to the truth."

"Yes, my lord."

Casan leaned in conspiratorially. "Truth is important, isn't it, Anlise? As is trust. So, how do you feel about all those whispers, eh?"

The girls eyes flared as if someone had put a spark to a torch.

"I always smile," she said proudly, "to all of them. Cryso, Cook, even the king. None of them think twice about me, especially Mistress Caralon. I looked after her last spring before the army marched. I pitied her, then, but she takes on airs now."

"And so I assume you don't much like service in the palace?" Casan inquired.

"I serve Mistress Eleni because I am told to, my Lord Prelate. I stomach the work though it grates bending to one who just months previous made her living sewing dresses for the likes of me and my sisters!" She gasped, hearing the anger in her own voice and perhaps fearing she had gone too far.

"I'm sorry, my lord," she whispered, hanging her head. "I try for humility, but I am a poor vessel."

"Never think that, child. As you believe, so you are fit."

She preened at that.

"But she is our king's intended," Casan tested.

"Our king does not believe. She has bewitched him!"

"And would you save him from this witch?"

"If I could, I would do anything."

Casan reached into his vestments and pulled out something wrapped in fine cloth. As he lay it down on the bench beside the girl part of the cloth slipped away to reveal a dagger blade.

"The Lady Eleni left this when she came to visit," he said pointedly. "Would you care to return it for me?"

He smiled at the flash in her eyes as she took up the package.

Faith is so biddable.

He walked unaided back to his offices in the library, buoyed by better spirits and the scent of the incense perpetually burning.

Incense works well enough, but I prefer a different kind of smoke.

Eleni finished proofing a last page and handed it to Drue to dry and add to the sheaf of reports destined for the next council meeting. She rubbed weariness from her eyes as she left her seat to go check the night from her window.

"That should be enough for tonight, Drue, I'm sure you've had enough."

"I could do a bit more, lady Eleni." His tired eyes gave the lie to his attempt.

"Thank you, but no. You've been a hero all this week since the king left. I don't know how I could have finished these without your help."

Donari had ridden out a week removed from her confrontation with Casan to escort supplies to Avarran's men. Meetings with members of the council and wedding arrangements taxed Eleni's time. Drue truly had been Renia sent.

"I enjoy this work, lady," the boy insisted. "And thank you for letting me read your history. I especially like the stories from, master Edri." He paused. "You know, I went to his grave that night looking for you when you went to your old house."

"Did you? And what did you think?"

"It was nice. There was a little girl there, putting flowers by the stone. I remember that fire, lady. Much was lost."

"Much more than just Edri's stories, Drue. That is why I write as I do, to preserve them for us."

"Really? The little girl said the same thing. She knows our Devyn, too."

"Pevana is a closer place than we think, Drue. That is why it is so special."

"But we are in trouble."

Eleni sighed, drawn to the young man's innocence and curiosity.

"Yes, we face troubles. My history and the king's efforts are all part of it, the young and the old, rich and the poor, you, me, Devyn; we are all engaged alike."

"Connected."

"Exactly."

Drue ran a finger over the topmost page on the pile. "All this is important, then," he mused. "What the girl, Tasia, said makes more sense now."

"What did she say?"

"She said Kembril needs more than flowers on his grave. He needed shade."

The reference to the Tree brought old emotions back. She looked with new eyes at the child next to her. He and the ubiquitous Tasia were Pevana's future.

"Drue, you surprise me," she said, ruffling his hair. "And this Tasia sounds like a spark."

"I guess. Anlise came up, said something cross, and sneered at the flowers. Tasia ran off. Lady, could I take some flowers from your garden down sometime? If we are all connected---"

"Then perhaps the palace should do its part. That is an excellent idea, Drue. Take some down in the morning."

"Thank you, mistress, I will. I think Edri was more important than people realize. I think stories are important. My favorites are the ones about Minuet."

"I agree with you Drue. And when we get through these troubled days, you and I will make sure to record all the stories. Perhaps when Devyn Ambrose returns he will grace us with some of his own. He was Edri's special student, you know. He is the one for the old myths."

"He has been gone a long time."

"Since when does three weeks mean a long time?"

"I'd gotten used to seeing him since the king returned. He talked to me. I like him."

"He is dear to me and the king, as well. He went on a journey for us, an important task. I suspect we will hear something soon."

Drue rose, pushed in the chairs and tidied the table.

"You will need some fresh ink tomorrow, lady Eleni. Should I see to it now?"

"No, thank you. Go get some, no, wait." A flare of light as from flames appeared in the city below. Eleni started to remark then froze as another fire surged upward over near the city's land gate. Then a third, off to the left near the harbor warehouses.

No accident.

"What is it, lady?"

187

"Drue, I need you to find Cryso and tell him there is fire in the city. Then get to the captain of the guard and tell I give him permission to go out and help. When you've seen them out the gate, come back to me."

The boy dashed off, his footsteps fading even as alarm shouts from the city began filtering through the glass. She watched the flames rise, fretful and anxious to out and doing something, but Donari had been adamant she stay in the palace. Memories whispered of that earlier fire, the soot, the effort, the rain after, and then Donari. But Jaryd Corvale now moldered in southern dirt. Donari was gone. She would have to do what she could on her own. Despite the late summer heat, she felt a chill form in the small of her back.

Anlise came in, all fuss and solicitation with a tray. "My lady, Cryso sent me to look after you. He told me to not let you leave. I'm sorry, but he insisted. I took the liberty of getting you some tea." She placed the tray on Eleni's writing table and joined her at the window.

"Terrible," she commented. "Those poor people. Look at how the fire is spreading."

For some reason, the last thing Eleni wanted was more time with Anlise given the crisis developing below. "Thank you for the tea, Anlise, but I won't require looking after. I'll be fine. I'll have a message for Donari later. If Drue returns, send him to me, please."

Something flared behind the girl's normally placid look, quickly blinked away.

"At least let me pour you a cup and turn down your bed for you. I'll only be a minute."

"That will be fine, thank you." Eleni turned away to survey the lurid scene below. The blaze near the land gate had faded, but the one adjacent to the harbor showed signs of growing. She prayed for the people, her people. She felt less than useless. She went back in to wait for word and set about composing a note to Donari. He would have to know; it might bring him back earlier. A small mercy in the face of such suffering.

A tea cup steamed next her ink well. She took a sip, absently, not thinking about the incongruity of hot tea on a summer night full of flames. She dipped her pen and began writing. By the time she finished her first sentence she felt the tingling in her lips. A moment later her fingers struggled to hold on to the pen. Alarm flashed to her brain even as she felt her toes tingle and grow numb. She looked up and caught a glimpse of her face in the mirror that hung on the wall above her desk. Even in the half-light she could see the slackness of her jaw. Panic rose inside her, but her face remained an impassive, sagging mask. She tried to form words but managed only a half-slurred moan.

Her body felt heavy, but she could breathe. Her extremities and muscles numbed and grew useless, and her heart raced out of fear. A face loomed above, sneering and half-bathed in the dancing light.

Anlise.

"Yes, my lady," Anlise whispered, waving a dagger. "Poison, but don't worry; it won't kill you. The Lord Prelate wanted you to feel the point of your own blade. A nice symmetry, I think.

"You will find talking difficult for awhile. I gave you just enough to take away your limbs and your voice. In the end, I think you will get the point," and she giggled and brandished the blade. "Quite funny, don't you agree?" She moved to Eleni's other side and bent close to whisper in her ear. "He wanted me to tell you how foolish you have been, thinking yourself secure in Donari's shadow, trusting in his apparent victories. You cannot escape the judgment of heaven. No matter how brazen your behavior, accounts will be squared."

Eleni groaned.

"Still trying to talk? Patience, my lady. My turn, this time."

Tears formed in Eleni's eyes unbidden and began to flow down her cheeks as she took in the enormity of the moment. All her hopes, fears, everything hung in the balance as Anlise, Casan's fanatic tool, prattled on.

"You never asked much about my life, my lady," the maid went on. She ran the blade down Eleni's cheek, under her chin and along her heaving breasts. "Did you know my family specializes in growing medicinal herbs? No? Of course not. Why question the servants about anything, right?" She paused, frowning. "I used some of them to help you recover from your despair when your husband died. I was here then. I watched over you. Small thanks for that, eh? You leave, come back with my lord, and my family sells me to service for the honor of it all. I should have poisoned all of them before this, but maybe now I won't have to. The Prelate assures me Heaven's Grace will see to it in the coming days."

All the little ticks, all those previous thoughts dismissed came flooding back, and Eleni's tears thickened in rage and remorse.

Oh, Donari, love, I'm so sorry.

"Oddly enough," continued Anlise. "Your tears are the best way to flush the effects out of your body. You can actually still swallow, you know. Water would save you, actually, good, cool, clean water. Oh, I have some here. Imagine that." She disappeared from view for a moment, and Eleni heard the sound of liquid being poured into a cup. Anlise reappeared and held the vessel to Eleni's lips and dribbled a small measure into her mouth. Eleni's tongue worked, and she managed to swallow some and felt a lessening of the numbness around her lips and jaw.

Anlise brushed the blade along Eleni's right cheek again. "You have such beautiful skin. Should I slice some of it off and send it to Donari in a letter? The Annals of the King's Theology have a word for the likes of you and him: *presumptive sinners.* He, so bold and irreverent, did not see that heaven keeps watch. My Lord Prelate said so when I last talked to him. And you, did you know you actually sewed a dress for my older sister? Nice work for a common seamstress. And here you are, spreading your legs for our dear king, adding sin upon sin in your assumption of quality. And I get to do your hair and light your candles and refill your stupid ink-pot and make myself available at all hours of the night to ease your *trying* labors." She leaned in close. "And you never once asked me how I felt about it. No one ever asked me what I felt about anything; not my parents, not Cryso, no one. I was to serve for honor, but what about me? What about what I want? What if I wanted to be taken care of? No one cared to ask. Now they will have to, once I take care of you."

She dribbled some more water into Eleni's mouth. "You should be able to speak soon," she whispered. "Though shouting will be out of the question. I want to hear you beg before I stick you. Make a poem out of that tid-bit why don't you?"

Eleni swallowed more easily this time. She tested her tongue against her teeth.

"Anlise, this is madness," she croaked.

"By whose definition? Yours? Donari's? Your failed Old Ways Goddess's?"

"By all that is reasonable."

"Reasons. I have had enough of reasons."

"But you are helping evil flourish, Anlise. Donari wants peace."

"So does every thief when he gets caught in the act."

"You don't know what you are doing."

"Wrong. I knew exactly how much powder to put in your tea. I've cut a few herbs in my time, so blades like this one and I are familiar. The Prelate has shown me how I may serve, so I think I can put this where it counts. With you dead, Donari is doomed."

"Anlise, Donari is our best hope."

"He is a thief, and you are his whore. The Prelate says I can be the agent of divine retribution."

"Anlise, I am so sorry I ignored you." Eleni stared intently at Anlise's eyes, trying to see beneath the madness. "Killing me won't make things better. The Prelate is using you. Can you live with my murder on

190

your conscience? You are Pevanese, Anlise, how can you reject your home? Casan is an evil old man, child, he will requite your crime with your own blood. He has done so before. You must believe me."

"Don't try and wheedle me out of faith. Nice try. Didn't work. My *city* as you put it is a cesspool of pompous families and their secrets. I am called to greater things than changing your bedding and scraping bows in the hallways of the palace. I have a calling. I serve in the royal faith. I will be the vessel for the wisdom from heaven. And I am no child, mistress."

Eleni saw and felt the blade move beneath her chin and flinched when it pricked her skin. She willed her body to move and with a convulsion of joy felt her hand clench and feeling began tingling back up her arm.

"It is time for you to shut up and die," Anlise hissed.

Footsteps pounded down the hallway, a familiar pattern coming closer, slowing.

Drue.

Anlise turned away at the sound of the door opening in a rush to reveal Drue's flushed and startled face.

"My lady," he began, but the rest of his words died still-born as Anlise, with feral quickness, stepped forward and plunged her dagger deeply into Drue's throat. His momentum and the force of her blow combined to send the tip clear through the back of his neck and he stumbled, gurgling and dying, wrenching the blade from Anlise's grip as he fell into a side-table. Voices raised in the hall at the sound. Anlise grimaced in frustration and stooped, grunting, to retrieve her blade.

Eleni quailed as she turned her head to watch Anlise advance. The sounds in the hall grew louder. Eleni felt the posion's grip on her body lessen. Alise swung the dagger back. Eleni drew a desperate breath and screamed "Cryso!"as Anlise's blade plunged toward her face. She threw her left arm up, clumsily blocking the blow. The blade bounced off Eleni's forearm, slicing through the flesh all the way to the bone before coming to rest in her shoulder in the hollow space just below her collarbone. Pain welled white hot.

The force of the blow sent Eleni falling backwards out of the chair, upsetting the writing table and its candles and sending her piles of paper flying through the air. Anlise cursed, drew back the blade for another blow. A hand grabbed her arm and wrenched her off of Eleni

"Wait," Eleni gasped. "Don't--"

But she was too late, for Anlise, moving with desperate speed, threw herself on the guard's sword point. She was dead before her body slumped to the ground.

Eleni saw everything as through a prism of fear and pain. Her arm and shoulder throbbed as adrenaline leached away the poison's effects. With feeling came agony. With agony came darkness, rushing with preternatural speed even as Cryso's face loomed above her mouthing words she could not hear.

Chapter.21: Decisions

Donari and his escort descended on the church on the university grounds in a clatter. The note from Cryso sent him and a small guard racing back to the city. The smoke tinged air and sight of Eleni's pale face and Drue's features contorted in death compelled him to act. He hoped to find Casan at his afternoon activities. Perhaps this one time his prayers rather than the Prelate's would be answered. Donari threw open the great wooden doors with a crash to reveal the old man kneeling in his false piety, surrounded by a cordon of red-robed acolytes. The place was a third full, and the penitents turned heads in alarm at the sudden intrusion.

Donari stalked down the center isle as his men fanned out to block the exits. One priest, more alert than the others, hurriedly scurried down the side of the nave to the arched way that ran beneath the bell tower. Donari motioned and four of his men followed the man. He wanted no untoward intrusions from that direction.

Some of Casan's attendants attempted to interpose themselves between Donari and their lord. Donari drew his sword and beat them about the shoulders with the flat of the blade, drawing grunts and screams as they fell away. Casan turned on his knees at the noise and scowled. Donari advanced a step up the dais. He and the decrepit old man faced each other eye to eye separated by the length of Donari's sword, point quivvering at Casan's throat.

Donari stared, transfixed by the gleam in Casan's eyes, which even as he faced three feet of cold steel, darted about the scene, as tough testing, sensing and analyzing what might yet be done. Donari fought down the fury that ran from his heart down to his sword's tip. The Avedun rage bubbled deep within him, restless, insistent, lusting to find its pointed expression. The image rose like a spectrous daydream, a thrust, a spray of blood, and it would all be over. He glared down the length of his blade at the man who plagued his days and knew that even here, now, at this crisis moment, he could not do it.

Casan made yet another throw of the dice. Defenseless and kneeling, he dared Donari to make him a martyr.

"My lord interrupts holy orders and brings weapons into sanctuary?" he asked quietly. "Do you think to spill blood here before the most holy?"

"Silence."

Casan blinked at the coldness of the order. "But how can I stay silent, lord, when you thrust yourself in here, disturbing my folk at their afternoon prayers? This is a holy, place, lord."

Donari deftly pressed his sword point under the old man's chin and raised it up to an uncomfortable angle.

"Murder is somewhat less than holy, I think. Anlise may have been your creature, but Drue was innocent. A child."

"I do not---."

"I said silence. I have had enough of your words." Keeping his blade in place, he half turned to speak to the congregation. "I give you leave to worship as you wish!" he shouted. "Though I question the sources of this faith, I do not dispute your rights to form your own opinions. But this man is no priest! Your Lord Prelate is a traitor and a murderer. He is a creature of power. I say, keep your faith if you wish, but this man will answer for his crimes. People, mutter your prayers in any form you like. If they give you peace and answer your questions, so be it. But remember the flames of last summer and two days ago! Remember the fallen, dead at this man's orders."

He turned back to face Casan and lowered his sword. He gestured to the nearest acolyte. "Get him up," he rasped. "I want them to see him take this like a man not an icon." He stepped back as the man helped Casan slowly to his feet. Raising his hand for attention, Donari called out the charges in a firm, royal voice.

"Hear me all you folk!" he cried. "Byrnard Casan, so called 'Lord Prelate of the King's Theology' is hereby charged with high treason against the Kingdom of Perspa. He is complicit in crimes against our person and our citizens. He has set in motion plots that have resulted in temple burnings, the Maze fire, slaughter and rapine on the war trail, the murder of Senden Arolli, and attempts on our own life. He is guilty of the accidental death of Tomais Caralon, a son of Pevana, and is responsible for the loss of many of your brothers, husbands and friends who fell in Roderran's war. His order set those fires two nights ago. Smell it! The stench still hangs over our city like a pall. He has tried for our life many times and suborned one of your own sisters to try and take the life of my intended, the Lady Eleni Caralon. These are not the actions of a holy man! They are the work of a man without a conscience. They are the after effects of evil, my friends, and have no place in something that tries to express itself as religion. Again, believe as you wish, but do so without the delusions of this man's cynical expression. You do not need him in order to find your peace."

He stepped down from the dais and motioned for his guards to attend him.

"Take him to the palace," he said quietly. "House him in the darkest room you can find. He is to have all comforts save light and discourse with his folk."

He turned to face Casan, who stood there defiant yet frail, his impotent rage a whisper of itself.

"You cannot do this," Casan hissed as he was led down the steps. "You will bring down just retribution. Gaspire will not--"

"The only reason you still live," Donari interrupted coldly, "is because Eleni still lives. You have failed for the last time, Casan. You have tried to breed darkness in your spite. Now you will have nothing but darkness until such time as I decide to try you. You are a criminal."

"Gaspire is coming, fool. He will take you down," Casan grated, but his voice had lost, forever, its rasp of authority. Now he was just an old man who needed help to walk upright.

Donari turned to his guard. "Take him to his cell." He motioned two others closer as the Prelate shuffled by. "Take charge of his offices and rooms. I want his correspondence collected, and taken to my study in the palace. Arrest his scribes for questioning. I want them cowed and suppressed until we can pull all their fangs. Casan was right in one respect; Gaspire is coming, sooner now once he gets word. I'd send the letter myself if it would make him try before he's ready. I will not leave any vipers behind if I have to arm and out against him."

He looked around the church, empty now save for himself and his remaining guards. "We will let this place stand," he said coolly. "But set crews to work on the bell tower. I want that insult pulled down. Save the bricks and give them to the Maze-poor; those stones have a history suited to the purpose."

Regardless how he might spin it, his actions in the church would cost him, but if it brought an end to the misery of Casan and his plots, then it was worth any price. He mounted his horse and clattered off after the carriage that now bore Casan to his cell. He wanted to see Eleni on the way to recovery before he could make his next moves. He scotched one snake, which still left him another to confront. He glanced up at the fall sky, a deep blue in a westering light. Soon, the weather would begin to change. Gaspire would come. Spring would see a changed world for better or for worse.

Thus, the message handed him when he dismounted in the palace courtyard did not surprise him. The missive came from Avarran's own hand and bore his seal. Its terse contents committed all of them to life or death. Gaspire's spears had been seen in the hills.

He allowed himself an hour to sit with a drugged and sleeping Eleni. He stared at her sleeping features, treasured the regular rise and fall of her chest, and took solace in her living. He had come so close to losing her. Before he left, he took up one of her pens. He would not wake her, but words spilled out along with the tears he had held back.

Love,
When you wake,
Note how the light diffuses through our window
To warmly bathe the coverlet.
And see, there, how wind from the bay
Filters through the garden;
There is a truth in that petal dance
That defies all augury.
Take heart, dearest, in the peace
We have sown there,
A source point for hope
Order out of turmoil.
Life.
Set it down for me in golden ink
Within the pages of your book—
How sight and smell, motion and light
Mixed to frame a dream
To see us through the night.
Remember.

He left her to take a light meal. In between bites he gave orders for a flying column to go with him to reinforce Avarran. The foot would follow after. No more time for vacillation. He ate quickly, chewing through bitter thoughts with each morsel. Eleni nearly killed, and by one of his own servants!

Cryso came to him, mortified, but Donari refused to accept his resignation. Rather, Donari cursed himself for a fool. He should have seen it coming. How could he hope to prevail when his enemies could strike within his own apartments? Cryso reported the palace staff in turmoil over Anlise's betrayal. But there, too, he restrained his wrath. He had to let Crsyo regain himself. There would be inquiries, but Donari doubted anything else would surface. The scene with Anlise held a note of finality about it. Casan would do no more wheedling from his black cell.

Anger and sorrow accompanied him on his way down to the courtyard. He missed Drue's bouncing presence. The lad had always seemed available when he needed him; never moreso than the night of the attack. The boy rushed back when he did at Eleni's request. If he had been delayed, or distracted, he would have been too late. His efficiency killed him. And yet his death allowed Eleni to deflect the blow just enough. The thought choked his spirit.

Senden, Drue. Is everyone who serves me fated to die? Is a crown worth such loss?

A servant handed him a message from the harbor master, reporting several small craft set sail within the hour of the church confrontation. The news suggested desperation and dismay rather than calculation. Casan's rats deserted him, and by the time they got to someone who might act on their news the great issue would already be decided.

For good or ill. Time is now the question.

He mounted, urged his mount to the head of the column and led them out through the citadel gate.

Eleni slumbered, dreaming fitfully in a revolving set of images tinged with lurid colors and distorted faces. She relived all the moments of her life in metaphor as she struggled to regain her lost strength. Anlise's knife blow missed anything vital, but she lost a lot of blood before Cryso and the doctor managed to stem the bleeding. Even her talk with Donari afterwards loitered in her memory as a surreal imitation of communication. So many blows to her happiness: Tomais' death, Senden, Drue's frozen surprise, Anlise's twisted fury.

When will this end?

She lay there in Donari's room, shoulder throbbing, weak and listless, missing his solid weight on the bed, and altogether wretched. She saw herself now as a burden; another care for Donari's already full plate. How could she feel herself worthy? And then Cryso brought her Donari's poem. She wept before she finished reading, and yet in the words all doubt vanished.

Casan had targeted her rather than Donari; a failing plotter's rash move. She considered her place in the drama of her life and found something there to be proud of after all. She loved Donari with a mature attraction bordered by reason as much as physical passion. They pushed each other. If they survived these days, she felt certain they would make a powerful pair. The image gave her hope.

She felt on the edge of destiny, their destiny, and adrenaline fluttered her pulse in spite of her weakness. She and Donari were part of the promise of the future. He had to prevail.

She lay there holding fiercely on to hope as she regained her strength. She called for pen, ink and paper, despite the bitter association with Anlise in the request. In order to still her racing thoughts, words as always served her as both quest and salvation:

> *The experience of pain makes us old before our time,*
> *Why are we in such hurry to grow old and die?*
> *I wish I could linger in my youthful dreams,*
> *Bask like a whale in the warm seas of innocence,*
> *And let the waters bathe me.*
> *And yet time makes me*
> *Succor my hopes and trammel up my conscious moments*
> *To assess these days with reason.*
> *Why must we always rush to act*
> *On thoughts?*
>
> *And dearly bought are all the lessons I've learned*
> *Through a maze of mistakes*
> *Miss-steps and missed chances.*
> *And in the end I surmise*
> *We suffer from our collective ignorance*
> *And bemoan our fates as*
> *Victims of chance, for*
> *The cards are marked,*
> *The judges unfair,*
> *The odds too high*
> *To expect victory or appeasement.*
> *But is that what the wise man meant*
> *When he said we all had days to see,*
> *Roles to play*
> *And things to be?*

When she finished, she put down her pen and surprised herself by weeping. She wept for Drue, for the hapless Anlise, for herself and Donari. Like the Goddess Renia, she wept for all of them.

Chapter 22: Lomillar: Birth of a crisis

Devyn and Talyior settled with the innkeeper to play that evening in his common room. They explored the lower levels of the city cautiously, trying to remain as inconspicuous as possible. For Devyn, the area around the bridge inn roiled with motion. A column of horsemen, with pack animals, streamed through to the causeway and the bridge. Armed men rushed about everywhere, groups of wagons clogged one side of the square waiting for the way to clear to head to the marshaling yards. They followed one such group and found a wide space of warehouses where men unloaded great sacks of flour. They hung back behind a large, heavily laden wain drawn by two oxen to view the scene. Rows of field ovens flared heat waves to add to the already warm day, baking hundreds of loaves of bread at a time. Other wagons held great bags of newly cut fodder that men placed in a frame attached to a fulcrum that lowered a weight to condense the mass down into a dense bale that men tied off and set alongside a growing pile of similar, cubical shapes.

"Gaspire must be close," Devyn whispered, "This much activity means that bread will be eaten soon. We've timed it close."

"And that fodder," suggested Talyior, "must mean he will be after speed. I wonder what has happened? We didn't see any of this intensity on the road."

"Yes, all this is to feed thousands, marching or riding. He might lack cavalry, as Donari suspects, but even nags will pull a wagon faster than a man can walk. Gaspire might be able to move quickly."

"I think we might want to head back," Talyior said, as their wagon cover lurched into motion. "Look at all the badges here. We stand out."

Talyior was correct. Collum badges dominated the scene, but he recognized some from Sor-reel and a few from Talyior's home province of Hallar.

"Yes," Devyn murmured, turning away casually. "Gaspire seems to have drawn bits from all over together."

"I don't like the numbers all this implies."

Devyn agreed. "True, but bread doesn't say much about the quality. Let's head back to the markets and see how the rest of the people seem to be doing."

They meandered back to the square and took a tour of the stalls there. And here they saw signs of that all was not prosperous. The folk about picked over stuff Devyn judged to be low quality. The food on

199

display appeared to be culls from the fields. Gaspire would have taxed the region to victual his force. Talyior grunted in disgust as they left the market behind to head back to the inn.

"Desopolis suffered badly from Casan's attack," he said. "But we made a good start at rebuilding right away. These folk seem stuck in old news. What is it they are missing?"

"Remembered faces, missed places at the table; all the stuff that comes from war," Devyn replied. "But mostly I think they miss what we have seen in Pevana and Desopolis."

"And what is that?"

"Leadership."

Devyn paused outside the inn doors.

"I think we'd better take care with what we play tonight, friend."

He took Talyior's solemn expression for agreement and went inside.

They played that night to a crowd made up mostly of off duty officers who liked to drink and gossip. They made it a point to keep sober and strictly avoid any language or tunes that would expose them to question. The requests for ribaldry and off color songs and the general tone of the ale-cup talk further confirmed Devyn's suspicions of an imminent move. From what he overheard, Gaspire sent out the call to assemble nearly a month ago, and over the last week training had intensified for the raw spears and inexperienced horsemen. A venomous undercurrent flowed beneath the talk; a genuine desire to destroy Pevana and her trumped up, traitorous king. They went to their beds that night unsettled.

"Tal," Devyn whispered, leaning over the edge of his bed. "I have a bad feeling about all of this. I should have seen it coming. Not much traffic on the road here, the poor quality of the troops we met back in Sor-reel. Gaspire has been busy, and I don't think Donari expected him to have such success."

"I agree," Talyior muttered. "The numbers and tone don't look good."

"As to that, I am not sure," responded Devyn. "But in our talks and planning, he always expected Gaspire to make a try before the snows. I foiled that archer's attempt on Donari the night before we left, and before that, Eleni. I suspect Gaspire has known all along how things have gone in Pevana. We took steps to watch the roads for Casan's letter carriers, but some must have gotten through."

"And we come to it. He's got men moving already. What more do we need to know?"

"The road."

"We know he will come down it, isn't that enough?"

"True, but timing remains the key. If we could learn Gaspire's timetable--" he left the thought unfinished. "Tomorrow, I say we split up and wander, see what sort of market is still maintained here. The camps on the far side of the river--"

"Can be broken down quickly. Face it, Dev, we know Amdoran is moving. What more could Donari need?"

"Lists of units, badges, numbers."

"Most of which we can guess at just from the crowd tonight and what we saw earlier."

Devyn hesitated to mention his other concern: Demona's pregnancy.

"There is one other thing I want to find out, if I can."

Talyior looked up at the changed tone. "That doesn't sound easy."

"Demona."

Talyior's features tightened, a shadow move in the dim candle light, and yet when he locked eyes again on Devyn, his expression remained neutral.

"Ah, I forgot about that little variable. That woman gets around."

"I need to find out as much as I can about her and the baby she carries." He paused. "Roderran's baby."

Talyior ran a hand over his face, sighed, and lay back on his pillows. "Demona and Roderran? Perhaps she should have come with me when I asked. Poor girl."

"Poor girl? You can't be serious. You do remember how that all ended, right?"

"Oh yes, but she was powerful, Dev. I think part of me always knew how it would end. I'm not sure how I feel about it, actually."

"What are you looking for? What of Lyvia?"

That brought a genuine smile. "One always hopes for closure, I suppose. But Lyvia has me, friend. I will stick to making notes about wagons and spears."

"Good," Devyn responded, relieved. "Lyvia will be pleased."

Talyior gave a low chuckle. "As to that, my friend, Lyvia is far more daunting than Demona in every way. Sleep?"

"You first. I want to put down some notes about the badges we saw coming up. I'll wake you in four hours."

Taylior rolled over without another word and settled himself for slumber, leaving Devyn awake and thinking. He stepped quietly over to the window of their room and used the light of the full moon above to write down some of his thoughts about his observations. While most of the great houses showed a presence, some showed more than others. He assumed Gaspire did not enjoy complete support for his cause, or perhaps the irregularity reflected the losses those houses suffered in the south.

Devyn's thoughts ran in circles as he scratched away with his pencil. Gaspire's numbers surely exceeded those Donari could bring to the field. Even forewarned and ready, it would be a near thing. Demona might be well along in her pregnancy by now. Would Gaspire wait for the actual birth? Not if he was as impetuous as Donari reported him. Everything he and Talyior noted in Lomillar spoke of impatience, and that fit Gaspire's temperament.

He shifted his pad to catch the moonlight, rubbed sleep from his eyes, and reshaped his pencil tip. Words once led him to protest the destruction of his people's faith. Indirectly, his words involved him in the great events that ultimately shook the region. He sat in the window now a far different man than the youngster concerned with dust and finding food, training horses for Malom Banley, and chasing nouns and skirts. A child of the Maze was never completely innocent. There were victims aplenty to account for, but in the end no one ever escaped sorrow. Kembril Edri burned because his faith placed him in the way. Everyone had a role, witting or unwitting, in the drama of the times.

He glanced over at Talyior, innocently asleep. He wanted to see his friend safe home to his Lyvia no matter the cost. Talyior had a love to live for. Devyn had a king. Donari might get other servants, but Devyn felt certain Talyior would never get another Lyvia, and she no other like him. He considered his options, thought of all that rolling stock and supplies.

I could do this alone if I had to. After all, I've learned a thing or two about the uses and abuses of fire.

The surety of his calculations calmed his racing mind somewhat and, surprisingly, almost magically, words came to him as he sat in the window marking time by the shadows cast by the westering moonlight. He knew Talyior would understand the message.

Shadows on the Wall
Cannot tell it all
Though we might wish to make it so.
Silhouettes fill the room,
Tenuous shapes in the gloom
Masking reason in the after glow--
Of a late summer's moon
And a faint, far-off tune
That reminds us of our youthful show
Of hope

202

And dreams
And all those things
That kept sorrow at bay.
And come what may
We all must face the day
When our choices have all bled away--
From the host of things we might do
To the one thing we must.

And in the end, when we measure
Accounts, losses and gains,
It is the finer thing to act
So that something good remains.
And the shadows on the wall
Cannot stop our fall
For they speak to us in silent riddles;
A fantastic pantomime
Of unexpressed information.
And so we fumble through our emotions
And trammel up our grace
To somehow find the will
And wherewithal to face
The task
That fate has set before us.
For there's always the one more thing to do
That says it all,
That one final offering
Before we join the shadows on the wall.

The moon's light passed by the window's opening by the time he finished. He rolled his notes up with the poem and stuffed them in Talyior's guitar cover against the strings, and then he gently woke his friend and settled himself to sleep for what remained of the night.

Devyn awoke to the sound of Talyior gently playing his guitar in the morning light. He took in the sight in silence then noticed the pile of his notes on the table next to Talyior's chair. A plate of bread, cheese and fruit lay next to the papers. Talyior paused at Devyn's movement.

"All quiet," he said. "It is about an hour after dawn. I went down earlier to piss in the alley and keep myself awake. There's food if you like and a little small beer, some water. And these," indicating the papers, "were in my guitar cover."

"Yes, what of it?

"Nice words," Talyior said. "I've been teasing a song out of them for a few minutes."

"Thanks. I found the moonlight inspiring."

"And this other stuff? Moonlight inspire that?"

"Insurance."

"Explain."

"I wanted to be sure to get what we have seen and talked about down on paper so Donari will know for sure."

"But we could tell him."

"Like I said, insurance."

"But if we get found with it."

"But *we* will not be found with it."

Talyior's brow darkened.

"What got to you last night? This smells of nobility. We go together you and I."

"Tal," Devyn began.

"Don't *Tal* me, Dev. You made a decision while I slept. I want to know what and why."

Devyn sighed, got up and sat down at the table across from his friend. He did not say anything for a moment, using the silence to munch a hunk of bread and pour a measure of the beer. He swallowed all subterfuge with the bread and a mouthful from the cup.

"We are in pretty deep here, Tal. We both know it. Our information is useless if it doesn't get back to the king. "

"Right, so we both take it to him."

"But getting out of here might not be as easy as getting in."

"We knew that when we came. Let's take a look today and leave tonight."

"We will, but if we somehow cannot, then I want you to get south as best as you can."

"I still don't quite understand."

Devyn looked directly at his friend and wondered if he understood himself, but he knew he had to give Tal an out. This went beyond nobility or love of a friend. It was for love itself and, therefore, correct. It was what a poet of Pevana would do. Plus, they might have to separate. His notes improved their chances. But he tried another gambit nonetheless.

"Demona," he said. "I need to confirm her condition, and Lyvia," he continued before Talyior could respond. "You are more at risk here than

I, Talyior. Lyvia needs you. I want you to lay low today. Let me do the snooping."

"Why?"

Devyn smiled.

"Tal, you're a hero, but you are still the son of a rug merchant. I have more experience."

"That's ridiculous. We've both seen our share of squabbles. I can handle it."

"Perhaps, but I can work this better alone, given the circumstances."

"I didn't come with you to have you protect me, friend. But I do agree that we should work apart today. This is a big place, and your notes are still mostly a guess. We can cover more ground separately."

Devyn took a long drink, considering. "On one condition," he said finally, burping for emphasis. "Stay away from the upper parts of the city. There are stock yards to the west of us, have a look."

"You want me to count cows?"

"And the pace at which they get slaughtered. If Gaspire wants speed, he will salt the beef and cart it. If he intends to leave soon, they will cull as many as they can."

Talyior pulled the beer pot over and refilled his glass. "Funny," he mused, staring at the foam. "For a minute there I thought you doubted me."

"I don't doubt you, Tal. I just know what you have waiting for you back home. This could get messy if we aren't careful. Sneak is my skill; you are good at love."

"I told you, Demona has no hold on me."

"So you say, but I'd rather you not run the risk." He rose, moved to the window to check the light. "I also think we should find another place to stay. This inn is too busy with military types. We may need several days to finish; less notice if we move around, maybe."

"What if the innkeeper here asks us to play again tonight?"

"We leave together this morning, baggage and horses, complain about the food, say we're looking for something a little more local to get the flavor of the place. Doesn't matter as long as we sound convincing."

They collected their stuff, made their performance downstairs to a barely interested innkeeper, they had taken pains to avoid showing their best stuff the night before, and joined the human stream moving further into Lomillar.

They passed on several places up the main road, but found a serviceable inn located next to an apothecaries shop over near the city's eastern gates. They agreed to play that evening. They stowed their gear and separated at the door.

"Remember," Devyn cautioned. "No love poems to strange women and keep to the sidestreets."

"Just be back here by sundown, Maze-boy, and we'll see who comes up with the best information."

Devyn spent the day wandering. He did not dare try and sneak his way into the palace grounds on the height, but he did what he could. He loitered at the market near the bridge for a good hour, surreptitiously listening in on the morning chatter. Gaspire's name was on everyone's lips. Demona had been seen occasionally, looking quite pregnant. Devyn heard muted grumbles about scarcities. On the whole, though, folk seemed to approve of Gaspire's moves.

He looked in at several ale houses, sipping small beer and keeping to the shadows as much as possible. From a stable boy at a hostel near the palace walls he learned the reason for the activity yesterday. The call had gone out recently to regions around Lomillar to gather food stuffs and provender and send them to the city. The boy dealt with the animals of two such trains; each one coming from even further away. The reference brought Talyior to mind. Devyn grinned at the image of his friend actually counting cows.

All the clues pointed to an early move. With his camps full and the weather nearing its turn, there was no way Gaspire could keep such a force inactive through the winter. With the son westering, Devyn headed back around the upper terraces of the city below the citadel walls, intending to meet Talyior back at their rooms. He reached a point just outside the apothecary's shop when a disturbance on the road near the gate sent folk scattering. Loud shouts to clear the way attended a carriage careening half out of control. Devyn tried to move, but a parked wagon blocked him. He pressed against the side and moved back to get around it as the carriage neared. In the back, several women hoovered over another slumped in the seat. Just before the rear wheel clipped his hip, Devyn thought he saw black hair tossing in the wind.

The blow sent him sprawling into the gutter. He lay there, stunned, while the escort pounded by feet from his face; all save one. A pair of boots dropped into his vision, someone grabbed his arm and helped him to his feet. Devyn's leg felt numb at first. He could put weight on it, but he suspected he would sport a nasty bruise soon. He blinked away the pain, and when his vision cleared he found himself looking at a youngish man, blond hair peeping out beneath a cavalry helm, with an earnest, blue-eyed expression.

"Are you all right?" the man asked.

Devyn did not answer at first; his attention drawn by another rider who approached from up the street.

"Hallan," that one said. "Hurry, we will be needed!"

The man who helped Devyn rise frowned. "They know their way to the palace," he said over his shoulder. "The sooner they arrive the better for the lady, with or without us. You follow, Sen, I'll be along shortly."

Palace? Hallan?

"Are you hurt?" the man asked again. "My apologies, but the lady was in a bad way."

"No, no, I'm fine," Devyn stuttered. "I mean, no, it hurts like Boriman's hammer got me, but nothing is broken."

"Good, good, then I'll be off." He frowned. "I have duties above, and likely questions to answer."

"Who was in the carriage?" As soon as he said the words, Devyn winced, cursing his foolish tongue.

"That is one question I perhaps should not answer," the man responded. "Hurts, eh? My name is Hallan. Yours?"

Hallan, that name.

"Uh, Kembril, Kembril Edri," Devyn offered, mind racing.

"I see you don't wear a badge."

"Yes, no badge. I'm a musician, from the coast. Come looking for a posting."

"Any experience with horses?"

Devyn smiled, more at ease now. "Some."

"I thought so. You have the stance. I lead my father's horse company. Come to the palace, leave your name if you are interested," he paused, "or if your leg allows."

"I will think on it, Hallan, was it?"

Hallan grinned. "That's right. Hallan, son of the Lord Hallaran of fief Hallar. Escort to pregnant women by day, intrepid cavalryman by night. Now, I am off. If your leg bothers you, at least you are in the right place." He pointed to the sign above Devyn's head: *Jonsur's Apothecary.*

Hallan mounted and trotted off, leaving Devyn stunned and throbbing in the street.

Black hair, pregnant, palace. Demona? Young man, Hallan.

And then he made the connection.

Balcony meeting: Eleni's report of the oath taking. Avarran praised him.

Devyn tucked the inference away and limped into the shop. He might as well get something to help the pain. Inside, he discovered an older, heavy-set man pottering about behind a counter, grinding something in a pestle.

"Well," the old man breathed. "That was close."

The comment put Devyn instantly on his guard. "Close?"

The old man kept grinding. "Sorry, saw the whole thing. Watched you talking with the officer. I figured you'd be in next. Leg hurt?"

"Bruise, just below the thigh. You are pretty observant, Jonsur?"

"Ah, yes, saw the sign from the gutter, did you? Jonsur Ginby, Apothecary. As for being observant, well, comes naturally in my line of work. Seen a few things over thirty years in this place." He leaned in conspiratorially. "Once sold contraceptive potions to the king's handservant, and later to one of the queen's maids! Astonishing stuff, astonishing!"

Devyn wondered if the man had spent some of those year's sampling his own handiwork. Jonsur emptied the contents of the pestle onto a slip of paper that he folded expertly into an envelop and sealed with a few drips from a candle.

"There," he wheezed. "Half tonight with water and the rest in the morning." He placed the paper on the counter.

"What if I don't want it?"

"Then you wouldn't have come in, yes? Besides, someone else will need it if you don't. This stuff keeps its potency. But you've a whiteness about your cheeks that suggests you will need it later if you'll pardon my saying so. It won't knock you out; this mix is just to take the edge off. Cost you a copper is all."

Devyn fished out the coin, alarmed and amused at the man's voluble way.

"Thank you, young man. Sorry to see your start in Lomillar be so uncomfortable."

"Start?"

Jonsur and waddled over to the till. "Thirty years, remember? I'm pretty good with accents, yours is a little different."

Devyn forced himself to a calm he did not feel as he pocket the powder.

"I am from Sor-reel, out by the mouth of the river. Musician. Just got in yesterday."

The apothecary gave him a quizzical look. "Sor-reel you said? My late wife came from the coast."

Devyn fought down an urge to panic. "Ah, that, yes. I've been told such like before. I had a tutor from Esda."

"Oh, yes! I have heard of that place. I thought you had something of the east in your voice."

"My family thought I might become a scribe. I compromised with music and poetry. My partner and I are playing tonight at the place next door."

Too much talk, Dev, but a musician that didn't advertise would be doubly suspicious.

Devyn moved to the open door. Outside a caravan of wagons rolled sedately down the street. Jonsur followed.

"I had my time wandering when I was young," the old man said casually. "I marched with Roderran's father." He gestured to the last of the wagons as it trundled by. "The army will need all that those can carry and more if they are to defeat King Roderran's cousin."

Devyn nodded sagely, as if in agreement. "To be sure you are right," he said. "Word in the camps says we will move soon."

"Very soon, I would say, given the length of that line. A whole slew of them rolled off a week ago. Not as big as that bunch, of course, but still, a goodly mess of them, I'd say."

They watched in silence as the last of the wagons turned off the main way and disappeared left, south, towards the marshalling yards above the river.

"Well, then, that's that," wheezed the apothecary by way of goodbye. "Best of luck to you, son. I've herbs to grind."

Devyn waved in response and stepped out into the street. He had seen enough and learned enough to settle his mind. He and Talyior needed to get out tomorrow if possible.

Luck, that man said. We are out of time, and we will definitely need luck.

He made his way down towards the inn where they stayed. Talyior waited for him in their room. Concern washed over his face when he saw Devyn's limp.

"Had a small accident," Devyn said to forestall the question. "Hurts a little. Got something for it from the Apothecary next door."

"Do you trust it?"

Devyn sighed as he lowered himself onto his bed. "He's a tradesman; we are the spies, remember? Yes, I trust it. Learned a few things too."

"Like?"

"Like lots of wagons to go with what we saw yesterday; something I want to check on tomorrow. I want a look at those warehouses by the river. We need to play tonight and get out of here with the late afternoon traffic tomorrow."

"In with the market, out with the market. Sounds good. How's your leg?"

Devyn flexed it, grimaced when his muscles protested. "I'll try this powder later. Sprinting might be a challenge, but I will be able to ride. How did you do?"

"Some really bad beer in a tavern by the western walls. Lots of cows, and lots of folks butchering them. You guessed right."

"Call me divinely inspired."

"I'd call you stupid if I weren't so glad to see you. You were late getting back. I was just about to go out and try and find you. What happened?"

"Carriage wheel clipped me," Devyn temporized. He decided to keep his guesses about who was in that carriage to himself. "I was on my way back here, actually. Like I said, accident."

Talyior spilled some water into a cup and handed it over. "Then have at that powder. Innkeeper wants us playing by the time they light the street lamps. You've time for a bite and rest."

Devyn fumbled some of the powder into the cup, swirled to mix, then drank it down. He lay back on the pillows, closing his eyes.

"Food later," he murmured. "Sorry about being late. You get to choose the song list tonight."

The next morning Devyn asked Talyior to lay low while he made one last circuit. Jonsur's powders worked, dulling the pain enough to let Devyn get through their sets and sleep after. He took the rest when he woke, massaged his leg to warmth and declared himself fit enough for anything.

Devyn made his reconnaissance and returned in the afternoon with more material for his notes. The innkeeper greeted him warmly.

"Well done, last night! That was a well-heeled crowd, drank me out of my best wine! So, you'll stay another night?"

"Can't," Devyn answered. "We've another engagement across the river in one of the camps."

"Is that so? Well, then, you'd better tell your friend."

"What's that?"

"Couple of palace types came and collected him an hour ago. Didn't say why. I know we had several of the maids from the place in here last night. Someone might have taken a fancy to him, like a private show?" He moved off, laughing at his own humor.

Devyn felt sick as he pounded up the stairs to their room. All of Talyior's things were there, trussed for the road, but his guitar and leather cover were missing. Devyn sat down, mind racing, wondering where they might have taken him. The Palace? The innkeeper's tone suggested their cover still held. Where? His eye strayed to his baggage. His flute poked out the top of his pack, unwrapped. That was not normal. And then he spied the slip of paper rolled tight and stuffed into the mouthpiece. He removed it. His heart skipped a beat when he read its contents scribbled in Talyior's hand:

Wanted both of us. Couldn't refuse. Too obvious. Play for 'the lady'. Summer houses, east wall. Get out, now. Demona?

Devyn went to the window. The sun was westering quickly, but it would not be full dark for a few hours. Time enough to plan, something; time enough, also, for Talyior to find himself in deep trouble. Devyn leaned on the sill, crisis gnawing at his calm, knowing he had to make a decision not just for himself but for everyone. Talyior knew it, however cryptic the note. He would understand.

But Talyior was not Maze-born. Loyalty mattered. Devyn was fine with his friend leaving for safety in the clinch because he knew he was more capable in a mess. Another Maze-trait from his youth. But he could not leave without making certain about Talyior. The innkeeper said he had been gone an hour. If he did not return on his own by dark, then something had gone terribly wrong. Devyn would wait out the light, make a show of leaving the inn, then find a place to stow their gear. He did notice a number of abandoned buildings in his wandering yesterday.

Then he would go find his friend.

Finding the house proved surprisingly easy. He left the inn just before sunset, mollifying the innkeeper with a silver piece for holding the room. He ambled slowly down the street, sniffing, and found a street that branched off the main way, left the built up areas quickly and climbed a gentle slope that revealed a line of wealthy houses at the top. A quick survey showed these properties ran to the edge of an escarpment. The street ran along this edge at first, and Devyn saw that the steep slope ran, brush-choked, to just behind the warehouse district on the first terrace above the riverbank.

There was a carriage parked in front of the first house on the right, a large affair surrounded by a low wall and a line of trees. His leg throbbed a little when he recognized it was the same one that had nearly run him over the night before.

Renia's Grace, but that has to be the place. I'd wager my life on it, or Tal's.

He turned away and rode back down to where the side street rejoined the main north-south way. He let the slipstream of traffic take him down the slope to another side street. Partway down he came to the building he had seen earlier: an old storage place long unused. He checked to make sure no one observed his presence before leading both mounts in through the loading doors.

He gentled both beasts with grain in the bags and tied them securely. Climbing to the second story, he found a window facing east. To his left and above, the row of houses perched on their slope. To his right and below, the dark shapes of the warehouse roofs ran in a line illuminated partially by torch light that denoted activity of some kind. He looked right, left, back again, an idea forming.

We might need a distraction, but first: that house.

He scrounged around and found an old burlap sack that contained the remains of an old horse blanket. He left the building and headed east to where it ended at the middle edge of the tumbled grade below the houses. He saw why it had been left alone. Too unstable for building, it provided a view for the houses above; a mottled green and brown deviation from Lomillar's continuous stone and timber.

But it would suit him just fine.

He climbed carefully down the slope, thankful for the darkness and the deeper shadows underneath the bushes and small trees that dotted the area. The torch-light near the warehouse loading doors revealed rows of unhitched wagons.

Gaspire's transport.

He reached the back of the wagon-park and wormed his way underneath the rearmost of them. It smelled of new grease and pitch-heavy pine. He took the blanket, tore it into strips, wadded up the sack and stuffed the mass under a wheel. He used his strike a light to pop sparks and blew until he got a small flame started. When it took, he shuffled back and headed up the slope. Even if he failed to find Talyior and they both died here, without his wagons, Gaspire's march south would be slower than he wanted.

He moved quickly, intent on a quick look at that house before his fire caused chaos. The light had grown by the time he reached the top. Faint shouts of alarm followed him as he slipped, vapor-like, over the low fence and onto the estate grounds. He slipped behind the tree line until he got right up to the house and crouched underneath some decorative shrubbery. Light flowed from a second story window, open to allow for the night breeze. He wiped sweat from his brow and waited. And then he grinned.

Renia's Grace, thank you, Goddess.

From the window above, light yet unmistakable, came the strains of Talyior's guitar.

Chapter 23: Birth

Demona woke from frightful dreams, to find Gaspire perched on the edge of her bed, his face a mix of concern and speculation. She sniffed; he smelled like horse and dust. That did not matter. He was there. There were twists to their connection, true, but the pain in her abdomen told her she needed someone. The sweat on her brow had nothing to do with the late summer heat. She reached out a hand, tentative, questioning.

Gaspire ran his gloves through his hand once, twice, a grin ghosting through his beard and dropped them on the bed. He took her hand and raised it to his lips.

"You look terrible. Did Hallan abuse you?"

"Is that all you can say?" She wanted to slap him but lacked the energy. "I'm in pain, you buffoon."

"You insisted on a day out."

But Demona was not interested in truth. She had to pee. She rolled herself out of bed and waddled over to the chamber pot. He surprised her by following and helping her down. Demona chuckled through her discomfort at her loss of dignity.

"Careful," she sighed when her water came. "We are going to look like an old married couple if we continue this way."

"Don't fool yourself, Demona," Gaspire responded, helping her up when she finished. "That's not possible. But whelp this king, and perhaps we can explore things."

He got Demona back to the bed. The baby rolled again once she settled on the pillows. She suppressed a gasp.

"I'm too uncomfortable to explore anything other than getting out of this stuffy palace and its snooping servants."

"If a move will help you bring this child to term, I will see to it."

"I'm also tired of your lousy attempts at gentility."

Her jibe produced a frown.

"I've never claimed to possess tact, woman," he said coldly, rising and pouring himself a glass of light wine. He stared at her for a moment before drinking. "I'm not used to being claimed so by a woman. You are a force. I have a list of concerns to deal with, and yet I find myself here."

"I'm sorry I distract you."

"That has been your intention all along. We have used each other to get to this point. The question is: can you finish the race?"

"I have no other choice."

213

"None of us do, anymore. We are committed."

"Tareegan doubts you."

Gaspire snorted, finished his glass and poured another measure. Demona watched him closely, gaging his reaction.

"He's old. He doubts everything, but he has given me men and supplies. You've figured out our arrangement, obviously: a necessary compromise. I will make him eat his doubts."

The pain swelled again. Demona arched against the pillows. Heat flushed from her core to her extremities. Agony. Agony. Agony. She reached out a hand, blind, desperate, encountered his shirt, gripped with preternatural strength, pulling him into her terror.

"Too soon!" she gasped. "Gaspire—"

She felt Gaspire's rough hand on her brow, heard his tense voice questioning, shouting for Tellis. She kept her body rigid as hands raised and lowered her. She sensed movement as an afterthought, opened her eyes for an instant before flinching away from the light. A change of air. More shouts, more movement, more pain. She groaned, swam back toward consciousness enough to make out Gaspire's voice.

"Have her looked after," she heard him say. "I need her!"

Shades whispered to Demona as she fretted in her fever dream. Voices, voices, voices spoke to her all at once, all consuming, incoherent yet insistent mutterings and laughter and cruel, cruel almost-words. Judgements personified afflicted her, the baby twisting in her womb joined them, accusing her of cruelty and vaunting ambition, squeezing her soul as it pushed against her uterine wall, pushing, pushing, downward, taking her downward, deeper into her personal darkness, a hellish domain peopled by Sevire's taunting ghost, Roderran's demanding face, and Gaspire's wooly cheeked intensity.

She felt herself separate from her body. With ethereal eyes she hovered over the woman who lay bloated, supine and sweaty on the bed. She bore only a passing resemblance to her memories of herself. She had been made for summer dalliances and daring trysts, a self-constructed daydream, a passionate image of sex and wantonness. But now she saw the changes and how her life and pregnancy worked her like a torture victim. She felt pity for herself: a husband dead, a lover lost, a baby fretting to term in a foreign city, a sensual object turned political chess piece. Her vision faded and she fell back down, repossessed by the frantic body below.

With each breath she fought for her life and the life of her child. All voices faded then, replaced by the plaintive, near-cry of the unborn babe, clutching at her like a drowning victim, pulling her, wanting her, needing, needing, needing everything she had left to give and more.

She moaned deeply in her fever dream half-aware and tossed her head back and forth on the sweat-drenched pillow. Something cool and wet bathed her face and arms, sponged her legs and feet. The moment's cool brought clarity. She took an easier breath, remembered where she was. She heard the sound of notes played softly, lilting, like poetry and the sound of laughter from happier days when she came close to love.

She opened eyes and confronted her past.

Talyior, or his apparition, sat next her bed playing a guitar softly. Demona blinked, but Talyior remained, stringing his random notes in a musical counterpoint to her disjointedness. Then he hummed along with the chords and slowly, slowly, his tuning calmed her. Her face relaxed, her body tension lessened. She sighed. He altered his cadence and by degrees seduced her, as he used to before, into a similar rhythm. He began singing along with the notes. The sunset turned the light in the room eerily red before fading altogether. One of her maids entered with two lit candles, surprised by the changed atmosphere. She placed the candles on a stand and left. Talyior played on, and Demona's body responded as did the troubled soul she bore within.

Though weary beyond belief, Demona refused to let her eyes close. She drank in the reality of him as he played. The lullaby he crooned took her back to her youth, to that brief time before she lost her childhood innocence, a time when kindness had still been possible. Talyior's words reached into her, ephemeral, like his touch, as though from a well-spring of grace that knew nothing of power, betrayal or fear. For perhaps the first time in her life, Demona recognized the sound and intention of goodness.

At the same time, she understood he played for life because he sensed death in the room. Hers.

Demona reached out a timorous hand to touch his knee. He opened his eyes at her touch and confirmed her suspicions.

Fear. Death. Pity.

She stared at him for a long moment poised on the edge of such an awful recognition, and then it did not matter.

"I thought I was dreaming," she said weakly, her voice a shadow of its old, sensuous timbre.

"No dream," Talyior answered, continuing to play. "I always knew we would meet again. We've come a long way from that last afternoon at Gania's, love."

She smiled at the memory. "You--" she began but lost the rest of her words to a sigh. She frowned. "Sevire told me you were dead," she whispered. "And then he, and then the king, and, and." A tear formed in her eye and ran down the side of her face. Her body tensed, and she ran a hand over her belly as though trying to placate the baby inside her. "Not yet, not yet, not—yet--little one," she gasped between clenched teeth.

Talyior played for her as she fought against the contraction. She struggled against rising panic, raised a hand to forestall him rising to go get help. One breath, another, a third and the contraction passed. She looked at him, shaking her head slightly in wonder.

"How do you come to be here? Now?" she asked in a weak voice. "And I so fat and in need of a bath and combing?" She forced out a breathless laugh before continuing. "Talyior, my Tal, my poet, who has learned to play so fine. How? Why? Have you met my lord Gaspire? He will be regent to my son, who will be king, a king, I tell you, even if he lacks patience and wants to come early to claim his own."

"Ah, Demona," Talyior whispered. "You have come a ways since Pevana. Consort to a king, and I still just a wandering poet."

She fixed her eyes pointedly on his, quite clear and focused, and stopped him cold.

"I have been a slut to Power," she said in a stern, objective tone. "And I have survived only because of luck and Roderran's seed. I fear this baby will kill me with his birthing. What?" she asked. "No rejoinder from my daring wordsmith?" She glanced beyond him to see stars birthing in the night sky. Talyior played on.

She touched his knee again, stopping him.

She looked into his eyes and saw for a moment the woman she could have been had fate been kinder to her. She judged her life then a failure, a quest for sensual culmination as a surfeit for real love. In the end, her physical vitality only made her desirable, an object of passion but ultimately passionless in any deeper context.

I am always the promise, never the fulfillment.

It suddenly seemed appropriate to her that she now lay there, wracked by a process her life had made impossible for her body to complete. Pain took her again, and she clenched her eyes tight against both the tears and the truth and lost time.

She opened them again when the wave passed. She looked at him, taking him in one last time.

"I'm sorry," she whispered.

A spasm took her. She cried out at the smell of the water and blood that broke from her.

Demona's cry brought the maid rushing in with towels, two others following with steaming basins. With her last consciousness Demona watched them push Talyior back out of sight. And then she and they set about their woman's work.

Sorry, sorry, sorry, for so many things. Talyior, my little one, Roderran...Talyior...

Gaspire sat at his desk in the study of his summer house. Directly above him, Demona's moans came as vague, fretful background noise interspersed by the sounds of a guitar played softly. Demona's maid, Tellis, had seen fit to bring in a musician to try and soothe the woman's distress. For the last hour, chords and groans competed for dominance with the issue constantly, distractingly in doubt.

He growled as he crunched a sheaf of papers into a ball and tossed them into the fireplace grating. No flames existed there to curl the fibers into ash. Bad news needed to burn. But that was the only kind he received. His brother lords sent notes advising caution, suggested herbal cures for Demona, or questioned his dispositions. Commanders complained about training and supplies. Kenton Reece continually pestered him with pompous requests.

Everything came to a head with Demona's crisis. So much depended on birthing a child. The realization came as a shock to Gaspire. He had gotten used to Demona as gradually biddable, getting rounder and needy. Her condition served as a backstory to the tale of his preparations. Now she lay sweating in the house's best bed, and each moan reinforced her central importance to their cause. He had made preparations for a replacement months ago; sound judgement in his view and Casan's. But now, his force nearly set and the way south clear, he vacillated between conflicting emotions. The battle rage simmered, ready, a familiar sensation, powerful. But the sounds from upstairs reminded him that he had come to care for the woman and the unborn child. And that was a strange, new sensation, temporizing, unfamiliar and powerfully unsettling.

For a cavalryman balance meant everything. To lose one's balance meant death in a fight.

But what happened when one lost one's heart?

The sound of boots outside the door brought him back. Hallaran, Lord of Hallar, and his disappointing son, Hallan entered. Gaspire scrutinized father and son as they approached to take chairs before the desk. Hallaran, of an age with Tareegan, still possessed the proud posture of a veteran fighting man.

"You are late," Gaspire fumed.

"And yet I am here," Hallaran mouthed serenely. "And my nephew and my son have been here."

"Small service that," Gaspire retorted. "A parade ground popinjay and this one. Seemingly useless for easy tasks like entertaining women."

"No need to get insulting, Amdoran. Women and battle are equally unpredictable. Leave the boy out of it. He rides well, but pregnant women are quite beyond him."

Another extended moan filtered down from the bedroom, reinforcing Hallaran's point and deepening Gaspire's frustration. He was in no mood to be conciliatory.

"And yet you sent Reece first. You place small trust in your heir."

"Or perhaps less trust in you that I should risk my last son. You'll have to excuse an old man's sentiment."

"We lack the time, Lord Hallar. Demoana comes to her time early. We need to move. Think on it. We will have a king or a corpse by morning. A still birth with the army in camp would be disastrous. And yet a sickly child struggling to survive the winter could be a deeper failure. I think we should move, now."

"Tareegan gave me some of it. A risk."

"Tareegan agrees with me. I want Donari to meet me in the open. If he hides behind his walls I'll burn his valley barren. I need you to see to your nephew and his men. Be ready to march."

"And Hallan?"

Gaspire looked at the younger man, took in the resemblance, wondered if the mettle went beyond the surface. In his day, the father had been a formidable fighter.

"What is the status of your remounts?"

"One for each trooper in the company, another score extra."

"Less than ideal."

"More than men were lost at Lyranden, lord."

Gaspire scowled. "No need to remind me, boy, but you will take to the hills with what you've got. When the army marches, I want you forward and on the flanks."

"Scouts?" Lord Hallar barked. "He's the one remaining cavalry wing commander we've got, outside of yourself. Small task for my heir, Amdoran."

"And until he proves himself worthy of more, that is how I will use him."

Hallan looked as if he wanted to say something, but seemed to think better of it. He stood and put a hand familiarly on his father's shoulder.

"Father, farewell. It seems I have duties to attend to."

The father patted the hand on his shoulder, a gesture Gaspire found oddly out of place, almost effeminate.

Love? The boy is the last of his sons. Too bad he is also the least of them.

Hallaran waited until his son left the room.

"You ask much of me, Lord of Collum," he said thinly. But though he may have meant the words an accusation, Gaspire heard old age in them.

"I ask much from everyone, my lord," Gaspire responded. "The realm requires it."

"This effort could see the end of my house."

"If Donari rules, Hallaran, all our houses will suffer. But I am not so pessimistic. Don't let your aching back rule your counsel."

Another moan loomed down from above, which rose at the end to a near scream. This time, Gaspire could not help but look up.

"From the sound of it, this will be a testy king we birth today. In that he will surely be his father's son." He locked eyes with Hallaran. "Will you ride with me? Tareegan on my left, you on my right. Donari will fall before us like wheat to the scythe."

Hallaran nodded. "I've one more battle in me."

"Good! That is all I intend. I suggest you rest. We ride at dawn."

Hallaran left. Gaspire paced over to the window that looked out over the city to the south and east. The horizon showed a deep, dark blue with stars. Campfires clustered on the terraces climbing up the southern riverbank. Directly below him, the warehouse section glowed, affirmation that his orders to load and ride were being followed.

And then Demona gave a shriek of pain and terror that broke his calm and sent him rushing for the stairs. Fear and anger fought with dismay and compassion each step he took.

In his haste as he entered the master bedroom, Gaspire ignored the stranger backed into the corner, his eyes drawn to the demented creature trying to give birth on the bed. Demona's final labor sent her into convulsions as her body rebelled at the tasks demanded of it. She began to bleed as her womb tried to contract and expel Perspa's future king, but the baby remained trapped inside her. Gaspire watched her thrashing weaken, as she passed into a keening, half-frantic, half exhausted state. The maid, Tellis, held one of Demona's shoulder and attempted to bathe her forehead.

The change in Demoana's appearance astonished Gaspire. Her face had gone deathly pale. She gripped the bed sheets as though hanging on to life itself. Her hair, usually lustrous, lay sweat soaked and ropy on the pillows. She smelled of blood and death and lost promise. Compelled, Gaspire knelt by the bed, pried one of her hands loose and held it in his own. He sought for words to bring her back. Another wave of pain took her, and she arched her back nearly crushing Gaspire's fingers with the power of her agony.

"Demona! Come back, come back--I need you." Something in his voice got through, for she rolled her head over to face him as the most recent pain wave receded. She looked at him with dull, distant eyes, blinked, recognized him, and almost smiled.

"Gaspire," she whispered, "here, too? Such a collection for my little king."

"I'm here, woman, Demona." He tried to soothe but knew he failed, for he had no experience; the tenderness in their connection always tinged by an earthy coarseness. Gaspire understood horses better than women. Demona sighed and closed her eyes. He kissed her hand, lingering over the knuckles, aware for perhaps the first time what their situation actually meant.

I would raise this king, but I want her more.

"Can you save the child?" he asked the mid-wife.

The old woman, with Demona's blood caking her arms up to her elbows, shook her head and shrugged.

"The baby comes too early, lord, and is twisted around the cord. It won't move for me. In fact, I feel no life in it now when I try to shift it. All's amiss here, lord, and I fear we will lose both of them."

"Save them," Gaspire grated. "Save them, woman. Save her."

The mid-wife showed her bloody arms. "My lord, there is nothing more I can do. She bleeds, badly. I cannot rip the child from her now. She grows too weak now to push."

Gaspire rose, defeated, and let Demona's hand slip from his. He stepped back. Then Demona tightened, face drawn back in a breathless scream. Her look appalled Gaspire, and he wondered if she would ever draw air.

And then Demona did.

"Talyior!" she gasped, reaching out beyond Gaspire. "Talyior help me, please! Tal--" But her last word ended as still born as her baby, for she gave a great cough and blood flowed from her mouth as something inside her ruptured fatally. She fell back, expiring, onto the pillows. Her womb gave one last spasm and pushed out the malformed son of Roderran Avedun in a rush of fluid and blood; dead even before it had a chance at life.

220

The commotion and Demona's final outburst stopped Gaspire in mid-stride. He looked to where Demona reached and noticed the musician for the first time.

"Who are you?" he growled. "How did she know you?"

"I, I," stammered the man as he backed toward the window.

Gaspire took a step towards him and as he did so his foot scrunched down on some paper that crinkled in the sudden silence of Demona's demise, and the noise made Gaspire look, bend down and gather the papers up.

"What is this?" he asked, scanning the pages. "Music?" Understanding spread over his face as he realized what he read. He stepped back, reached for his sword and drew breath to call for his guards.

But he never managed that shout. The stranger, gripping his instrument like a club, aimed a viscious blow at Gaspire's head. The women in the room screamed. Gaspire swung up his off-hand to fend off the blow and half succeeded. What should have knocked him senseless only smashed into his face and sent him reeling back across the bloody mess of Demona's birthing bed. Before he could recover, the stranger swung both legs out the window and dropped out of sight.

Gaspire regained his feet, grabbed a cloth and pressed it against his ruined nose, and staggered to the window. At first he saw nothing. It was as if the man had disappeared altogether. He thought he saw two shapes leap over the low fence at the back of the estate. He shook his head to clear his vision, looked again, saw the unnatural, pulsating glow from the marshalling yards by the warehouses. He stood amazed, mind racing with anguish and thoughts of treachery.

Heavy footsteps pounded on the stairs behind; Hallan's voice came through the door.

"Lord Amdoran! Fire, fire lord! Among the wagons!"

Gaspire's head throbbed, and he snarled against the pain. He turned away from the window and took a last look at Demona's bloody figure. He lingered at balance point. Rage grew with the glow behind; sorrow swelled in the scene before him. He pulled the cloth away to reach for another. A droplet of his own blood fell to join the pool collected in the hollow of Demona's throat. He blinked, once, at the image. It seemed a fitting farewell.

Someone pounded on the door. "My horse!" he shouted. "Be ready to ride when I come down!"

He made to leave, then paused at a touch on his elbow. It was the mid-wife, holding the bloody, malformed mess of Roderran's child half-wrapped in a bloody sheet.

"It was a boy, indeed, lord," she said, timorous and weary. Behind her, Tellis looked on, cloth held to her own nose against the smell. "What are we to do with it?"

A desire to revenge himself for the chaos caused to his plans filled Gaspire then. He glanced down, confirmed the sex, took the child and placed it next to Demona. In the same motion he whipped out his dagger and expertly slit the mid-wife's throat with a back handed slash. Stepping over the woman as she collapsed, he did the same to Tellis when she drew breath to scream. They had used an oil lamp to illuminate Demona's laying in. Gaspire tossed it, still burning, on the bed.

He closed his eyes against the rising flames for a second; sought for and found a way to reconcile his rage and sorrow.

Farewell, lady, ambition helped us start. Revenge will help me finish.

A good commander adjusted to setbacks. Flames, below and above, would serve to deflect any questions. Now, the image of those two silhouettes slipping over the fence took command of his attention.

Two. And one is named Talyior. She knew him. Why?

Jealousy, another new emotion, attached itself to his motivation. He stomped downstairs, ignored Hallan's questioning glance.

"Leave it," he growled. "Treason. The musician was a spy." He dabbed his nose again. "I'll repay him for this in time. We ride. Now."

Talyior crashed into the bush under which Devyn hid; its branches and Devyn's shoulder helping to save his friend a broken leg. He grabbed Talyior's shirt and hauled him upright, fending off the panicked blow Talyior aimed at his head.

Above them, footsteps rumbled in the house, and the sound of Gaspire's voice, at first a little groggy, gathered force and volume as he raged.

"Can you run?" Devyn asked. "Things will get a bit hot here real soon."

"Of course," Talyior gasped.

"Then follow me. Keep low and head for the shadows beyond those trees. With luck we should be able to get across the bridge before they close it."

"Horses?"

"Saddled and close. Run!"

They ran off even as the alarm rose behind them.

They made it back to the abandoned building without being seen. They could hear the sounds of crying voices and running feet as folk took up the cry about the fire. Devyn took a moment to check the saddles of both horses.

"Demona?" he asked as he retightened a girth strap on his own horse.

"I figured you would follow," Talyior answered.

"And?"

"Dead," he answered. "She died trying to give birth. Blood rushed out of her mouth at the end. They wanted me to play for her to calm her. Then a hairy brute, the maids called him Lord Amdoran, came in, right at the end, and--." Talyior's voice shook as the trauma of the moment took hold.

"Hey," Devyn urged. "Keep hold, Tal."

"But it was so unreal, Dev, the last thing I would have expected."

"Tal, she made her choices."

"I know, but she looked so helpless at the end, and that Gaspire fellow looked so, so decided."

"And the child?"

"Stillborn. Nothing that hideous could live, I think."

"Which means Gaspire does not have the symbol of his revolt."

"He found your notes."

"All the more reason for us to get out of here while things are riled up. Are you ready to ride?"

Talyior answered by walking his horse out the double doors. Devyn followed and mounted in the lane before leading them back to where it connected with the main street.

They rode out into the stream of traffic confident in their anonymity despite the full moon and lamps that hung from shop doors along the street. Down the slope, they could see a crowd gathering under lamplights near the tavern where they had spent their first night. The cluttered roadway there forced them to push their way through as best they could.

The fire's confusion drew the curious and the concerned to choke the square at the beginning of the causeway, but they managed to work their way without challenge through the press and, with the smoke and flames still rising from the warehouse district to their left, made their way onto the causeway and over the bridge.

Devyn spared a glance over his shoulder as he clattered over the span behind Talyior. The whole scene now seemed too fantastic to fathom. And then his horse's hooves passed from the bridge timbers to the solid ground of the southern bank and the moment faded. He urged his mount alongside Talyior's. Once beyond the outlying buildings that sprawled at the end of the causeway, they turned off to the east to avoid the camps they passed on their way in to Lomillar.

They rode carefully in the darkness, keeping the lights of the camps off to their right as they picked their way out of the river valley. Devyn reined in as they crested the last bluff. Behind them smoke rose into the night as an eldritch line against the full moon's pale light. While they made their ride over the bridge and up the slopes, the moon cleared the hills to the east. Now, the moon's light waxed bright enough to make out horsemen on the bridge.

"Like as not those are for us," Devyn said, leaning over to pat and gentle his horse.

"If we have to ride cross country, it will be a race."

Devyn laughed and straightened in the saddle.

"Well, then," he chuckled. "I think both of us know a thing or two about that."

Talyior gave a brief snort in return. "At least this beats running along rooftops."

Chapter 24: Southwards

Devyn and Talyior picked their way in the night through the broken country to the south of Lomillar. Dawn of their first day away from Lomillar found them cold, wet, and tired with badly blown horses. They took shelter in a shepherd's bothy at the base of a small hill. No farms dotted the region because of the rocky, thin soil; perfect for sheep and other kine but less so and too far away from population centers to bother growing cultured crops.

They took what rest they could. The bothy proved abandoned and in the early stages of decomposition, but it served for their first fireless camp. The next day they turned back south and west, heading for the King's Road. They needed to get in front of any troops Gaspire might have pushed ahead of his main body. They wanted speed, but fate seemed to turn against them after their escape from Lomillar; whenever they tried to sneak back to the road they encountered groups of northern horsemen.

It quickly became apparent to them that the patrols were part of an ever widening pattern. Their southward progress slowed to a crawl. Hopes faded for a mad race down the main road with news and time enough to make adjustments. The patrols forced them to go round about, even back tracking once to avoid a particularly large group. They had been lucky. Trotting down a track running through some trees, they heard the jangle and creak of armor behind them. They had just enough time to swing out of the way behind some bushes. A score of riders passed wearing Hallar colors. Devyn took a long look at the tall man who rode at their head and recognized Hallan.

"Tal, do you ever get the feeling we not as independent as we think?" he whispered.

"We make our choices."

"True, but what if we are mostly directed?"

"Not really the time for more of your fate philosophy, Dev. If we keep seeing signs in everything, we won't get anywhere."

"Or we get to where we were meant to be. I've seen the blond fellow before and read about him back in Pevana. I suspect there's a design in all of this."

"A pretty bloody, dangerous one, then."

"Agreed. Troubling, but I still wonder."

They waited till the group rode out of earshot and changed direction, but the result was the same. They came across two more squads. The first sky-lined, riding along a ridge; the second, unmounted and clustered around a waterhole. Both groups wore Hallar colors. They made sure to walk their horses back and around before moving on.

"Gaspire has the hunt after us," Devyn said. "So far, that is three separate times and none the same. He must have a whole company out looking for us."

"Hunting or herding?" asked Talyior. His voice sounded tired. "We aren't making time."

"Agreed, but we still make south, regardless. The ground grows more broken now. We have been climbing. There will be game trails ahead that might serve us. Let's walk our mounts till dark and find a hole somewhere. Tomorrow, maybe, we can break for the pass."

The next day they rode through more broken ground. Great boulders, cracked and weathered, dotted the slopes, and beyond these trees began to appear in clumps and lines that indicated water. As the afternoon turned towards evening, they ran into another group of hunters plodding along a stream bed. While Talyior kept the horses quiet in a clump of bushes and scrub oak, Devyn crept up to where he could observe them. He watched the line of horsemen disappear downstream and around a bend before he slipped back to Talyior.

"They've gone," he said quietly as he mounted. "They looked like they have been in the field for awhile. They bore Gaspire of Collum's badge. We must be getting close to the road. Hallar all about and Collum in front. Not good. The hunt is well up, my friend."

"What do you know of the road?" Talyior asked, urging his horse in behind Devyn's as they moved out from under the trees.

"Not much, really. It is well kept all the way. There is a winter shelter at the high point, according to Donari and his maps. No one I talked to before I left had ever heard of any easy paths through these hills. Towards the spine Avarran told me the land gets rocky and jumbled; a fit place for hunters after elk, perhaps, but not a place for tired horses and spies to make fast time."

"How long before we come to the king's troops? We may run out of food before we crest these hills. Coming hungry and late does not sound appealing."

Devyn grinned. "Coming late would take hunger out of consideration, Tal. But we should make it. There will be camps at the base of the hills, and I suspect Avarran has scouts placed to watch." He scanned the horizon. "But we must still be leagues away yet from that sort of help. Gaspire has kept these parts under a strong guard."

"No one said this was going to be easy."

226

"True, but what if it proves impossible? At this rate we will miss the battle we are supposed to be warning our folk about." He let his horse pace into the center of the stream that slipped over its rocky bed in a lazy fashion. Afternoon sunlight broken by clouds fell in beams over the region and one such bathed the place where he and Talyior let their horses drink their fill. Under different circumstances, something much less desperate, Devyn would have called the spot pretty. He stretched and considered their alternatives.

"Let's follow this back west," he said, gathering up his reigns and pulling his horse away from the water. The beast ruckled a little unhappily but gave in to Devyn's gentle pressure on the bit. "That last bunch must have a camp upstream. We need to get back closer to the road, I'm thinking. Come on. It will get dark in a few hours. Maybe we will see a way through this tonight."

He prodded his horse back over to the shallows near the bank and began working his way upstream. By the time they passed around a bend upstream the sunlight failed, masked by clouds rolling down the ridgeline. The stream still gurgled along but absent its momentary glamour.

Gaspire Amdoran let his horse keep pace with the men marching alongside. His nose still throbbed but the blasted bleeding finally stopped. Getting out of Lomillar proved difficult. After collecting Hallan, Gaspire had hopes of sealing the city and starting a thorough search for the two men he saw slipping away from the summer house. The wagon fire led to a stampede of draft animals into the lower city. It took hours to control the flames and tally up the losses. In that time all thought of a quick pursuit faded.

And yet Gaspire still thought the whole night, expensive and chaotic as it was, could not be deemed a total loss. Demona and her child were dead, but so were the two witnesses to the event. The offending house was now a smoldering ruin easily blamed on treachery. Gaspire allowed himself a small grin, thinking of how he made use of that mess. Tareegan and his old man's caution were wrong. Moving was far better than waiting. With the fires put out, he sent word to break the camps. By the time they contained the flames, the men had started marching down the road. The lack of transport meant they would go a bit slower and hungrier, but those things happened in war.

His throbbing nose brought images of the blood pulsing from Demona's ravaged womb and the spray from Tellis's throat. He knew he would suffer ill dreams from that event. Tellis, Tareegan's creature, he tallied up as a necessary casualty. In the end, he had disliked the woman almost as much as Demona did. Demona was the far greater loss. Blood soaked her lips and front in the end; her appearance completely at odds with the sensuous and voluptuous woman that claimed him in ways no other woman had before. Even now, his loins stirred at the thought of her despite the finality of her passing. There were times with her when he felt poised on the edge of something unfamiliar, fine and passionate. She had nearly consumed him; he had almost loved her. The pain behind his eyes reminded him just how close the affair came.

But in the end, he was a warrior more in love with power than anything else. He was not made for sentiment. And yet he had to admit to himself that, if things had gone otherwise, he would have submitted to her and what they might have been together. Gaspire shuddered, both in grief and relief, unused to such direct honesty. He kicked his horse into a cantor and tucked his memories away for another time; remorse was just too unsettling and got in the way of more immediate needs. Like finding those two spies and killing Donari. Victory would go a long way to assuage both grief and rage. His sword hand clenched tighter on the reins.

Talyior, whoever you are, you better hope someone else takes care of you before I do.

Gaspire's pace allowed him to course the column until he came to the front. He slowed his horse to a walk beside a dusty Kenton Reece stumping along at the head of his men.

"You will need to quicken your pace," Gaspire said. "I need you in the hills as soon as possible."

The look Reece gave him held a mixture of sneer and respect. They had not spoken since Gaspire ordered him out to the camps to prove his vaunting.

"My men would march faster if they didn't have to pack everything on their backs. Where are our wagons?"

"A regrettable accident. I've taken measures to replace what we can."

"We would also march faster on full bellies. Where is our food?"

"Some of it burned along with your wagons. You will just have to adjust along with the rest of us."

"If you want us to fight, feed us."

"Watch your tone, fool, and get your men forward. Do that, and I will see to it your men get their fill."

Reece scowled but nodded acceptance. He made one curt order, and his column increased their pace. Gaspire moved out the way to let them pass. A squad of riders crested a small rise next to the road and made their way down to their position. Their leader drew rein alongside and saluted.

"My lord Amdoran."

"How does your hunt, Hallan?"

Hallan removed his helm and gloves and ran his fingers through sweaty hair. "I'm not sure, my lord, since I am not sure what we are looking for, exactly. You say you saw two men fleeing your house. They might have made out of the city ahead of us. We found sign at dawn two days ago to the east, but we were so late getting over the bridge due to the fires there was no telling how old it was."

"Anything to the west?"

"Nothing lord. Plus, there are more farms to the west. None we questioned reported anything unusual."

Gaspire considered Hallan's news. "Keep at it while we are still here on the flats. You see your cousin up ahead there? He's double-timing it to get in place. I have a company of spears near the heights. If you chase shadows, we lose nothing as long as we get over the hills. If that sign you report was them, then we might trap them. If they are indeed stuck back in Lomillar, we also lose nothing."

"Except worn out horses and riders."

Gaspire gave him a scathing look. "At times you follow after your cousin. I question his competence, too."

Hallan leaned away from the words as if avoiding a blow. "Too, lord?"

"You heard me. He might be a fool, but you fared poorly with Demona."

A little color rose in Hallan's cheek at the mention of the dead woman's name.

"Ah!"Gaspire chided. "Trust me, young man, you never stood a chance against her even if it was for just the one day."

"I regret her death, lord."

And that sobered Gaspire. "I do, too," he said. "And I blame those spies you don't think you are chasing for her death."

"And the child?"

"Looked after by wetnurses," Gaspire lied.

"Then, if we chase shadows, we do so for a reason."

"Exactly. I will avenge her passing, Hallan. I need you to expend yourself and your men to make me certain of my course. What is the state of your force?"

"Tired and hungry. I've several broken horses. So far the remounts are serving."

"Hunger seems a preoccupation, especially with your cousin."

"My lord, may I speak freely?"

"Well, you pass your cousin there, at least. What?"

"My cousin thinks me incompetent, but he was not at Lyranden Bridge."

"We share that evil memory."

"And I was there, after, lord."

"Yes, what of it?"

"I got most of those men back home, lord. By the end we subsisted on roots and grasses. I came to know them. They deserve better than Kenton Reece."

"You have a higher opinion of your worth than I, Hallan. I have to trust you, in part because you were, as you say, at Lyranden Bridge. I've no one else. I will not apologize for your cousin," he finished. "He does me a service."

"He's going to get most of his men killed. I grew up with some of them. Reece is a peacock, and you know it."

"Careful, young man. No more nattering. We've a job to do. Work with him."

"As you wish, my lord." But the look he gave suggested Hallan had more to say.

Gaspire urged his horse closer.

"No smirch on your character, lad. You did well to get your men home as you did."

"I did what my duty dictated. I do so, now, lord. I saw death such as I never thought possible at Lyranden Bridge. I lost better men on the march back than the ones Reece pummels up the road ahead. I am my father's son, Lord Amdoran, but I sometimes wonder if he returns the favor. You call Donari usurper, reject him out of hand, but you were not at the oath-taking. I read honor there, lord, I'll not deny it."

Gaspire calmed his ire at the mention of his cousin's name. But even he could see the genuine quality of the young idealist before him.

"Will you find these spies for me?"

"If they are truly out there, my men and I will find your spies."

"Will you fight for me when the time comes?"

Again, the irritating hesitation. Gaspire snarled and put a hand to his dagger.

"I said, will you fight when the time comes?" he repeated.

Hallan nodded his head, once, deferentially. "I will fight, lord, to save as many of my men as I can. I will fight for my honor, the honor of my house and Roderran's heir. If that means I fight for you *when the time comes,* then yes, I will. More than that, lord, I cannot, will not say. I went south out of a sense of honor and duty, but I came back doubting both."

Gaspire almost drew the blade, but thought better of it. In a way, he felt easier about Hallan's genuine doubt than he did about Reece's uncertain confidence.

"Well enough," he said, forcing his voice to a casual tone he did not feel. "I will accept that. Find your honor, find me these spies, and I will overlook the questions you have of me. Now, off and do your duty."

Hallan reset his helm and gloves and swept his men back over the rise. Gaspire watched him long after he disappeared from view.

Devyn and Talyior made their way up the water course with as much care as they could, walking their horses and making sure all their gear remained securely tied. The late afternoon sun beat down on them, lending an almost fae quality to the stream. Butterflies danced in sunbeams, late-season gnats swarmed to the warmth. The water bubbled over its stones, singing its song among the roots and dead wood snags. They walked along the northern bank, for as near as Devyn could tell, it ran through its little valley from west to east. Devyn fought against the daydream spell. He knew they had to be nearing the road. He expected to meet up with their pursuers every time they turned around a bend.

He checked the sun again and forced himself to step carefully, deliberately, spiting his deep need for speed. Time moved against them here. Devyn could only guess at Donari's preparations. Scouts about the heights, surely, and perhaps they might have fresh mounts to lend. Avarran might be out in force. Any number of other things, most of them negative, presented themselves to his mind.

The way ahead widened around a bulging rocky lump. West and above, Devyn spied the tops of two hills that spoke of a pass. They were close. Beyond the open space, the stream began climbing up rocky terraces to other tree choked spaces, almost ravines, as it climbed to its ridge sources.

They climbed up through this close space, forced to splash along in the stream itself when things got too narrow. Devyn could tell they climbed up through the gap between two of the rises that made part of the ridge. The sun dipped behind a hill shoulder, bathing them in shade. A breeze developed, sending leaves cascading in a gentle shower of color, cooling the sweat upon their brows. They cleared the narrows and regained the bank when the way widened. The widening turned into a meadow ringed with trees. Another streamlet percolated out from a ravine to join their own. Devyn paused. He did not like the open space. He dismounted, motioned Talyior to do the same and walked his horse in amongst the bushy undergrowth. Devyn waited, shaking his head at Talyior's questioning look.

The water murmured contentedly about them. A moment. Another. Devyn held his own breath, strained to hear. Then a twig snapped, the sound coming from up the ravine, followed almost immediately by the altered water sounds that spoke of horse hooves in water. And from out the ravine opening plodded a small file of mounted men, their voices raised in jocular, casual conversation.

Through the skein of leaves, Devyn watched the group assemble at the streambed. They wore Hallar badges, and for the second time in three days, Devyn recognized their leader. Hallan sat his horse not thirty yards away.

"It's nearly sunset, Hallan," one rider commented. "We've seen nothing on this leg. Nothing since those few prints back by the spring. East and down, sir? Or west and camp. We can make the road easily."

"There's several of us whose mounts have loose iron, lord" said another.

"And yours looks near lame, sir, if you pardon me saying," said a third.

Devyn ducked instinctively when Hallan scanned their hiding place and checked the light.

"Agreed, Farly," he said finally, dismounting. "Head up stream. Make camp near the road. I'll have to walk Gryphon behind you. That last stumble seemed to unsettle him."

"Shall we stay with you, lord?"

"No, go on. We will be fine. I'll give him a rub and we'll be on directly. Get something hot in a pot for me."

Hallan's men urged their horses along the bank and soon passed out of sight and sound around a bend. Still, Devyn held back, gentling his horse, willing it to silence, waiting.

Hallan loosened his saddle girth and led his mount to the stream to water it. Devyn noticed the right foreleg seemed to plant tentatively. The wind freshened, rising to an audible rush as it coursed downstream. Hallan bent to examine his horse's leg, and under cover of the wind and Hallan's inattention, Devyn made his choice.

He handed his reins to Talyior and moved out into the open. Talyior followed. Hallan did not hear their approach as he massaged and soothed, but his horse did. When it sidled away, he spun quickly, sword drawn to confront them.

Devyn stopped just out of sword reach and drew his blade.

"Well met, Hallan," he said. He kept his off hand up, palm out. "I hear the fishing is good in this stream."

Hallan kept his blade up but frowned at both the words and their tone. Then he looked closer and comprehension bloomed.

"You! You are a long way from the apothecary shop, what was it, Kembril? Or was that a lie?"

"A necessary deception, given the circumstances." He gestured to include Talyior. "We had need."

"And I assume your companion left a guitar behind in Lomillar? You killed her, man, and the child."

"Wrong, friend," Talyior disputed. "The babe died stillborn. Demona just before. I was there."

"Gaspire said otherwise, and he was there, too."

"Yes," Talyior replied. "And how is his pukish face?"

That brought a smile, a look Devyn remembered from their first meeting. He relaxed, lowered his blade a little.

"Now, Talyior," he soothed. "Let's have more respect for our betters."

"Gaspire sports a shattered nose and a grim disposition," Hallan offered "He was quite clear. Why should I trust your word over Lord Amdoran's."

Devyn decided to press. He had seen something in that brief encounter in the street back in Lomillar, and he had studied Eleni's account of the oath-taking carefully.

"There it is, isn't it," he urged. "The doubt that has been nagging you since Pevana?"

"I have no doubts about my duty."

"And if Demona's child still lived, I would agree with you. Poet's tell stories, Hallan, but we also tell the truth. Poet's honor: my friend has it right. The child is dead. What does that do to your sense of duty?"

"My father wants revenge for my brothers. Donari betrayed them."

"Like you, he made a hard choice, one forced on him by Roderran's foolishness."

Hallan's blade swung back up. "This is hardly the place to debate policy. Gaspire wants your heads."

"He has to catch me first," Talyior hissed. "Dev, we are wasting time."

"Dev? Is that your real name?" Hallan asked, turning. "And as for catching you, well, I have help still within shouting distance."

Talyior took a step forward, but Devyn raised hand to stop him.

"Now, man, let's be calm about this. I am Devyn Ambrose, aide to king Donari of Perspa."

"Donari's title is debatable. And you are a spy."

Devyn persisted. "The king spoke of you, most positively, after the oath-taking when the army made it back to Pevana. You made a hard choice, friend."

Hallan said nothing, looked a question.

"You are far from home, Hallan," Devyn continued. "And this is not a noble task you've been given."

"I go to war at the bidding of my father and the council of lords. Gaspire sent me to keep you from reaching Donari with your news. Men will die if you reach your destination."

"Men are going to die anyway," Devyn answered. "But don't you think they should die for the right reasons?"

"That is not my concern."

"Blindness? Ignorance? Are these noble things?" Devyn sheathed his sword and stepped back. Talyior came alongside, frowning, but lowered his point as well.

"What are you doing?" he asked.

"Giving Hallan a chance to make the choice he really wants to, if he could see his way to making it."

"I could shout out." Hallan said, edging a bit to his left. His horse, sensing threat from the other two horses had sidled away out of reach.

"You should have done that already if you thought it would work, but I wager we've talked long enough for them to get too far away." Devyn dropped his hand to his belt. "Choose. Your horse has a bad leg. There's two of us. Choose."

"If you kill me you won't make it," Hallan responded, lowering his sword point until it rested on a tree root that poked a shoulder through the dirt. "I do not want to die here, gentlemen, but I am not quite ready to turn traitor, either."

"That word has some troubling associations," Devyn said quietly. "You are a good man; I suspect a just man, as well. I serve Donari because he is a just king."

"Gaspire has---"

"Duped the whole region," Talyior finished, sheathing his blade. "I knew Demona, Hallan. We were lovers once. She reached out her hand at the last, not to him, but to me. My name was on her lips at the end not Roderran's or Gaspire's. He has lied to you in this."

"Spies." One word only but now doubting.

"Out of service not choice, just like you, I think." Devyn let his hand slip along his belt to his sword hilt. "Now, choose."

"How can I take the word of spies and strangers?"

Devyn frowned. "Enough of this. We will be going. Aide us or try and stop us. The choice is yours. Are you ready to die?"

"What you suggest is treason."

"To whom? You have seen and heard Donari. How could service to one such as he be treason?"

"You trap me with words."

"We give you a chance, with words," Talyior asserted. "Have you heard nothing? Gaspire has lied to you. Roderran's bastard is dead."

Hallan's sword rose.

"I'm sorry, gentleman," he said sadly. "But I can see no way out of this. Will you come quietly?"

Before he finished his question, Devyn and Talyior both drew and advanced. Hallan swung wildly in a futile effort to gain space. With a flick of his wrist, Devyn neatly sliced into Hallan's forearm, causing him to drop his blade. Talyior lunged into the opening, reversed his blade, and smashed the pommel into Hallan's jaw, snapping the man's head back. As his eyes glazed over and his knees buckled, Devyn hit him on the forehead with the flat of his sword, giving him a convincing gash that immediately began welling blood. Hallan was out before he slumped to the ground. Blood pulsed from his forehead and a badly split lip.

"Did we kill him?" Talyior asked, leaning over Devyn who knelt to check. Though bloody and unconcsious, Hallan still breathed.

"He'll have a sore head and arm, and easy answers for any questions he may encounter."

Talyior led their horses over. "Tie him?" he asked, handing over the reigns to Devyn's mount.

"No, leave him. That is the least we can do for him. Poor fool. If we leave him, maybe he can make up his mind. I would hate to have to kill him."

"What about his horse?"

Hallan's mount trembled off to oneside, right leg held just off the ground, refusing to accept weight. It was obviously afraid but unwilling to leave his master.

"He won't let us touch him, but I don't think he will go far. Hallan will need him when he comes to."

"Now what?"

Devyn considered while he mounted. "I think we are out of options," he said, turning his horse upstream. "Did you notice how tired he looked? We've led them quite a chase, it seems. This lot is heading for the road. We follow. Try to get by them. A last sprint."

"But for how long? We don't know what else is up ahead."

Devyn laughed. "You want to quibble now?"

"What was it you said back in Gallina? *Lark's over?* Or something like? Lead on, Dev. Just tell me when to go."

They followed the stream west into fading sunlight as the sun set behind the mountains. They neared the end of the little valley cut by the stream just as true dark began to form in the low spots between the slopes that framed the road. They saw the firelight of the camp in time to stop and observe. The wind came out of the west and the horses, tied in line, did not smell them.

The scene appeared relaxed, quiet. Apparently, Hallan's men had yet to miss him. Devyn looked over his shoulder and nodded. It was time to go. Devyn spurred toward the horse lines, avoiding the small slope that led to the road. He drew his sword and almost casually sliced through the tether, upsetting the horses and scattering them satisfactorily. Gathering speed he sliced a tent line and leaped his horse over one of the fires. Men shouted in alarm and scurried out of the way. Talyior thundered through the chaos and joined Devyn on the roadway.

After days of frustration it had almost been too easy. They rode off into the darkness. Even if those behind managed to set out in pursuit they could not hope to catch up with them. They let their horses run and hope ran with them. They put some distance between themselves and Hallan's force and slowed their mounts to a road-eating canter. An hour passed, their horses tired, but they kept on. The terrain steepened. They rode on.

Right into the last patrol.

They were fortunate in that the group they encountered had yet to receive word of the general pursuit, but they still posted sentries. They rode down one, but the other raised the alarm. They burst through the skein in a flurry of shouts and sword blows at shadows. They came closer to the pass with the pursuit right behind them. Devyn's horse stumbled on an uneven spot and nearly threw him. It slowed to a halting walk despite his heels in its withers. He dismounted. Talyior doubled back, his horse's chest a heaving, frothy mess.

"Come on!" he shouted. "We are almost to the top."

Devyn patted his horse's neck. She had been a game filly, but he could tell she was done. The stumble must have strained something in her right foreleg for the horse refused to put any weight on it.

"It's no good, Tal. She's done for now. Can't even walk."

"Then climb on behind me."

Just then the moon, fading from its fullness of a week ago, broke through some clouds and shone down on them. Devyn shook his head and smiled, objective, despite the tension.

"Don't be silly," he said. "She can barely take you." The sounds of pursuit grew close. "I know this seems like a bad poem. Do you remember that fool from the competition finals? Ha, maybe he was not so much a fool after all."

"You cannot be serious, Dev."

Devyn waved him off. "You know what was in my notes. You know what Donari and Avarran need to know. Go. Tell them."

"Devyn, no!"

"I'll give you a little time. Maybe I can slip away from them in the darkness. I'll be okay, really. They will probably ignore me anyway. Go."

"I can't."

"You have to. You have to explain to Lyvia why you broke your guitar even though it was for a good cause. Now go." He drew his sword and gave Talyior's horse a great slap on the rump. Neighing in pain and fear, it leaped away and galloped off into the night, taking Talyior with him whether he wanted to or not.

Devyn gave a rub to his horse's damaged leg and judged that she could do one more thing for him.

"Okay, love," he said gently, remounting." No more running for you tonight. All I need is you to give me one or two steps and a little courage, okay? Yes?"

Pounding hoofbeats drew closer. Devyn turned her slowly with his knees, taking a small pleasure in the remembered skill.

Then he drew his dagger, re-gripped his sword and waited to greet what came around that final corner. He needed to at least give Talyior a chance to escape. Once alerted, any defense the Pevanese could muster would be all to the good. The hoof beats grew closer. Devyn considered his options. His horse could not move. Those who chased them could deal with him and still catch up with Talyior. He thought quickly and dismounted just as a group of mounted shadows spurred into view. They shouted as they noticed him blocking the road.

Devyn gave his horse a final caress on her bloody muzzle. "Sorry dear," he whispered. And then he plunged his dagger into her jugular vein and ripped his blade free in a shower of blood. The mare reared in terror and pain before collapsing in the road, legs flailing the air as she bled out. The northerners reached her at that moment and she tripped up two of them in her death throes. Devyn backed away after cutting the mare then lunged forward and, with grace borne of desperation, slashed the necks of the two riders, pinned beneath their fallen horses.

Devyn kept moving as the others plunged about in a confusion of neighing horses and cursing riders. He dodged a wild sword blow and took that man in the groin as he passed. He pirouetted from the thrust and slashed the leg of another and kept swinging his blade to block yet another blow from a rider who managed to curb his mount. For a moment Devyn had the whole troop in a sidling, screaming turmoil. Adrenaline lent his sword arm a feral quickness, and his blade sketched a silvery death dance in the moonlight. A glancing blow to his shoulder shook him back to reality and he dove underneath a rearing horse and took off to the east, running like a deer through the broken trees. Horses pounded in pursuit, but in that terrain he held the advantage. The ground sloped downward. The sound of horse hooves faded. He kept running, exulting in his sudden, unexpected success.

Then he half-tripped on a tree root, glanced off a rock and stumbled through a bush. He put a hand down to recover his balance but met only air. With an involuntary yelp he tumbled through the dark for a sickening three seconds before meeting branches and then the ground. The impact drove the air from his lungs. He kept falling. Then his head slammed into something that did not yield and sent him into complete darkness.

Chapter 25: Price of a King's Crown

Gaspire crumpled the letter disgusted and delighted. Donari's spies were over the pass but pursued. He called for his armor, his horse, and grabbed the messenger.

"No time for written response. Can you remember what I tell you?"

The man nodded. "Ye, yes, my lord," he stammered. "I, I have been trained."

"Right then. Back up the road you go. Tell Kenton Reece to get his parade ground fools up the slope. Tell him I will be right behind with my spears. Tell him to make them run!" He shoved the man in the direction of his horse. Gaspire did not wait to see him mounted and off. His officers collected at his shouted summons.

"We need to close up with Reece and the Hallarese," he said. "Don't bother with the silly tents. We will likely be fighting and dying before dawn. Others will bring up what we need. Get your men suited up and on the road. Double time it! If the Pevanese are in the pass in numbers they will slow us down. That will not happen, hear? Not happen!"

He turned away to allow his servants to help him arm himself. By the time he finished strapping on the final greave, his column of spears had already assembled and tramped off. He and his escort mounted up and followed. Well-being, absent since Demona's death, rose in him as he spurred his horse to speed. He understood combat; grieving served no useful purpose now.

He led his small troop around the footmen and quickly up to the region of the summit where they ran into Hallan's disrupted campsite. Several large fires burned to illuminate the clean up. In the half-light, the younger man, blood stained bandage on his forehead and another on his arm, met him on the road. Dawn was a whisper of light in the east.

"They came up a watercourse from the east," Hallan said, coldly. "We made camp to block the road, sent a small group ahead to the top of the pass to scout. My apologies, lord, but they surprised me, road through like a storm and scattered our mounts. Word came back from the top. It seems one of them got through. The other made a mess of the pursuers and used the dark and confusion to run off to the east."

"Yes, I know," Gaspire snarled. "I had a message from Reece. Poor work, sir, poor. I expected better from you."

Hallan raised his wounded arm as if in explanation.

239

"None of that," Gaspire interrupted. "I'd rather you dead in the effort to capture or slow them. Wounds are no badge of honor to me. Where is your cousin?"

"He marched through here an hour ago, while I tended to myself and my other wounded. I sent men whose mounts were still sound up with him."

He paused, attention drawn south by a faint noise. Gaspire gentled his horse, followed his gaze and listened likewise. From up above in the stoney narrows of the pass the sound of men's voices raised in anger and the metallic clang of swords filtered down to them as a summons.

Gaspire cursed. "Well, it looks like your cousin has found something. Send word to my men coming up behind to hurry. From the sounds above, I'd say Reece is already engaged. Damn! The Pevanese beat us to the spot by an hour." He made ready to ride off then paused. "Have your men prepare torches if they can. Have them ready to light when my column arrives. It will help speed them up in the darkness and show Reece's men help is on the way."

Gaspire spurred away, putting the younger man out of his thoughts. He had a battle to win. He and his small group reached the pass to find a full scale encounter in mid-career. Reece's men faced a similar number of Pevanese spearmen in the level space of the pass. Dawn's light lent a hint of clarity to the violent confusion. Line crunched against line. Reece sent his men rushing forward as Gaspire reined in next to him. Bodies littered the roadway. Gaspire noted with some chagrin that most of them bore the Hallar badge.

"We came up just in time to support what was left of Hallan's scouts. They pursued a single rider right into a mounted southern patrol. They got cut up pretty badly and fell back. By the time we got here, that lot stood to line across the road."

"And you seem to be bleeding men, Reece," Gaspire cut in. "Can't you break them?"

"I've numbers only, lord. And as you can see, there is no room to flank them. It has been beat and push for almost an hour. We are moving them."

"Too slow."

"Get me more weight. Your spears might tip the balance."

Gaspire checked the area. The pass crested in a narrow space maybe a hundred paces wide on either side of the road. The Pevanese line stretched from end to end like an armored cork in a bottle. In the pale light he could see their line's thickness: two or three men deep at the most.

"Maybe three hundred," he muttered. "Yes, I agree, Reece. Keep pressuring them, but rest as many of your men as you can. My lot will be up soon. We will have them two or three to one then. They will have to give way. If my memory serves me, once through the pass the ground about the track widens. Their line will thin as ours swells."

"Yes, my lord." He turned away to give orders.

Gaspire, for all the fire and expectation of his ride, remained a spectator to the conflict. He considered the grinding horror of the shield wall a terrible waste of men. He likened the scene to a nightmare collection of tinkers all beating on their pots and pans at the same time, making a terrible din, with the only sign of progress the odd fallen body or wounded man crawling backward out of the press. Gaspire had men enough to waste, especially Reece's puffs. He only lacked time. He sat his horse out of arrow shot and tapped his gauntleted hand on his thigh, marking the minutes as dawn turned to morning, waiting for his men to come up so he could begin killing in earnest.

His nose throbbed anew but faint, a reminder of the way Demona's pulse fluttered and failed when he last held her hand.

"Water!" Gaspire wiped the sweat from his brow. Someone pushed a waterbag into his hand. He drank and spit. Noontide sun now bathed the slopes about the pass. A morning's worth of fighting, of grunting, pushing, futile charging, of beating and taking blows, resulted in a slow, unsteady progress through the narrows of the pass. Reece's force suffered at first. Parade ground techniques just did not pass muster in the heat of real battle. The losses slowed when Gaspire's more capable Collumese arrived on the scene, and their weight in numbers created a terrible inertia that now, as the space about the road widened, reached its tipping point. Gaspire had yet to strike a blow himself. He directed from behind; at times forcibly shoving men into place and screaming at them to get them moving forward. The small Pevanese force blocking the road vexed him. They refused to give way as they should. They forced him to expend time and men with their false bravado. They had to know his forces far outnumbered them. Their sacrifice confused him. They needed to flee or die faster.

A line of double teamed wagons drew up in the pass, spilling men dressed in Sor-reel colors. The sight sweetened Gaspire's next swallow. Tareegan was doing what he did best back down the slope, organizing and collecting the needed troops and transport. The new arrivals formed up, waited expectantly. Gaspire mounted his horse and trotted back to where his men faced the enemy. Fifty yards away, the Pevanese linked shields after retreating to gain space to reform their lines. From his vantage Gaspire got a good look at them. They, too, had suffered in the sun and dust, their ranks thinned by attrition and the need to cover more ground to avoid getting flanked. Behind them, down a long straight slope, Gaspire made out a milling mass of cavalry; not many, but more than the squad he possessed. He smiled grimly. Those troops could cause damage if once they found room to maneuver. Without room, they became observers as their brothers took the brunt of the fight.

"Enough watching," Gaspire muttered to himself. "If I can break that line here, those horsemen may annoy us, but they won't stop us." He sidled his mount closer to Kenton Reece, who looked up at him dusty and blooded from trading blows in the front ranks. Whatever the man's limitations, Reece still possessed a ferocious native courage.

"Right," Gaspire said. "I've a mass of spears behind us just at the summit. I've sent word for more to come up. See the Pevanese? They fall back to regroup, but you are not going to let them."

Reece nodded. "My men are tired, lord, but we will break their line for you."

"Your men are fools, and you are a fool, but you and they have served my purpose, Reece."

"My lord!"

"Save it! Save it! You've one more task, and it is simple enough for even you to accomplish. Reform your lines with mine. When I give the word, send them all against the right side of their line."

"But that will expose our flank! Lord Amdoran---."

"Let me finish, damn you! As you make your rush, the companies behind us will surge into the gap. The road is wider here. We have bled them enough for the push."

"But they have horsed spearmen!"

"Of course they do, fool, but we will roll them up as we go. Break this line and they can fret themselves all the way back down these hills, man! One more push."

Reece's eyes cleared. "You are killing us," he said, his voice suddenly coldly aware.

Gaspire laughed at that. "Yes, I am. Very astute of you. But at least you still have your honor. Get to it, now, and good report of you goes off to your uncle! And that is better than your sore-headed cousin, Hallan. If you want to finally put him in his place, break that line."

Reece scowled, saluted and stomped off. Gaspire looked over again at the Pevanese line. They fought well and showed solid training. He wondered who led them. He focused on the horsemen behind their lines and found his answer. A man with a tall helm separated himself from the group and rode across the front of their line, obviously redressing their formation and exhorting them to new effort. Then he turned and pointed directly at Gaspire with his sword. They locked eyes and Gaspire recognized him.

"Ah, so that is why they stand so," he whispered. "Well met, Captain Avarran."

He stared at his adversary, anger building anew at both the honor and the insulting situation. Donari's best faced them with a tithe of his strength and delayed him.

"Well then, Avarran, you Pevanese shit," he snarled, drawing his sword to signal Reece to advance. "It is time to be done with you."

Donari halted his column near a low place in the river bank. All around him men led their tired mounts down to the water. Two days hard riding separated them from Pevana's walls. Somewhere behind them, the massed foot paced it out; everything now hung on what Donari would find once he reached Avarran's camps. The message reported spears in the hills.

Donari let his horse finish and climbed back up the bank. He checked the saddle girth and squinted against the late afternoon sun setting behind the western mountains. In addition to the members of his guard culled from the citadel, with him rode all he could muster from the decimated Pevanese horse herd: barely two companies of indifferently mounted horsemen, something under a hundred all told. It was a pitiful total, but with Avarran likely embattled against long odds, he had no choice. He prayed strength ahead and speed behind.

A single horseman riding quickly emerged from the sunset haze. Donari expected news, but what came to a frothy, exhausted stop next to him surpassed all surprise; the lone horseman proved to be none other than Talyior Enmbron.

"Oddly enough, I am not surprised to see you," Donari began when the young man slipped from the saddle. "You here smells like a Devyn move."

Talyior smiled grimly, his dusty face making his teeth whiter by comparison.

"Good guess, sire," he responded. "His mount came up lame in the pass. I tried to stay, but the fool spanked my horse and forced the issue. He's too noble by half."

Donari nodded agreement. "More than half, I suspect. What news, then?"

Talyior gestured ahead toward the marching foot. "You seem to have pre-empted my news, sire, and luckily so. Gaspire is in the pass with over 7000. Avarran has taken his men into the narrows to meet him."

"How long ago was this?"

"Devyn and I ran into scouts late yesterday afternoon. More trouble at sunset in the pass. I rode like the wind, found an advance squad halfway down. I made the camp by morning. After that, I raced east and Avarran marched north."

Donari checked the sun's position. His foot soldiers would take at least two more days to cover the distance to Avarran's camp. They would never make it. He motioned an officer close.

"Get them out of the river. I want them walked and warmed before we try to ride. Avarran is up against superior numbers and will need support. We go to see what we can do for his flanks if he cannot hold the narrows."

The officer saluted smartly and moved off. The companies quickly reformed and started off down the track, leaving Donari and Talyior alone.

"So, tell me your other news," Donari ordered. "Help me to see what foolishness my cousin brings with him."

Talyior reviewed the events of his and Devyn's mission, walking alongside the king and what remained of his guard. Talyior's report of Demona's death in childbirth, and the loss of the babe, left Donari strangely unmoved. Demona's death did not touch him; she had allowed herself to become a tool of powerful men and paid the price. He also felt no remorse for his little, stillborn cousin, for by that small tragedy he might yet avoid a greater. Talyior wound his tale down, ending with his last sight of Devyn. The grief in Talyior's voice did touch Donari, deeply. The two young men shared a bond that reminded him of his relationship with Senden. Devyn gone would be a double blow, for Donari knew how Eleni would receive the news back in Pevana.

"I choose to assume Devyn is alive," he said quietly through a strangely clenched jaw, "for Eleni's sake if not my own. Do you the same, please. We four---." He paused to breathe back a sob. "We have shared too much of the sadness of all this folly."

244

"I will try, sire." Talyior's whisper hinted at suppressed emotion. "But Gaspire has so many, and we—."

"Are too few?" Donari finished. "Right enough, but I'd rather do this here and spare Pevana a siege. Blame my impetuous Avedun blood. I have just enough of Roderran in me to value confrontation when it is necessary. Just now, I need to get word to those who come behind. Get your beast some water and continue on."

"But I want to fight!"

"Your horse is done in, Talyior. I have none to spare. Attach yourself to the foot if you like. We will all have more fighting than we would like soon enough."

Talyior fell silent and dropped back. Donari walked his horse and chewed on Talyior's bitter information. Grudgingly, he accepted that he partially underestimated his cousin, or those like Tareegan of Sor-reel who advised him. He assumed the lack of news from the north a reflection of Gaspire's bullying ineptitude. In fact the man had prepared behind a screen of well-placed scouts, like the ones he and Avarran encountered earlier, that kept inquisitive southern eyes at bay and discouraged northern deserters. Or more chilling, perhaps there had not been any who might have wanted to expose those preparations. Always, in the back of his mind, Donari fostered the notion that eventually the people of the north would see through Gaspire's false revolt; that they would recognize the disaster that had been Roderran's rule. They would see him as the better man. Every man of sense, no matter how much he may protest otherwise, wants to be liked, even a king.

Donari's column found Avarran's camp empty, gates opened, the village nearby abandoned. They continued on, urging their tired mounts to as much speed as they dared on the climb into the hills. They heard the sounds of battle filtering around a sharp bend in the road, well in, but distressingly below the summit. Donari ordered most of his men to stay behind and rode ahead. Around the corner they saw Avarran's embattled force stretched out, blocking the way at the top of a long, straight slope. Donari led his men up the road. Avarran paced back and forth behind his lines. Off to the left and back a little clustered a small group of riders; all that remained of Avarran's cavalry company. His tired, dirty face twisted in surprise when Donari dismounted beside him.

"Sire! You come upon a wish. My man made good time, then."

"He did. I set everything in motion as soon as I heard. The foot are out and marching. Talyior found us yesterday. I've all the riders I could scrape together. Less than a hundred, I'm afraid. I've twenty with me. The rest are back beyond the bend."

"Talyior ran into one of my forward patrols. That bunch drew first blood. I marched as soon as Talyior made it to me. We came in time to stiffen my men. It was darkish, early morning stuff. We saw nothing of Devyn Ambrose. I'm sorry, sire."

"He was your friend."

Avarran grinned, a flash of white at odds with the grime. "Taught him how to use a sword. Tried to teach him a little sense. He was never more at home than when he was in trouble."

Memories flashed of former days when that young man's misadventures with words assisted Donari's own designs. Donari saw something in him then, Senden saw even more, and yet in the end Donari could only hope that somehow the boy had found another kind of Maze to disappear into.

"We have lost much, Captain, for this crown I wear. I wonder---."

"Never doubt, sire," Avarran interrupted. "We are here because of what Ambrose and Enmbron achieved. We can't let remorse lead us to question. Now, your coming is timely, sire, but we will soon have need of numbers. Look there," he pointed at the northerners. "They pulled back to reform. And there's more come up behind them. Gaspire has something in mind. Soon now, I think."

Donari checked the Pevanese line. It looked tragically fragile. And yet as men grew aware of their king's presence, backs straightened, spears beat on shields and a ragged cheer began.

"You've done well, brothers!" he shouted. "You have made them hesitate at least! My thanks!"

"Thank you, sire," Avarran acknowledged. "We have stung them repeatedly, but we are bleeding now. If we lose this ground, we will have to fall back quickly. Once they gain the slope here, that will only add to their weight in numbers."

Donari surveyed the ground and agreed with Avarran's assessment. He thought back down the road. The ground leveled off around the bend where his cavalry column waited. If Gaspire broke them here, it would be carnage, a running slaughter all the way back to the camp in the flats. Donari checked the sun. Avarran had bought them a full day at cost, but it would not be enough: the foot were still at least two days away.

"This is a dangerous moment, Jason," Donari said. "And I don't have enough with me to tip the balance."

"You here raises the risks, too, sire. Look, our northern friends have finally figured out who you are."

The activity up the road intensified as a whole group sidestepped to the right, allowing space for a troop of well-armed foot soldiers who advanced behind a waving standard of Collum. Donari squinted against the light and picked out the armored figure of his cousin, Gaspire Amdoran, pointing directly at him.

Donari mounted. "I am here in support, Jason. What can I do?"

"Leave your squad with me and fall back, sire. We are target enough without you."

"Agreed, though I hate it. What will you do?"

Avarran mounted, raising his hand in a rude gesture at the northerners.

"Amdoran thinks he is going to break us in a moment. He expects us to run. I've been watching him through all of this, sire, and he is getting impatient. Why else would he use his own men here, now? So, we will do the unexpected; we will charge."

Avarran turned away, motioning an aide close.

"Pass the word along the line. At my call, we charge. No reserves. We all go. Sire," he said, swinging back. "Add your riders to mine and send them in after us. When we sting them, they will screen our way back down this slope. Send them, sire, and then ready what is left around that bend. We will have need very soon."

Avarran trotted back to the center of his line, faces turned to him expectantly. Again, the man's sense of command struck Donari as something truly powerful.

"Eyes front!" Avarran rasped. "Give nothing away."

Donari trotted his troop to swell Avarran's few. He saw Gaspire rise in the saddle, raise his arm as if in command. The northern mass began to pace forward, a spear length, another, yet another. War shouts swelled from their ranks.

"Now!" Avarran shouted.

At his command the Pevanese sprang forward, covered the distance in a rush to crash into the enemy ranks. Caught off guard, whole groups fell beneath the charge, Avarran's men piercing deep, screaming defiance, creating bloody confusion. For a moment the issue hung like a smoke ring, death undulating, and then Donari sent the squad of cavalry, as a breath of desperate air, racing in from the flank. The pause became a rout as the pressure to the Pevanese front eased. Men yelled, slashed, died. The hindmost bled away in a swarm.

Donari followed, drawn by the rank courage of the moment to disregard Avarran's wishes and his own logic. He plunged into the melee, sword drawn and biting. Gaspire's stunned, raging face appeared before him, and he spurred his horse through the press, swung his blade in a mighty arc that Gaspire met with a clumsy block. The shock of the blow separated them, the flood of fleeing, fighting men acting like a current. Gaspire spurred out of harm's way.

And then into the void raced a handful of northern cavalry. They slammed into the remains of his own, and what had felt like victory turned instead into bloody chaos. Donari wrenched his horse's head around. By common consent his men streamed back the way they had come, back, leaving the roadway strewn with northern and southern dead. Behind him his squad of cavalry reformed, creating a milling, dancing line as they tangled with their counterparts. Donari caught a glimpse of the foremost among them; a tall man with blond hair spilling out beneath a dented helm and remembered.

Hallan.

Gaspire cursed, stunned frozen in the saddle as the Pevanese broke their line and charged, slamming into Reece's men on their flank, exploiting the gap created by Gaspire's ordered side-step. He admired the fool's hope courage of the action even as he sidled his horse back and right to avoid the press of their spears.

The Pevanese rolled up Reece's men and crunched against the men of Collum. Men fell screaming. Spears and now arrows flew thick in the air, taking more. The northerners began to break. Donari's hated face swam before his, sword poised for a killing blow, and Gaspire had to make a desparate swing with his own blade to block it, wrenching his horse around in the process.

He fell back. Men streamed back with him. The small contingent of Pevanese cavalry moved against the broken mass, riding down and spearing men at will, the scene one of utter chaos. Reece ran by Gaspire, screaming, the left side of his face spouting blood from a deep slash. Gaspire tried to stem the tide, swinging from side to side, rage and fear at war within him as he processed Donari's sudden appearance.

He is a ghost.

The Pevanese mounted spearmen cleared the space before him, reformed and prepared to punish Gaspire's hopes further. He cast about in search of support and realized his dangerous exposure. The Pevanese horsemen moved forward. Gaspire saw his death in their intent. He wrenched on the reins again, and as he turned his horse he caught sight of Hallan of Hallar at the head of his handful of mounted men thundering past him. Gaspire turned to watch them crash into the Pevanese, upsetting their formation, knocking men from saddles. He looked for Donari, found him spurring free of the ground.

Hallan's sudden action stemmed the chaos. In the pause, Gaspire's men came up and rolled into the Pevanese who broke in turn and streamed back down the slope. And kept going, seeking distance and space in which to reform. Gaspire urged his men on as they ran screaming to the fray, line after line, a growing mass of metal and malice sweeping down the road to keep up the pressure. At the front of it, Gaspire made out Hallan and what was left of his squad, swords out and darting, leading the way.

Gaspire moved out of the way as the rest of his army filed by. Then he followed, picking his way down a road that suddenly sprouted dead and wounded men like spring weeds.

Avarran's gamble in the pass bought him the rest of the day. Night fell before either side could remarshall their troops. Donari bowed to Avarran's angry criticism and kept station with the foot soldiers. Avarran led Donari's doughty squadron in charges time and again to stem the advance. Men fell. Horses took lame and were slaughtered in the road to clog the way. Again and again, Donari rued the losses at Lyranden Bridge. But Avarran's stratagem worked. Donari reformed the column behind the tenuous protection. Rain fell at dusk, further dampening the pursuit. Donari and Avarran's survivors spent a cheerless night huddled in their cloaks in line across the roadway.

The morning brought a muddy resumption of the pummeling. The day passed in a series of desperate, temporary stands against the swelling northern numbers. Time and again Donari's men reformed, linked shields, took the shock and held for ever shortening moments, and time and time again Avarran's riders extricated them. Through it all Donari's men marched and fought an orderly manner. And yet the line of dead and dying lengthened with each mile, and the slopes about the road widened as they descended towards the flats. They came finally to a space where they lacked the numbers to anchor their flanks. The northerners rolled into them, those flanks buckled, and the retreat became a rout.

A bare remnant reformed on the far side of a small streamlet that gurgled underneath a single span bridge. Donari sat on his horse grim and stoic as what was left of his mounted screen filed by him on the bridge. Avarran was the last one to cross. Down the road, what was left of Avarran's command struggled to maintain order. Up the road the sounds of the Perspan mass preceded their appearance. Less than a score of riders remained. They spread out along the bank to either side of the bridge.

Avarran sported a bloody bandage on a thigh that seeped around the bindings. His face, pale beneath a dented helm, bore gashes and gore as well. Donari sat free of wounds and felt guilty for it.

"Sire," Avarran began, voice cracking with exhaustion. "Please, my king. Enough. Once they gain this span they will finish us. You need to go."

"We go together."

"Brothers!" Avarran shouted to the riders that remained. "Please get the king back to the others. This is no fit place for him."

"First man to touch me loses the hand." And yet even as he said it, Donari knew he would go. He had thousands marching at his orders. Dying here to honor a friend would be less than useless. He had risked much staying for as long as he did. It pained him to agree with Avarran.

"Donari."

The use of his given name startled him. He looked closely at Avarran, saw the signs there and nodded.

"Right," Avarran said quietly. "I think you understand. This leg is all but useless, and my horse is lame. I'm done running, Donari. Go."

"What do you hope to achieve alone?"

"I'd rather die here than bleed out on the road. This is as good a place as any."

"And not alone, King Donari!" A small group of riders separated themselves from the others. They were all that remained of Avarran's original squad. The foremost of them spoke. "We will stand with our captain. He is right, sire. You must go, now."

Still Donari hesitated, unwilling at the last. The northerners spilled out onto the road from around the last turn before the bridge and decided his course for him.

Clouds above crouched over the scene to repeat the previous day's rains. Somehow, the idea of Renia's Tears to grace the moment seemed appropriate. He moved his horse off the bridge, took a last look at the northerners swelling for the charge.

"Thank you, brothers," he said around a clenched throat. "Let us pray we have done enough for light and love. Renia's Grace on all of you."

He spurred away. Behind him the sounds of battle rose. He looked over his shoulder, saw Avarran strike once, twice, before disappearing beneath the rush.

Tears came in earnest then as Donari urged his tired mount to more speed.

Chapter 26: Two prodigals

Water rushing in the beginnings of a small flash flood woke Devyn where he lay unconscious in the ravine. He blinked and tried to focus, but his badly concussed vision refused to clear. He made out vague outlines of rocks and tree branches set as shadows against a grey background. He felt the water's pull strengthen as the land collected the bounty of the rain storm and sent it percolating and flowing down, seeking a collection point from whence gravity and the land's slope could send it downward, ever downward until it joined the river and added its volume on the way to the sea.

The rising water pulled at him and threatened to dislodge him from the rocks where he lay, bent uncomfortably, between two large basaltic boulders. His head ached and his hair felt sticky as if from dried blood. He moaned and tried raising his head. He ached all over; his body felt like a bruise. But the water insisted he take notice or drown. He forced his arms to reach back over his head and found he could get a purchase on the rocks that bracketed his position. He managed to pull himself back, inch by inch, up and away from the water's grip. He grew aware of a deep chill and shivers took control of his body. The water rose against his thighs, reluctant to give him up. Despite the agony in his head and his body's weakness, Devyn kept reaching and pulling, hands scrabbling for holds on the rocks and tree roots that clustered at the lip of the ravine.

He managed to get a leg underneath him and pushed up further and then found a lodgment for his other foot and so leveraged himself even higher up the bank and felt the water's questing pull lessen and pass away. Stars swam before Devyn's eyes as he fought against the spasms that wracked his body. The short climb exhausted his meager resources, and he slumped back against a tree root and lost himself in darkness. He did not mark the sudden rise and fall of the flood. It passed while he lay, a frothy, jumbled temporary torrent in search of a way down and around the hill.

Surreal water dreams perplexed his dark slumber. Renia's tears bathed his hurts then threatened to drown him. He felt himself adrift amid towering waves that alternately bore him up then crashed down upon him, plunging him so deep he despaired of surfacing, his lungs burning for air. And yet when he attempted to breathe, expecting to feel the rush of water death, nothing of the sort happened. He woke and realized he lay on the ground near a small puddle of new fallen rain where his exhalations caused minute ripples across its small expanse. And in that small water he thought he saw one of Minuet's arrowheads pointing straight at him, and then Renia's voice, like the faint sound of waves held in sea-shells came to him.

"Breathe child, sleep, live. Let the waters of life ease you. Sleep. Sleep. Then wake. Wake to your fate, child."

When he woke, he found his vision normal, but his head still pounded and his body felt like he had been run over by an ox team. He checked himself and discovered all his appendages worked and that he could stand. Fever made such an effort questionable, but he knew it was move or die. He had no idea how long he lay in the ravine; his last clear memory a collage of horse hooves, sword blades and the nothingness of his fall. But he was alive and still free, which meant he needed to find out if Talyior made it through and if there was anything left to do. He still retained his sword. He wondered what became of the young man, Hallan, he and Talyior encountered by the stream. Despite his condition, Devyn felt somewhat reassured by the fact his mind still worked and that he still had questions. He needed answers, so he stumbled off down the ravine, moving slowly at first, fighting down the shivers and struggling with weakness in his legs and arms. He kept moving, following the last remnants of the flood, hoping that its trickle at least led southward.

It did. Devyn kept moving, unwell but still mobile, and so cheated death for a time. That was enough for now.

Devyn stopped repeatedly to clear his head. In time the ravine dwindled down to a gurgling watercourse and swung back to the west around the shoulder of a hill. The sun setting drew him on until he collapsed under a bush. As the light faded, he drifted off into a sleep troubled by fever dreams and memories.

Once again, images paraded before him in repose, disjointed and macabre, and yet his sleeping self made sure of their import. His father accosted him with the face of a leper, shaking a hand that lacked three fingers. His mother leered at him, laughing hysterically even as a dark shape spread shadow hands around her neck and squeezed. Pevana's children walked by him in a solemn procession with bound hands and tongues pierced with what looked like candles from a King's Theology altar. And the little girl, Tasia, who had warned him of Tolimon in the bell tower, looked directly at him and tried to speak, but Devyn only heard the sound of her tears that dripped from her cheeks to fall on his outstretched hand. He heard screams of horses and faint echoes of the war cries of men and stars fell from the sky. The old scars on his forearms ached with remembered flames, and he thought he might have cried out once, but all was metaphor in his wandering dreamland. Kingdoms rose and fell like tidal surges and time became a reality trapped within the confines of an hour glass.

He awoke at daybreak, weak, hungry yet clear headed, a need to hurry nagged him though he could not tell the reason. He struggled to his feet and continued his travail. He followed the watercourse and soon it passed out from underneath its screen of trees and joined another rivulet and grew back into a brook. After stumbling around a turn and picking his way through a tumble of rounded boulders and water-weathered stones, he found himself on the edge of a battlefield a furlong away from a small bridge. He staggered out from his cover, drawn by the profusion of humped shapes littering the area. He recognized northern badges among the dead, but the greater number sported the dolphin insignia that said they belonged to Donari's men, most of them lay facing south. He felt hope fade like a wave retreating.

This was no battle. Rout, rather.

Devyn put aside hope to scrounge food from the pack of one of the fallen and took a hunk of stale bread. From another he scavenged a water bottle which he refilled at the brook near the bridge. The food refreshed him and brought some strength back into his limbs. He looked around the scene; he was the only one alive. He wondered how bad had been the defeat here, whether it would be worth it to follow in the wake and perhaps do his part. He wondered if Talyior was still alive.

He crossed the little culvert bridge and saw a familiar shape lying on the side of the road next to the stiffened carcass of a horse he remembered. Sorrow took Devyn as he smoothed away a strand of bloody, matted hair from Avarran's face.

"So it truly was defeat," he whispered, and then he wept and faced more memories. Avarran and Kembril Edri, the pillars of his life, now lost to the horror of the times. Edri showed Devyn how to survive Pevana's Maze and gave him the power of words. Avarran taught him the use of the sword and to live with honor. Their relationship that began with Avarran chasing an impish Devyn about Pevana's streets grew into a fast friendship. Save Talyior, Donari, and Eleni, there was no one alive who Devyn could say he respected more. The sight of his friend's face frozen in death's grimace felt world ending and darkness threatened anew. Pevana without Avarran's steady nobility and firm ways: unthinkable. And yet Devyn thought the same thing when Senden died.

Time paused for him. He existed as a thought suspended, frozen, like his friend's face in death. A breath. Another. Silence. And then his pulse began to beat its cadence. A gentle breeze tufted his hair, caused a caricature of life as it brushed Avarran's battered temple. He followed the line the hair made, saw Avarran's sword, broken near the haft. He gathered the pieces and laid them on Avarran's chest. Devyn knelt, touched his friend's cold brow a last time. Unbidden, like an unexpected gift, came a snatch of an old song Avarran had liked. In a voice that grew with each word, Devyn sang:

And in the end all is made the same
If your days run to ruin
You've only yourself to blame.
It's like working all week
To pay for the dance
And then acting sorry you came.

You have to make the world care
With a gift of your passion.
And you have to take the dare
To make a lasting impression.

Let your hair catch the breeze
Set your course as you please
If Fate knocks you down
Shout defiance from your knees.

There's no one to bar your passage
Save your own fear
Anyplace free would be better than here.
So go...

His voice faltered as the gift bled away.

"Any place free," he muttered, rising unsteadily to his feet. For Devyn that meant Pevana.

An image from his fever dreams flashed to him, Minuet's face mouthing words, and then he saw the horse nibbling grass that grew just beyond the burm next to a corpse whose hand, frozen in death, still retained its grip on the reigns. It nickered when he drew close and tugged against the restraint of its fallen rider but calmed when he talked to it and gently patted its muzzle. Something of his former timber when he worked at Malom Banly's must have come through, for the beast permitted him to mount though the effort made him woozy. Then he and the horse, both orphans of war, plodded down the road looking for the tragedy that made them so.

He came to the remains of a village and a small military camp set up, he thought, to guard the fords. Here men still groaned from wounds or called out to him for help, but he forced himself to ignore their pleas. He had a battle to find.

He could see no one had crossed the fords. Whatever fighting that took place ran down the northern bank of the river. Devyn heeled his horse into a quick walk and left the smoldering scene and its dying men behind. Later he reined in, drawn by the sight of a face he recognized. It belonged to a man who attempted to mount a horse but whose wounded leg defeated him when he put weight on it to lift his good one to fit a foot into the stirrup. The horse sidled, and the man fell with a gasp of pain and frustration. Devyn walked his horse over, grabbed the reins of the restive beast and looped them through his own horse's bridle strap. Then he dismounted, knelt down and helped the man sit up.

"Well met, Hallan," he said quietly. "Could you use a little help with your horse?"

Hallan stared at him, dumbfounded. "You," he managed to croak at last. "How?"

"Yes," Devyn answered, "me. Sorry about your nose. And yet you look like you received worse, after. You will sport a fine bump there for the rest of your days once the bruises fade. I can't say it will be an improvement, but it does make you a bit more rugged looking."

Devyn's tone, so at odds with the scene, brought a wry grin to Hallan's face, which fell to a wince from the pain of his swollen lips.

"You could have killed me back there," he said. "Why didn't you?"

"I did not think you needed killing. We just wanted to get by your squad. Besides, I figured why spoil the fun for some other fellow, but you seem to lead a charmed life."

"Charmed. That is not how I would describe it."

"But you are alive. There seems to have been fighting. What can you tell me of it?"

Devyn put a hand to his forehead to rub a sore spot, and his fingers came away bloody. Hallan winced when he saw the blood. Devyn noticed the reaction. "Yes," he offered, "I missed it. Had a bit of a fall, you see. So, we find each other damaged but still alive. I think that calls for some sort of truce, don't you think?"

"I do not think I want to kill you, Devyn Ambrose," Hallan said. "Besides, my sword broke in the last cavalry charge."

"Cavalry? Tell me, what has happened?"

Hallan's expression faded. "We pushed your troops down from the pass. I guess your partner, what was his name? Talyior? Yes? Well, I suppose he got through. Your folk came up to meet us in the narrows. King Donari was there."

256

"The King, here?" Devyn interrupted.

"Yes, that surprised me, too. He nearly got to Lord Amdoran, but I think I foiled him there. Odd." He paused, a strange expression, almost rueful, ghosting over his face before he continued. "For a whole day we beat against each other's shields. Eventually, we came to wider ground, and Gaspire managed to get most of his army in place. Your men broke. I saw Avarran fall; he was a brave man. I came to respect him on the march back after Lyranden Bridge. They pulled him down. They weren't gentle."

"That much I gathered. I found him at the bridge."

"Yes," Hallan mused, remembering. "He tried to hold the span by himself, I think. The rest of your folk ran. We came after. About a mile or so further on from here what remained of your horse companies hit us in mid-career. I lost control of my mount in the melee after taking a blow to my leg. The silly thing ran back here before tossing me. That was last night. I have been trying to remount since morning." He looked up at Devyn, his face respectful behind its ruined nose and bruises. "Your men fought well," he finished. "They fought very well, but in the end numbers told and we won the field. What remained retired with Donari behind your cavalry with Gaspire and his force close behind." His voice faltered and trailed off.

Devyn sat back on his haunches, testing Hallan's story, weighing it against the burden of his own responsibilities. He liked this man and understood why Donari spoke so highly of him. He took a drink from his borrowed water bottle and shared it.

"Well," he sighed. "We come to a choice again you and I. What are we to do?"

Hallan paused, looking keenly over the bottle's rim.

"I suspect," he answered carefully, "if you were to get me in the saddle, that if we ride half a day east we will find what ever battle that remains to be fought."

"And what then?" asked Devyn. "Will we square off and start trading blows?"

Hallan laughed at that, breaking the tension of the moment. "I think we both have come close to death since we first met, and I doubt either of us will be the death of the other."

Devyn snorted in response. "Good answer. Let me bind that leg of yours and get you up. Then we shall see what there is to see up ahead."

Nightfall caught Devyn and Hallan short of their objective, and neither wanted to blunder into guards from either side in the dark, so they agreed to share a night's camp and make their choices in the morning. They turned their tired horses away from the river and climbed the shoulder of a hill until they came to a hollow fenced by alder trees with a spring that pooled in a low spot before cutting its way out through the eastern end. They staked their horses near the water and managed to light a fire. Devyn suspected they were high up and far away enough to avoid detection. For a truce camp it was a good location. They shared what food they had been able to scrounge, saw to each other's wounds, and carefully felt out each other's story.

Devyn found much to respect though it troubled his thoughts.

He assumed Hallan struggled with deeper questions, which likely waited to perplex his sleep.

The half-full wineskin Devyn found in Hallan's saddle bag helped lighten the mood.

But in the morning, Devyn woke alone. He shifted himself as quickly as he could, tightened the girths on his horse, and struggled into the saddle to follow.

"And what did you choose, Hallan?" he muttered as he spurred up and out of the hollow.

Once they reached the level spaces near the river, the Perspans widened their front and rolled forward like a wave. They filled the area from the last slopes to the river bank like a wall of spears intent on chewing up anything that got in their way.

And nothing did.

Gaspire let them go secure in the columns that now marched down from the hills to his ranks. The river guarded his right flank and the hills his left; their treeless, rolling slopes offering little in the way of cover for anything numerous. Every league Gaspire's rabble claimed from the ruined camps behind them meant a wider region for maneuver. More room to swamp Donari and his presumption of power.

And so he let them go, a rolling undisciplined mass, heedless in their rush, arrogant and confident after their victory in the hills. Gaspire tamped down the little voice in the back of his mind that whispered caution, that suggested the line of dead moldering on the road back up to the hill pass reflected strength not desperation, that Donari was still dangerous in any context.

"Go on, Reece, you ugly bastard," he muttered, quieting the whispers in his mind. "Run into something tangible for me."

Just before sundown Reece did. Sounds of fighting came back to the main host as an afterthought, a distant clamor and alarm as of thunder

258

heard rumbling too far off to be of concern. But the rabid survivors of that clash told of a sharp encounter with Pevanese horse.

"Not a large force, lord," a bloodied Kenton Reece reported. They rolled us up smartly enough. But then they spurred away rather than take advantage."

"And what does that tell you?" Gaspire kept his voice droll.

"That the southerners are out, my lord."

"How very astute! That hole in your cheek seems to have improved your wits." Gaspire dismissed him with a wave and turned to his guards. "Spread the word. Camp here. Full sentries. Links between units. The bastards are out there, likely shitting their breeches over what's coming for them. Set up my tents here next the road and let the lords attend me."

"Fires, my lord?" one asked.

"Absolutely! Make a constellation of light for Donari's hill skulkers to see and report. I want him visited by his ghosts and fears tonight."

Gaspire was well into his second glass of wine when Tareegan and Hallaran joined him in his tent to toast their success. And yet Hallaran insisted on scowling over the rim of his cup.

"You are smug, Gaspire." The rasp in his voice obvious. "But you've Donari yet to best tomorrow. That was but a portion of his strength."

Gaspire laughed derisively and tossed a roll at the older man. "He cannot hope to hold me here," he scoffed. "You saw him in the hills, skulking behind the real fight. Even the surprise of his horsemen did not have a lasting effect. We stopped them. Donari hasn't the mounts here to annoy us tomorrow. We will grind him up. He is too proud, the fool, to try and meet us so far from his city's walls."

"We have no appreciable cavalry to guard our flanks, Gaspire," Tareegan interjected.

"What of it? That was barely two companies today. We stung them afterward. I tell you he spent them to save that rabble. Tomorrow will be spear to spear, shield to shield. What horse we have left will do fine on our northern flank."

Hallaran growled into his cup, muttering disagreement.

"I'm too old for fights such as this, Lord Amdoran. And yet what I saw yesterday disturbed me. You showed credible skill in the contest in the hills, but you lost control of them after."

"I gave them their heads, my lord, as a reward for their hard labors."

"And look what happened. Reece tells me there were losses. My men, lord."

Gaspire frowned in mock concern. He did not enjoy the older man's too cautious attitude. He sounded like an old woman. Gaspire wanted his men; he did not need either the father or his only remaining son. He noted also that son's absence since the fray at the bridge.

"My lord," he asked, his voice silky and sarcastic. "Where is your son, Hallan? Perhaps if we have questions about our own available horse, we should ask him?"

"I have not received word of nor from him since he left Lomillar to chase your spies."

"Yes," Gaspire retorted. "And made a poor job of it. His incompetence led to our troubles in the pass."

"But I am told he led the charge that turned the thing for us. Deny that truth, lord."

Gaspire grunted, hiding his disgust with a generous swallow from his cup as he remembered that close call. Donari had almost seen to him. Hallan's charge stemmed the Pevanese attack. Plus, the young man fought in the forward press for the rest of the chaotic day. Gaspire owed him, yet he declined generosity.

"No word? And Kenton Reece bears noble wounds. I am well-pleased with your nephew, despite his limitations." He sipped again to swallow the lie. "How strange that a son should be outshone by the cousin. I recall Hallan came late to the fight in the hills. Too intent, perhaps, on scouting to fight? I also recall seeing bandages on his arm and forehead. Wounded, but I wonder how he got them?"

Hallaran's expression darkened as if suppressing an angry retort. He slurped from the cup and kept his silence.

"I will send a party back along the way we came," Gaspire soothed. "If he fell they will surely find him. Hold up, man. Tomorrow we will see an end to this."

.

Darkness finally drove Donari from his saddle. The rolling defeat after Avarran's fall at the bridge had tasked him like never before. Only a desperate ambush by his mounted few, stiffened by two score of the more able-bodied footmen, managed to barely blunt the pressure from Gaspire's unruly mob. His survivors met up with the van just before dusk. The army went into a doubtful camp with the news of Avarran's death spreading from campfire to campfire like rumor.

Donari's knees nearly buckled as he dismounted. He gripped his saddle to keep from collapsing. Thankfully, his tired horse waited patiently as he regained himself. The poor beast had gashes and small cuts to front and both flanks. He patted its mighty shoulder.

"Many, many thanks, Boce', great heart. You saved my life today." He gave the reins to a waiting horseboy. "Mix in a little spirits with his oats. He earned them."

"Yes, sire," the boy said. "And I know where I can get some salve for these slices."

"Thank you, son, and if you see Drue—." He stopped. No. That was not right. Drue was dead.

"Sir?"

"Nothing, child, I'm all but done in. You may go. Rub him for me, and then find yourself something for the night."

Donari staggered to tent prepared for him. He spied his favorite camp chair and what looked like a wineskin looped over the arm. He eased himself down, took a long, bitter drink and tried to will his mind to consider life and rule without Avarran as his rock. For as long as he ruled Pevana, Avarran had been captain of his guard. It was Avarran who saw to the care and training of Pevana's military units. It was Avarran who led the army back from Roderran's defeat and Avarran who melded the fragmented groups who swore fealty to Donari into a cohesive, confident force. Donari took small solace that he and Avarran had guessed correctly: this was Gaspire's one and only gambit.

And yet the cost is too high. Avarran!

Donari toured the fires of his men that night and bore that cost as best he might. He walked the camp, talked to his men and took their measure. What he sensed pleased him. Avarran's survivors had not infected the others with fear and defeatism. Rather, they clustered about him, reassured him with their firmness and asked for a chance to avenge their fallen leader.

"I was with him during the march south to Lyranden Bridge," an older veteran said. "Cool as clean sheets the whole time, sire. And on the way back, Renia bless him, he kept the peace and the pace. No one else could have done that."

"You should have seen him in the pass," asserted another. "They were swimming around us, but you wouldn't have known it. When he ordered that charge, ha! But you were there, too, sire, you saw! I thought we might have done for them, then. But they was just too many, King Donari, just too many."

"Yes, men, I was there. You did well. All of you did so well," Donari said. "We have a chance. I could not ask for more. You more than repaid Avarran's faith in you."

"We aren't done yet, sire," the veteran replied. "There's a few of us left that want another crack at those rebels yonder. Avarran never blinked, and neither will we."

"But many of you are wounded. You've a nasty gash yourself," Donari countered.

The man waved off the notice. "A scratch. A lucky thrust, but I skewered the bugger that gave it to me. I'll not let it keep me from the lines, my lord. Like I said, me and the boys have talked it out. We owe it to Avarran to see it through. We owe it to you, too, lord."

"I do not hate those men," Donari responded. "I want to end the killing."

"It's not about hate, sire," the older veteran gushed. "It's about defending what is right. We are your men, lord. And if those men don't see it, then we will sting them until they do. Some's going to die, but that's the way of it. They make their choices, as do we."

"The morning will see an end, regardless. My thanks for your service, men."

"As my grandad used to say: *It is too late to change your mind once the arrow has been loosed.* We are here to see to it, sire."

Donari could not find words for a further response and bowed himself away overcome by such confidence and loyalty. He sent a bit of the wine from his tents back to their fire before taking to his own blankets. If this proved his last night of peace, then so be it. He was in the company of heroes; not even the glow from Gaspire's camp could take away that power.

Chapter 27: The Last Day of Peace

Eleni Caralon, shadowed by a hovering Cryso, strolled along the citadel battlements in the September afternoon sun. Eleni moved carefully, right hand and arm held gently but firmly by Cryso, along the crenellations until she reached a bench seat placed on a raised platform to provide a view over the battlements. She settled back with a sigh and looked out to the lands to the west.

What she saw formed the core of a kingdom. To the south of the little river that pierced the Pevanese valley the lands ran mostly flat, folding into downs and slopes as they neared the highlands. To the north the land spread out in rolling acres sliced by alluvial masses that buttressed the rocky hills. The region's beauty of tilled fields and farms below the river and the ordered rows of vineyards above appealed to her, had always, but differently now since her ascencion. It and the ring on her finger were a promise; a promise that now faced ruin thanks to Casan and Amdoran. Casan deserved what Donari did with him. No martyrdom for him locked away in a windowless room in the palace, alone in the dark with his plots, cut off from his pens and power.

That left Gaspire Amdoran.

Eleni wanted an end to the mess. She wanted Donari and she wanted a child. She wanted her words and she wanted the scene laid out before her eyes to be real and not illusion.

Eleni took in a deep breath and wondered how fared Devyn Ambrose and his friend, Talyior Enmbron, gone now for nearly three weeks. She hoped they were safe. She looked north to the hills and tried to imagine them riding south with the news Donari needed so desperately.

But her imagination would only take her so far, and the effort tired her. She sighed again, and at the sound Cryso sat down next to her.

"Tired, my lady?" he murmured deferentially. "Perhaps we should get you back to bed."

She looked at him, moved by his concern and marveling yet again at the depth of his devotion to Donari, and through him, her. Calm and efficient, Cryso added his own special weave to the tarton of love Eleni sensed growing daily.

"Not just yet," she answered finally, blinking and smiling away his concern. "The sun feels good, and I need to breathe."

Cryso relaxed and leaned back in the bench seat.

"A few minutes more, and then it is back to bed with you."

She sighed. "More of Donari's secret orders for me?"

"Among a small handful, lady, but none of them secret. He worries for your recovery."

"And I appreciate your concern, Cryso, really. You've been so kind to me."

Cryso bowed his head. "I serve House Avedun, mistress, and you are now part of that house."

"Not yet," she countered, twisting the ring Donari placed on her finger when he announced his intentions. "And likely never if things go ill."

Crsyo lightly touched the gem gracing the band.

"This stone declares otherwise, lady. The people don't require a ceremony to cement their love. Neither does Donari. You are his queen in all ways that matter to him, to us. I serve you now as I have served him heretofore. Command, lady."

"Could you make time stop?" she asked softly. "Make all the clouds stay away, turn Gaspire into a pliant priest and Casan into a doting grandfather?"

Cryso laughed gently and snapped his fingers imperiously. "Of course, done! And what else?"

"That will do, for now," she countered. She found the sound of Cryso's laughter humanizing and compelling, like a glimpse inside a special room where folk locked away their deepest secrets. Her days since the spring had been so full of watch and ware, her joys small and stolen by comparison, that real mirth came as a surprise, a spiced poignancy to be cherished.

Time would not stand still, Gaspire would not seek peace and Casan was as far removed from grandfatherhood as the cruel god Boriman from kindness. She and Donari, Cryso and Devyn, all of them seemed fated to see great things done, kindnesses and cruelties that echoed the cataclysms that occurred between the gods of their land. Even Renia's tears, benison that they were, had their source in eternal tragedy.

In the darkness of his room, the Lord Prelate Byrnard Casan raged in silence and bitter gall. He sat in an overstuffed chair placed next to a trundle bed. He knew that only because when he reached out his foot he could feel its wooden frame. He strained to note some sort of shape or landmark to orient himself. Nothing. They made the space totally dark, going so far as to place rugs against the door to block out the last ribbons of light that might penetrate into the room. For all intents and purposes, Casan sat in a coffin. He could think and fret and rage and no one would care. He chose to do so in silence. If they had listeners at the door, then he did not want to give them the satisfaction of hearing him rave.

And assailed by memories and images, Casan did rave in a heart clenching, chin quivering fashion. Roderran's shade came to him and showed him the great rent of the death wound Sylvanus gave him, asking him how, why, what could have allowed such an imposition to happen? And Jaryd Corvale paced before his mind's eye holding his head before him like a chalice that dripped blood and gore. And it, too, asked him questions about how it came to be that he stood there with a severed head, victim of such a blow from a stripling like Devyn Ambrose. Why was it, both shades seemed to ask, that they should fall to a southern dilettante and a silly wordsmith? How was it possible that Donari could prosper so when served by such lesser men as those?

Casan forced himself to consider answers to those questions as he sat there, stewing in his bitter disappointment, and what he came up with only made him feel worse. Donari the better man? Such a thought, unthinkable in the past, loomed plausible as he fretted in the dark, powerless, lightless, alone. *King* Donari. Even the consonants of the two words together caused him pain. And that woman, so proud, so arrogant, so insidiously fortunate! He heard her voice in his head most often now; every syllable dripped perfume and acquired power. She lived, and Donari loved her; acted like a man, finally, for her, and that was the most damning result of the whole affair.

Casan clenched his hands and shook them. But that deeply recessed and attenuated part of his mind, where the vestiges of reason lay locked away and forgotten for nearly fifty years, now whispered otherwise and questioned whether Casan shook his hands out of conviction and wrath, or palsy and uncertainty?

He only had one hope for an end to the madness: Gaspire. Donari's actions meant news, and Casan felt the rumor in the stones of horses pacing, men marching. A lifetime in conflict left Casan innately aware of such things. War. They could shove him into this dank hole, but he still knew and that knowledge meant they did not have total power over him. Not yet. But defiance, empty and ignored, was all he had left. He blinked, tried to imagine light and could not. His pulse quickened unnaturally and he felt a dull pain in his shoulder. He dropped his hands and massaged the spot with weak, boney fingers. For the first time in his long, duplicitous life, Byrnard Casan had run out of options.

Eleni sat at her writing table and struggled to find words. Despite the dramatic changes in her life, she kept to the duties Donari first gave her back in those dark days after Tomais' death. Eleni strove with her pen and store of words to set down a version of the truth for posterity. And as events flowed, changed, intensified so had her devotion to the task. She recognized the temporary quality of history and the perils of mythmaking. She determined Donari would not suffer misinterpretation though he marched with his men to uncertain fate.

Eleni forced herself to stay objective. She ignored the dull ache in her shoulder, tamped down the rage at the man responsible and wrote as much of the truth for which she could hold herself responsible.

She dipped her pen anew and froze.

No! First Tomais, then Senden. Renia, goddess, please, not Donari, too.

She put the pen down, rose carefully from her writing table and moved over to the window. It faced west, overlooking the bench seat on the citadel battlements where Donari took his leave of her. Beyond that now precious vantage, the valley of Pevana reached back along its river and hill ridges to the mountains beyond. All her remaining hopes lay out of reach. Her shoulder ached, keeping company with her heart, punctuating her sense of helplessness in the face of things. She had grown so used to *doing* that *not doing* pushed her toward panic. She felt as trapped by her body, ignorant and alone, as Casan locked away in his darkened room. She paused at the thought, momentarily intrigued by the realization that the old fool's presence in the palace actually made her feel safer.

How odd. I lose Donari to duty, gain Casan as a charge, and yet somehow it all fits. Let him sit in his darkness until the end.

The sight of a lone rider racing quickly up the road to Pevana's Land Gate snapped her attention back to the present. Such a rider meant news. She followed the rider's progress, then looked once more westward and noticed for the first time the line of smoke on the horizon's edge. Something burned there at a place towards which Donari marched if he was not there already. Fear washed over her, and her shoulder protested at the change by pulsing anew. That sent her reeling back to her chair to wait for the message she knew would come.

Eleni listened for footsteps in the hallway, recognized Cryso's measured rhythm and tred. He entered after a faint knock on her door. Eleni composed herself for the worst.

"My lady," Cryso said carefully. "We have received news."

"Yes," Eleni responded, her voice tight yet restrained. "I saw the rider. Please, tell me, is it Donari?"

"No, lady. Donari sent him. The king lives."

Eleni sagged in partial relief. "I saw smoke on the horizon, what of that?"

Cryso nodded. "There has been battle in the hills. Avarran contested the pass with Lord Amdoran's men."

"And? The smoke?"

"Avarran is dead, lady. One who saw him fall met up with Donari's force a day ago. The northerners burned a village near the river ford." He paused.

"What else, Cryso? Tell me."

Cryso sighed, meeting her intent gaze with eyes softened by age and pity. "Yes, lady, there is more. Avarran had time to prepare a defense because he received word of the northerner's intentions."

"Devyn Ambrose and Talyior Enmbron," Eleni snapped. "They returned?"

"It would appear, lady, but--."

"But? But what? Cryso, be clear."

"The messenger said word reached them from a lone rider. Talyior, mistress. Devyn Ambrose remained behind in the pass. He has not been seen since."

Eleni slumped in her chair. Not the worst news, but almost. She ticked the names off in her mind like a list of doom: Tomais, Senden, and now Devyn. Fate took all the most precious from her. And yet Donari lived.

But he was alone now.

The urge to fly to him overwhelmed her, and she cursed her weakness. Her shoulder throbbed, and she fought down the wave of queasiness pushed upward from the new life surging in her womb.

What chance for my babe if Donari falls?

"Cryso!" she snapped.

"My lady?"

"What force did Donari leave in the city?"

"A few score here in the citadel, some to guard the sea and land gates."

"Send them."

"My lady?"

Conviction swelled. "What good walls with none to hold them? Send out word, now, throughout the city. Spread this news. The people need to know."

"But, lady, they might panic."

267

"Cryso, you've spent too much of your time in these quiet halls. I believe otherwise. Get every nag, work horse, drey mule, everything that can move and the folk to ride them out. Let the people choose, Cryso. Those who can fight, go. Let the others man the walls if they will."

"But what use will they be?"

"Maybe little, maybe nothing, Renia knows. But Donari makes a gesture with this battle, Cryso. Perhaps we can make our own."

"We? But lady, Donari's orders—"

"I'm sure you will find at least one beast capable of pulling the small carriage. Don't argue with me, please. I have to go, if for nothing else, at least to see, to know. Waiting is worse than death to me. Now, go see to it and send word when all is ready."

Cryso left. The power of her outburst cooled, faded back to fear, and shadows crept into her thoughts and darkness settled around her heart and squeezed. She felt faint. So much death. Talyior alive. Donari, alive. And then the other bit of the message returned to her.

Devyn. Gone. Possibly.

She hung her head and tears fell. One of them dropped onto the page she had been working on before, smearing a letter in the name she wrote there: *Devyn Ambrose.*

The coincidence sent her riffling through her basket of papers. At the bottom she found them, Devyn's scribblings from when he was Malom Banley's horse boy. She recalled trying to return them during their ride back to Pevana after Lyranden Bridge, but he made her keep them, calling them part of a life he no longer lived. And so she had, and worked them into her ever expanding account of Pevana and her people. She was poet-seamstress, stitching people into her life with well-crafted words; the only way she knew how to keep them. She wrote to draw them closer to her, and in that desperate composition she came to understand them and the magic they worked, an extended metaphor of love and connection.

She read over Devyn's poems and musings again, caressing the pages as though touching the memory of him. In so many ways, those words were the frame of the wider tale in which she and everyone else played a part. Donari went to contest the truth of Devyn's words for all of them. More tears splattered the page, for she realized then that, ultimately, words were the beginning and ending of everything.

She wiped away her tears, dipped her pen anew, and went back to writing.

She had to.

For herself, for Devyn, for Donari.

It was the only way she could keep them alive.

Saymon Brimaldi wiped down the counter of his serving bar and used the rag to dust off the little oaken beer keg. It was a copy in miniature of the great barrels and casks that lined his storage rooms at the back of his establishment. He had been hard put to it to find that little jewel, shoved out of the way and hidden behind a row of last year's vintage. He wiped it down carefully and contemplated what sort of evening he could expect. Most of those that would enjoy it now marched under arms westward. He intended to send the little keg off to the king in one of the supply wagons. If Donari could not come to the beer, then Saymon would send the beer to him.

Saymon spent most of the summer hoping Donari would come to the Cup in disguise just like old times, but nothing of the sort happened. The closest thing to a royal visit he got were the infrequent meetings with the poet, Devyn Ambrose. And once, the Lady Eleni, the king's betrothed. Those felt more normal but in the end unsatisfactory. Hence the keg, which he filled with some of his finest and Donari's favorite. He tapped the bung-hole secure and hefted the liquid package and took it outside to the boy waiting with a wheel barrow.

The lad, one of the Maze children who of late earned change hauling bricks away from the bell tower demolition, gave him a knowing look when Saymon wedged the keg in the barrow with a spare rag.

"Now Bastin," Saymon said, tossing him a coin. "Make sure this gets down to the Land Gate. There is a line of wagons collecting there with food for the army. Tell the officer in charge who this is for. This stuff is too good for muleteers and drivers."

"Who is it for, then?" Bastin piped, pocketing the coin and hefting the barrow handles to test its balance. "It's a nice little thing, isn't it? Must be for the quality because something this dainty wouldn't last long in the tent lines."

Saymon chuckled and gave the boy a gentle cuff as he turned to go. "Look you, rascal," he said pointing at the keg. "See the design burned on the top? That's the Avedun dolphin that is. This goes to King Donari and no one else. Can I trust you to see this gets on the right wagon? I can't leave to do it myself."

The boy nodded confidently and set off. Saymon watched him until he turned right off Lampwright's Street onto the main way down to the gate square. Bastin and his little sister, Tasia, belonged to the group that frequented the gravesite of the old beggar, Maze-poet Kembril Edri. After Donari's return, Devyn Ambrose set them to watching the city for him, and some of the information they gleaned during their city-wide wanderings made its way to the palace through Saymon and the *Golden Cup.*

Saymon took his good mood back inside with him. His new serving girl, Sanya, the baker's daughter, sat in the corner suckling her child born less than two months ago. Her man fell in the southern fighting, and while her family accepted the addition, she had come to him anyway looking for more work to take pressure off of her family's charity.

She noticed his glance and made shift to stop and get back to setting up for the evening's trade, but Saymon waved her off.

"Nah, nah," he eased. "Let the little fellow get his fill. There's time yet for crockery, Sanya. Lucky fellow, that one, to have such bounty at his disposal. Almost makes me wish I had my second childhood!"

Sanya reddened and yet smiled at the ribald compliment. Saymon saw to it that none molested her when she worked, and he found he did not mind having the child about during the day. To him, the whole scenario seemed almost normal. They were not lovers, and yet he knew she appreciated his forbearance. She possessed mettle enough to prosper even with his clientele. She always held her own delivering her family's baked goods in the past. She now settled into the rhythm of the place. It felt like peace, missing since before all the temple fires began several years ago.

He gave her a last wink and returned to wiping down his counter. He felt good, satisfied. Perhaps if the days ahead promised more such feelings, he might actually get his own chance at Sanya's beautiful breasts once her son finished with them. It had been a good day despite the uncertainty of the coming conflict. Donari was in the field with his men. Saymon sent a prayer to Renia to grant his king the victory. Victory meant peace, which meant better business.

Bells tolling and the sounds of folk rushing about in the street came to Saymon through the kitchen door as he put the last bit of carrot into that evening's stew. The disturbance sent him out through the common room to the street where he met a nearly breathless Bastin.

"What is it boy? Where is your barrow?"

"Saymon! I got your keg down to the gate, but a messenger came from the palace just as I was about to leave. The Lady Eleni and the council are sending all able and willing to aide the king!"

"What?"

"I heard a watchman in the square. Anything that can bear a rider, draft-horses, nags, yearlings; all are to assemble in the gate square and ride. Every man who can find a spear or blade to follow."

"So much for peace," Saymon muttered, looking around as folk collected to take in the news.

"What, sir?" Bastin asked.

"Hm? Nothing, lad. I suggest you find your sister and get home. Things will be strange about the city."

"Is this bad?"

"Child, it has always been bad. We have just avoided seeing it."

Saymon looked down at the boy, seeing in the scruffy face the sum total of the desperate venture. If Donari failed, they all failed. Suddenly, his notion of beer to the king seemed silly and presumptuous. The news that reached the palace must have been tragic for such a response. Eleni's face loomed before his mind's eye along with a memory of a certain, magical night of poetry and revelation. Desperation had driven her to jump tradition before. This was no different. Saymon stomped back inside certain Eleni's love and intuition set all in motion.

He waved off Sanya's questioning look and headed to the storeroom next the kitchen. He rooted behind a line of boxes, feeling for and finding the shaft of an old spear. He took an even older, dented, rusty helm from a hook near the door. Helmed and armed, he returned to the common room and tossed his keys to Sanya.

"Promotion, girl. Watch the place until I come back. And if I don't--."

"Saymon, you can't be--."

"No time for sentiment, girl," he interrupted, moving to the door. "Make sure Bastin gets his sister home. It's time to fight."

Chapter 28: Battle at the End of Innocence

Dawn broke clear and cold over the opposing forces. Donari called for his armor early and set out to see the rain drenched ground first hand. Men woke stiff and hungry, rolling from their blankets with ungracious grumbles. The prospect of death at the end of the day lent an added chill to their morning ablutions.

Donari understood histories reported the numbers who attended the death dance and listed the fallen and tried to compress their stories within the confines of a chapter or a verse. But the real truth went beyond words, for who can really know the mind of a man whose life faced definition by a blade's sharpness or a spear's length? All the scribes could do is collect generalities and attempt to shed a pale glow of understanding on the things that percolate in the mind of a man on the cusp of eternity.

Eleni, dearest, you might try, but I am glad you aren't here just the same. Be safe, love.

Talyior loomed up in the half-light, already armed with a dented cavalry buckler on his shoulder. Donari looked at him now and saw a tie with his old life; that something magical about his city and its poets before politics boiled up trouble. Donari found he missed those days. Words. Rhyme. Life a different, casual cadence.

"I am glad to see you here, poet. Seems fitting somehow."

"I needed to be here, sire, for Devyn. I've done with spying. Time to fight."

"I wish the affair could be settled by words. You gave good blows with yours in the finals that time. Seems like a distant memory, now."

"And yet blood came from those words, my king."

"Blood was always going to come, Talyior, never rue the words. Devyn didn't, Kembril Edri didn't. Perhaps we fight for more than this crown on my helm. Perhaps we fight for Pevana's poets as well."

"I'm sure Lady Eleni would agree! My king, I refuse to think this trial will be the end of all that. Words will always be."

Something in Talyior's tone clicked for Donari. Eleni always made the connections. As care and concern drove him further away from his words, she served as his link to that better, finer thing. He realized his life had always been a conflict. The sun, poking its face over the horizon east, brought forth whispered words:

There is a battle at the end of innocence
When a man struggles to make sense

Of all the things that stress
His calm in the test,
Revealing all he is or ever was
Without recourse or just because.
It is so for all as a life decree
And, ultimately, all we can seek,
Is to find a way to end our days
Free.
And in Peace.

"A fine sentiment, sire," Talyior said. "Is that a challenge for a duel later?"

Donari chuckled, which ended in a sigh. "Would that were all I had to risk," he said ruefully. "Gaspire and I have an appointment this morning. But after, after, then I will gladly test rhymes with you."

"I read something once about *words before blows*," Talyior said, bowing. "But I confess I did not expect such from you, my king."

"Words will always be part of my path, young man, moreso than blows in any case. You remind me of my own past, young man. I fear I give the moment poor effort this morning, however. Doubtless you, Devyn or Eleni could do better."

"Not so, my king!" Talyior protested. "Devyn and I recall a certain prince who was a poet of Pevana. It appears he lives still. I'll take your words for a royal command. None of us are innocents anymore, but we will gain freedom and peace, lord, depend on it!"

"I wish your Devyn were here with us," Donari said. "I never had the chance to tell you how sorry I am."

"He knew I had Lyvia to consider. He always thought two lines ahead of me, in truth. And yet none of it matters if we don't hold here. I miss my friend, sire, but his choice just reminds me of my own. I want my Lyvia. I want a family. I want roots. And if I have to cut my way through all of those fools to get my chance, then words will have to wait for blows. I've a sword, my lord, and a borrowed buckler, and I know how to use them."

"What if I asked you to stay back? What if I asked you to take Eleni aboard your ship and sail south if we lose here?"

Talyior shook his head in respectful denial. "Hard orders, my lord. I would send word to Espan to do just that at your word, but this poet intends to fight for his poet-king. And, trust me, Lyvia would understand." His expression turned wry. "She wouldn't like it, but she would see the need."

273

"She must be quite a woman," Donari offered. "But I would expect such from Sylvanus's daughter." He looked at the younger man in new found respect. "You and he are more alike than I first thought," he continued. "And I say again, I am sorry if he is lost. I hold myself responsible."

Talyior chuckled. "Oh, yes, Lyvia more than matches me, sire. And, again, I say don't give up on Dev. As long as I have life and fight in me, I refuse to give up hope."

"Eleni was correct about you," Donari said, laughing. "She told me your poems had a spirit in them that sounded like mirth. I see now what she meant. Your words hearten me, Talyior. If we prevail today, we shall match words. I promise. Since you insist on fighting, see to your horse, and ride with what is left of my cavalry."

"I'm not afraid, sire."

"Of course you are. So am I. I don't doubt your courage. I want you away from the press. Choose your moment and strike a blow with them."

Talyior bowed at that and set off on his new task. Donari watched him walk away and then continued his tour. Around him now the camp began to ripple with activity as men armed themselves and stamped their feet to get their blood moving, hefted spears, tested shield straps, and felt the sharpness of sword blades. Donari called for his horse and stood in the stirrups to address them.

"Brothers! We will see hard strokes today. Remember for whom you fight. It is not just this crown or the standard of my house. You fight for all who would see peace in this realm. You honor me with your presence here. We are Pevana's sons. All those behind bend all their thought to us today. Let that strengthen your limbs. I will not cozen you with high sentiments! I am not certain if we are meant to change the world or just be a part of it. But let us face what comes bravely. Have courage, my friends, and we will prevail."

Donari lowered himself into the saddle and walked his horse out of the camp, the Pevanese mass following to spread out to their positions.

Activity from across the fields greeted their own, and the two armies shook themselves out into line. Within minutes the remaining flower of Perspan manhood faced each other across a narrow front that stretched from the escarpment about the river to the rise of the hill slope to the north. All waited for the word.

It came without fanfare, for things had gone long beyond words. A single horn sounded behind the northerners. Spears clashed on shields. With a feral growl the mass rolled forward. The Pevanese dressed their lines and waited for them.

Renia save us. They are two to our one.

The Perspans swelled closer.

Two hundred paces. A hundred. Fifty.

Donari let a page lead his mount behind the lines. He dismounted, drew his blade and sent final thoughts winging homeward and heavenward.

Jason, Senden.

Thirty paces.

Devyn.

Twenty paces. War cries. Horns.

Eleni. Love.

Ten. A screaming rush.

Life.

The lines met.

Donari paced along his line, just out of reach of the vicious, grinding fray. A page kept pace leading his restive horse by its bridle. Men died fighting where they stood with no respite, no shuffling of lines to relieve pressure or fill gaps. All around him men fought beyond the point of exhaustion, metemorphized expressions of agonized sinews attached to reddened blades. Shields disintegrated from the press of blows. Men abandoned them to swing their blades two handed, cursing and crying, fighting and dying. The ground turned slippery with blood stomped into the turf to create a muddy morass in which men slid and faltered, rose and recovered, pushed and got pushed back in turn, gasping, grunting, stumbling over fallen foes and comrades with unrelenting ferocity. The battle line took on the qualities of an undulating wave lapping at the shores of death.

Whenever Donari tried to enter the line, his men pushed him back, reducing him to a spectator, useless save to urge them on to greater effort. The Pevanese ranks thinned and began to step back as if by design. Donari loosened his sword in its sheath and tightened his shield strap.

Soon. Soon now.

The noise rose as the northerners, too, sensed a weakening in the Pevanese line. Donari thought he heard his hated cousin's voice urging his troops to greater effort. He caught a glimpse of him off to his right, a large, bearded terror screaming at the top of his lungs, his battle lust obvious, his sword already blooded. Donari felt the force of Gaspire's hate like a physical blow. Though his cousin's men fought and died in alarming numbers, the force of his will held them to the task.

The line to his front took a step back. Another. And all along the line Donari could tell the issue had reached its tipping point. He drew his blade, forced his way to the front of his men to add his thrusts to the madness. His world collapsed to a space a yard in front and a pace to either side. He felt the shock of his blade against bone and shield as a summons to vent his despairing wrath. He screamed defiance. Blood not his own splashed against his face, half blinding him. Another step back. Then two more. Then a separation; a moment's pressure release, like that of the elastic split flesh makes when scored by a knife before the nerves send pain winging to perplex the brain.

His men tried to remove him from the fight, but he shook off their hands, snarling. He would not flee, could not, dare not; the thought of flight a coward's suicide. He faced front, swept his gaze back and forth along the line and saw the same result everywhere: raw courage beat down by too many foes.

It seemed to Donari then that all his hopes might pass as victims of a cruel, cruel joke.

So this is how goodness leaves the world?

He pushed the thought aside and forced himself to think clearly in the face of chaos. His men now retreated steadily, no longer biting back but huddled behind shields, responding to blows forced upon them. A motion off to the right drew his attention. What was left of his cavalry, Talyior in tow, chose their moment. They swam in amongst a sea of spears, and from his vantage Donari saw the effect of their charge as a rippling wave among deep waters that rolled across his front momentarily stopping the Perspan press.

He saw Gaspire again, mouthing words the din of battle rendered inaudible. A large mass of men formed up before him, led by a red haired, ferocious giant. Gaspire pointed his sword directly at Donari, and with that motion those men linked shields and rushed the line, smashed against his exhausted men, broke through, making the space around Donari a melee of single combats.

And then all thoughts ended for Donari, his sensations limited to the shocks he felt in his sword arm when his blows landed and the growing numbness of his shield arm as he received them. He fought with a completeness to his motions, laying about on all sides; every blow for Senden, Avarran, Devyn and Eleni. High. Low. Beat. Beat.

When his arm burned too much to respond to his commands, he stepped back out of the line, spent and out of breath to discover that the battle had turned into a fluid thing that now swept them to the flats before the river ford. He leaned on his sword and tried to make up the status of his line, but everywhere he looked he saw northerner and southerner fully engaged, an interminable cacophony of clanging, defiant blows.

But the Pevanese line could no longer hold the bank. Donari watched in growing horror as a great press of northerners pushed his men aside, reached the fords and then turned back to begin rolling them up. Encirclement was only a matter of time. Donari swung back to the right. His cavalry, their charge long since spent, now fought amid a sea of foes. Spears casually plucked men from saddles with the dexterity of a monstrous child picking petals from a field of flowers.

And then the red haired giant Donari glimpsed earlier loomed before him, gore flecked blade raised and rushing for him. Instinctively, Donari parried the blow, responded, drawing blood and a satisfying look of doubt on the man's face. Then the presumptuous quality of the moment came clear to him. The man was large but no swordsman. He parried another blow, another, like reading sums in a text, and then he recognized the parade ground rhythm. Anticipating, he slipped inside the man's guard and, gripping his blade short, thrust it once, cruelly efficient, in under the ribs and deep into the man's chest cavity.

"My kingdom will not fall to trash such as you," he snarled. The man grunted once, pulsed blood from a slashed cheek, stiffened against the firmness of Donari's steel and then fell into death with a metallic crash.

Donari wrenched his weapon free, tried to clear the sweat from his eyes, but all he did was smear blood across his brow. He blinked, the world misted grey, and in the grey he thought he saw an Avedun banner swim through a haze of dust and water droplets. And then his feet felt a different rhythm as of hooves pounding, mounting with speed along the river bank near the ford. And then the sounds of the fighting around him changed timber.

He blinked away the glammor to find Gaspire poised before him, helmless, shieldless, his blade gore-flecked and in his eyes the red hate of death.

Donari raised his own blade as best he could, recognized the moment's appropriateness, and prepared to defend himself, his crown, his love, everything.

"Let's finish this, cousin." Bloody spittle foamed Gaspire's lips.

"You can't win. We know about Demona's babe."

"Then I'll finish you, at least."

"You will always be least."

"Not if I outlive you." Gaspire stepped forward, smiling, redolent in his violent arrogance and swept a blow low at Donari's feet. Donari sidestepped away, aware that his cousin, taller, heavier, would want to beat him down in close quarters. Gaspire rounded on him, swung viciously at Donari's head. Donari's desperate attempt to block only succeeded in deflecting it and he felt the shock as Gaspire's blade glanced off the tip of his battlecrown. He backstepped, blocked yet another blow.

"Is that all you have?" Gaspire spat. "I had more challenge from Demona!"

Donari answered him with a clever feint low and thrust to the midsection. Gaspire's mail blunted the blow, but the impact drew a gratifying painful grunt and a backward step. Donari followed up this slight advantage with rapid swings. Both blades rang with the demented music of their collision. Gaspire parried with difficulty at first and then with growing ease and confidence as Donari spent himself trying to keep up the pressure.

Donari's breath began to come in gasps. His sword arm burned like one of Casan's temple fires. Gaspire turned his last, feeble blow and actually laughed out loud.

"I take back my last comment," he chortled. "You've done slightly better than Demona, but only just. Time to die, cousin."

His sword crashed against Donari's feeble guard. Donari staggered back. Gaspire flowed forward, inexorable, death's wave come to swamp all life and hope. Gaspire's next blow numbed Donari's arm and sent his blade spinning off out of sight. Donari hugged his arm, struggled to keep his feet and meet his death with honor. Gaspire swung his sword back to deliver the killing stroke. And then he stiffened unnaturally and stared with stunned incredulity at the end of the sword poking out from his side. His own blade fell to the ground. He turned, tottering, to see who had betrayed him. And there, grimfaced and favoring a wounded leg, stood the last remaining son of the Lord of Hallar.

"You!" Gaspire gasped. "You traitor!"

"Not anymore," said Hallan. "Not anymore."

Gaspire glared and waved his hand in a vague gesture as though attempting to keep his balance. "You insult your house, dog," he spluttered. "Your father will--." But as he drew breathe to finish his curse he coughed a splatter of blood, his expression slackened, and he fell dead, face-first, into the mud.

"Wrong, my lord," Hallan responded quietly, stooping to remove his blade with a tired grunt. "My father is dead, and I am now all that is left of our house." He knelt with difficulty before Donari, holding the hilts of his bloody sword out in supplication. "Forgive me, my lord king, for my tardy oaths. Take my sword, sire. My life and my House are forfeit to your justice."

Donari stood in stunned silence that spread throughout the field as men took note of the drama that just occurred. All around the din of battle faded to the sounds of men calling for retreat, crying out for mercy, exulting in sudden, unlooked for victory. Donari stepped forward, took the hilts of Hallan's sword in his off hand.

"Oaths so well-spoken are never tardy," he said. "Arise, Sir Hallan, Lord of Hallar, and enter into my peace. We have much yet to do, and I have a Lord's portion reserved for you. Though he rejected my peace, I still grieve at your father's passing."

"As do I, my lord," Hallan said. "Yet he died in folly." He nudged Gaspire's corpse. "This man's folly. He fought for a lie. They all did. The lesson is bitter, my lord, but I would rather live in wisdom than follow error."

"So you know. Devyn told you?" Donari asked. Hallan nodded. "And would you still have offered fealty had the child lived?"

Hallan paused at the hard question. But Donari had the young man's oath, which bound him to answer. Donari waited, observing in the young man's expression ware and concern in equal measure and knew how he should respond if fate would have reversed their roles.

"I might have, sire, truthfully. I told Demona I would fight to give him a chance at life, but life never gave him a chance to put me to the test." He paused, as if stunned by his own honesty. Then he met Donari's eyes squarely, as if he came to a fine conclusion. "In truth, my lord, I feel I was always your man though it took me over-long to find my way."

Donari laughed, a tired, gentle release of tension and care, fear and sorrow, and all within ear shot laughed as well and men put up their arms and the horrors of the time passed like a wave receding from the shore. Talyior trotted up, dismounted and shook Hallan's hand.

"I'm glad we only winged you, my Lord Hallan," he chuckled. "I only wish Devyn were here to see this."

Hallan returned the grip. "I left him before dawn. I owe him my life twice over, it seems. He found me yesterday, weak and bleeding behind the pursuit. He bound my leg, and we followed after. I needed to make my own choice. He was still vague from a blow to the head. I left him sleeping."

"He's alive?" Talyior asked. "Alive? Where? Where did you leave him?"

Hallan turned to point north but dropped his arm in mid-gesture. There, picking his way through the corpse-littered field rode Devyn

Ambrose. He bore a wan smile on his face when he dismounted. He took in the scene, turned to Hallan and said, "Nice choice."

The space around them cleared as men moved off to search out the wounded. Officers marshalled others into companies to pursue Gaspire's remnants. Some of the group milling about caught his attention for their irregular attire and equipment. One man passed carrying a pitchfork, another bore a large cudgel, the kind used by bar bouncers. None of them had any armor. Then two men walked by leading draft horses of all things. The great brutes had blood and mud up to the fetlock.

"What is this?" Donari mused. "Who are these?"

No one answered him. He stumbled in the mud and had to put a hand down to steady himself. Once he regained his balance the answer to his question froze him. The royal carriage, drawn by two of the oldest horses Donari had ever seen, lurched to a stop before him. Eleni leaned out the window ashen-faced, lips aquiver.

Joy, anger, love and relief swept through Donari in an instant. He threw off his gloves, stepped up to the window, grabbed Eleni's face with his grimy hands and kissed her, deeply, crushingly, taking life from her lips in one long all consuming moment.

"Well," she gasped when he broke away. "I wasn't expecting that. I was sure you'd be angry."

"Oh, I am," he assured her. "Very cross, in fact. Cryso will much to answer for."

"You will leave him alone, Donari. I made him."

"So all of that was your idea?"

"I had to come. I had to send—."

But Donari kissed her silent, oblivious to the crowd that looked on.

"It was terribly foolish," he whispered after. "But a risk worthy of you, my dear, however disobedient. But then that's the real question, isn't it?"

"Question?"

"The only way I will get you to truly listen to me is to marry you."

The afternoon passed on to twilight as all who yet lived on the field from both sides set about succoring the wounded and burying the dead. Only a tithe of Gaspire's followers fled, and Donari's cavalry rode down most of those before they could reach the dubious safety of the hills. None of the northern lords who supported Gaspire lived. They found Tareegan among the piled corpses of the last fight, and Hallaran among the fallen near the river bank. Great changes would come to the northern fiefs that winter. A few fugitives chose outlawry over fealty, but the vast majority of the survivors took their knee and gave the oath once they learned how they had been suborned. And all took heart in the mercy Donari showed; so different from Roderran but no less forceful in the expression of his will.

That evening Donari, Eleni, Hallan, Devyn, and Talyior shared a fire, a wineskin, and pulls from a little keg of beer someone produced from one of the supply wagons. Donari half-wondered if Hallan was surprised at the familiarity of the others, for the young man held his tongue. And yet, as the wine flowed, Donari watched him grow more at ease. Hope takes getting used to.

So will peace.

Talked rose and fell with the flames as the night deepened. Around them men from both sides mixed around other fires and tentatively, diplomatically; a welcome replacement to the blows previously traded. The night's chill, the herald of deeper cold to come helped cool the men's ardor even further. Stars shone down for the first time in over a generation on an entire region at peace.

Chapter 29: Transition

Byrnard Casan, Lord Prelate of the King's Theology, communed with his past in the darker shadows of his room in Pevana's palace. His eyes had long since ceased to note the absence of light. He gibbered quietly to himself, talking in his strange language to the faces he saw distinctly hovering before him. Time did not matter in that unworldly conversation. The shock of his shabby treatment, the utter disdain with which Donari dealt with him quite unhinged his old, devious mind. Casan did not mark them, all his attention focused on his visitors. Once again, Roderran's pale face mouthed surly, disgusted words, and Jaryd Corvale's head hung suspended in the air, its hair clutched in the hand of his headless torso.

Casan stuttered nonsensical words, and his visitors repaid him in kind. Plans past, present and future bounced around in the darkness between them. Casan smiled into the blackness and spittle dribbled down his chin.

"I will get Donari yet! Gaspire is coming, and once he gets here Donari will die and that pompous bitch will pay with her dignity and we will set this city alight and drink to the dance of flames!"

He jabbered his invective in a stream of drool laden syllables, crafting, shaping, willing his desires into reality. And the images came to him: glorious flames that leapt from building to building, consuming everything within seconds, reducing the streets of this shabby, tawdry, pretentious slum to ashes.

A pulse began to beat again in his temple, but he ignored it. His right hand began to shake and a pain formed in his shoulder and he labored to breath. His heartbeat took on a staccato rhythm that graduated to a thumping, discordance. He raised his left hand and clenched his wizened fingers into a fist that shook although, with the darkness so complete, he could not really tell.

"Gaspire is coming!" he screamed.

And then he saw Gaspire before him with a hole in his side that oozed blood. The throbbing in Casan's temple intensified; the pain in his shoulder grew to a white hot agony. Gaspire's bloodless face mouthed something important, but Casan was too preoccupied with eternity to notice.

Donari took a last pull from the skin, his lips pleasantly numb, and passed it on to Devyn.

"Last pull for me, sire?" he said. "Then I offer this toast: To the Grace of Renia's Peace for all of us and all we love. Long live the King!" The others about the fire roared their approval. And still others around nearby fires took up the call and soon refrains rolled throughout the host.

Donari listened until the cries faded then sighed and leaned back contentedly. "Peace, but at such a cost? Can we call it victory?" He looked across the flames at all of them, took Eleni's hand in his, and decided that, yes, it was a victory. "We will need to find new leaders to help Hallan in the north, and we will build a road through the hills to tie us all together. We have to," he finished. "Otherwise this will have been an empty triumph."

And that was how he processed the events of the day. He had preserved his crown, eliminated a direct threat, and now turned his mind to healing. In his mind he began framing the wording for the proclamation he would send north and south. With Sylvanus's help he would make plans for glory. He glanced at Talyior across the fire light. He and his Lyvia would figure into those plans as well.

"My friends, we rest here at the end of hard days and the beginning of new tasks. I wonder, what do you think, Devyn?"

Devyn suppressed a burp and rubbed his temple as though trying to rub away a painful spot. He stared at the flames dancing above the coals, and Donari wondered if he saw a million words there waiting to find their proper order. Donari did. Devyn looked up from the flames, a wan smile spread across his face.

"I think," he said finally, "that Eleni will need a lot more ink for her pens."

Afterward

Devyn paused in the shadow of a building on the edge of the cleared space about Kembril's grave. The celebrations from the great wedding spilled out to the city and the people swarmed the squares, alehouses and wine shops to talk about the great event. But Devyn craved a different kind of party. He slipped away as soon as he could, but the sight of Tasia dancing reminded him of an important promise. As he drew closer, Tasia began singing in time with her steps:

Once upon a time, once upon a time
The stories always say there is a once upon a time.
Once a upon a time, once upon a time,
The King and Lady joined their hands, once upon a time.

And the people all laughed and sang, they all laughed and sang
Once upon a timeless time the people laughed and sang.
And the women strew flower petals, and the men all sang in tune
Once upon a happy time beneath a late fall moon.
Once upon a time, once upon a time
The stories always say there is a once upon a time…

And as she finished her circuit she bumped into Devyn's legs. The collision sent Tasia sprawling, and she landed with a thump on her backside.

"Tasia," he said, kneeling down to help her up. "Does your mother know you are here alone? Where is your brother?"

Tasia accepted his hand and stood up, stunned and rapturous all at the same time.

"My, my mother is busy with the baby," she stuttered. "And my brother and his friends are down behind the *Cup* helping in the kitchens. But you came back! You came back!" She clapped her hands beside herself with joy. "You said you would come back and you did, and the king has found his queen and the bad men are all gone, and, and Tolimon is gone because the bell tower is gone! I saw them tear it down stone by stone! But you came back! I knew you would because you promised me a story, and everyone knows a poet's promise is a story that will be told. Isn't that so?"

Devyn laughed. There was a reception at the palace, and he promised to meet Talyior for an hour of words at The Cup, but a promise was indeed a promise. He sat down with his back against the fence just as he had done in the spring. Tasia settled herself in front of him expectantly. Her face glowed with a receptive light, and Devyn could see that words would figure in her future. There would always be poets in Pevana.

"Okay," he said. "How should I begin? I owe you a story, and a promise is a promise as you say."

Tasia giggled and clapped her hands.

"Start like you are supposed to, silly," she said. "Once upon a time…"

"Right, then here we go." But Devyn paused, and he thought of Senden, Kembril, Avarran, his friend Talyior with his Lyvia, and he thought of the joy that was deepening even then in the Palace on the hill. He wondered at the wonder of it all and took it in like a great breath of life, and began:

"Once upon a time there was a city noted for the quality of her poets…"

About the Author

Photo credit: Grace Eide-Gabriel

Mark Nelson is a career educator and for the last twenty-two years has been teaching composition and literature at a small high school located in the rain shadow of the Cascade Mountains in eastern Washington State. He is happily married to his best friend and fellow educator and together they have raised three beautiful daughters and one semi-retired cat. Words, music, food and parenting permeate his life and serve as a constant source for inspiration, challenge and reward. To temper such unremitting joy, Mark plays golf: an addiction that provides a healthy dose of humility.

www.ingramcontent.com/pod-product-compliance
Lightning Source LLC
Chambersburg PA
CBHW030652260626
47157CB00007B/2616